Belfast's Shankhill Road: in the darkness ... ed,
knowing she would come . . .

So begins one of the most terrifying works of fiction
ever written about Ulster. Based on the author's own
experiences this is by far the most realistic 'Ulster'
novel ever published, but where does fact end and
fiction begin?

Kane is not just a run-of-the-mill IRA gangster. He
is the organization's main hit man – a cold, ruthless
loner. He is also something else even more terrifying
. . . a suspected killer of women – seductive young
women who happen to be Protestant.

Sergeant Nevin Brown's suspicions turn to certainty
as he finds himself tracking a man who kills for both
political and sexual reasons. But Kane is clever . . .
very clever. How else could he get away with killing for
so long?

☆　　　☆　　　☆

Henry McCallion had a long and varied military and
police career. He joined the Parachute Regiment in
1970 and served seven tours of duty in Northern
Ireland. He saw service in Belfast, Londonderry and
South Armagh.

Mr McCallion later joined South Africa's equivalent of the SAS and was wounded in action. In 1980 he
joined the SAS and returned to Ulster. He also took
part in the Falklands War.

He later joined the Royal Ulster Constabulary and
his personal experiences are vividly evident in the
pages of this book.

# DOUBLE KILL

## Henry McCallion

Temple House Books

Sussex, England

Temple House Books
is an imprint of
The Book Guild Ltd

Temple House Books
25 High Street,
Lewes, Sussex.

First published 1992
© Henry McCallion 1992
Set in Baskerville
Typesetting by APS,
Salisbury, Wiltshire.
Printed in Great Britain by
Antony Rowe Ltd.,
Chippenham, Wiltshire.

A catalogue record for this book is
available from the British Library

ISBN 0 86332 770 2

*The policeman stood at the golden gate*
*His head was bent and low*

*He gently asked the man of fate*
*Which way he had to go*

*'What have you done?' Saint Peter asked,*
*'To gain admittance here.'*

*'I served in the Ardoyne below*
*For many, many a year.'*

*Saint Peter threw wide the gate*
*And gently pressed the bell.*

*'Come inside and choose your harp*
*You've had your share of hell.'*

\* With apologies to the original author.

This novel is dedicated to all members of the Royal Ulster Constabulary, past and present. Men who do a thankless task, in a troubled land.

# Glossary of Terms and
# Phrases Used in this Book

**ACC** – Assistant Chief Constable.

**ASU** – Active Service Unit. A term used by the IRA to describe its men when on operation. Could be as few as one or as many as twenty men, but normally about three.

**ATO** – Ammunition Technical Officer. Bomb disposal officer.

**Black Bastard** – Derogatory name for RUC officers. Taken from old style black uniforms and black overcoats.

**Drogue Bomb** – IRA hand thrown grenade. Styled on a Second World War stick type grenade.

**DCI** – Detective Chief Inspector.

**DI** – Detective Inspector.

**DS** – Detective Sergeant.

**E4A** – Elite RUC surveillance teams. Specially selected and trained personnel. Experts in both urban and rural surveillance.

**Felix** – Old army radio term for bomb disposal teams.

**Fenian** – Derogatory name for a Catholic. Taken from early forerunners to the IRA.

**Garda** – Irish Police.

**MI5** – Military Intelligence. Mostly responsible for running informers and collating and collecting information on terrorists.

**MO** – Modus Operanda. Taken from the Latin. A criminal's method of operation, his trade mark.

**MSU** – Mobile Support Units. Usually used in riot control situations.

**OP** – Observation Post. Sometimes covert.

**Peeler** – Derogatory and slang name for an RUC officer. Taken from original police force formed by Sir Robert Peel.

**PIRA** – Provisional Irish Republican Army.

**Prima Facia** – Latin, an open and shut case.

**Prod** – Short for Protestant.

**Provos** – Short for Provisionals.

**Ruger Revolver** – Canadian manufactured .357 double action, six shot revolver, standard RUC issue.

**SB** – Special Branch.

**Skipper** – Slang name for police sergeant.

**Stiff** – Ulster slang. To cross or even kill a person.

**SOCO** – Scenes of Crime Officer. Specially trained RUC officers trained in collecting forensic evidence at crime scenes.

**Taigh** – Derogatory and slang name for a Catholic.

**To house with weapons** – Covert army and police term meaning 'To get a suspect located' or 'To get a suspect located with weapons'.

**TOIL** – Exchanging time worked for time off.

**UDA** – Ulster Defence Association. Para-military legal Protestant organization.

**UDR** – Locally recruited British army regiment.

**UFF** – Ulster Freedom Fighters. Very violent proscribed Protestant terrorist organization. A 'flag of convenience' for the UDA.

**UVF** – Ulster Volunteer Force. Proscribed Protestant terror group. Heavily armed and relatively well organized and trained.

# 1

Belfast 8.30 pm, Shankhill Road, Friday, Week One.

In the darkness he waited, knowing she would come. He'd
targeted her for three weeks, watched her routine, she'd pass
his hiding place within minutes. Already beneath his trousers
he was starting to get an erection. Soon his medicine would
arrive, soon the fire within him would be fed. Anticipation
poured through him like an intoxicating drug. Keeping his
breathing deep and even, he readied his body to strike,
drawing on his years of combat experience, preparing himself
for the swift and savage action that was near.

Lynn Moody closed the door of her Leopold Street home
and glanced up at the darkening sky, heavy with rain clouds.
Every city had its moods, Belfast was no exception. It could be
happy or sad, busy or quiet, tense or relaxed. Involuntarily the
pretty eighteen-year-old shivered; it was as if the city was
waiting. Turning she walked quickly towards the main Shankhill Road.

Her Fridays had fallen into a comfortable routine since she
had met Martin; they had been going steady for nearly four
months and met regularly on Fridays at 8.45 in the Beaton
Docket, a lively city centre bar. After a few drinks and a chance
to swap their respective week's gossip, Martin would take her
late night dancing at Pips night club. Invariably they would
end up at his city centre flat. Last week they had sex for the first
time, only her second sexual encounter. For Lynn it had been a
totally satisfying and fulfilling experience. Her mind filled with
thoughts of the pleasures to come, her head bent against
steadily falling rain as she walked swiftly down the dimly lit
street.

His attack was so sudden, she had no chance to cry out.

9

Clamping a forearm across her throat, he cut all air supply to Lynn's lungs. Half lifting, half dragging, he pulled his struggling victim into the alley's darkness.

Lynn kicked backwards, panic and fear giving her added strength, but his grip on her throat only tightened. For a moment unconsciousness threatened, its black oblivion offering her an escape from her terror. Then he spoke. 'Don't scream, don't struggle and I won't hurt you.'

He produced a knife and passed it in front of her eyes; previous experience had taught him that this usually stopped a victim's struggles. She kicked once more, he tightened his grip and pressed his knife point into her neck, drawing blood. Again the voice came, this time firmer. 'Don't struggle, if you struggle I'll cut your face to ribbons.'

Lynn stopped kicking, his voice terrified her more than the knife, it was cold, emotionless. His grip loosened on her throat, thankfully she drew air into her straining lungs. He spun her around, involuntarily she almost cried out. Her attacker loomed above; in the darkness he seemed to have no face. She realized he was wearing some kind of black mask.

Watching her he knew she was totally in his power. Slowly he passed the knife in front of her eyes, enjoying the look of terror that contorted her face. Placing a hand on her shoulder he forced his, now unprotesting, victim to the alley floor. Keeping the knife pressed against her throat, he hiked up her dress and removed her panties. 'Dear God in heaven,' Lynn thought. 'Don't let him hurt me, I'll let him do what he wants, but please don't let him hurt me.'

She felt rather than saw him unbuckle his trousers; roughly his knees parted her legs, he reared up above her as he entered her. She turned her head, as he rode her with long even strokes, loathing for him rising like bile in her throat. His breath quickened as he climaxed. She felt him move off her, sensed him kneeling between her still parted legs.

With a move, made all the more savage by its suddenness, he plunged his knife into her chest. It smashed through the protecting ribs and punctured her heart. Again and again his arm rose and fell, ripping and tearing, long after his victim ceased to move. Finally he rose from her still form, his breathing quick and heavy. With a wrench, he tore the black balaclava from his face. 'That's another one for you Ma,' he whispered to the still alley.

Stuffing the balaclava under his black jacket he checked the still empty street, his blond hair shining in the dim light, satisfied, he left his hiding place and the broken ruin that had been Lynn Moody.

☆　　☆　　☆

Etna Drive, Ardoyne Area, Two Hours Later.

Larry Martin, Officer Commanding what the IRA called its A-Company Belfast Brigade, checked his watch; it was 10.35 pm. Turning he spoke to Quin, 'Where the fuck is Kane?' Martin's voice betrayed his anger and concern, so much depended on tonight. Quin shrugged his shoulders in reply, it was his first operation, he held a Colt .45 unconvincingly in his right hand. Martin cursed again and turned back to look out of the window.

Up until now everything had gone exactly to plan. Quin and two other young volunteers had taken over the house two hours ago; they did not even have to show the guns they carried, just the sight of them, all wearing balaclavas and the warning that they were from the IRA, was enough to scare all in the house into submission. All six members of the family were being held in an adjoining bedroom by one member of Quin's group, while the other was organizing the diversion. Mary O'Niel had arrived promptly at 10 pm, an AK47 assault rifle hidden beneath her coat. It leaned against the far wall, awaiting Kane.

Martin checked the room again, the curtains had been drawn and a thin slit cut in them. From the street below they would appear normal, but a sniper had a clear field of fire through the open window. A sofa had been dragged to its edge and a chair upturned on top of it to provide a stable platform for the shooter. He nodded his head, satisfied. All was set, they just needed Kane; it had been Kane's return that had con-vinced Brigade to allow tonight's ambush. He checked his watch again.

'Where the fuck is he,' cursed Martin to himself. An image of Kane came unbidden into his mind. God how he hated the man, hated his reputation. Kane the man who never missed,

11

hated the look of hero worship on the faces of his ASU when Kane entered the room. There was something unhealthy about the man, a look in his eyes that made Martin's flesh crawl. He shook off the feeling and concentrated on the escape plan.

He would leave as soon as Kane arrived. After the shoot, Quin would remove the rifle, while Kane headed through a maze of back gardens and alleys to a waiting car. Mary O'Niel would be waiting with a pram for Quin, and would transport the rifle to a hide. If there was any trouble the gun would be ditched; guns could be replaced.

'Kane will get the credit for this, if everything goes well,' he thought with disgust. 'What the fuck just as long as he gets the job done.'

With no sound to announce his approach, Kane stepped into the room. Martin watched as he walked with cat-like grace to the waiting AK47 and checked its action. Protests died unspoken in Martin's mouth. Kane's quiet professionalism impressed even him. Without speaking to the gunman he walked to the door and opening it he looked at Quin, and smiled. 'Nothing can save them now,' he said.

11 pm Crumlin Road, Belfast, Same Night.

Tennant Street police sub-division was universally recognized as being one of the hardest policing districts in the whole of Ulster. Not only did it cover the fiercely Loyalist Shankhill Road, and several other militant Protestant estates, but also the hardline Republican Ardoyne, an area so dangerous it could only be safely patrolled in strength, usually with army back-up patrols.

In order to deal with the unusual problems posed in trying to police this IRA stronghold, the Ardoyne Patrol Unit had been formed – specially selected officers whose main job was to get to know the area, its residents, its streets and, of course, its terrorists.

On this Friday night four members of the six man patrol sat in their heavily armoured 'Tangi' Landrover. Sitting in the front seat was Constable Edward Magill, a senior constable with ten years service. As the vehicle's observer he would deal

12

with any calls during their turn of duty and, of course, any subsequent paperwork. For this reason the role of observer rotated through the patrol, regardless of rank or length of service.

In the rear seat two gunners Constable Tony Addams a stocky, hard working, Belfast man in his late twenties, a Sterling sub-machine gun resting across his knees, and Constable Billy Campbell, a tall lean, soft spoken married man in his early thirties. Campbell carried an M1 carbine with a thirty round magazine, its butt in his hand while the barrel rested on his toe cap. Both were half asleep, they had less than an hour to kill before the end of their shift.

The radio interrupted their reverie. 'Delta Tango 98 from Delta Tango over.'

Magill lifted the handset with a sigh, 'Delta Tango 98 send over.'

There was a slight pause. 'Delta Tango 98 we have a report of youths breaking windows in a parked car in Etna Drive over.'

Magill looked at his driver, Constable Kelly, who nodded his completely bald head and swung his huge vehicle in a tight turn. For several weeks there had been a series of seemingly random acts of vandalism against cars in that particular area of the Ardoyne. Magill spoke again into the radio handset. 'What cover do we have, over?'

'There's a call-sign from Delta Oscar on its way to back you up, over.'

'Roger out,' Magill answered.

Magill was content. Delta Oscar was the call-sign of their neighbouring sub-division, Oldpark. He knew and trusted the men from the station. In minutes Kelly pulled up behind the wrecked car.

'Arrival Etna Drive,' Magill reported.

Using the overhead spotlight Magill surveyed the Ford Orion in front of him, it had obviously been badly damaged. There was still no sign of the Oldpark vehicle. 'Delta Tango from Delta Tango 98, I can confirm the vehicle is a red Ford Orion, no number plate visible, over.'

'Roger Delta Tango 98, if you can get me a VRM, I'll close it down until tomorrow.'

Magill surveyed the dark street; not more than six feet from him lay the vehicle's number plate. He came to a quick decision and turning he spoke to his two gunners. 'I'm going out to have a quick look at that number plate over there.' He indicated with a jerk of his head. 'I want to be in and out fast OK?'

Both men nodded without replying; swiftly they opened the back door and ran into covering positions on opposite sides of the street. Magill started to open the heavy passenger door.

Across the road, Kane sighted on Magill as he left his seat, tracking him as he walked the short distance to the discarded number plate. Kane waited until Magill stopped. As he started to bend, Kane fired twice. Both shots hit just behind the right ear and exited through the bottom left of Magill's jaw. He fell heavily but felt nothing as his head smashed into the concrete road surface; he was already dead.

Changing aim swiftly. Kane sighted on Addams, kneeling in a doorway almost directly opposite him. Echoes of his first two shots were still rebounding from wall to wall, while the curtains in front of him hid the gun flashes. Addams was starting to rise, having no idea where the shots had come from when Kane fired again, three shots in quick succession. Two hit the rising man on his protective body armour, but the third smashed into Addams' open mouth, blowing out half his skull as it exited. His unused sub-machine gun fell from nerveless hands.

Below and slightly to Kane's left, Billy Campbell was completely confused by the two sets of shots. Thinking himself under fire from both ends of Etna Drive, he ran from his safe position in the doorway towards Kelly's armoured Landrover.

Kane was preparing to withdraw when Campbell ran into view; ignoring the frantic shouts of Quin behind him, he took aim at the running RUC man.

Campbell became aware of shots landing around him. The distance to safety seemed to lengthen, his legs became heavy and everything started to slow down. A giant hand grabbed his right shoulder and spun him in a half arc, so that he tottered drunkenly on one leg. Simultaneously he was hit again, in the left leg and throat. Falling, he tried to scream but only a grotesque spray of bright red blood erupted from his throat.

From inside the Landrover, Kelly watched in horror as his friend rolled in agony, unable to do anything but scream for assistance on the radio.

Kane turned, satisfied, handing the AK47 to Quin, and raced down the stairs. Already, in the distance sirens could be heard. Once in the back alley Kane split up from the two younger volunteers. Sprinting down an adjacent back garden and through a conveniently open back door, he discarded his black boiler suit and balaclava. Stepping outside he found a black taxi waiting for him. A short drive took him to the Shamrock Club where at least six witnesses would swear he had been in the club all night.

Several streets away a foot patrol of the Royal Green Jackets, responding to the Etna Drive ambush, almost knocked over a young girl pushing a pram. Watching them as they raced down the street, Mary O'Niel smiled and continued to push her sister's baby towards the weapons hide for the AK47 it concealed.

12 Midnight, Republican Press Bureau, Falls Road, Press Release.

> At 11.05 pm an Active Service Unit of 'A' Company Irish Republican Army, ambushed a patrol of RUC gunmen operating in the Nationalist Ardoyne Area. At least three gunmen were seen to be hit. The ambush is in response to the increasing harassment of Nationalists by Crown Forces and their Loyalist allies in North Belfast. Locals are warned to stay away from all security force patrols as further attacks are planned.
> Signed P. O'Niel, Press Officer.

Carrickfergus, just outside Belfast, 1 am Saturday Morning.

Nevin Brown reached groggily for his radio alarm, but the buzzing continued. Realizing it was the telephone, he picked it up. 'Hello,' his voice sounded hoarse, even to his own ears.

'Nevin, is that you?' a familiar voice answered.

Nevin forced his eyes to focus on the illuminated face of his alarm clock. 'I hope so otherwise there's a stranger in my bed.' He finally registered the time, 'Inspector it's 1 am.'

'I'm aware of the time Sergeant Brown,' Detective Inspector Cotton, his immediate superior, answered.

The tone of his voice made Nevin sit upright, sleep banished completely from his brain. 'What's happened?' he asked.

He heard DI Cotton take a deep breath. 'One of our mobiles got hit in the Ardoyne, about two hours ago, we have two dead and one critical – ' He broke off as an unheard voice asked him a question. Nevin could hear him saying, 'OK, OK,' then he was back on the line.

'On top of that I've got a separate murder scene in Leopold Street, a young girl raped and stabbed. You're one of the few Detective Sergeants I know who wouldn't be drunk at 1 am on Saturday morning.' Nevin grimaced involuntarily, both men knew why he didn't drink any more, 'Can you come in?' Cotton asked.

'Give me an hour,' Nevin said.

'OK see you then,' Cotton said and hung up without further comment.

Picking up the standard issue .357 Ruger revolver he always kept by him, Nevin strode to the built-in closet and selected a pair of lightweight slacks. Hopping on one leg as he pulled them on, still barefoot he made his way to the bathroom, glancing at his reflection in the mirror. He shook his head, there were bags under his deep-set blue eyes and his hair looked like it had been combed with a hand grenade. He looked much older than his thirty-five years. 'You're a sorry sight, Brown,' he said aloud.

At least the wash and shave made him feel more awake. Returning to the bedroom he completed dressing and went downstairs. In the hall his pet Doberman Pinscher, King, lifted its head in enquiry; satisfied he dropped his head with a sigh and went back to sleep. Nevin paused to pat the huge dog. 'You've got more sense than me boy,' he said softly.

It took only a couple of minutes to make a pile of toast and a mug of tea; past experience had taught him to eat before reporting for duty, you never knew when you would get the chance again. Balancing his makeshift snack precariously, he made his way back to the sitting room and, switching on the TV, found the CEEFAX news headlines. It jumped straight out at him.

'POLICE KILLED IN BELFAST AMBUSH.'

Munching through his toast, he dialled the code for the full story and read,

> 'A police patrol was tonight ambushed in the Republican Ardoyne area of Belfast. At least two constables are known to be dead and a third seriously injured. Police did not return fire.
>
> In a separate incident, an eighteen-year-old girl was found stabbed to death in the nearby Loyalist Shankhill Road area; police have not said whether or not the killing was sectarian.'

Nevin swore aloud and wondered who the dead officers were. King padded into the room and put his huge head on his knee, begging a slice of toast. He fed him his last slice and gave him a playful tug on the ear. 'I won't be seeing much of you in the next few weeks,' he said shaking the dog's head between his hands.

Fitting the Ruger revolver into a shoulder holster, he threw on a casual sports jacket and left by the back door. He would ring his next door neighbour at a sensible hour and get him to feed and exercise King. Once outside he checked the street and satisfied it was clear, dropped onto his hands and knees and checked the underside of his Ford Escort car -- an everyday precaution for all RUC officers, given the IRA's love of undercar booby traps.

His drive to Belfast took less than thirty minutes. He kept his window rolled down despite the now steadily falling rain, allowing the cold morning air to clear the last vestiges of sleep from his brain. The streets were deserted as he drove along the Crumlin Road, past Crumlin Road Prison, its walls grey and grim in the dim light.

Turning into Tennant Street, he stopped at the huge electronically-controlled security gates and allowed the sentry to see his face; as they swung open a second sentry approached, armed with a Sterling sub-machine gun. Nevin recognized him at once and driving his car forward he stopped next to him. 'Hello Peter, what can you tell me about the ambush?'

The part-time policeman's face was drawn by a mixture of

sorrow and anger, 'It's bad news Nevin. The bastards killed Edward Magill and Tony Addams; Billy Campbell's been shot up real bad, last we heard he was listed as critical.' He paused to let the information sink in. Nevin looked up into his face. In the five years he had known part-time Reserve Constable Peter Taylor it was the first time he could recall having heard him swear. 'If you hear anything about Billy will you let us know?' He jerked his head towards the sentry box, 'Eddy Gardner is inside, he and Billy play snooker together.'

Nevin glanced towards the concrete and steel sangar in time to see an anxious face appear. He felt Peter's hand on his shoulder and looked again at his worried face. 'Eddy's taking it real bad,' Peter said in a low voice. 'You'll likely hear anything first being CID and all.'

'As soon as I hear anything I'll let you know,' Nevin said.

Peter nodded his thanks. Nevin rolled up his car window and drove into the station complex past the squat red brick main building, still bearing bullet marks near its flat topped roof where a UVF gunman had fired on a long removed army sentry post. A page of Irish history long forgotten by most. Parking his car, he strode quickly across the rear car park and made his way to CID general office, situated on the second floor. Organized chaos greeted Nevin as he entered. Phones rang incessantly, threatening to overwhelm two young CID aides left in charge. One of them, Billy Boyd, gave Nevin a weak smile. Placing a hand over his telephone he said, 'The boss wants you in his office asap, skipper.'

He grimaced and nodded towards the still covered telephone. Lowering his voice he said, 'I've got Hart on the other end. He wants all the answers.' He shrugged helplessly and rolled his eyes. 'I don't even know the questions.' Removing his hand he spoke into the receiver. 'Yes sir, of course sir.' Winking at Nevin he rolled his eyes in mock exasperation.

Nevin returned his smile with heartfelt sympathy. Detective Chief Inspector Hart was head of divisional CID and was almost universally disliked by all. An obese, arrogant man, he had well earned his nickname, Heartbreaker. Giving Boyd an encouraging thumbs up, the detective headed for his DI's office. Knocking he entered quickly. DI Cotton stood with his back to Nevin, studying a large scale map of Tennant Street area. Two large red pins, one in Ardoyne, one in Leopold

18

Street, marked the murder scenes. Without turning Cotton spoke. 'Glad you got here so fast Nevin. I'm sorry to drag you out of bed, please sit down I won't be a moment.'

Sitting, Nevin studied his immediate superior. Standing at just over six foot, broad shouldered and slim hipped, his jet black hair cut fashionably short, DI Brian 'Billy' Cotton cut a smart figure. Turning, he sat down opposite his senior DS. Nevin noted signs of stress on Cotton's normally handsome face. There were worry lines at the corners of his naturally hooded eyes, fatigue wrinkled his low forehead, the normally firm straight mouth beneath his slightly hooked nose drooped tiredly. Despite fatigue's ravages it was a face that still radiated strength and character. In his early forties, Brian Cotton could normally pass for thirty-five; tonight he looked his age and more.

Brian returned Nevin's frank stare. They had worked together for five years and held each other in mutual esteem. In DI Cotton, Nevin knew he had a tough, methodical and totally dedicated superior, who could, if the occasion demanded, be totally ruthless. Cotton, in turn, knew Nevin to be a truly gifted detective who could have insights of true brilliance, even if he didn't always follow laid down police procedures.

'OK, here's how things stand at present,' the DI said, tiredness obvious in his voice. Briefly he outlined events, speaking slowly to allow Nevin to take occasional notes. It amounted to little more than what he already knew. Pausing, Brian lit a thin cigar and carried on. 'Dessi Anderson was DS on call; he's got the Ardoyne scene. The army's in there in strength, providing cover. All available agencies, SOCO, mapping and photography, are tied up with him and will be for some time.' Shaking his head ruefully he glanced down at a sheet of paper on the desk. Reading from it he carried on. 'They've got a lot to cover, a house take-over, ambush site, not to mention what looks like three separate escape routes taken by the shooters.'

Flicking ash from his cigar into an ashtray on the table, Brian took a sip from a plastic cup next to it. Screwing his face up with distaste he went on. 'The second murder scene is in Leopold Street; it takes second place to the Ardoyne, so don't expect any help for at least a couple of hours. At the moment a DS McFarlan from Castlereagh is in charge.' He looked up at

Nevin. 'Control sent us every detective on duty they could spare, do you know him?'

'I think so,' Nevin replied. 'I did my CID initial course with a DS McFarlan. It must be the same man. He's good.'

The DI nodded. 'I'm sure he is, but he doesn't know either the locals or the area.' He flicked his right index finger at Nevin. 'That's why I want you to take over. I'll give you Billy Boyd to help you. McFarlan has a D.Con. with him. As soon as you get there start a house to house enquiry.'

'Will they open their doors at this time of the morning?' Nevin interrupted.

Cotton fixed him with an unswerving stare. 'One of their own has been killed; they'll open up all right.' He continued his briefing, telling Nevin what little he knew of Lynn Moody's murder. He finished by saying, 'McFarlan will give you all the details on the victim; at the moment all I have is a name, Lynn Moody. A police woman from the night section is with her family. Let McFarlan deal with that side of things; you concentrate on the house to house, use your local knowledge and see what you can pick up.'

Nevin nodded his head, standing. 'I'll get right on it.' Turning he headed for the door. From behind, Brian's voice stopped him, softer, no longer a superior, a friend asking a question. 'Nevin, when I called you, were you alone?'

Involuntarily Nevin stiffened, then gave a short humourless laugh, glancing back at his friend. 'Yes.' Smiling at Brian's sympathetic shrug he opened the door and stepped back into the general office. Walking quickly to his desk, he removed his personal folder from its drawer. 'Billy.' He shouted across the room without looking up.

Caught in the act of picking up yet another ringing phone Billy Boyd froze and looked up. 'Yes skipper?' he answered.

Looking across at his young aid's concerned face Nevin smiled. 'Let me take you away from all this,' he said throwing a set of car keys which Billy caught deftly. 'Get the car ready, you're coming out with me.'

A relieved smile spread across Billy's face. Without further prompting he stood and threw his coat on. Hurriedly shoving his Ruger into a holster on his belt and picking up his personal folder, the short roly-poly apprentice detective raced out of the room.

20

By the time Nevin had signed out a personal radio, Billy had an unmarked CID car waiting for him. As they passed back through Tennant Street Barrack's huge security gates, Nevin asked Billy to pause while he told Peter Taylor that he had no fresh news. Promising to keep the part-timer informed, Nevin nodded to Billy to carry on. It was a short drive to Leopold Street. Stopping at the outer cordon, manned by members of Tennant Street's own mobile support unit, Nevin was aware that every house in the narrow street had a lighted window.

'Brian was right,' Nevin said to himself.

Leopold Street formed a part of the Shankill known as the Woodvale. It was a semi independent off-shoot, its people traditionally tight lipped and wary of authority, preferring to solve their own problems.

At its east side a peace wall, or environmental wall as the city planners liked to call it, separated this fiercely Loyalist area from the neighbouring and equally Republican Ardoyne. In all the tragic years of violence, this small area had seen more than its fair share of victims, but none like tonight's.

With Billy at his heels Nevin made his way to a taped-off alley entrance and spotted a familiar figure. 'Ray, Ray McFarlan,' he shouted with genuine warmth. 'I thought it was you.'

DS Ray McFarlan accepted Nevin's outstretched hand in his own huge farmer's paw. 'Always a pleasure Nevin,' he said pumping the hand enthusiastically. A big, burly, sandy-haired Ballymena man, you could cut his broad country accent with a knife. Many a professional criminal had been deceived by his outward appearance, but behind it lay a mind like a steel trap.

Nevin managed to extract his hand before any bones were broken. 'What have you got for me?' he asked with a slightly pained smile.

McFarlan took a deep breath and looked down at the clipboard in his left hand, suddenly a professional policeman. 'It's a bad one Nevin,' he said, his voice suddenly strained. 'The body was found at approximately 10 pm by a local beat patrol, Cons. Brady and Herron.' He looked up at Nevin and jerked his head towards a nearby parked Hotspur Landrover. 'I've kept them here so you can talk to them.'

'Thanks, I'll do that after I've seen the body; anything else?' Nevin asked.

'Not much, doctor pronounced life extinct at 10.30 pm,

21

preliminary cause of death given as multiple stab wounds. There's also evidence of sexual assault. We're still waiting for SOCO and mapping to get here from the Ardoyne.'

'They're going to be some time yet,' Nevin interrupted. 'We'll just have to get on without them. I don't suppose anybody saw or heard anything?'

McFarlan shook his head. 'None that have come forward as yet, we've been waiting for you to start the house to house. You want to see the body now?' he asked.

Nevin nodded and followed him into the alley. A short distance inside its gloomy interior McFarlan paused by a blanket-covered form and waved a hand. Immediately light flooded into the alley from a parked Landrover. Turning he spoke to Nevin, his voice strained, his face stern. 'Brace yourself lad, this is not pretty.' He lifted the blanket.

Involuntarily Nevin's breath caught in his throat. In his fifteen years of service he had seen death in all its ugly forms. His friends' and colleagues' bodies torn and shredded by bomb and bullet. Suicides by rope and electrocution, bodies bloated by drowning, the heart rendering grief of a cot death. Nothing, nothing, had ever been like this.

Lynn Moody's body looked like it had been ravaged by a wild animal. Her face, frozen in death, held a grotesque look of utter horror. Momentarily, Nevin felt light-headed and a wave a nausea swept over him. From what seemed like a great distance he heard McFarlan's voice. 'Her name's Lynn Moody, age eighteen, only child, lives at 112 Leopold Street with her mother, father dead. She was on her way to meet a boyfriend when she was killed . . . '

Anything else that McFarlan said was blocked out by a buzzing in his head. Nevin stood quickly and almost fell. McFarlan steadied him. Fighting down his rising gorge he stumbled back into the street. Steadying himself he sucked huge gulps of air into his lungs. Looking up he saw McFarlan's concerned face close to his. 'You all right lad?' he asked softly putting a reassuring hand on his shoulder.

Nevin nodded, 'I'm sorry,' he said.

McFarlan smiled sympathetically. 'Don't be lad.' He patted him on the shoulder. 'It hit me just the same; you OK now?'

Nevin nodded and taking another deep breath he said, 'Right, me and Billy will handle the house to house. Ray you and – ' Nevin looked enquiringly at a second detective who had appeared at McFarlan's shoulder.

'Eddy McBride.' He offered extending a hand.

Nevin accepted it. 'Nice to meet you Eddy.' Looking back to McFarlan he continued, 'You and Eddy interview her mother, usual thing, any boyfriends.' He made a casual gesture with his right hand. 'Has she broken up with anybody recently, threats made by ex-boyfriends etc., OK?'

Both men nodded soberly. Interviewing the distraught mother of a recently raped and murdered young girl was not a prospect anyone would relish.

'Is the women con. still with her?' asked McFarlan.

'As far as I know,' answered Nevin.

Without further comment, both Castlereagh detectives moved off on their thankless task. Alone with Billy, Nevin called the two uniformed beat officers over. Both were known to him. 'What about you Martin, Jeff.' He offered the traditional Ulster greeting to both men.

'A bit better now skipper,' answered Martin Herron, a tall thin senior constable in his early forties, his eyes involuntarily drawn to the covered body in the alley.

Nevin nodded his sympathy. 'Which one of you actually discovered the body?'

'Me,' Jeff Brady offered, a few years younger than Herron and overweight. His normally jolly fat man's face wore a troubled frown. 'We had stepped into the alley for a smoke when I all but tripped over . . . ' His words died as the memory of his horrific discovery flooded back, making his face contort with pain. Regaining control he looked at the detective sergeant, 'I'm sorry, I've got a daughter that age.'

'It's OK, I understand; just two more questions, are you quite sure of the exact time you discovered the body?' Nevin asked, keeping his voice businesslike and calm.

'Positive,' Martin Herron replied at once. 'As soon as Jeff found her I checked my watch.'

'OK, just one more question,' he said glancing at Billy to make sure he was taking notes. 'Did either of you hear or see anything unusual, at any time during your shift?'

Both men shook their heads negatively. 'No, everything was very quiet until we . . . ' Jeff Brady offered pointing back into the alley.

'Right,' Nevin interrupted to prevent Brady dwelling on his gruesome discovery, 'that's all for now, get yourselves back to the station, make a statement, and then knock off for the night.'

Looking more than slightly relieved, both constables walked back through the security cordon. As they ducked under the white tape sealing off Leopold Street, Brady gave a fleeting glance backwards at the alley entrance and its tragic contents.

For several seconds Nevin was quiet, watching both men disappear. Finally he turned to his young aid, his eyes hard. He said, 'I'm going to find the animal that did this Billy, and when I do, I'll nail the bastard to the wall.'

Watching his superior, Billy Boyd felt hairs start to rise on his neck. In his eighteen months of CID attachment, he had grown to like, trust and admire Tennant Street station's senior detective sergeant. Never had he seen him become personally involved in a case, until now. As Nevin led him up the dimly lit street to begin their enquiries he said softly to himself, 'I hope so skipper, I really do.'

As any police officer will readily tell the uninitiated, investigations, especially murder investigations, are not solved by discovering a single vital clue. In real life detectives do not, as a general rule, find a speck of mud that is only found in one part of the country, a convenient button that eventually leads a resourceful sleuth to discover a murderer's identity.

No, real life detectives solve crimes by a combination of back-breaking routine questioning and methodical collection and processing of evidence. What occupied both men for two full hours was just that. Door to door, routine questions: were you home? Did you hear anything unusual? Did you know the victim? Routine questions that form the backbone of every murder enquiry.

DI Cotton had been correct. No door had remained barred to them. Helpful as everyone wanted to be, they had drawn a complete blank until Nevin knocked on a door that was vaguely familiar. Stepping back he was confronted by a familiar figure. 'Well, well, if it isn't Martin Hewitt,' Nevin said with mock seriousness, 'I'd forgotten you lived on this street.'

Martin Hewitt blinked twice behind his rimless glasses as he returned Nevin's stare. Only 5′ 6″ tall, his thin frame still managed to contain a prominent pot belly, a fact barely concealed by his thin, off-white vest and shabby grey trousers, held up by broad red braces. A slash which passed for a mouth broke into what was meant to be a smile. 'Mr Brown isn't it?' Hewitt replied, his bullet-shaped skull, with its close cropped grey hair, moving up and down as he spoke. 'You'll be coming in for a cup of tea, won't you?' Without waiting for a reply he turned and led both detectives into the house.

Nevin exchanged a glance with Billy and then jerked his head towards the retreating Hewitt. Gingerly both men followed. Surprisingly Hewitt's front room proved to be both clean and tidy. The small man stood with a teapot in his hand. 'Milk and sugar?' he asked pleasantly. Nevin nodded without replying. Watching Hewitt scurry back into his small kitchen, he mused that in any other society the small man might be considered a figure of mirth, someone to poke fun at, but not on the Shankhill!

It was well known throughout the whole of Protestant North Belfast that Hewitt was a member of the violent para-military UVF, one of the most organized, heavily armed and violent Protestant terrorist groups operating in Ulster. What was not so well known, but suspected by the RUC, was that he was responsible for at least two sectarian murders and was currently intelligence officer for the organization. No, nobody on the Shankhill Road laughed at Martin Hewitt, not twice anyway.

Hewitt returned with three cups of hot tea. 'Sit down, sit down please,' he said with urgency. Both detectives settled themselves in Hewitt's large comfortable armchairs, Billy with an audible sigh of relief. Accepting one of the offered cups, Nevin glanced over Hewitt's shoulder. Mounted on his mantelpiece was a tapestry. Two black clad figures rested rifles in solemn salute; below was an inscription:

IN PROUD AND LOVING MEMORY OF
LT COL LENNY MURPHY
A SOLDIER OF ULSTER.

Unbidden a face jumped from the past into Nevin's memory. Lenny Murphy, Shankhill's 'master butcher', a psychopath whose reign of terror was still talked about in whispers, as if fearful of his return, even from the grave. A man who inspired such fear and control that he was able to walk into a crowded bar, select a victim and shoot him dead in front of a dozen witnesses. Finally his own organization grew weary of his excesses and set him up for assassination by the IRA.

'The Provos may have pulled the trigger but your own people loaded the gun.'

'Did you say something Mr Brown?' asked Hewitt.

Startled Nevin realized he had spoken out loud. 'Sorry,' he said quickly, 'just musing; you knew Lenny Murphy didn't you?'

The UVF man glanced over his shoulder. 'Ah Lenny,' Hewitt said nodding, lost in thought for a minute as he studied the memorial to the dead killer. Looking back at Nevin he said with a sad smile, 'He was a true soldier of Ulster.' Conviction rang true in his voice.

Billy Boyd opened his mouth to make an angry retort but a barely perceptible shake of Nevin's head silenced him. Flashing an angry glare at Hewitt's back he lapsed into a sullen silence.

'Well that's the past Martin. I suppose you've heard about the girl's murder?' The detective asked, knowing that nothing happened anywhere around there without Hewitt hearing about it.

Hewitt paused before replying, his eyes perpetually blinking behind his glasses. 'Aye a bad business, bad indeed.' He moved to lean his back against the unlit fire. 'I was over with the mother, she's in a terrible state. She was a good girl, Lynn, stabbed wasn't she?' Hewitt's watery gaze fixed on Nevin.

All good detectives get a gut reaction when they are on to a scent; Nevin had one now. Hewitt knew something! Keeping his voice casual he replied, 'Yes, were you in all night?'

'Yes.'

'Alone?' asked Billy, making notes.

'Yes, all night.'

'Did you hear or see anything suspicious?' asked Nevin.

Hewitt rubbed his unshaven chin. 'No not tonight.'

Knowing that something was being kept back, Nevin rose and crossed the room. Behind narrowed eyes he leaned close to Hewitt and said coldly, 'This has nothing to do with the organization, this is a young girl, raped and stabbed. Now let's have the truth, all of it.'

26

Their eyes locked for several seconds. Turning, the UVF man shuffled to a sideboard, found a cigarette and lit it. Turning back to Nevin he said, 'OK, my people had a meeting here last Friday, at about 8.30 pm. One man was late; when he came in he said he saw a man down by the alley watching the house.'

'The same alley Lynn was killed in?'

'Yes.'

'Who was the late arriver?'

'Now Mr Brown I can't tell you that . . . '

'Listen, Martin,' Nevin's voice was colder than a December frost, 'I want to know everything, or you just won't believe how much trouble I can make for your people.'

Hewitt hesitated for a second, only a second. 'OK, but this isn't going to be used against us?'

'I'm only interested in the girl's murder, not the UVF.'

Hewitt sighed. 'OK, his name is Billy Moffit, he lives in Crimea Street.'

'What did you do after Billy told you about the man?'

'We piled out and searched the area, didn't find anything. Billy got a bit of stick. I didn't give it much thought until now.'

Nevin looked over at Billy who nodded to indicate he'd got everything.

'Anything else?'

'No Mr Brown, that's all, honest.'

Realizing he had got all he was going to get and that he would get no written statement, Nevin led Billy back out into the street. Closing the door, Hewitt pursed his lips thoughtfully and walking quickly to his phone he dialled a number from memory. When it was answered he said, 'I want to speak to Colin.'

Outside, rain cascaded down, making life difficult for all. By 6.30 all of Leopold Street had been checked. SOCO and all other relevant technical agencies, had poked, dusted, mapped and photographed Lynn Moody's remains. Sitting in his car Nevin had a short conference with Ray McFarlan, who filled him in on what Lynn's mother had said. It wasn't much. There was a knock on his passenger window. Nevin glanced out to see a uniformed officer. Rolling down the window he had a piece of paper thrust at him.

'Message from your DI. All CID officers to be back at base

for a briefing at 9 am skipper.'

'Thanks, when is the body being moved?' he asked.

'Should be any time now.'

'Thanks again,' Nevin gave the drenched officer an encouraging grin, watching with sympathy as he returned to his place in the cordon. Turning back to McFarlan he said, 'Ray will you and Eddy hang on here until the remains are moved?'

'Sure, we'll get a lift back with the cordon and see you back at base.'

'Good, I don't think there'll be any problems, but give me a call over the air if there is.'

Both men got out into the pouring rain without replying. Nevin shook his head. 'Who'd be a peeler on a morning like this?' Turning to Billy he said, 'Right let's go talk to Mr Moffit.'

Billy Moffit was a slim unkempt youth whose personality matched his appearance. His temper was not improved by being awakened at 7 am, a previously unknown time to him. 'What do you want at this time of the morning?' he asked with barely concealed contempt.

Nevin took a couple of seconds before answering. 'It's about the meeting you had at Martin Hewitt's house last Friday night.'

'What meeting? I don't know what you're talking about.'

He tried to close the door, but Billy jammed it open with his foot. Nevin shook his head in mock sadness. 'Listen Billy either you talk to me here, or I'll arrest you and we can talk at the station.'

'On what charge?' Moffit tried to appear unconcerned, but failed.

'Oh, let's see.' The detective rubbed his chin in mock contemplation. 'Withholding information! Hewitt told us you were there. Now don't screw around with me,' he advanced on him, his face hard and menacing. 'What did you see?'

'OK, OK, if Martin told you I was there, I was there.' Moffit crumbled, 'I saw a man, I thought he was watching Martin's house.'

Nevin nodded to Billy who took out his notebook. 'What did he look like?'

Moffit shook his head. 'I didn't see his face; he wore an anorak with the hood up, but he was a big bloke, broad

28

shouldered; fair scared me to death, just the sight of him.'

'You didn't see his face at all? Hair colour anything?'

'No, it was dark.'

'How come you came to see him in the first place?'

'Well I was just going into Martin's house when Lynn Moody came out; she's a girl who lives across from him. I was watching her walk down the street when this fella came out of the alley.'

'Why were you watching Lynn Moody?'

Moffit leered at Nevin. 'She's got a great set of legs.'

'Not any more.' Nevin watched him closely. 'She's dead, murdered.'

Genuine grief flooded Moffit's face. 'I can't believe it, I only saw her yesterday on the bus coming home. I can't believe it.'

Nevin exhaled. 'This man you saw in the alley, you say he stepped out after Lynn passed?'

'Yes, he looked after Lynn then up the street.'

'Do you think he saw you?'

'No I was in Martin's hallway, I don't think he saw me.'

Nevin's eyes narrowed. 'He only came out after Lynn passed,' he said, more to himself than Moffit. Looking back at the UVF man he said, 'Just one more thing, where were you last night, between 8.30 and 10 o'clock?'

'I was in the Berlin Arms all night, with some mates. You don't think I ... '

Nevin interrupted him, 'No I don't. I just have to ask. I'm going to need a statement from you, can you come round sometime this morning?'

'Aye I'll come round after nine, that OK?'

'Dead on, Billy, just ask for D.Con. Boyd here all right?'

In the car Nevin told Billy to return to Tennant Street. 'What do you make of that, skipper?' he asked, starting the engine.

Rubbing a thumb nail against his bottom lip, Nevin took a second to answer. 'I don't know, yet.' He flashed a quick glance at his young aid. 'But it seems too much of a coincidence to ignore, make sure you get that statement, OK?'

Back at the station, Billy left him, rushing off to catch up with some paperwork. He checked his watch. He had an hour. Time for some breakfast. Normally the canteen would have been half empty but last night's events had caused an influx of unexpected customers. Troops from various regiments jock-eyed with mobile support units and local police for food and space. Nevin grabbed a prepared meal and found a seat at one of the noisiest tables. Gary Howe, a burly Scots ex-marine commando, was having a volatile argument with several other officers.

'I tell you the man isn't bloody well invincible; we had him on the run back in '73; killed one of his ASU and nearly got him,' the Scot was saying.

'Oh, and how do you know it was him?' asked one of his MSU antagonists.

'Because military intelligence confirmed it, that's why.'

Before any more debating points could be scored, a message over the station's loudspeaker system called all uniformed officers to a briefing. Gary hung back.

'What about you skipper?' he asked cheerfully.

'Fine Gary, shouldn't you be going?' he asked indicating his retreating comrades.

Gary laughed and took a sip of tea. 'They won't miss me for a moment.' His face became serious. 'This bastard Kane has got them all scared.'

'I know.'

'No you don't skipper. Ever since we were told Kane was back from America they've been like a load of turkeys waiting for Christmas.' He shook his head and snorted with contempt. 'Waiting for the axe to fall.'

'He doesn't scare you?'

Laughing Gary got to his feet. 'No,' he said, turning to leave. 'I know he's human, not a ghost.'

Watching the Scot disappear, Nevin munched through his breakfast, not tasting it but needing nourishment. He thought about what Gary had said and about Kane, Butcher Kane, the bogeyman all policemen were scared of. 'Yes we'll get you Mr Kane, but how many of us will you "butcher" before we do?'

Finishing his meal he made his way to CID general office for his 9 am briefing. Seeing Ray McFarlan he made his way to the burly Ballymena detective's side, collating and updating his notes.

Promptly at 9 am DI Cotton accompanied by DCI Hart, head of Divisional CID, entered the room; all fell silent as DI Cotton called for order. Hart surveyed his assembled CID officers. Standing at just over six foot tall and immensely overweight, he had none of the fat man's usual jollity. Small brown eyes stared stonily from beneath thick eyebrows. His small ears and nose, totally out of proportion to his huge head, gave him a porcine look. His ego and arrogance matched his bulk.

'We'll hear about the Ardoyne incident first, DS Anderson.' Hart's voice was unusually high for a man of his bulk.

DS Anderson, a tall, ramrod straight, Belfast man stood at the back. In a clear, firm voice he outlined his initial investigation into the previous night's police murders.

'First people to arrive at the scene were a back-up mobile patrol from Oldpark Station. They secured the area and rendered first aid.' He checked his notebook, 'They arrived at 11.10 pm, army patrols arrived in strength a few minutes later. A hot pursuit by a patrol into 34 Etna Drive revealed a family held captive and a firing point in the upstairs front bedroom.' He looked up at Hart. 'I talked to the family, husband's name . . . '

'Don't give me every detail sergeant, just an outline,' Hart interrupted.

Anderson shrugged and looking back at his notebook, 'The house was taken over at approximately 8.30 pm by three armed men, I don't think any of them was the actual shooter . . . '

'Why do you say that?' Hart interrupted again.

'I'm coming to that, sir; the householder said all three were young and nervous, probably first timers. The examination of the firing point revealed a platform made up from an upturned chair. The curtain had been split, just enough to give a field of fire. In all eleven shots were fired by a single gunman, eight hit three separate moving targets. Whoever the shooter was he was no first timer.'

'Kane!' an unseen voice said. There were mumbles of agreement.

'That will be enough of that, this is a briefing, not a gossip shop,' DI Cotton interjected angrily. Silence returned.

'That's why I don't believe any of the takeover team was the shooter, it was too professional.' Anderson looked at Hart enquiringly and received a curt nod. 'Follow up by dog teams revealed three separate escape routes, but they all petered out.

Forensic is so far negative, they all probably wore boiler suits and surgical gloves, so I'm not hopeful. No news on the gun yet, but its probably an AK47. Follow up searches on known PIRA suspects, all negative.'

'Thank you Sergeant Anderson.' Hart's voice managed to convey a feeling of contempt.

Hart outlined his follow-up investigation, a special incident room was set up, a huge house to house enquiry and search operation, with army back up, was organized. DI Cotton was given authority to arrest both Kane and Martin under section 12 of the Emergency Provisions Act. He finished by asking, 'Any questions, any points.' Silence greeted him. His small eyes rested on Nevin. They had crossed swords before. Hart said, 'Let's hear from Sergeant Brown.'

He began by outlining Lynn's movements on the last night of life, described her body's discovery by Herron and Brady, and gave the preliminary medical evidence.

Finally he came to his conversations with Hewitt and Moffit. Hart listened, his face impassive.

'Is that all Sergeant Brown?' asked the DCI.

'Yes.'

Hart nodded and without saying anything managed to convey the feeling that he could have done better. He gave the senior detective three men, including Billy Boyd, all that he could hope for under the circumstances. 'Concentrate on any ex-boyfriends, lovers etc., all right sergeant?'

'What about what this man Moffit saw?'

'I don't put much store in that. If Moffit did see somebody it was probably something to do with the UVF meeting, not the girl. By the way report that meeting to SB. Any other points anybody?'

Nevin remained standing. Hart glared at him. 'Is there something else sergeant?'

'I'm sorry, sir, but I believe Moffit . . . I think we should . . .'

'Sergeant I don't care what you think. I've given you my directions.'

'But sir what if . . . '

'Don't but me,' Hart was half out of his chair, 'I run this Division not you, do you understand!'

Nevin opened his mouth to make an angry reply. 'I'm sure he does, sir; sit down Sergeant Brown and see me later,' DI

Cotton interjected.

He glanced at his friend and superior. Cotton gestured with his right hand, motioning him to sit down. He did so, reluctantly. Hart gave him one last baleful glare and resumed his seat. Cotton took over, detailing detectives the every day mundane tasks that consumed most of their time.

Later in his office the DI studied Nevin across the desk top. 'Just what were you trying to do in there, get yourself suspended?'

'That fat, arrogant, excuse for a police officer . . . ' Shaking his head, he stared Cotton directly in the eyes, 'He's got as much idea of how to run an investigation as I have of flying a plane.'

'He runs Divisional CID.'

'I don't care if he is God Almighty, he has no right . . . '

'That gives him the right.' He held up a hand to prevent another outburst. 'Nevin, he already wants you off this investigation.'

'WHAT, I'll . . . '

'SIT DOWN,' Cotton almost shouted. Nevin sat down and took a deep breath. The DI gave him a second to calm down. 'Its OK, I'm keeping you on the case.' He smiled at Nevin sardonically. 'I told him you were my best investigator and our DCI didn't like that.'

'Thanks.'

'Don't mention it. I happen to think it's true, but it's not going to do either of us any good if you go and get yourself suspended, is it?'

Nevin shook his head, a smile returning to his face. 'All right, I'll be good.'

'Fine, you know he's never forgiven you for the Maginnes affair.'

Nevin laughed, almost a year earlier there had been a series of violent armed robberies in North Belfast. Hart had arrested a well known local criminal, James Maginnes, on suspicion. Two days later Nevin had cracked the case. Hart had been made to look a fool and had never forgotten it.

'Well I had better go and start proving your faith in me is justified.' He stood to leave and the telephone rang. Watching, he saw colour drain from Cotton's face, heard him give a curt 'Got that' and replace the receiver. 'What's wrong?'

Cotton looked up at him pain and anger on his face, 'Billy Campbell just died.'

☆ ☆ ☆

Foster Green Hospital Mortuary, Belfast, 3 pm Saturday.

Rubbing his eyes to ease them of pain, Nevin felt like death warmed up. He'd managed a few hour's sleep, snatched in a friend's room at Tennant Street, but hardly enough. Smells assaulted his senses, a mixture of antiseptic, preservatives and decaying flesh, never would he get used to them.

His eyes were drawn, as if by a magnet, to Lynn's body, naked and obscenely stretched out, her face still bearing a look of horror.

Two attendants moved around the table on which she lay, cracking occasional jokes to each other. Nevin had long ago realized that this was occupational therapy for them; without it both might go mad. Behind him a door opened. Dr Ealing, pathologist for Belfast City, entered, a tall elegant man in his early forties, his jet black hair greying at the temples and haughty good looks adding to the authority of his position. He strode directly to the detective and looked down at him. 'Detective Brown isn't it?' His voice was upper class Belfast Irish.

'Detective Sergeant.'

'Ah yes, Detective Sergeant,' he corrected himself with a slight smile. 'You have the necessary paperwork?'

He handed him the official form P1, required in all sudden deaths. Ealing glanced at it and then the corpse. 'You can identify the deceased?'

Nevin exhaled and looked at her. 'Yes its Lynn Moody, DOB . . . '

'That's OK, sergeant, just the formal identification; that's all, you can go, unless,' he looked at the body and back to Nevin with a slightly superior smile, 'you want to remain?'

He shook his head and retired to an adjoining waiting room and spent his time completing his notebook and journal. A full two hours later Dr Ealing joined him. Striding to a wash basin he scrubbed his hands and addressed the detective over his shoulder. 'I hope you're taking notes detective sergeant. I don't

34

like to repeat myself.'

'Carry on any time you're ready Doctor.'

'Cause of death was multiple stab wounds, eight in all, any one of which would have proved fatal. Murder weapon was a twin edged, very sharp instrument, about six inches long, two inches broad at the hilt and tapering to a needle point, probably a knife.' He turned to face Nevin towelling his hands vigorously. 'You getting all this?'

'Yes, please carry on.'

'There was evidence of a sexual assault, actual penetration and semen remains. I've taken smears and sent them for analysis. That will give you the blood type of her attacker. There was also bruising around her throat, indicating she was grabbed from behind; from the angle and shape of the bruises I would say her attacker was considerably taller than her.'

'How much taller?'

'I'm a pathologist, not a magician,' he shrugged. 'She was 5′ 6″, her attacker was at least five inches taller; that do?'

Nevin nodded. 'Anything else you can tell me?'

'Her attacker was abnormally strong; depths of the wounds show considerable force was used; one blow actually severed her sternum.' He looked uncomprehendingly at him. 'Breast bone,' the pathologist explained.

'Abnormal strength! Would you say her attacker was some kind of athlete?' asked the detective.

Abruptly Ealing sat down. He rubbed both hands over his face, slowly pulling his fingers down over his eyes, nose and mouth. 'An athlete sergeant?' He shook his head slowly, 'No, I haven't seen wounds like that in twelve years of pathology. If you want my opinion,' he fixed Nevin with an unswerving stare, 'you're dealing with a madman.'

# 2

---

Tennant Street, CID Interview Room, Monday 10 am.

Martin Sheedy sat across from Nevin and Billy, looking both tired and sad. 'This interview is going to be taped, Martin,' Nevin was explaining. 'For the record I want you to state your name, age and address.' Sheedy did so. 'I also want you to state that you are here of your own accord, is that true?'

'Yes.'

'I am Detective Sergeant Brown.' Nevin inclined his head towards Billy, sitting taking extra notes next to him. 'This is Detective Boyd. We are investigating the murder of Lynn Moody.' Nevin paused studying Sheedy, he was hardly more than nineteen. 'What was your relationship with Lynn?'

'I was her boyfriend.'

'You had arranged to meet her last Friday?'

'Yes, we always met on Friday night, in the Beaten Docket.' He shrugged. 'She was normally as regular as clockwork.'

'What did you do when she didn't turn up?'

'I stayed in the pub until about ten, then went around to Pip's. I thought she had stood me up.'

'Were you her only boyfriend?'

Sheedy's eyes narrowed. 'What do you mean?'

'Was she seeing anybody else?'

Sheedy erupted across the table, grabbing Nevin by his shirt front. 'You black bastard, she was a good girl!' He started to shake Nevin. 'Do you hear me, a good girl!' Billy started to rise, but Nevin motioned him to remain seated. 'She was a good girl,' Sheedy started to cry. He dropped his head and sobbed uncontrollably.

Later, Nevin sat alone with Billy, his hand massaged tired eyes. 'What do you think skipper?'

36

Nevin shook his head and sighed. 'He had nothing to do with it, nor did her first boyfriend, what's his name?'

Billy checked his notes. 'Allan Davies.'

Nevin sat for a second, thumb nail rubbing his bottom lip. 'Billy, ninety-nine per cent of female rapes and murders committed in this province are done by persons who know, or are known by, the victim.' He looked at his aid. 'I keep remembering what this man Moffit claims he saw. Maybe he didn't know Lynn at all.'

Billy looked confused. 'What kind of man would rape and stab a young girl?'

Nevin remembered Dr Ealing's words. 'Maybe a maniac.' He stood. 'Maniac or not, I'm going to find him.'

Fate is a strange task master. At almost exactly that same time, in two completely separate parts of North Belfast different sets of ruthless people were meeting. Their deliberations would drive Lynn Moody's murder from Nevin's mind; for their agendas were, murder!

☆    ☆    ☆

Tyndale.

Of all of Shankhill Road's satellite Protestant estates, Tyndale had by far the worst reputation. Filth ridden, narrow roads were home to some of Ulster's worst and most violent men. Many black and terrible deeds had been done in its dark alleys and dim lit streets in the name of 'Loyalism'.

Set high on a hill on its outskirts, commanding a dominant view of the area, was the grandiose named Tyndale Community Centre. A long single storey building, which could only be approached by a single road, it was in fact an illegal drinking club run by the local UDA. Its rear opened on to an expanse of low rolling hills, used as a rubbish tip by estate residents.

In a rear room of this building, reserved for 'special customers', sat seven men; their faces bore the stamp of casual cruelty. All had been drinking. One man in particular dominated. When he spoke, everybody listened, he was William John Bing.

A squat, muscular, powerfully built man, his nose had been broken by more than one punch. Naturally hooded eyes, behind tinted glasses, studied each man as he spoke. He had joined the then fledgling UDA soon after it was formed and, by a combination of natural leadership and a physical savagery that was legendary, soon rose to command the organization in Tyndale.

It was during this period that he earned his nickname, 'The Window Cleaner'. Accompanied by a single accomplice and carrying a ladder, he would go to an intended victim's home and lean it against an outside bedroom window. Climbing up, he would gently knock on a window. When its curious occupant answered, Bing would shoot him twice, slide down, and make his escape.

Using this tried and trusted method he had by 1983 killed twenty-one men. Behind him, his huge bulk making the chair on which he sat look too small, was Billy Dixon. He was Bing's strong right arm; his devotion to him was almost child-like. It was his only child-like quality.

'So everything is set for Wednesday?' Bing asked, looking at his second in command, Mick Mickmichael, seated on his right.

Mickmichael, a tall thin hatchet-faced man nodded. 'I pick the guns up from Bob, bring them here and give them to the boys.'

Bing turned to Robert McCrum, an ex-sergeant in the UDR who had been discharged after two rifles in his charge had 'gone missing'. He was Bing's quartermaster, his bald head and hooked nose giving him the appearance of some hideous bird of prey. Behind his back he was nicknamed 'Bald Eagle'. 'What have you got then?' Bing asked him.

'A .45 Colt automatic and a .357 revolver.'

Bing nodded satisfied. 'Are you sure he'll be there at twelve, Andy?' He spoke to a tall, blond haired man, whose natural good looks were marred by a weak chin and mouth.

'Absolutely sure, he always covers for the other drivers while they have lunch.' Andy Prentice was their unit's main intelligence collector. When stopped by either police or army he took great pains to be polite. His primary job? To find and set up victims for assassination.

Pursing his lips, the UDA leader switched his gaze to two young men, both barely eighteen. 'You pick up both guns, Trevor OK?' Trevor Boyd, a huge hulking youth nodded without replying. 'Then you meet Steve, and you both take a bus into town.'

'Why don't we get a taxi?' Steve Morrison, a slightly built weasel-like teenager asked.

Bing smiled and looked around his men, shaking his head in mock sadness. This was their first killing, they had a lot to learn. 'Because,' he spoke slowly, as if to a child, 'taxis sometimes get stopped at roadblocks; buses seldom do.'

Both youths nodded. Bing went on. 'Remember to wear gloves at all times and to burn the car afterwards. One last thing, and this is very important.' He smiled at his two potential killers. 'Don't do anything until you get Andy's call.'

He threw wide his arms and laughed. 'After all we don't want to kill the wrong Taigh, do we?'

Around him, his men burst into a collective roar of laughter.

☆    ☆    ☆

Ardoyne.

While one killing was being planned in Tyndale, in Catholic Ardoyne, a better trained, better armed, and equally ruthless band of men were meeting. Their purpose was to bring normal life, such as it was in North Belfast, to an end.

It was their safest house in Ardoyne, only used for very important meetings. An old couple, with absolutely no Republican connections, owned it. Outside, a ring of Fidelious Clarke's Int. and Security ASU provided protection.

Larry Martin sat facing his three ASU commanders: Sean Hughes, head of his bombing team and second only to himself in Ardoyne PIRA; Fidelious Clarke, a veteran Republican who had been nicknamed 'Stiffer' when younger because of the amount of people he had killed, and 'Butcher Kane'. Behind them sat Mary O'Niel, the unit's main courier and weapons carrier.

On his release from prison, a year ago, Martin had found his organization in North Belfast in complete disarray. Starting from scratch he had reformed his volunteers into three totally separate ASUs; one under Hughes, responsible for bombing; another under Clarke to provide security and collect intelligence. It was his shooting ASU that had given him the most trouble. Its operations had been near disasters, with weapons lost and, in one case, a volunteer captured. It had only been with Kane's return that he had found the perfect man to lead it.

'First let me tell you the result of me and Sean's visit across to the West yesterday.' Martin smiled. 'Brigade have given us the green light, thanks to Kane's job on Friday. We are now to mount an all-out offensive in North Belfast.'

Hughes, Clarke and Mary O'Niel laughed. Kane remained as impassive as ever. 'Now Sean, what about next Monday's job?'

'Everything is set, the explosives are already in place; all we need to do is run out a command wire. We'll do that on the night.'

Martin smiled. 'Good job, now any questions before we discuss future operations?'

'Yes,' Clarke spoke, 'what about Carmichael?'

'Whose Carmichael?' Hughes asked.

Martin laughed. 'He's a UDA man, got a snooker club at the top of the road. Stiffer wants to hit him.'

'That's supposed to be my job,' Kane said, his voice low and firm.

'The bastard's recruiting kids for the fucking UDA. That threatens this area. That makes it my job.' Clarke angrily stabbed a finger into his chest. 'I can still hold up my end in an operation.'

Before Kane could reply, Martin interrupted. 'It doesn't matter. Brigade don't want any trouble with this bastard Jackson on the Shankhill. Now if you could find him, that would be another matter.'

'I'm trying,' Clarke's mouth dropped, 'but he's hard to pin down.'

'Keep trying, now any other questions?' Martin looked around. Silence greeted him. 'Right then,' he smiled broadly, 'future operations.'

☆   ☆   ☆

Tennant Street CID General Office, Wednesday 1 pm.

As in all organizations, CID officers had their pecking orders.

Detective inspectors had their own office, detective sergeants got a whole desk, full detectives shared a desk. CID AIDs, like Billy Boyd, fought for a drawer in which to store the mountain of paperwork every officer acquired.

In view of the fact that he was helping him with investigating Lynn Moody's death, Nevin had invited his young aid to share his desk, but only, he had stressed, for this one case.

Nevin was studying the forensic report he had received that morning. It had established that Lynn's killer had O-negative blood. He looked over at Billy. 'The more I think about this, the less it makes sense.'

'What do you mean skipper?'

Nevin rubbed his thumb nail across his bottom lip. 'Let's suppose that our man is the man our friend Moffit saw OK?' Billy nodded. 'What do we have then; a big, broad shouldered man with 'O' Negative blood. With me so far?'

Again Billy nodded. 'Let me ask you a question. How did he know Lynn was going to pass that alley at precisely that time?'

Billy thought for a second. 'Because he watched her. I thought we'd already established that. Moffit saw him the week before.'

Nevin slapped his hand down on his desk. 'Exactly, he watched her, but not for just a week, he couldn't have established her routine in that time.' He shook his head. 'No our killer planned this for some time.'

He was silent for a second, thinking. When he spoke it was more to himself than to Billy. 'Almost like a military operation.'

Their deliberations were interrupted by Inspector Cotton who burst out of his office. 'Nevin, Billy, get up to that quarry at the top of Crumlin Road; a uniformed patrol has just found a body, shot several times.'

As he got to his feet Nevin said, 'That's all I need right now!' Picking up his folder, he ran after Billy.

☆    ☆    ☆

Belfast City Centre, One hour earlier.

Dial-a-Cab was a Catholic-owned and run taxi firm, operating out of Carlisle Circus on Belfast's Crumlin Road. Taxi firms in

41

Belfast, if not exactly owned, certainly paid money to whatever para-military organization controlled their area. For this reason their drivers were often seen as 'legitimate targets' by opposing factions.

If a caller was to ask for a cab to a hard line Protestant address, he would be politely told that none were available and given a Protestant taxi number.

'What time do you want to take your lunch break Sean?' Eamon Bradley, the firm's dispatcher asked.

Sean Grady, bald and overweight looked up from his *Irish News*. 'I'm not bothered, any time after one.'

In his early years, Grady had been a volunteer in first the Official and then Provisional IRA. A heart attack and general ill health had forced him to stand down from 'active' service. He still helped out when he could, carrying messages and occasionally guns in his taxi – a practice his firm knew nothing about.

He liked nothing better than to have a jar with new bloods and tell stories of his early exploits. Whenever a Republican died he always attended the funeral. Unfortunately for him, this had resulted in his face appearing several times in local papers. Before Bradley could say anything else, a man walked in. Sensing a potential fare Eamon walked over to him. 'Yes?' he enquired.

'Got change for the phone?' the man asked, handing over a five pound note. Disappointed, Bradley exchanged it for coins. Smiling at both men, their visitor walked out, crossed the road and entered a phone box. Dialling a number from memory, he waited for a reply. When it came he said, 'He's there, ring now.'

Without waiting for a reply he replaced his receiver and walked outside. Looking across at Dial-a-Cab, Andy Prentice smiled and turned to walk up Crumlin Road and home. Almost immediately Bradley's phone rang. 'Dial-a-Cab, can I help you?' Bradley answered.

'Any chance of a taxi to Ardoyne?'

'Where to exactly?'

'Butler Walk, the name's Cassidy.'

'From where?'

'Me and my brother will be outside Robinson's.'

'Dead On, Mr Cassidy, he'll be there in five minutes.'

Bradley replaced his phone and looked at Grady. 'Two from Robinson's to Butler Walk, Ardoyne.' He handed over a slip of paper. 'Do this and then take a break, Joe will be back shortly.'

Grady nodded and shuffled off without replying. It was only a few minutes drive to Robinson's, a popular city centre drinking bar used by both Catholics and Protestants. As he pulled up outside, a huge youth approached him. 'Dial-a-Cab?'

'Cassidy for Ardoyne?'

'Aye.' Jerking his head, he was joined by a second smaller youth and both got in. Grady drove back down Royal Avenue but as they neared Crumlin Road, a police road block stopped their path.

'Black bastards,' Grady said, as he was waved on, failing to see both his fares stiffen and then relax. He was approaching Flax Street, one of Ardoyne's main entrance routes, when Grady felt the larger of his two passengers lean on his seat.

'What's black and brown and looks good on a fucking Taigh?' Grady's heart stilled. 'A Doberman Pinscher.' Trevor Boyd screwed his Colt .45 auto into Grady's neck. 'Keep driving fatty, all the way up the Crum.'

Grady's hands shook as he gripped the steering wheel. Morrison leaned forward and patted his shoulder. 'Don't worry, all we want is your car.'

Unconvinced, Grady now desperately wanted to find a police or army road block. He did not know that several bogus calls and bomb scares, sent by UDA members, had drawn most patrols away from their route. They drove round Crumlin Road's giant 'horseshoe' bend.

Boyd said, 'Take the next turning on your left.' Grady's heart sank as he turned; it led to an old disused quarry. He had dumped bodies there in his early years with the IRA. Boyd was out almost before their car had stopped and, wrenching open Grady's door, he pulled him out.

The taxi driver fell to his knees. 'Dear God, Oh dear God.'

Grady's hands were clasped almost in prayer. 'I'm an old man, boys, what harm have I done you?'

Boyd looked at his companion and grinned. 'These Provos are all the same, big men in numbers, but get them on their own and they turn to jelly.'

Morrison nodded, his eyes fixed on their pleading victim.

43

'Please boys, pleas . . . ' Without warning Morrison fired his revolver twice. Both .357 soft lead rounds hit the kneeling man and threw him onto his back. Boyd stepped forward and standing spread legged over Grady, fired five rounds into his face and body.

For several seconds neither man moved, then Morrison grabbed his bigger partner's arm. 'Come on,' he urged.

With a last look, Boyd turned and jumped into Grady's taxi. As they drove back towards Tyndale he turned to the smaller UDA man. 'Do you know what I liked best?'

'No, what?'

Boyd grinned, his eyebrows lifted. 'I liked it best when he begged.'

☆    ☆    ☆

Nevin ducked under a string of white tape, sealing the quarry entrance. Followed by Billy he walked over to a slightly built man, in a dishevelled, ill fitting, brown suit. 'What have you got for me, Danny?'

Danny Edwards, Tennant Street's SOCO man, stood and shook his head. 'Not a lot Nevin.' He smiled, his pinched features making him look like an ageing pixie. 'He still had his wallet on him,' Danny handed it to Nevin. 'As you can see, his name is Sean Grady and he was a taxi driver. Dial-a-Cab, on Carlisle Circus. Only one set of tyre tracks in and out, so I'd say they brought him up here in his own car.'

Nevin checked to see if Billy was taking notes, his young aid was scribbling furiously. Edwards went on. 'He was shot seven times. I've found five .45 auto empty cases, so at least two gunmen. Come and see this.' He gestured to Nevin and pointed down; crouching he could see faint marks on either side of the dead man's body.

'The shooter who used the .45 stood with his legs on either side of the victim's body. He'll almost certainly have blood on his trousers and probably traces of this quarry dirt. Also, with that leg span, he must have been quite a tall man.'

'Any chance of getting a foot imprint and taking a plaster cast?' Nevin asked.

'No, ground's too hard.'

'Skipper!' They were interrupted by a shout from behind.

Turning, Nevin saw a uniformed constable running up towards him. 'They've found Grady's taxi, burnt out in Tyndale.'

Nevin shook his head. 'Another stupid sectarian killing.' He turned back to Edwards. 'See if you can dig up anything more here, Danny, then check his taxi in Tyndale. I don't suppose you'll get much but have a look.'

Edwards nodded. 'I'll take some soil samples, just in case you do get a suspect.'

'Good man, try and let me have something in writing before you knock off. Come on Billy.' He turned towards their car. 'Let's go and retrace our friend's last few hours.'

☆    ☆    ☆

Tennant Street. Same day, 5 pm.

They'd retraced Grady's last call, talking first to his dispatcher Bradley, and then to staff and customers at Robinson's. They had no leads, no one could remember seeing anybody get into a taxi around midday. Nevin clapped Billy on his shoulder. 'Go and put a few details down on paper for DI Cotton, then knock off. I'm off to have a word with Special Branch.'

Walking up only one flight of stairs, instead of his usual two, Nevin stopped at a reinforced steel door with a combination lock and knocked loudly. The door was opened by a long haired young man who was only vaguely familiar to him. 'Yes?'

'I'd like to speak to your DI, tell him it's Nevin Brown.' The door was closed abruptly in his face. Nevin felt slightly miffed. A few seconds later it was just as abruptly opened again by a tall broad shouldered man with flaming red hair.

'Come in, come in,' Detective Inspector Bill Dodds ushered him in. 'Don't bother about him.' Bill gestured towards a slightly crestfallen young man. 'He's a new boy, doesn't know the ropes yet.' Leading him to his office Dodds gestured towards a chair. 'Sit down, what can I do for you?'

'I'm investigating this Grady killing, can you help?'

'I've been expecting somebody, so I've got his file out.'

'He was known to you then?'

Bill's eyebrows shot up. 'Oh yes, our friend Grady was quite

45

a boy in his younger days.' He opened a brown folder and read as he spoke. 'Suspected of at least two murders in the early seventies, but was stood down due to ill health. He was still on their auxiliary list. We'd been keeping an eye on him, we suspected him of moving weapons.'

Nevin took notes. 'What about his killers, any ideas?'

'His car was found in Tyndale, that would mean Bing and his merry men, he runs that rabbit warren.' He fell silent for a second. 'I've heard a few whispers and,' he smiled, tapping his nose with a slender finger, 'I do have sources up there; let me dig around, if I can find out anything I'll leave you a note OK?'

'Thanks Bill, I appreciate it.' He started to rise.

'Just a second, nothing for nothing; as it happens I wanted a word with you.'

Nevin sat back down suddenly curious. They had known each other for over ten years. Dodds had been his first DS before being promoted into Special Branch. He was one of the shrewdest and most determined men the detective had ever met. 'How can I help Special Branch?' he asked with a smile.

Dodds steepled his fingers and studied him. 'You're investigating this girl Lynn Moody's murder?'

The smile left his face. 'That's right, why?'

Dodds ignored his question. 'Is there anything strange about her death?'

It was Nevin's turn to think. 'There's plenty strange about it, but nothing that I would have thought would have interested SB. Now why do you ask?'

'You know Colin Jackson of course?'

'The main buck cat of the UVF?'

Dodds nodded. 'He's taking a personal interest in this girl's death, and what interests him,' Dodds tapped his chest with his index finger, 'interest's me.'

'Well I don't know why, but if I come across anything you'll be the first to know.'

Bill seemed satisfied. He looked down and then back up at Nevin. 'You ever hear from Sharon?'

Even after all this time, her name still brought a stab of pain to his chest. He shook his head. 'No, last I heard she was over the water, London I think.'

Bill grabbed his arm. 'Nevin it's been a long time; my wife's got plenty of friends, she's always asking me to invite you over. Why don't you come for dinner and meet one or two?'

Nevin smiled and stood. 'Thanks but I really am too busy, maybe later.' He walked to the door and paused, 'Will Ardoyne PIRA retaliate for Grady?'

Bill laughed without humour. 'He was one of their own; when they find out who killed him, they'll hit back, hard!'

Confirmation on Grady's killers was not long in coming. At 10 pm that evening a caller rang a local Protestant newspaper; using a recognized code word he read a short statement.

> 'Sean Grady was today shot by the UFF, he was an active member of the IRA and was active in targeting Loyalists.'
>
> Captain Black
> UFF

Ardoyne, Thursday 9 am.

Larry Martin tossed his *Irish News* into a corner and walked purposely to his telephone. He dialled a number from memory.

'Yes.'

'Is that you Stiffer?'

'Yes, who's that?' Clarke's voice was tired.

'This is Larry, you remember that job you wanted to do last Monday?'

'Yes,' Clarke replied, his voice more eager.

'Do it.'

Tennant Street, CID General Office, approximately the same time.

As usual they had gathered for their morning briefing. DCI Hart was incensed that neither Kane nor Martin had been arrested as yet. 'Why Detective Sergeant Anderson have you not arrested our two top IRA suspects?' Hart asked, his voice barely in control.

'Because, sir, I can't house Kane. Martin is easy to find, he's just moved into a new house, but Kane,' Anderson shook his head, 'it's like trying to find a ghost.'

'I don't want excuses, Sergeant, I want both those men arrested within a week and questioned about the Ardoyne murders, do I make myself clear?'

'Perfectly sir,' Anderson said and sat down.

Hart gave the luckless Detective Sergeant a malevolent glare and turned his watery eyes on Nevin. 'Now Detective Sergeant Brown, what have you to tell us about your investigations into the Lynn Moody and Grady murders?' There was just a hint of sarcasm in his voice.

Nevin stood, 'As far as the Moody investigation is concerned we have no real leads but,' he thought for a second about mentioning the mysterious man again but decided against it, 'but we are pursuing every line of enquiry. As for the Grady killing, as you know it was claimed by the UFF. I saw Inspector Dodds of Special Branch last night and he left me a note.' He glanced down to read it. 'A well placed source has indicated that Trevor Boyd was one of two men involved in Grady's killing.'

'What do you intend to do about this information?' Hart interrupted.

Nevin smiled. 'I have already obtained a search warrant. I intend to go immediately to Boyd's house, search it, then arrest and question him.'

'Have you arranged uniform back-up?' DI Cotton asked.

'Yes, sir,' Nevin glanced at his watch, 'it will be ready at 9.30 am.'

'Good Sergeant Brown, I think you can be excused from the rest of the briefing, don't you sir?' The DI glanced at Hart.

For a second the big man said nothing, then slowly nodded his head. 'OK Sergeant Brown you can go.' Flashing a smile of thanks to Cotton, Nevin nodded to Billy and left. Swiftly both detectives made their way downstairs to the station briefing room. Six uniformed constables were waiting for them. Nevin gave them a quick briefing, detailing tasks and the reason for their search. He ended by saying, 'Now I don't think we'll be lucky enough to find a weapon, but keep your eyes peeled for blood-stained clothing, gloves, anything at all that might give us a lead. OK let's go.'

They piled into two grey armoured Landrovers and made their way to Boyd's Tyndale Green home. Two uniformed men ran to cover Boyd's back door while Nevin and Billy, accompanied by two more, approached the front. 'What a dump,' Billy observed, glancing at the filth-strewn streets.

Nevin nodded and knocked. It took several thumps and a loud, 'It's the police, open up,' to rouse Boyd.

'What the fuck do you want?' Boyd snarled as he opened his door. Wearing only tracksuit bottoms, his bare top revealed a mass of rippling muscle.

'I have a warrant to search your house,' Nevin showed his warrant as he and Billy forced their way past.

'Come in, come in,' Boyd said sarcastically throwing wide his arms, 'I've nothing to hide.'

Within seconds Boyd's house was being searched carefully by Nevin's uniformed colleagues while he questioned his suspect. 'What were you doing yesterday between 10 am and 1 pm?'

'I was in the Tyndale Community Centre.'

'Any witnesses?'

'Plenty, Robert McCrum, Billy Dixon, Martin Mickmichael.'

Nevin smiled. 'All good solid citizens.' Beside him Billy made comprehensive notes. 'Now exactly what time did you arrive there?'

'How the fuck should I know? Nine thirty, quarter to ten,' he shrugged his massive shoulders. 'I couldn't say for sure.'

'Bit early for you, I mean you're still in bed at,' Nevin glanced at his watch, 'at ten past ten?'

'I was up late last night,' Boyd gave a sarcastic grin.

Before Nevin could ask another question a uniformed officer came from upstairs. 'Skipper I found these on top of his bedroom wardrobe.' He handed Nevin a pair of thin cotton gloves.

Holding them between thumb and forefinger Nevin asked, 'These yours?'

'What if they are?'

'Detective Boyd note that at 10.11 am precisely the suspect admitted owning a pair of black woollen gloves.'

'What is this?' Boyd said belligerently, but his voice held a note of concern.

49

Before answering, Nevin carefully bagged the gloves, with a label bearing his initials and time. Looking up he smiled. 'I don't suppose you've heard of carbon tests but if you have you'll know that a scientist can test those gloves and tell us if somebody fired a gun wearing them.'

Boyd's face now bore a distinctly worried look, but he said nothing. Nevin let the silence grow, sometimes it was better than questions. It didn't last long. 'Skipper.' A second constable entered from Boyd's kitchen, holding a pair of blue jeans in his hands. Nevin studied them for a second and looked at Boyd. 'These yours?'

'So what?'

'You wearing them yesterday?'

Boyd sneered, 'What if I was?'

'Billy record that at,' he checked his watch, '10.13 suspect admitted owning a pair of blue jeans and wearing same on previous day.'

'What the fuck's going on here?' Boyd was now definitely worried. Nevin stepped closer and showed him a leg of his jeans. There were two tiny spots of blood near the bottom.

'There's blood on them.'

'So I cut myself.'

Before answering he carefully bagged and tagged Boyd's jeans. 'That might be true, but you see we have this process called genetic finger printing. It can identify a person's blood.' He paused and looked at Boyd. 'If that blood is Sean Grady's, it's as good as finding his finger prints on you. Also,' he smiled, 'we'll probably be able to match soil samples from the quarry.' Stepping towards the door he said to Billy, 'Arrest him and get him dressed.'

Billy stepped forward saying, 'Trevor Boyd I arrest you on suspicion of murdering Sean Grady. You are not obliged . . . '

Bill got no further. Without warning Boyd threw a vicious left hook which felled the advancing detective. Screaming he charged for the door. Only one thing stood in his way – Nevin Brown. He had never been one for unarmed combat, but as the screaming giant rushed towards him, Nevin threw an uppercut which had all his body behind it. Connecting with Boyd's chin, there was an audible click, like two billiard balls meeting.

Boyd seemed to be trying to do two things at once, go forward, and fall back. He did neither and sat down with a

50

thump. In seconds two uniformed constables had pounced and had him handcuffed. One looked up with frank admiration, 'Great punch Skipper.'

Nevin blew air noisily out of his lungs and shook his head. 'A lucky punch I can assure you.'

They got a struggling Boyd to his feet. 'You black bastards, he was a bloody IRA Taigh, you should give me a medal.'

'I'll take that as an admission of guilt, take our hero outside.' A cursing Boyd was dragged out. Nevin helped up a dazed Billy. 'You hurt?'

'Only my pride,' Billy laughed.

As both detectives stepped outside they were met by a stern faced constable.

'There's been another shooting, about ten minutes ago, it looks like a PIRA revenge killing.'

☆     ☆     ☆

Ardoyne, one hour earlier.

It had not taken Fidelious Clarke long to set up his operation. His men had been targeting Carmichael for weeks and knew his routines perfectly. The UDA man ran a snooker club, which was a front to launder money for his organization. Invariably he would arrive at his club an hour before opening time, to check stock and club equipment. Clarke had two men scouting both Carmichael's club and the surrounding area for security force activity.

He waited for their call with two other members of his ASU, a driver and a back-up gunman. Outside their safe house a car waited for them; it had been taken from a family nearby who were being held by three younger members of his unit until their job was completed. The phone rang, Clarke picked it up. 'Yes.'

'He's there and all's clear.'

'Fine expect us shortly.' He hung up and looked at his younger volunteers. 'He's there, don't forget what I've told you. Let's go.'

Colin Carmichael sat in his rear office going through his club's invoices. When he had agreed to run this club for the UDA he had never thought it would entail so much paper-

51

work. 'Still,' he thought to himself, 'it keeps the wolf from the door.' Situated in a rear room, his office had no windows and only one door. Visitors had to traverse the entire club to reach it.

Outside, a dark maroon Vauxhall Cavalier drove slowly past, did a U-turn at the top of Ligonel Road, drove slowly back and parked outside Carmichael's club. Clarke got out carrying a Berreta sub-machine gun and a second man followed armed with a Smith and Wesson .38 revolver. Hardly breaking stride Clarke kicked open the club's door and rushed in.

Seated in his office Carmichael thought somebody had thrown a brick through his window. Standing, he rushed to his door in time to see two armed and masked men rushing at him. 'Oh Christ, no,' he screamed and tried to use his body to bar the door.

Both gunmen hit it running, throwing Carmichael into a corner like some rag doll. Lying, Carmichael brought both hands up in front of his face. 'No boys, not me,' he pleaded.

Clarke opened fire with his sub-machine gun. It's 9 mm bullets smashed through the UDA man's hands like a hot knife slicing butter. Sections of Carmichael's face became distorted as large chunks of flesh were torn off. Turning, Clarke covered their retreat. His back-up man rushed past him to the prostrate man. Placing his revolver against his head he fired two shots at point blank range, leaving a gaping hole in Carmichael's skull. 'Out,' shouted Clarke.

Both men turned and ran swiftly to their waiting car. In all, the entire incident had taken exactly thirty seconds.

At 3 pm that afternoon, a press release was issued by the Republican Press Bureau. It read-

'This morning an Active Service Unit of the 3rd Battalion Provisional IRA executed a high ranking UDA officer. This man was responsible for planning attacks on innocent Nationalists. Let this attack serve as a warning to all such organizations that we will not tolerate such attacks.'

Signed P. O'Niel
Press Officer.

☆　　☆　　☆

Tennant Street, 11 am Friday morning, the second week.

The two days following Carmichael's murder had not been easy ones for Tennant Street's officers. Local press and politicians from both communities had lambasted them, pointing out that one in four of all people killed during the present troubles had died in their area.

On top of this Inspector Dodds's Special Branch team had issued a strong warning that Ardoyne PIRA were planning a series of attacks and all personnel were to be on high alert.

Uniformed patrols were increased and all sections put on twelve hour shifts. To say that everybody was tense, was by far an understatement.

Nevin sat at his office desk, a mountain of paperwork covering it and threatening to engulf him. He had spent all of Wednesday and Thursday interviewing Boyd. The UDA man had made a full admission about his part in Grady's murder but had refused to name any accomplices. Despite all his efforts all he got was, 'If I tell you any names I won't last five minutes inside.'

He rubbed his eyes. For a second the whole futility of it struck him. A young man, barely eighteen spending the best years of his life behind bars because some madman had given him a gun and told him to kill a perfect stranger. He shook his head, all for some obscure cause that wouldn't make a blind bit of difference twenty years from now.

Sighing, he put away Boyd's file. He had a case against him and all he needed to do was write up his reports. Forensic identified the blood stains on Boyd's jeans as being the same type as Grady's; they had been sent over to England to be genetically fingerprinted, but he was sure it was Grady's. Boyd's gloves had shown traces of gun oil and carbon, proving they had been worn whilst firing a gun. Even if Boyd retracted his confession, he had more than enough to convict him in court.

Lynn Moody's murder had been pushed to one side by recent events. He picked up her file and glanced through it. He was still no nearer to discovering who was the mystery man, seen a week before her death. He read the forensic report again. A lot of it was too technical for him to understand, but they were certain her killer had O-negative blood. What had he got? A big man, abnormally strong, with O-negative blood.

'You can get taken away by the men in white suits for talking to yourself.' Startled, Nevin looked up to see a smiling DI Cotton.

Slightly embarrassed he said gruffly, 'It's the only time I get a straight answer.'

'Busy?' Cotton asked, his voice innocent.

'Snowed under.'

'That's a pity.' Something in his voice made Nevin look up.

'OK, let's have it, I know that tone.'

'I'm sure I don't know what you mean,' Cotton's smile broadened. 'There is one thing.'

'Yes,' Nevin said, expecting the worst.

'There's this American doctor, an expert on criminal psychology, she's giving a lecture at headquarters tonight at 7 pm.'

'So what's that got to do with me?'

Cotton handed him a piece of paper. 'All senior detective sergeants and possible promotion candidates to attend where possible. You qualify on both accounts, so you're elected.'

'You can't be serious. I've got too much work to do.'

'Don't we all,' he dropped his voice, 'Kane and Martin were picked up an hour ago; everybody is going to be busy with their interview and checking their stories.'

'That's a waste of time and manpower, those two are professional terrorists, you'll get nothing out of them,' Nevin said with disgust.

Cotton sighed, 'I know but our lord and master wants them interviewed. You're the only one not involved, so you get the pleasure of the good doctor's lecture.'

'No way I can get out?'

'Afraid not.' He leaned over and patted Nevin's shoulder. 'Look on it as two hours of easy overtime.'

'Thanks a bunch,' Nevin replied with little enthusiasm.

☆     ☆     ☆

Knock, Headquarters of The Royal Ulster Constabulary, 7 pm that evening.

Arriving ten minutes early, Nevin spotted Ray McFarlan and

slotted into a seat next to him. 'What about you Ray?'

'Fine Nevin, I hear you got a result on the Grady murder, congratulations.'

'More luck than anything,' Nevin conceded.

'What about the Lynn Moody investigation, any progress?'

Nevin shook his head. 'Not much, I should be working on that instead of sitting here listening to some half-baked American fossil telling me her theories on criminal behaviour.'

'I take it you haven't seen Dr Sterling?' McFarlan said, a sly smile on his face.

'No and if I had my way . . . '

Whatever Nevin was about to say was interrupted by a door opening behind him. The sound of high heels clicking made him turn his head; his jaw dropped. 'Some fossil eh?' McFarlan whispered in his ear.

Doctor Marrianne Sterling, PhD, MD, walked elegantly towards the rostrum. There was more than one gasp of surprise. At thirty-one, she was an extremely attractive example of her nation's womanhood. Her shoulder-length auburn hair framed a face that, while not classically beautiful, held both intelligence and character that would interest a man long after mere beauty had faded.

A severely cut black two piece outfit could do little to hide the exciting contours of her body, while the legs below her knee length skirt would have done justice to many a movie star. As she mounted a short flight of stairs to the speaker's platform there was a low wolf whistle from behind Nevin.

Doctor Sterling flashed an engaging smile, 'Thank you, it's always nice to have admirers.' Her voice was low and throaty, with a cultured Bostonian accent.

Nevin realized he was holding his breath. Beside him McFarlan whispered, 'She can diagnose me any time.' For some insane reason he felt jealous, then concentrated on her speech.

'The subject of this seminar is, "Psychotic disorders associated with post-combat syndrome".'

She smiled again and her audience was captivated.

'Those are very big words, gentlemen; what they mean is the reactions some of our soldiers had when exposed to long periods of action in Vietnam. I have conducted long studies into several of these case studies and I believe we can learn many valuable lessons from them.'

Once Nevin had got over his shock, he found her lecture both interesting and absorbing. First Doctor Sterling outlined several 'case studies' of GIs who on their return from active service in Vietnam had gone on murderous rampages.

After a short break, she went on to outline the warning signs of such behaviour. Her lecture completed, she invited questions from the floor. A hand went up. 'Doctor Sterling,' said an Inspector sitting two rows in front of Nevin, 'from your observations do you believe any of the troubles your police forces have had with American GIs might surface in our soldiers serving in Ulster?'

Dr Sterling thought for a second before answering. 'It's hard to see that happening, at least to the same extent as we have witnessed in the States. Your soldiers here are under constant threat and this is having an effect. Witness the dramatic rise in suicides in army and police personnel.'

She paused, considering her next words carefully. 'However your troops are not, as ours were in Vietnam, called upon to kill on a practically daily basis. Put simply, your troops would have to kill regularly to suffer the same effects.'

A second hand was raised. 'You indicated in your lecture that many of the worst cases you studied came from disturbed family backgrounds. Do you believe these people would have become killers if they had not served in Vietnam?'

'That's a good question,' Dr Sterling conceded. 'When you are dealing with mental disorders there are not hard and fast rules. There is no doubt that many of the victims we saw coming back from Nam would have developed psychotic symptoms regardless of their service in the war. However there is no doubt that sending people with troubled backgrounds to serve in the war was a bit like mixing nitrogen and glycerin.'

She looked at her questioner directly. 'You see, all psychotics need a trigger to set them off. In many cases the Vietnam War was just the stimulus they needed.'

Final questions centred around the thorny question of treatment or punishment, with Dr Sterling fighting her corner well. The seminar ended with a standing ovation.

Nevin sat in his chair as the room emptied. A small group of admirers gathered around Dr Sterling firing questions which she fended with skill and dexterity while making her way to the door. When her questioners had thinned sufficiently, he pushed his way forward.

'I enjoyed your lecture very much.' His own voice sounded strained to his own ears. Her dark blue eyes surveyed him with a frankness he found disturbing.

'Thank you.' She looked at him enquiringly.

'Brown, Detective Sergeant Nevin Brown,' he offered, feeling himself blushing like a schoolboy asking for his first date.

She started to walk past him. 'Excuse me, I don't want to be pushy but I'd like your advice on a case I'm working on,' he stammered quickly.

She turned back to face him. 'Are you serious?' Her eyes searched his, there was a slight edge to her voice.

'Yes, perfectly.'

'What type of case?'

Nevin suddenly realized they were alone. 'A murder case, a young girl, I really would like your advice.'

Curiosity replaced suspicion on her face. 'Why do you think I can help you?'

Nevin shrugged. 'Without appearing big headed I'm reckoned to be a good detective, but nothing in this case fits anything I've ever come across.'

Marrianne studied the earnest face in front of her. She had initially thought his approach an attempted pick-up. Now she realized he was serious. 'OK, I'm staying at Queen's University for two months.' She delved into her handbag, found a card and wrote a number on it. 'You can get me on this number, give me a ring and we'll talk.' With that she turned and left an open mouthed Nevin Brown standing alone in an empty hall.

☆    ☆    ☆

Tennant Street, Saturday 6.30 am.

It was still dark as Nevin pushed his way through the station's front door. He collided with a burly figure travelling quickly in his direction. He heard an oath in a thick Scottish accent. 'Sorry, Skipper, didn't see you,' Gary Howe apologized.

Nevin laughed, 'No harm done, Gary.'

'What's CID doing in at this time? I thought 6.30 was

unknown to you lads.' Howe's voice was filled with mirth.

'Paperwork, Gary, I'm trying to clear a mountain of it on my desk.'

'Your trouble, if you don't mind me saying, is that you're a work-a-holic; me I'm off on a week's leave after this shift.'

'You finishing now?'

'No such luck.' He jerked his head towards two huge army armoured Landrovers, surrounded by a group of soldiers. 'I've got to babysit that lot on a house search in Ardoyne.'

'Whose house are you searching?' Nevin asked curiously.

'Fidelious Clarke's,' Howe said in disgust.

Nevin shook his head. 'That's a waste of time, Clarke's too long in the tooth to keep anything incriminating at his home.'

'Don't tell me, tell the army anyway.' He pushed past Nevin. 'I must be off.'

Walking swiftly across to his waiting troops, Gary gave them a cheery 'Hello', greeted by a few mumbled replies. He got into the lead Landrover accompanied by an officer and several soldiers and found himself seated next to two older men, wearing dark green overalls. He tried to strike up a conversation with one of them. 'Nice to see somebody my own age along, I sometimes feel ancient going out with army patrols. I haven't seen you and your mate before, you just posted in?'

Shooting a quick glance at the officer opposite, the man turned towards Gary. 'We're Battalion Int. Cel., just out for this one job, the regular search team is away on leave.' His voice was cultured and distinctly unfriendly.

'Pardon me for asking,' thought Gary.

Swiftly the two vehicle patrol swept into Ardoyne and stopped outside Clarke's Eskdale Garden home. As soon as the vehicle stopped, soldiers burst from its doors to take up pre-planned positions. Accompanied by his two unfriendly friends in green overalls, Gary went straight to Clarke's heavy wooden front door and banged on it. 'It's the police, open up.'

Several minutes passed before a voice asked, 'What do you want?' Suspicion, anger and sleep were mixed in its tone.

'RUC, open up.'

Waiting outside, Gary heard a profanity and footsteps; an eye appeared at the door's spy hole. Slowly heavy bolts were drawn. Opening his front door, Fidelious Clarke stood dressed in a black tracksuit. 'What the fuck do you want at this time of

58

the morning?'

'Now, now Stiffer,' Gary used Clarke's old nickname, 'we don't want any unpleasantness, read this.' He handed over a piece of typed paper. Glancing down Gary read from an identical document.

'This house is being searched under section 12 of the Northern Ireland Emergency Provisions Act 1988. You are requested to comply . . .'

'OK, OK,' Clarke snarled and stepped aside. Four soldiers walked in; two who had been in Gary's vehicle searched downstairs, while two dressed exactly the same went upstairs. 'You'll find nothing here,' Clarke shouted at their retreating backs.

'You can go where you want Stiffer, feel free to supervise the search as you see fit.' Clarke glared at him and stamped upstairs.

Gary looked at the front door. Behind its wooden front was an armoured steel back with four huge securing bolts. A steel gate sealed off the upstairs from downstairs; should an attacker somehow gain entrance he would still be unable to reach Clarke upstairs.

'What a way to live,' Gary thought to himself. Shaking his head he walked into the downstairs living room. It was being searched thoroughly. One member was removing the back of Clarke's TV set. Gary was about to talk to him when his partner called him over. 'Have a look at these will you?' He held up two books.

Gary crossed and looked at them. *The Anarchist's Cook Book* and *The Undeclared War*. Gary shook his head. 'There's no law against these.' His eyes narrowed slightly. 'He should know that,' he thought.

Behind his back, the second soldier removed a very small electronic device, no bigger than a fifty pence piece, from inside his overalls and installed it inside the TV set with practised precision. By the time Gary turned round, he was securing its rear cover.

'I was just about to say, I hope you don't break that. I'd hate it if we had to buy Mr Clarke a new one,' Gary said.

Replacing Clarke's TV set he looked up at Gary. 'Don't worry, it will work properly.' Looking past the policeman, he spoke to his partner, 'I have to get a torch from the APC, won't be a tick.'

Once outside, he strode quickly and purposely to his APC. Soldiers surrounding Clarke's house made way for him respectfully. The officer in charge waited for him and opened its doors for him. Once inside he removed a green bag from under a seat and removed a small radio set. Flicking a switch he listened intently.

A smile crossed his face. He could clearly hear Gary Howe's voice saying, 'Are you and your mate always this talkative?'

His companion replied, 'We're just tired, that's all . . .'

He flicked another switch and picked up a radio handset. 'Zero Mike, this is Zero Oscar, over.'

Many miles away, in Lisburn barracks, a voice answered. 'Zero Oscar, Roger, send over.'

'Zero Mike, have installed Charlie One, are you receiving over?'

There was a slight pause, the man began to sweat slightly. 'Zero Oscar, this is Zero Mike, receiving Charlie One strength five over.'

'Zero Mike Roger closing down, out.'

The MI5 man replaced his radio set and sat for a second in silence. Then his normally impassive face broke into a grin, 'Bingo,' he said enthusiastically.

# 3

Monday, Tennant Street, 3 pm.

Nevin had worked like a man possessed to clear his paperwork. He had rung Marrianne Sterling late on Saturday and, much to his surprise, she had suggested they talk over dinner on Monday. All CID officers, like their uniformed counterparts, were pulling double shifts due to the recent terrorist upsurge of violence.

It had taken a lot of help from Billy Boyd, plus dire threats of either transfer or resignation, to elicit a solemn promise from DI Cotton that he could have Monday night free.

Fighting his way through his last pile of papers he was suddenly aware his superior had joined him. 'Now this is what I call dedication,' Cotton said, seating himself on Nevin's desk and idly swinging a leg as he talked. 'In at the crack of dawn, working all day and,' he winked to Nevin's colleagues, 'giving up his spare time to consult an expert on criminal psychology.'

'I think she can give me some advice about the Lynn Moody murder,' Nevin replied, keeping his head down.

'Oh really?' Cotton said, his voice casual.

'Yes really,' Nevin looked up, his face starting to flush.

'I've heard she's quite a looker?' Cotton studied his finger nails innocently. 'That wouldn't have anything to do with having dinner with her I suppose?'

Nevin laughed, trying not to bite. 'Honestly it's strictly business.'

'Well it's a dirty business,' Cotton leaned over and patted Nevin's shoulder, 'but somebody has to do it.'

Nevin was spared further embarrassment by the entrance of Inspector Bill Dodds. 'I'm glad I caught you Brian, Nevin,' the Special Branch man said; his voice held a note of concern. 'I think you should know Kane and Martin are out, they were released this morning.'

'I thought they'd be held for the full five days,' Nevin pointed out, plainly irritated.

'No point, we couldn't get a peep out of them, both had a dozen witnesses to swear that they were in the Shamrock bar when our patrol was ambushed.'

'All good solid citizens no doubt?' Cotton said dourly.

'More like good solid volunteers in PIRA,' Dodds conceded. 'There's something else,' he went on. Not only Cotton and Nevin were listening, every officer present hung on Dodds' every word. 'We have good information that an attack is imminent. I'll be giving a full security brief tomorrow but until then,' he glanced around the room, 'everybody be on your toes.'

With those hearty words he strode from the room leaving a thoughtful band of CID officers behind him. 'OK,' Cotton said, his voice firm, 'you all have work to do, let's get to it.'

Nevin looked up into his superior's concerned face. 'Don't even think of cancelling my night off.'

Cotton smiled, 'Don't worry, you're safe.'

☆     ☆     ☆

Ardoyne, One hour later.

Larry Martin drove his second hand Ford Escort along Ardoyne Avenue, Sean Hughes by his side. 'Well I'm glad you haven't wasted any time while I've been inside.'

'No,' Hughes replied, his voice holding a note of pride. 'Everything is set, the explosives are in place, all we have to do is run out the command wire tonight.'

'Good, your people are all set for the come on?'

'No problems there; we've been watching the place for a week.'

Martin nodded his head with satisfaction. 'Everything is going to plan with your attack tonight, and Kane's a week on Wednesday. We'll have shown Brigade that we can maintain our offensive.'

'Why is Kane so adamant about doing his job on a Wednesday?' Hughes asked, clearly irritated.

Martin shrugged. 'Search me but he won't be budged.' His

eyes narrowed. 'There's something about Kane that's not right, I don't know what it is . . . '

'Fuck, a road block,' Hughes interrupted urgently.

Ahead of them, two police Landrovers blocked the road. A police sergeant waved them to stop. Within seconds both men were out of their vehicle and being searched. Martin recognized most of his searchers; they had stopped him many times before.

Early in his terrorist career Martin had rebelled against the security forces' continual stop and search tactics. This had resulted in several fights and his eventual imprisonment for assault, his first prison sentence. Now he accepted police and army stops as part of his job, answering questions mechanically, saying no more than he was required to do by law.

He watched, dispassionately, as his car was thoroughly searched. As OC of his unit he made it a rule never to carry a weapon or document. The search completed, both men got back into their car, refusing to be drawn into casual conversation. 'Bastards,' Hughes remarked as they drove off.

'Never mind, Sean,' Martin gave a short humourless laugh. 'You never know, you might get one of them in tonight's operation.'

Hughes laughed also. 'Yes wouldn't that be a laugh?'

As they stopped outside Martin's Jamaica Gardens home, the IRA chief turned to his second in command. 'There's just one thing, Sean, I was on the phone to the chief of staff this morning. He was a bit upset you didn't join us for a drink after the last meeting.'

Hughes flushed. 'I had to see an old friend. I only get the chance to see him when we visit the west.'

'Are you sure it's a "he?" You looked a bit flushed when you met us later.'

Hughes's mouth dropped open and he flushed even more. Before he could reply Martin clapped him on his shoulder.

'There's no need to be embarrassed. If you've got a bit on the side over in the west good luck to you.' He opened his car door and winked at Hughes. 'It will be our secret.' Stepping from his car Martin failed to see Hughes's face take on a look of real concern.

☆     ☆     ☆

Queen's University, 8 pm.

Nevin sat in his car outside the university's accommodation building where Marrianne had rooms. He felt both excited and nervous as he waited for her to appear. She had sounded quite pleased to hear from him; now, however, he felt like a teenager on his first date. He spotted her as she walked towards his car. He tried not to stare, it wasn't easy!

Marrianne wore a stunning black dress, short enough to show more of the elegant legs that had caused such a stir at her lecture. A white jacket, with stylish padded shoulders, set her outfit off to perfection.

Nevin got out to greet her. As she approached he took a deep breath. 'Discipline, Sergeant Brown,' he said to himself. 'Remember this is strictly business.'

He extended a hand towards her, 'Good evening Dr Sterling.'

'Marrianne please.'

Her touch sent an electric current up his arm. 'Nevin,' he mumbled, trying to cover his shyness. He stood for a second, mesmerized by her beauty.

'Are you going to open the door?'

Recovering he said, 'Oh yes.' As she elegantly got into his car, Nevin cursed himself. 'For God's sake get a grip of yourself; you're starting to look like a fool.'

Pulling on his seat belt he flashed her a quick smile. 'The restaurant isn't far.'

She smiled warmly. 'I'm glad, I haven't eaten all day and I'm famished.'

Nevin looked away quickly and tried not to put her right leg into gear.

Their meal was excellent and Marrianne proved to be an ideal dinner companion, having an uncommon knack of knowing when to talk and when to listen, and to be good at both. Nevin relaxed as their meal progressed. He had chosen a good restaurant, The Saint and Scholars, partly because it was near to Marrianne's rooms, but mainly because it served some of the best food in Belfast.

'You know when I told people I was coming to Belfast, they were appalled,' she paused to take a sip of wine and shake her hand excitedly, a gesture Nevin found utterly charming. 'You would have thought I was going to Beirut or Afghanistan.'

'We do have that sort of reputation but, as I'm sure you've seen for yourself, most people never see anything of the troubles.' He took a sip of mineral water as he was on call and couldn't drink.

'But three officers from your station were killed last week, weren't they?'

A look of sadness drifted across Nevin's face. 'Yes but this scale of violence is unusual, especially in my part of Belfast. It's just that certain people have returned to my area and are spreading their own brand of hell.' Unbidden an image of Kane flashed into his mind.

'Do you know who these people are?'

Nevin smiled. 'Of course I do.' He tilted his head on one side and observed her. 'I'd be a poor detective if I didn't.'

'Then why,' she asked, her voice firm, 'don't you stop them?'

Nevin lowered his head and shook it slowly. He gave a short laugh and raising his head he locked eyes with her. 'Knowing something and proving it in a court of law, are two entirely different things.' He brought his thumb nail up to rub his bottom lip. 'I know who killed my three friends last week, but I'll be damned if I can prove it.' His voice was edged with bitterness.

Marrianne knew she had touched a raw nerve and swiftly changed the subject. 'You said you wanted my advice on a case?'

'Ah yes.' Nevin's thumb nail was working overtime on his bottom lip. He took a second to collect his thoughts. 'I'm investigating a young girl's murder, her name was Lynn Moody.' Swiftly he outlined what he had learnt so far.

'You see,' he ended by saying, 'I keep coming back to this man who was seen a week before Lynn's death. I believe he was the killer and if he was, one,' he counted out points on his fingers, 'he watched her for some time, probably more than one week, because he knew her routine.'

She nodded in agreement.

'Two,' he counted out a second digit, 'that means her attack was planned, you agree?'

She nodded again.

'Then three,' he took a deep breath and blew it slowly out, 'her attacker meant to kill her from the very start.' He shook his head. 'This was no rape that went wrong; whoever killed Lynn Moody planned it like a military operation.'

He paused to let his words sink in.

'Now what I want to know from you is, what kind of man does that sort of crime and,' he gave a rueful smile, 'how do I go about catching him?'

She was silent for several seconds, considering his words. 'Have there been other attacks similar to this one in the past?'

'You should be a detective, that was the first thing I checked.' He shook his head. 'Nothing like it before in Ulster.'

'How far did you check?'

'Right back to 1973.'

It was Marrianne's turn to shake her head. 'That is unusual.'

'Why?'

'If you're right about the girl's death, then you're dealing with a *psychopath*.' She studied him across the table. 'That's a very misused word. Your true psychopath cannot tell right from wrong; in fact your right is very often his wrong. Many are highly intelligent and,' she smiled and shook her head, 'contrary to popular belief, they don't secretly want to be caught.'

She took a sip of wine. 'Just the opposite in fact, they will go to any lengths to remain free.'

'So that they can go on killing?' Nevin asked.

'Just so, once started on a killing spree they will go to any lengths to continue it. We call them "serial killers" back in the States. Many are caught purely by accident.' She frowned. 'But something puzzles me about your killer.'

'What's that?'

'This killing was far too well planned and executed to be his first; killers, even psychopaths, have to learn from experience.' She shook her head slowly. 'No, he must have struck before.'

Nevin worried his bottom lip. 'My thoughts exactly; but if he has, I can't find it.'

'Perhaps you're looking in the wrong place?'

Nevin inclined his head thoughtfully. 'Maybe you're right.' He paused, thinking. 'Tomorrow I'll try contacting the mainland police.' He rubbed his bottom lip and half to himself said, 'Perhaps I am looking in the wrong place.'

'I have some additional data back at my rooms; would you

like to take me home and I'll show it to you?'

Nevin's jaw dropped, 'Me take you home?'

'Yes,' Marrianne laughed, 'why not?'

'No reason, it's just that . . . ' He flushed and stood hurriedly to hide his embarrassment. 'Never mind.' He shook both hands in front of him, 'I'll pay the bill.'

She watched him retreating back with a smile and, shaking her head with amusement, followed him to the door.

Seated in her comfortable rooms, Marrianne spent two hours going through some of her research material. Files littered a small coffee table in front of them. 'You asked me earlier, how to catch this man; this is how you catch him.' She tapped one of her files.

'In every case I've studied, there is always one consistent factor. Every one of these killing rampages was set off by some kind of trigger. Find what triggered your man and,' she tapped him on the chest to emphasize her words, 'you'll find your killer.'

Nevin nodded, impressed by her knowledge and involuntarily he yawned. 'I must be boring you?'

'No, no,' he protested smiling, 'you've helped me tremendously, but two hours of murder and mayhem are enough for anybody.' He smiled wanly. 'Tell me something about yourself. How did someone as lovely as you get interested in studying mass killers.'

'Thank you.'

'For what?'

'The compliment, I'd begun to think you hadn't noticed.'

'Oh I noticed. I've been trying not to stare all night. You really are quite beautiful.'

'Thank you kind kind sir,' she inclined her head, 'two compliments in a row, I'm honoured.'

She was silent for a second, watching his face. 'As for why I studied criminal psychology, that's easy, my father was a professor in human psychology at Yale and mother was a practising psychiatrist.' She threw her hands up in mock surrender. 'What chance did I have?'

They both laughed. 'What about you, was your father in law enforcement?'

'Dad a peeler?' He shook his head. 'Good heavens no, he worked in the shipyards all his life. My mother died when I was

67

ten and dad worked every hour that God sent to send me to a private school.'

Marrianne's brow furrowed. 'What's a peeler?'

'The first police force in England was started by Robert Peel. They were called the Bow Street Runners, but everybody called them peelers after Peel himself.'

'Oh I see, where is your father now?'

'Retired, he lives in Bangor, that's a town just outside Belfast. I see him when I can.' He smiled wistfully. 'I'm an only child, it can get lonely at times.'

'What, no wife, girlfriend?'

For a second a look of intense pain flashed across his face.

'I was, she left me, two years ago.' He dropped his eyes. Marrianne could almost feel his pain. 'She was younger than me. I was studying for my inspector's exam.' He looked back up into her eyes. 'You know love is like some bright new shiny ornament, to keep it shining you have to take it down and polish it regularly.' He shrugged and smiled sadly, 'I just forgot to take it down and polish it.'

For a second he was silent, then he shook himself. 'What about you, husband, boyfriend?'

She shook her head, smiling. 'No, neither, my life is my work. I always seem to be too busy for anything as complicated as a permanent relationship.' It was her turn to look a little sad. 'There was someone once, a long time ago.'

'What happened?'

'He died.'

For several seconds neither spoke, then, taking him completely by surprise, she leaned forward and kissed him lightly on his lips. 'You know,' she said in a low voice, 'it was her loss.'

She was very close to him, her lips parted invitingly. He took her face between both his hands and kissed her gently, feeling the soft warmth of her kiss. The telephone rang! She gave the ringing instrument a withering look. 'I won't be a second,' she smiled.

'Hello.' Puzzled she looked across at Nevin, quizzically.

'It's for you.'

Rising he smiled in apology. 'I'm sorry.' He shrugged his shoulders. 'I'm on call and I gave them your number.'

Gingerly he took the phone and said, 'Detective Sergeant Brown.'

68

Marrianne saw his smile fade, colour drained from his face; his voice was hard as he said, 'OK I'll be in within ten minutes.' Replacing the phone he turned to Marrianne. 'I have to go,' his voice was strained.

'What's wrong Nevin?'

He shook his head, pain etched lines in his face. 'They've just murdered another one of our constables.'

☆     ☆     ☆

Ardoyne shop fronts, one hour earlier.

As a result of public pressure, in the wake of the upsurge of terrorist activity, extra patrols had been stationed at potential flash points in an effort to prevent further outrages. At night most were made up of part-time officers, who only came on duty at 7 pm and terminated at 2 am, commanded by a regular constable.

One such patrol, commanded by Constable Martin Smyth, sat in a parked Landrover in Twaddle Avenue, its crew more asleep than awake. Their position was strategic and dominated a major trouble point. Smyth yawned and stretched his arms; he'd been on duty for over twelve straight hours and still had two to go. 'Quiet tonight,' his driver Reserve Constable Eddy Gardner observed.

As if on cue their radio burst into life! 'Delta Tango 94 armed robbery in progress at Ardoyne shop fronts!'

'You would have to tempt fate,' Smyth said in disgust as Gardner started his engine. Picking up his radio handset he answered. 'Delta Tango 94, Roger, responding.'

Within seconds they pulled up outside a late night take-away restaurant. An agitated middle-aged man ran to Smyth's passenger door. He opened it warily. 'There were two of them, one had a gun, you've just missed them.' His words tumbled out, almost incoherently.

'Calm down now, sir,' Smyth spoke slowly and made notes.

'You've just missed them, they ran that way.' He pointed towards Ardyne Avenue.

'Fine, sir, can you just give me your name,' Smyth asked keeping his voice controlled.

'Sean McManus, I own this restaurant.'

'Fine, now how much did they get away with?'

McManus shook his head, 'I don't know, I haven't checked the till yet.'

'Just a second please,' Smyth picked up his handset, 'Delta Tango from Tango 94, arrival Ardoyne shop fronts, confirmed armed robbery, full details to follow, out.' Turning he spoke to his two gunners, 'Give me some cover while I'm in the shop.'

His two covermen raced from their Landrover, one across Crumlin Road, one into a shop doorway next to McManus's Restaurant. Smyth followed McManus into his shop. As both men entered the doorway, the world exploded.

Inside his Landrover, Eddy Gardner was aware of a blinding flash and thunderous noise. Numbly he stumbled from his driver's seat; there was something wet on his face and putting up a hand, he was surprised to find it came away covered in blood.

There was nothing left of the doorway in which one of his comrades had taken cover. Shuffling towards it he tripped over a bundle of rags and fell heavily. Looking down, it took him a second to comprehend what he saw, then he began to cry. It was Peter Taylor and he had no head.

☆ ☆ ☆

Tennant Street Canteen, 8 am Tuesday.

Nevin forced himself to eat, exhaustion had robbed him of any appetite. His follow-up investigation into Peter Taylor's murder had been extensive, but had yielded few clues as to his killer's identity.

He had been hard pressed to contain both his, and his fellow officer's, anger during the operation. Normally hardened men, they had been enraged at the barbarous murder of such a well-liked and respected man.

'What about you Skipper?' a familiar voice boomed.

Nevin looked up to see Gary Howe making his way towards him. 'Gary, I thought you were on leave?'

'I was, but my skipper rang me last night and asked me to come in, most of my section are exhausted.'

'I know how they feel,' Nevin rubbed his eyes tiredly.

'You look like death warmed up, had any sleep?'

'Not much, I co-ordinated last night's operation.'

'What exactly happened?'

'Well from what we can gather, it seems they staged a robbery to draw one of our mobiles into a pre-planned bomb trap. A twenty pound semtex bomb had been placed in an empty shop next door to McManus's restaurant. They'd run a command wire through the shop and across an alley behind into a vacant house.' He took a sip of tea. 'They must have had someone across the road with a radio; as soon as McManus was out of danger, they detonated the bomb. Peter was standing in the doorway of the shop.' He shook his head. 'He never stood a chance; it's a miracle we only had one killed.'

He paused for a second remembering the night's scene of carnage. 'Eddy Gardner is in hospital, he's got a deep cut on his forehead and is in shock. That's the second close friend he's lost in less than two weeks.'

'Bastards,' Howe said with feeling.

Nevin nodded in agreement and both fell silent, lost in their own thoughts.

'Well at least this is one job they can't blame on fucking Kane.' Gary spat his name like a curse. 'Kane's a shooter, he never touches explosives.'

'It sounds like you have something personal against Kane?' Nevin asked, suddenly curious.

'You might say that.' The Scot's face hardened, 'He killed my best friend. 22 April, 1973, I was in the same patrol. Kane's ASU jumped us on the New Lodge Road. My patrol commander and best friend, Ian Hunter, was shot dead.' He stared at Nevin, 'You might say I had something personal against Mr Kane.'

'It was a long time ago.'

Howe nodded. 'I remember it like yesterday, Ian getting killed and finding that wee girl stabbed up in Duncairn Gardens.' He started to rise.

Nevin grabbed his arm, restraining him. 'What girl?'

'A girl we found stuffed in the boot of a car up behind Girdwood Army Camp. The Provos killed her, said she was an informer or something.' Howe started to rise again, but Nevin's grip tightened.

'Tell me everything you can remember about that day.'

'Skipper I've got to go, my patrol is waiting,' Howe protested.

'Never mind your patrol. I'll square it with your inspector and sergeant. Tell me about that day.' Nevin's voice would brook no arguments.

Howe shrugged. 'OK if you insist, where do you want me to begin?'

'From when you found this girl's body.'

Howe thought for a second, remembering back through the years.

'Well we were heading back to Girdwood camp after a patrol . . . '

☆     ☆     ☆

22 April 1973, North Belfast, 3 pm.

Corporal Ian Hunter studied the black Cortina, parked in a side street of Duncairn Gardens. Its registration number struck a cord in his memory. He checked with base; it was stolen all right. He called second in command Gary Howe to his side. 'That car's been stolen in the Ardoyne; base don't want us to go near it, they've tasked ATO and want us to cordon the area.'

'Christ! We would have to find it near the end of our patrol.' He grinned at his best friend. 'Why do you have to be so damned efficient?'

'Just get the cordon set up Gary. Felix won't be long. It's been a quiet day.' He gave Gary a playful slap on his shoulder.

Felix was not long, only twenty minutes. 'What have you got for me?' the army bomb disposal officer asked Hunter on his arrival.

'That car over there,' Ian pointed out the black Cortina, 'it was stolen in Ardoyne this morning and we don't want to take any chances with it.'

'Quite right; that's what we're here for. I'll have it cleared for you in a jiffy.'

Ian and Gary watched as what looked like a miniature tank was wheeled out of ATO's armoured personnel carrier. Attached to it were both a miniature remote controlled camera and a Browning automatic shotgun.

Using his remote control ATO directed the wheelbarrow, as it was nicknamed, towards the parked car. First he blew off both car doors and checked its interior by using the camera, then he blew off the bonnet and boot. Satisfied no quick release booby traps were in operation, he donned his heavy protective body armour.

'You going to check it now?' asked Ian Hunter.

'That's what they pay me for,' replied ATO.

Watching him walk away, Ian turned to Gary. 'I wouldn't do his job for any amount of money.'

Looking like a spaceman ATO checked first under the car's bonnet, then inside and finally the boot. Despite his heavy clothing, both men saw him stiffen. He motioned Ian and Gary to join him. 'Jesus Christ!' Ian exclaimed looking over ATO's shoulder.

A young girl's body lay, foetus-like, covered in blood. Several deep stab wounds could be clearly seen in her chest and stomach. Gary felt sick. 'What kind of animal would do that?'

Removing his helmet, ATO shook his head. 'It beats me; you'd better call the RUC.'

☆    ☆    ☆

After covering their police colleagues while they dealt with the dead girl, Ian and Gary's patrol returned to their Girdwood base for a well earned rest. Now they waited for Corporal Hunter to brief them for their night patrol.

Hunter appeared from his intelligence briefing and gathered his men around him. Swiftly he outlined his intended patrol route, showing where he intended to set up roadblocks and points of particular danger.

'All patrols report the area particularly quiet, that might mean nothing, or it might mean they're up to something. Keep on your toes, stay tight; let's not give these bastards an opportunity to have a go at us.'

Turning, he was about to lead them to their loading bay when a thought struck him. He turned back. 'Oh yes, there's something else you might like to know; that girl we found this afternoon,' Hunter glanced around at his patrol, 'the fucking IRA claimed her death, said she was an informer.'

There was a growl of anger from his men. 'That's right, now

73

you know what kind of animals we're up against.'

Hunter led his patrol from Girdwood and crossing Antrim Road they headed for New Lodge Road, keeping well spaced and moving with speed and skill. Ahead of them was a major road intersection, dominated by high tower blocks. In one of these tower blocks, Artillery Flats, Kane and another IRA volunteer, Seamus Cassidy, waited for them. They were the point of a triangular ambush. Once they initiated it, the other two would in turn ambush any patrols coming to the ambushed patrol's aid.

Kane held an AR18 Armalite loosely in his hands, watching the intersection below intensely. Beside him Cassidy held a .303 bolt action Lee Enfield rifle; he was nervous and kept fidgeting. Without taking his eyes off the road junction below, Kane said softly, 'Stop moving, you're upsetting my concentration.'

Cassidy was upset. He was, in theory, Kane's superior. This was only the younger man's third operation, while he had been on 'active service' for over two years. 'Don't tell me what to do,' he hissed angrily, 'I'm in charge here.'

Kane turned to look at his older companion. Cassidy suddenly felt a wave of fear. Even in the darkened room, Kane's ice cold blue eyes bored into his. Involuntarily he moved back. 'If you keep on moving, I'll shoot you myself.' A very faint smile crossed his lips. 'Then you won't have to worry about the Brits.'

Cassidy swallowed involuntarily, suddenly more scared of Kane than anything outside their room. He tried to say something in reply, but no words would come out of his dry throat. Kane turned his head to study the intended ambush site.

'When this is over, I'm telling Scullion I'm not working with this maniac again, nephew or no nephew,' Cassidy said to himself, but kept perfectly still, not wanting to upset Kane again. Beside him Kane said softly, 'I think we have company.'

Below Hunter knelt against a corner and scanned ahead using a Tri-Lux sight mounted on his SLR rifle. Tension hung heavy all around him like a thick blanket, causing hairs on his neck to stand on end. 'They are out there, I can feel it,' he said softly to himself.

Across New Lodge Road, Gary Howe also knelt, giving cover to his friend. Both were aware that this junction was very dangerous. Gunner Curtis had died at this very spot, the first army fatality in Ulster. Signalling to Gary he was going to cross, Hunter stood, gathered himself, and sprinted for cover across the wide open junction. In the flat above, Kane and Cassidy fired together as Hunter came into sight. Despite having the more accurate rifle Cassidy missed his running target, but three .223 rounds from Kane's Armalite hit.

Ian Hunter was sprinting at full speed when something that felt like a hammer smashed into his right leg, whipping it from underneath him. He fell heavily, loosing his grip on his rifle. A searing red hot pain shot through his body from his right thigh. Forgetting his rifle, he grabbed his wounded leg in both hands. Even in the darkness, Hunter could see a fountain of blood gushing from a gaping hole. He was aware of more shots landing around him. 'Gary I'm hit,' he shouted through gritted teeth.

Howe could clearly see gunflashes from the ambushers' weapons. Bringing his own rifle up he returned fire. His first three rounds were tracers which arched gracefully towards Kane and Cassidy's position, marking it clearly for the rest of his patrol. Around him other marines started to return fire.

Above them Kane emptied one thirty round magazine at the patrol below. He had two magazines taped together and coolly he turned to reload and continued to fire. Cassidy was trying to work the bolt on his .303, but his shaking hands jammed it. Throwing the now useless weapon from him he stood, intending to flee. A 7.62 round hit him just below his chin, blowing out half his skull as it exited. For a brief second he stood on tiptoe, then fell full length on the floor.

Lying on his back and still holding his injured leg in both hands, Hunter was aware that he was getting weaker; he could feel his life's blood draining from him. 'Gary, Gary, I'm hit,' he shouted and even to himself his voice sounded faint.

'Put some fire down, I'm going for Ian,' Howe shouted to his patrol. Dropping his own rifle he ran for Hunter. Reaching his friend he threw him onto his back in a fireman's lift and ran back towards cover. Around him his patrol laid down a concentrated burst of suppressing fire. Kane took aim at Howe's back and squeezed the trigger of his rifle. A dull click sounded, his rifle was empty. Around him the flat was starting to disintegrate as heavy fire from below became more accurate.

A bullet narrowly missed his head. 'Time to go I think.'

Casting a disdainful look at Cassidy's body, he dropped to his stomach and, holding his rifle tight to his chest, rolled across to the door. Reaching it, he crawled through on hands and knees.

Once outside he ran to a refuse chute and paused to stuff his rifle and gloves into it. Below in a basement a weapons carrier was waiting to transport the weapon to a hide. Satisfied, he ran for safety along his pre-arranged escape route.

In the relative security of a doorway, Howe worked on his injured section commander's leg. He had covered both entry and exit wounds with dressings but bright red blood still poured out from under them. He guessed that the femoral artery had been severed, blood was everywhere. He'd already called for assistance and given his radio to another patrol member while he worked on Hunter's leg. He heard a heavy burst of automatic fire in the distance. 'What's happening?' he called to his radio operator.

'Gary, the ambulance coming for Ian has been shot up; they are trying to fight their way to us.'

Another burst of heavy firing could be heard in the opposite direction. One of their satellite patrols, trying to come to help them, had also been hit. 'There's nothing for it,' Howe said to himself, 'I'm going to have to try a tourniquet.'

Using a broad six inch bandage, he improvised a makeshift tourniquet, trying to stem the seemingly endless flow of blood. Hunter's face was deathly pale; he was lapsing into unconsciousness. Howe grabbed his friend's shirt front and shook him. 'Fight it Ian, fight for fuck's sake; it won't be long.' Hunter's eyes flickered open briefly; he tried to say something and failed, he gave a weak smile and closed his eyes.

'How long before that fucking ambulance gets here?' Howe shouted to his radio operator.

'Not long, five minutes at most.'

In fact it was ten minutes before the armoured ambulance could reach them. By then it was far too late. Corporal Ian Hunter, Royal Marine Commando, was dead.

As they lifted his still form, a small group of women gathered at a nearby street corner. A woman, old enough to be Howe's mother, shouted in a harsh Belfast accent, 'That's one less Brit to worry about.'

A ragged cheer went up from her group. It was all Gary could do to restrain his patrol. He glanced across to the small crowd, some were actually dancing. 'Come on,' he said to his enraged men, 'let's get back to base and leave those scumbags; it's what Ian would have wanted.' With a last contemptuous look at the still cheering women, Gary turned and led his patrol away.

☆   ☆   ☆

Some four hours later, Kane sat in a safe house in his native Ardoyne. Around him other members of his ambush party sat; some were quiet, others talked in excited voices. He sat alone, keeping his own council. Leo Scullion, his uncle and commanding officer of Third Battalion, walked in. He looked at Kane. 'I'm sorry to hear about Seamus.'

'He went down fighting,' Kane lied.

Scullion nodded. 'He died a soldier's death, you did well.'

Kane made no reply but smiled. His uncle walked to him and placed a hand on his shoulder and turning he addressed his assembled volunteers. 'I think we have a star here,' he glanced back to Kane and gave him a paternal pat on his shoulder. 'Congratulations, you've killed your first Brit.'

☆   ☆   ☆

Tennant Street Canteen.

'And that's the whole story,' Gary Howe finished.

Nevin sat for a second, his mind racing. 'I want you to write me out a statement, putting everything you've told me in writing.'

Howe shrugged his shoulders. 'Anything you say Skipper, but what's this all about?'

'I'm not sure it means anything, yet, but I want your story in writing as soon as possible.' Nevin's voice was thoughtful.

Howe stood. 'I'll get it to you before I go off today. Now I must get back to my patrol.' Turning, the Scot strode away.

Alone Nevin sat deep in thought, tiredness banished from him. An horrific thought was taking place in his mind. 'Find the trigger,' Marrianne had told him. Maybe he had done just that. Standing he raced upstairs to CID general office. Quickly he donned his shoulder holster and threw a sports jacket on over it. Walking to DI Cotton's office he knocked and poked his head around the door. 'Can I be excused this morning's briefing?'

Cotton looked up. 'Something important?'

'Yes, could just possibly be a lead in the Lynn Moody investigation.'

'Sure, you're excused; anything you want to tell me?'

'Not yet, let me run a few things down first.'

Cotton nodded and Nevin raced out, almost colliding with a startled DCI Hart. 'Where's Sergeant Brown off to?' he asked, entering Cotton's office.

Without looking up Cotton said, 'He's doing what he's good at.'

'What's that?' Hart's voice was unfriendly.

Cotton looked up and smiled, 'Being a detective.'

☆    ☆    ☆

RUC Records Office, Knock, Belfast. Two hours later.

'And you've tried both stations and computer records?' she asked for the second time.

Exasperated, Nevin took a deep breath. 'Yes, as I've already told you, station records for 1973 were destroyed in a mortar attack. Computer records only go back to 1975; everything before that is only statistical detail. I need to see the actual file, I need details.' His voice betrayed his impatience.

She looked at him over her horn-rimmed glasses. For a second he felt like a schoolboy talking back to his head teacher. 'I'm just trying to be thorough Sergeant Brown.'

Angela Murray, the Ayatollah of records branch, was a woman used to getting her own way. Looking down at the prim sixty-year-old's stern features, he decided on a tactical retreat. 'I'm sorry Miss Murray, but this is really important.'

She nodded her head, mollified. 'OK, Sergeant Brown, let's see what we can find.' Moving around file laden shelves, Angela Murray tutted. 'The problem is Sergeant . . .'

'Nevin, please.'

A smile lit up her face, totally transforming it. 'Nevin,' she

78

conceded, 'the problem is that we don't have a name.' She patted him maternally on his arm, 'But don't worry, if it's here I'll find it.'

True to her word, she found the file – a full two hours later. 'Here it is,' she beamed in triumph, handing Nevin a thick buff coloured file.

'Is there somewhere I could read this?'

'There's an office at the end of this gallery.' She pointed to a grey door. 'You can use that.'

Nevin opened and read the file's covering report:

On 22 April, 1973, an army patrol discovered a black Ford Cortina parked in Duncairn Gardens. The vehicle had been stolen in Ardoyne earlier that day. An immediate security operation was put into operation and an army bomb disposal team declared the car clear by 5 pm.

The car was found to contain a female body stuffed in its boot. The deceased was later identified as Margaret Hamilton, thirty-four years, 24 Jamaica Street, Ardoyne, a Protestant married to a local Catholic. A postmortem revealed that she had died as a result of multiple stab wounds.

At 9 pm on the same day a caller, using a recognized code word, called *The Irish News* and stated that Mrs Hamilton had been executed by them because she was an informer. The caller also stated that they would take action against any other informers they discovered.

To date, no one has been caught for this crime.

Leafing through the file's pages, he noted Dr Edward McMullan had carried out the postmortem. Several other factors were evident. Mrs Hamilton had been killed earlier that day, it was also obvious that she had been put into the car after her death. Finally he found himself thumbing through a glossary of photographs. There were views of the car with its tragic remains. With a start, he found himself looking at Margaret Hamilton's postmortem photos. Her face held that same identical look of horror he had seen on Lynn Moody's. Transfixed, he sat for several minutes, staring at the dead face.

Finally he shook himself out of his reverie and, picking up the phone, dialled Foster Green Hospital. It took fifteen minutes to locate Dr Ealing. 'Do you know you've interrupted me in the middle of a lecture Sergeant Brown?' Irritation was obvious in his voice. 'This had better be important.'

'Do you know a Dr McMullan?'

'Of course I do, he was my predecessor here at Foster Green, why?'

'Could you find out his present address for me?'

There was a slight pause, Nevin waited anxiously. 'Sergeant Brown, the names and addresses of former employees of this hospital are strictly confidential. I cannot give out that type of information without proper authority.'

'I quite understand that, sir, but this is an emergency.'

Again there was a short silence. 'Could you give me some indication as to what this emergency is?'

Nevin thought quickly. 'I can't explain fully but it is connected with the Lynn Moody murder.'

'I don't know,' Ealing said doubtfully.

Nevin began to lose patience. 'For God's sake, Ealing, it might help me stop another Lynn Moody,' he shouted.

There was an icy silence and for several seconds Nevin thought he had gone too far. 'Can I ring you back?' Ealing said eventually.

Nevin gave him his telephone number and the line went dead. He sat for ten anxious minutes watching the phone, willing it to ring. When it did, he grabbed it instantly. Swiftly he noted down McMullan's address. 'One thing Sergeant Brown,' Ealing's voice was cold.

'Yes?'

'This had better be important.'

Dr McMullan lived in a comfortable detached house, just off Belfast's exclusive Malone Road. Nevin heard him approaching long before he opened his front door. Leaning heavily on a walking stick he studied Nevin's warrant card, having to adjust his glasses twice. Looking up he smiled. 'Come in, come in.' His voice was surprisingly firm.

Nevin followed him into a large comfortable sitting room. He accepted a deep armchair opposite McMullan. 'Now young man, what can I do for you?' Nevin explained his interest in Margaret Hamilton's death and its possible link to his present investigation. 'So you think both murders are linked?'

Before Nevin could reply, McMullan went on, 'It hardly seems likely, considering the time between both deaths.'

'I know it seems a bit wild but there is another connection.'

'Care to tell me what it is?'

Nevin shook his head and gave a short humourless laugh. 'If I did, you really would think I'm crazy.'

Dr McMullan studied for a second, then smiled. 'Lucky for you I keep copies of all my major files.'

Standing, he shuffled to a huge writing bureau and, opening a drawer, he removed a large red book. Flicking through he muttered, 'Ah yes.' Turning to Nevin he said, 'Follow me.'

The detective followed him to his study, its walls covered with files and books on criminal pathology. McMullan shuffled from one file to another, occasionally picking one up, only to discard it. Finally he said, 'Here it is!' He looked at Nevin. 'You'll have to forgive me, my filing system is not what it once was.'

Both men returned to McMullan's sitting room. 'Right Sergeant let's begin. I won't bother you with personal details, that's all in your police file, OK?'

Nevin nodded, producing a note book.

'Death was due to six deep stab wounds to the chest and abdomen, any one of which could have proved fatal. Murder weapon was a sharp instrument, at least six inches long, double edged, width at least two inches at its base, tapering to a needle point, probably a knife.' He looked up at Nevin. 'Helpful so far?'

'Very.'

McMullan continued. 'From the angle of the wounds it was established that the victim was standing when the first two blows were struck; the rest were administered while she lay on the ground. It was also established that her killer was taller than her.'

'Hold it please Doctor, how tall was she?'

'Five foot nine inches.'

'Could you estimate the height of her killer?'

'Oh yes, the wounds inflicted while she was standing show clearly that he must have been at least three or four inches taller.'

'Go on please Doctor,' Nevin urged.

'Well, let's see, not much more really. Her killer was physically strong.'

'Could you be a little more specific Doctor?'

'In what way?'

'When you say physically strong, what exactly do you mean?'

McMullan studied his file. 'Well one of his blows severed her clavicle and punctured her lung.' He looked up. 'The clavicle is your collar bone, here.' He tapped his chest near his neck. 'It was severed completely by the blow; that would take great strength.'

'Abnormal strength?'

'Yes.'

Nevin was silent for a second, lost in thought. 'I've only one last question Doctor, was there any evidence of sexual assault?'

McMullan studied the detective for a full minute before he answered. 'You have to remember, Sergeant, we were not investigating this murder as a sex crime. The IRA admitted killing Margaret Hamilton.'

'I realize that, sir, but was there any evidence of a sexual assault?'

'Margaret Hamilton had sex shortly before her death; there was no bruising around the vagina to indicate forced entry. I concluded that she had sex willingly and that it was not connected with her death.'

Nevin felt disappointed. 'I don't suppose you took a smear for analysis?'

'As a matter of fact I did, just in case.'

Nevin smiled. 'Then you know the blood type of the last man to have sex with her?'

'Yes, obviously.'

'I'll bet you it was O-negative.'

Doctor McMullan paled slightly, 'Yes it was.'

Nevin nodded. 'Could you let me have a full written report covering everything you've told me?'

'Yes of course,' McMullan said, still shocked.

'Could I use your phone please?'

'Yes, it's in the hall.'

Nevin made two calls, the first to DI Cotton. 'Glad you called in,' his superior sounded tired, 'how is your lead working out?'

'I think I'm making progress,' Nevin answered.

'Anything you want to tell me?'

'Not just yet Brian, let me run with this for a bit longer. There's someone I want to talk to this afternoon, do you need me back at the office?'

'No if you think you have a positive lead I trust your judgement; there is one thing, it's Peter Taylor's funeral tomorrow. I'd like you to represent CID at it.'

'I'd be honoured, what time?'

'10 am at Roselawn.'

'I'll be there, see you later.' He hung up and called his second number.

Marrianne Sterling was summing up to a psychology class when she was informed over the intercom that she had an urgent telephone message. 'Well, class you get reprieved ten minutes early.' There was a gentle ripple of laughter. 'Class dismissed.'

Going to her office she took the call. 'Hello.'

'Marrianne, is that you?'

'Nevin, it's lovely to hear from you.' Her voice held genuine warmth.

'I need to talk to you as soon as possible, can you get away?'

'Yes of course, where do you want to meet?'

'Could you come out to my house in Carrickfergus?'

'Yes, give me directions.'

She wrote down his instructions. 'I'll see you there in an hour.'

Later, sitting in his front room, Nevin outlined all he had found out, omitting nothing. 'I'm sorry,' he concluded, 'but you're the only person I could turn to for advice.'

She smiled. 'That's OK, it is my work after all. So you think this IRA man Kane killed both girls?'

'Yes.'

'Couldn't it just be coincidence?'

'As a detective I don't believe in coincidences; the similarities between both deaths are striking. One,' he held up a finger, 'both girls were killed by a tall man with abnormal strength. Kane is six foot two and is a fitness fanatic. Two,' he held up a second finger, 'both victims had sex with a man who has O-negative blood. Kane has O-negative blood. I checked. Three,'

83

he held up a third finger, 'the weapon and type of wounds inflicted by it are identical.'

He paused to let his words sink in. 'Now what I want from you is your professional advice; could Kane be some kind of psychopath?'

Marrianne stood and walked to his window. Without turning she spoke. 'There was a syndrome we found in certain GIs in Vietnam. We called it The Double Killer Syndrome. Very few cases were actually documented, although it's possible that it was more widespread than we thought.'

She clasped her arms around herself as if cold. 'One case in particular comes to mind. It concerned a master sergeant in the navy SEAL's.' She turned to look at him. 'Have you heard of them?'

'Yes they're some kind of Special Forces aren't they?'

She laughed. 'Not just Special Forces, these were the creme-de-la-creme. Hand picked, specially selected and trained. America's best. No mission was too dangerous or tough. They did everything, including Operation Phoenix, the assassination of suspected VC supporters inside South Vietnam.'

She sighed. 'And Master Sergeant Mark Kramer was one of their top men. Highly decorated, Congrational Medal of Honour, two Silver Stars, three Purple Hearts, the works. They might not mean much to you but to the American military, they mean everything.'

She delved into her handbag and pulled out a cigarette. 'I'm sorry. I'm trying to give up but I need one right now.'

She joined Nevin on his sofa.

'Because of who they were and what they did, SEALs were one of the VC's top targets. Kramer and a buddy were out on local leave, drinking in a Saigon bar. A bar girl recognized Kramer's friend, enticed him upstairs and knifed him. Kramer heard him shout, ran upstairs and found her with the knife in her hand.'

She took a pull on her cigarette and looked at Nevin. 'Kramer killed her with his bare hands. That's what triggered him. He started killing bar girls before he went on operations. By the time he was finally tracked down, he had killed twenty-five girls. You see, nobody wanted to believe a hero like him was guilty.'

Marrianne looked away, lost in thought for a second.

Stubbing out her cigarette she continued. 'My father sat on the medical tribunal that ruled he was unfit to plead. I've interviewed him myself. He's highly intelligent, like many psychopaths, and totally without remorse. Just the opposite, he's proud of what he's done. He once told me killing bar girls "got his eye in" for operations and that's why he was such a successful soldier.'

She fell silent. 'Do you believe Kane could be like Kramer?' Nevin asked at last.

'Perhaps. There are obvious similarities; both are under immense pressure daily; both are required to face the stress of killing on a regular basis.' She looked at Nevin. 'That's an important factor. Psychopaths see killing as a natural thing to do; that's why they often make good soldiers.'

'Or terrorists,' Nevin commented.

'Precisely; but if Kane is suffering from the same syndrome as Kramer then there are two very important factors you may not have considered.'

'What are they?'

'Firstly Kane will kill again. There's no doubt about that but far more importantly where are his other victims?'

Nevin shook his head and looked puzzled. 'I don't understand, what other victims?'

She sighed and explained. 'Once a psychopath is triggered, there is no way he can alter his set pattern of behaviour. If Kane killed Margaret Hamilton in 1973 and then went on to kill for the IRA, it would have been impossible for him to wait eighteen or so years to kill Lynn Moody.'

Nevin was horrified. 'You mean . . . '

'Yes precisely,' she nodded, 'where are the bodies of his other victims.'

☆   ☆   ☆

Wednesday 9.30 am, Roselawn Cemetery, outskirts of Belfast.

Nevin had not got much sleep. Marrianne's revelations had plagued him through the night. People were already gathering as he drove through Roselawn's huge gates. A tight security cordon had been thrown around the cemetery to protect Peter Taylor's mourners.

Recognizing friends from his station he went over to them and was swapping gossip when they were interrupted by a serious-faced constable from the security cordon. 'Could you move right back to the far corner of the cemetery, we have a suspect car outside the main gate.'

Nevin followed his friends to a safe distance. Standing next to a uniformed member, he listened as events unfolded. Peter Taylor's funeral cortege had been delayed and diverted by a string of bomb scares along its intended route. Stolen cars had been placed at strategic points, bomb warnings were coming in thick and fast by callers using recognized IRA code words. Even as he listened there was a tremendous explosion near the front gate. The suspect car had exploded as it was being investigated; six officers were injured, miraculously none seriously.

It was to be a further three hours before the dead constable's funeral procession arrived at Roselawn cemetery. The IRA were later to issue a statement saying that, 'Unless Crown Forces ceased their harassment of Republican funerals they could not expect to bury their own dead in peace.'

Reserve Constable Peter Taylor, Royal Ulster Constabulary, robbed of the sanctity of life, was denied dignity in death.

Tiger's Bay, North Belfast, 1 pm the same day.

Mary Kirkpatrick walked confidently towards her two bed-roomed terraced house. Her hips had a natural swing that had brought her many a wolf whistle. She was a source of constant gossip amongst her neighbours. At thirty-two her figure was still good; her long legs, amply showed off by short skirts, were usually encased in black nylon stockings.

Dyed blonde hair, tied back in a neat bun, somehow made her look accessible. Divorced, she lived alone with her two children. Wednesday was her favourite day, not only was it a half day from the clothing shop at which she worked, but her two children were at her mother's until four o'clock.

Opening her front door she gave an audible sigh. 'Home at last.' In her hall she stretched. Time for a cup of tea before *Neighbours*. The Australian soap opera was her favourite TV programme. Closing her door she failed to see a tall, broad shouldered man, his anorak hood hiding his face, watching her from across the road.

Orange Cross Club, Shankhill Road, 10 pm that evening.

Colin Jackson watched the man's face as he told his story. In a dimly lit back room, he and three other men present wore black balaclavas to hide their identity. Jacky Hewitt and the man sat in front of the four hooded men. He motioned Hewitt to come and sit next to him. He whispered into Hewitt's ear. Hewitt spoke for him.

'So what you are saying is that Larry Martin has just moved into a new house at 9 Havana Gardens. What kind of front door does it have?'

'Just a normal plywood two by four, but it has heavy bolts top and bottom.'

Jackson whispered again. 'No steel or macralone plating?' Hewitt asked.

'No, but I've heard that he's going to get it armoured and reinforced shortly,' the man answered.

Jackson whispered again. 'Tell us about the letter again,' Hewitt said.

'I was giving cover while his house was being searched, prior to his arrest. There was a letter on a table in his front hall. It was from a solicitor called James Fennel. He said in it that he was coming to speak to Martin at 3 pm next Monday.'

Jackson leaned across to Hewitt again. 'You're absolutely sure about both the time and day?'

'Definitely sure,' the man replied, his voice firm.

There was silence for several long seconds and the man began to sweat. Finally Jackson made a motion with his hand. Hewitt smiled and said, 'Thank you very much for the information and we will try and put it to good use. We know where to find you if we need you.'

The man stood up, aware his audience was over. Walking to the door he paused and looked back. 'All I want is justice.' Without waiting for an answer he turned and left.

With him gone, Jackson and his three top gunmen removed

their hoods. 'Do you trust him?' Hewitt asked his CO.

Jackson smiled. 'Of course I do,' he laughed. 'He knows he wouldn't last five minutes if he lied to us.'

Turning to his gun team he said, 'Monday, that gives you four days to set it up; is that enough?'

'No problem,' one of them said.

Outside, the man pulled up his collar against the cold night air. Turning, he walked up Shankhill Road towards Tennant Street. A passing police Landrover beeped its horn as it passed. He raised his hand in acknowledgement; he was Eddy Gardner, part-time reserve police constable, RUC.

☆    ☆    ☆

Tennant Street CID General Office, Thursday 3 pm.

All day Nevin had poured over statistics sent to him by various law enforcement agencies, from as far apart as Interpol in Paris to Scotland Yard in London. There was no history of female homicides with anything like the MO of his present case. If Kane was a double killer, he could find no trace of his activities.

His phone rang. 'Detective Sergeant Brown, can I help you?'

'It's Marrianne, are you busy tonight?'

Involuntarily Nevin smiled. 'As it happens I have tonight off, what did you have in mind?'

'Well,' she dragged the word out, 'I thought we might have a bite to eat at my place, and maybe a couple of drinks.'

'That would be nice.'

'Yes I thought so, then I thought we might make love.'

He checked the room, everything looked normal. Glancing at his pile of paperwork, he thought, 'It must be too much work, I've finally cracked.'

'Nevin are you there?'

'Yes, yes could you say that again, the part after . . . ' He looked around, his colleagues were staring at him. 'Never mind,' he said quickly, 'I'll be there at eight, is that OK?'

'Fine,' she said sweetly, 'I look forward to seeing you.'

He still had the phone in his hand when DI Cotton passed. 'What's the matter Nevin?' he asked. 'You look like you've just won the pools?'

☆    ☆    ☆

Queen's University, Accommodation Rooms, same day 9 pm.

She had made a lovely meal, ginger beef on white rice, followed by her own special peach melba. Over coffee they talked and laughed, sharing secrets and stories. When they went to bed, it was as if they were old lovers.

At first they made love frantically, hungry for each other, two people deprived of physical love, desperate to be fulfilled. Then, their initial passion spent, they made love again – slowly, passionately, each trying to discover in each other something they both thought they had lost, forever. Finally, exhausted, they lay in each other's arms and talked, as lovers do, of their own pasts.

She told him of her high school love, a college football star, found dead, over-dosed on cocaine. 'Nobody knew, we never suspected he was an addict.' He felt her shudder. 'We just found him one morning, lying there dead.'

For a time he held her, then told of his twelve months after Sharon left him. About trying to drink himself to death and sleeping with every girl he could find, hurting himself and them more. 'It all came to a head one night. My DI found me dead drunk on night shift. He took me up to the gym, threw me in a cold shower, and slapped me sober. He told me, "Wise up, or get out!"'

He laughed, 'He took me home with him next day and kept me there for three months.'

In the darkness he shrugged and pulled her closer. 'I haven't been drunk or with a woman for twelve months.'

She reached up to pull his head down and her lips found his softly. When they parted she whispered, 'Nevin I'm glad we found each other.'

# 4

---

Tennant Street, CID General Office, 9 am Friday third week.

Nevin arrived early and got through some paperwork. He sat, his open diary across his knees, awaiting the morning's briefing. Briefly his mind drifted back to last night's events and a smile drifted over his face. DCI Hart walked in with DI Cotton. 'Ah well,' he thought, 'back to reality.'

Hart began, as usual, by asking each of his detective sergeants to outline any progress on their respective cases. He kept Nevin to last. All eyes turned as Nevin stood. He began by outlining his investigation into Sean Grady's killing, Trevor Boyd had been remanded without bail on a charge of murder and other related offences.

'What about the Lynn Moody investigation?' Hart interrupted him.

'I'm following a definite line of enquiry.'

'Oh really?' Hart leaned forward slightly, 'and what is this line of enquiry?'

Nevin thought for a second before replying. 'At this moment in time I'd rather not say.' He paused and added, 'Sir,' as if it were an after-thought.

Hart's face turned several shades redder. When he spoke his voice had risen to a higher pitch. 'Well I want to know now! What is this so-called line of enquiry?'

Before Nevin could reply, DI Cotton intervened. 'With all due respect, sir, Detective Sergeant Brown has kept me informed of his progress to date, and I agree with him that it is too early to reveal what line his enquiries are taking.'

Hart turned to look at DI Cotton. 'Why?' he asked flatly.

'There are sensitive matters involved, sir, above and beyond the actual case itself.'

Hart pursed his lips. By backing Nevin the DI had put him in a quandary. If he carpeted his senior sergeant, he was also going to have to bring his Chief of Detectives in Tennant Street up on charges as well.

'Very well,' Hart turned back to face Nevin, 'but I hope for both your sakes this line of enquiry proves fruitful. I'll speak to you later, Inspector.'

After the meeting Cotton caught Nevin's eye and jerked his head towards his office. 'Do you know why I did that?' he asked as Nevin closed the door.

'No.'

'I did it to prevent my senior detective sergeant and my CID Director from having a stand-up fight in front of junior officers. Now what the hell are you up to?' he sat down opposite Nevin.

Nevin dropped his head into his hands and massaged his face. He looked back up to his friend and superior. 'I can't tell you Brian.' He held both hands up as Cotton opened his mouth to make an angry reply. 'Hear me out please.'

DI Cotton nodded and remained silent. 'There's more involved here than just the death of one girl, much more. If I tell you what I know, what I suspect, you will have to go to the authorities, you won't have any alternative. I need more time, please believe me.'

Cotton removed a cigar from a packet on his desk, lit it and dropped back his head to blow smoke towards the ceiling. He looked back to Nevin. 'OK,' he said eventually. 'Thank God you've had a result in the Grady murder. I can use that as a lever with Hart. I'll keep him off your back for two weeks. After that . . . ' He made a cutting gesture across his throat.

'Thanks Brian, I won't let you down.' Nevin stood and headed for the door.

'One other thing.' Cotton's voice halted him. 'I rang your place last night. Were you out?'

'Yes I was, as it happens.'

'Is it serious?'

Nevin's smile broadened. 'Yes I think it is.'

Cotton slapped his hand on his desk top with delight. 'Thank goodness, it's about time. Is it anybody I know?'

'In a way, you brought us together.' The DI's face took on a puzzled frown. 'It's Marrianne Sterling, that visiting American doctor; you sent me to listen to one of her lectures.' Nevin raised his eyebrows up and down twice, winked and left.

Cotton looked at his closed office door, stunned. 'The lucky bastard,' he said softly.

☆ ☆ ☆

Antrim Road, 3 pm same day.

Kane and Martin drove past their intended target for a third time. 'What do you think?' Martin asked.

'Piece of cake.' Kane's voice was full of confidence.

'What time do you think is best?'

'Three o'clock, they change shift then.'

'I'd prefer to do it on a Thursday; that's the end of their working week, they'll be more tired, less alert.'

'No,' Kane's voice was firm, 'I want to do it on Wednesday.'

Martin was puzzled. 'Why Wednesday? What's so important about doing it on a Wednesday?'

Kane was silent for a full minutes. 'I want to do it on Wednesday. I've set it up for Wednesday.' He turned to face Martin. 'I'll do it on Wednesday or not at all.'

Concentrating on his driving, Martin was aware of Kane's ice cold blue eyes boring into the side of his face. He shrugged his shoulders, 'OK, if you want to do it on Wednesday that bad, we'll do it on Wednesday.' He shrugged again, 'It won't make that much difference in any case.' He flashed a quick look at Kane's stern features. 'We'll do it on Wednesday all right?'

Kane turned to look back out of his side window, calmer, more relaxed. Without turning his head he said, 'I just want things to go the way I planned, that's all.'

Martin dropped Kane near Gemma Court where he was staying with Mary O'Niel and drove off to his Havana Gardens home. Parking his car he went inside and, going directly to his front sitting room, poured himself a stiff whiskey. He pondered over his conversation with Kane.

He had never like the man. Despite his reputation, there was something that worried him, a feeling he could not put a finger on. Maybe it was just jealousy. Kane was after all the best gunman the organization had in Belfast. He laughed to himself. Who was he kidding? Kane was the best, the most reliable killer the IRA had ever had. Butcher Kane never missed!

Still his flesh crawled every time he was in Kane's company, there was something unhealthy about him. He would have to get Mr Kane watched. Yes, that was the answer. Fidelious Clarke was away for this weekend. When he got back on Monday night he would get some of his Int. and Security ASU to watch Mr Bloody Butcher Kane.

Martin sat for several seconds, contemplating his decision. He had to be careful. His own men worshipped Kane. He was a hero to them. Still it would do no harm to have him watched for a while. He contemplated writing Fidelious Clarke a note, then decided against it. Better to tell his veteran Republican in person what he wanted him to do. Clarke was a good man, devoted to the cause; he could be relied upon to do the right thing.

Monday, CID General Office, 3.15 pm.

He had spent all weekend pouring over his accumulated data, and still he could find no pattern. As a professional police officer he was conditioned to criminals setting a pattern of behaviour. Most offenders were traced by their modus operandie, their MO, the way they carried out their crimes. The set methods of operation that had brought them success in their past criminal exploits, and which they usually continued to use.

So far he could find nothing even remotely resembling any kind of sequence of events, let alone a pattern. He shook his head. Something Marrianne said came back to him. 'Maybe you're looking in the wrong place.'

Well maybe he was, he looked again at his piles of paper. 'It's here somewhere, it has to be.'

DI Cotton burst out of his office. 'Nevin, there's just been another shooting in the Ardoyne.'

'Don't tell me another one of our patrols got hit?'

'No, it looks like one of the opposition's been killed.'

Ardoyne, twenty minutes earlier.

The car drove slowly down Oldpark Road, its three occupants casual and relaxed. There were no police or army patrols to hinder them; all available personnel were dealing with a string of suspect bombs and cars scattered around the Shankill and Ligonel areas.

They parked their car in Havana Gardens and got out. Both were smartly dressed, one carrying a briefcase. They walked directly to number nine and knocked. Inside Larry Martin looked up from his paper and checked the time. 'That will be Fennel,' he said to his wife. Standing, he walked to his front door and paused, hand on one of the heavy securing bolts. 'Who is it?' he shouted.

Outside both men produced guns from under their coats. One held a double-barrelled sawn-off twelve gauge shotgun, the other an Ingram M10 sub-machine gun.

The shotgun holder fired first, his weapon blowing a huge hole in the thin plywood door. Martin took the full force of its blast in his chest and was blown backwards onto his hallway floor. Stepping forward, the second gunman pushed his M10 through the gaping hole and pulled its trigger. The vicious little gun emptied its thirty round magazine. Fourteen bullets hit an already badly wounded Martin, killing him instantly.

Moving with practised precision, both men turned and ran for their car. As he ran, the M10 holder changed magazines. Both dived into their waiting getaway car. People began to scream from their homes. A group of four youths ran towards them, armed with sticks, and tried to prevent their escape. One gunman leaned out of his window and fired his M10 again, hitting one youth and scattering his friends. At full speed the killers sped off up Oldpark Road to safety.

Martin's killing sent shock waves around his native Ardoyne. Groups of youths and young men gathered on every street corner. Police and army patrols, responding to reports of shots fired, were stoned. Stones turned to petrol bombs as news spread that the IRA chief was dead. A general riot broke out, with police and army patrols forced to fire plastic bullets to keep rioters at bay. Two army patrols were fired on by gunmen from Fidelious Clarke's Int. and Security ASU. Amidst almost total anarchy, Sean Hughes called a meeting of senior members of Ardoyne PIRA at Mary O'Niel's house in Gemma Court.

Hughes was now effective OC of Ardoyne PIRA. He paced O'Niel's front room. 'The fucking Prod bastards,' he screamed to his assembled men. 'He must have been set up by the bloody Brits.'

'What about retaliation?' Joseph Downey, Fidelious Clarke's right-hand man and in control of his ASU while the veteran Republican was away, asked.

Hughes stopped his pacing to throw a baleful glare at him. 'I've already been on to Brigade. They want to use Brian Turney's West Belfast ASU to hit back at the Shankill UVF.'

'Why?' Anthony 'Luger' Hardy, his own number two, asked, his voice angry. 'We can handle it. Larry was one of us. It should be us that get even with those Prod bastards.'

Hughes nodded his head. 'I said the same thing myself, but Brigade thinks it will be too risky for us to mount an attack from Ardoyne. Both the peelers and UVF will be expecting it; they think Turney's men have a better chance coming in from the west.'

'What about my operation on Wednesday?' Kane asked, his voice as unemotional as ever.

'That will have to be postponed for a week. We have to bury Larry and I want to bury him in style.' For the first time since he'd met Kane, he saw him express an emotion. Disappointment was written clearly across his face. 'You can wait a week, can't you Butcher?'

A very faint smile flickered briefly on Kane's lips. 'Oh yes, I can wait.' He looked up, his ice cold blue eyes locking with Hughes. 'I can wait,' he repeated softly.

Tuesday, 3 pm, Shankhill Road.

Retaliation for Martin's killing was not long in coming. James 'Gypsy' Jordan was standing outside the offices of the Popular Unionist Party when a dark maroon Ford Cortina with four men in it drove slowly by. He turned his head, as if to enquire who was in it. For the briefest of seconds Jordan was aware of his impending fate, then both gunmen opened fire. In all, forty

.223 rounds were fired; thirty of them hit Jordan in his chest and stomach, practically cutting him in half. The car sped up Shankhill Road, its occupants laughing and firing their weapons in the air.

Later that evening Nevin sat alone at his desk in CID general office. He was trying to clear as much of his paperwork as possible in order to give himself time to devote all his energies to the Lynn Moody investigation.

He sighed and stretched and wished that life could be like the fictional detectives he saw on TV. They only ever had one case at a time to solve. He had five major investigations, including two murders, not to mention reports and statements on several lesser cases. All of them had to be cleared to allow him time to pursue Kane's elusive trail.

Behind him a door opened and closed. He turned to see Inspector Bill Dodds striding towards him. 'Working late Bill?' he said in greeting. The SB man sat opposite him, tilted back his chair and put his feet up on Nevin's desk. 'Aye, Mr Jordan's tragic demise meant that I had to work late.' He rubbed his eyes, obviously tired. 'He was one of the UVF's old guard, not one of Jackson's young Turks.' He shook his head slowly. 'Jackson won't mind swapping him for Martin any day of the week.'

'Ardoyne PIRA were quick to hit back,' Nevin said, putting down his pen and observing his friend.

Bill scratched his head. 'I don't think they did it. The car used by the gun team was found burn out in Divis Flats. If you want my guess I'd say it was Brian Turney's West Belfast ASU that did the shoot.' He made a dismissive gesture. 'Not that I really give a damn. Jordan was a hood. The IRA and UVF can blow each other away to their hearts content. I'll shed no tears. It's tomorrow I'm worried about.'

'Martin's funeral?' Nevin asked.

Bill nodded his head. 'Aye, Ardoyne PIRA want a big military-style funeral; you know, black gloves, beret and tricolour on Martin's coffin, not to mention a uniformed guard of honour.' Bill brought his chair down with a bump and shook his head sadly. 'The ACC for Belfast won't allow a military-style funeral. He's got every available mobile support unit in the province on stand-by. We could see a pitched battle in there tomorrow.'

Both men were silent, considering the possibilities. 'Anyway,' Bill said, standing, 'I'd better be getting home. If things go as I expect, none of us will have much spare time over the next few days.' He turned to leave, then stopped, a smile on his face. 'That reminds me, I'm under strict instructions to invite you and your new girl friend, Dr Marrianne Sterling from America, over for dinner.'

'How in heaven's name did your wife know. I've only been going out with her for a few days.'

Bill smiled slyly. 'Elementary my dear Watson, the three fastest methods of passing information known to man are,' he held up three fingers and counted them off as he spoke, 'one, telephone, two telegram and three tell-a-woman.'

Nevin still looked puzzled. Bill sighed and explained. 'You told Billy Cotton, who in turn told his wife, who in turn told her sister, who in turn told her friend, who in turn told my wife's sister, who in turn told my wife.' He shrugged his shoulders, 'Simple really.' He patted Nevin's shoulder. 'Do me a favour and bring her round; my life will be hell until my wife meets her.'

Nevin laughed. 'Of course I'll bring her around.'

The SB man turned and walked towards the door. Over his shoulder he shouted, 'That's of course if we can remember what our homes look like by the time Martin's funeral is over.'

With those parting words he left, leaving Nevin to ponder on what tomorrow might bring.

☆   ☆   ☆

Ardoyne, Wednesday, 10 am.

Bill Dodds's words were to prove prophetic. Martin's funeral was due to take place at 11 o'clock. By 9.30 a large crowd had gathered around the dead IRA man's Havana Gardens home. Inside, top Republicans, including their current Chief of Staff, had gathered to form a guard of honour.

In response, some 300 RUC men ringed the house. Most of them were members of the force's elite mobile support units. Attempts at mediation by local churchmen had proved fruitless. Tension mounted as both sides awaited the appointed funeral hour.

At precisely 10 am, the Assistant Chief Constable for Belfast approached and knocked on 9 Havana Gardens. Hughes, representing Martin's family, answered. 'I'd like to speak to a member of the deceased's family please,' the ACC asked.

'I speak for them.'

Both swapped stares of thinly disguised contempt. 'I'm sure none of us wants any trouble . . . '

'Then get rid of them,' Hughes jerked his head towards the massed ranks of RUC men.

Pursing his lips, the ACC tried again. 'We don't want a confrontation . . . '

'Then get the fuck out of here,' Hughes interrupted again.

The police chief took a deep breath, and fought for control. He tried a new approach. 'OK, if that's the way you want it. We will not allow any para-military displays, no tri-colour, no black beret and gloves. Only six people may carry the coffin, everyone else will walk behind. Anybody seen in any kind of para-military dress will be arrested.'

It was Hughes's turn to fight for control. For a brief second he visibly shook. He almost threw himself at the police chief. Finally through clenched teeth he said, 'We will bury our dead in our own manner,' and slammed the door.

Turning, the ACC went back to his men and he called his individual commanders to him. 'Get your men ready,' he looked back at 9 Havana Gardens, 'there's going to be trouble.'

Five minutes later Martin's coffin, carried by six IRA men wearing dark glasses and black berets was carried out. On top lay a tri-colour, a black beret and a pair of black gloves. Twelve more IRA men, similarly dressed, emerged and tried to form a guard of honour. Police moved in, scattering the 'honour guard', and tried to remove all para-military trappings from Martin's coffin. They were, in turn, attacked by sections of the crowd. Batons were drawn, bricks thrown, a mini riot developed. Fighting became general.

Martin's coffin was taken back inside his home. Slowly some kind of order was restored. All day, both sides faced each other, each refusing to budge. As darkness fell, Hughes appeared, a megaphone in his hand. To roars of approval he shouted, 'Irish men and women have a right to be buried in a dignified way. We will not give up our Irish dead. Our day will come.'

That night violence erupted throughout the whole of Belfast.

Cars and lorries were hijacked in various areas. Amidst almost total mayhem, Nevin stole a quick minute to ring Marrianne. 'Listen love, I'll not be able to see you for some time. Everything is absolute chaos round here.'

'How long do you think it will last?' she asked, concern clear in her voice.

'I don't know. Both sides can't be seen to give in. I hate to think what's going to happen tomorrow. I have to go, bye for now, I'll ring you when I can.'

☆   ☆   ☆

Havana Gardens, Ardoyne, 10 am Thursday.

Crowds had swelled around Martin's home. Many people had come from as far away as Londonderry and Tyrone. Police estimates put them at somewhere near three thousand.

Police had tightened their grip around the former IRA man's home. Two ranks of heavily armoured RUC men stood flanking each side of his door. It opened. Martin's coffin, carried by Hughes and Kane, both wearing dark glasses and black berets, emerged, decked in IRA trappings.

It was only three quarters of the way out when police stepped in to remove its para-military decorations. Hughes and Kane started to back pedal, knocking over Martin's widow in the process.

☆   ☆   ☆

Mountain View Bar, Shankhill Road, 1 pm Sunday.

'Hello Eddy.'

Eddy Gardner turned to find Martin Hewitt standing at his elbow. 'What about you Martin?'

The UVF man put a confidential arm around Gardner's shoulder. 'I'd like a wee word.' He steered Gardner to an empty corner. 'How did you like the job we did on that IRA bastard Martin?'

Eddy Gardner looked nervously around the bar. 'Shush, for Christ's sake, somebody might hear you.' His voice was high with apprehension.

Hewitt shook his head slowly. He smiled, as if enjoying the part-time police officer's discomfort. 'Nobody will hear, we did a good job for you on Martin, don't you agree?' Behind his glasses Hewitt's eyes gleamed.

'OK, OK, you did a good job. I'm glad the Fenian bastard is dead, what do you want, a medal?'

'No, we want you to do something for us in return.'

Gardner closed his eyes. 'What have I got myself into,' he thought. Opening his eyes he looked at Hewitt. 'What do you want?'

'There's no need to be like that Eddy, it's nothing really. We just want you to keep your ears open about a case one of your detectives is investigating.' Hewitt paused, his eyes hard, his voice firm. 'We want to know everything about the murder of Lynn Moody.'

'That's a CID investigation. How am I going to find out about that?'

Hewitt stood up and put a hand on Gardner's shoulder. 'You'll find a way. We have confidence in you.' He patted Gardner's face gently. 'Now don't let us down, will you?'

Later that afternoon Hewitt met his commander, Colin Jackson, in the Orange Cross Club. 'What did he say?' asked Jackson.

'Oh, he'll do it all right; what choice did he have?'

'Good,' the UVF leader nodded his head in approval.

Hewitt was puzzled. He leaned towards his leader. 'I don't understand, Colin, why are you so interested in Lynn Moody's murder?'

Jackson was silent for several seconds. 'Let me ask you a question. What would happen if our people found out that a young Protestant girl was raped and stabbed to death by a Taigh from Ardoyne?'

Hewitt looked startled. 'They'd go crazy.'

Jackson nodded. 'That's right, no Catholic would be safe in North Belfast.' He looked at his intelligence officer directly and smiled. 'That would mean more recruits for us; after all we'd have to defend our womenfolk wouldn't we?'

Hewitt shared his commander's smile.

☆    ☆    ☆

Tennant Street, General Briefing Room, 9 am Monday.

100

As he looked around, Nevin was aware of just how tired everyone was. He had been lucky enough to have had Sunday off, and had spent it with Marrianne. Most of the others present had not been so fortunate; strain and fatigue were plain to see on most faces.

Instead of their normal morning routines, all senior personnel, both plain clothed and uniformed, had been called to a Special Branch intelligence briefing. Attendance was mandatory. All was quiet as Bill Dodds took centre stage. 'Good morning gentlemen,' there was a brief acknowledgement from the assembled mass, 'yes I know you're tired and I wish I could bring you some good news.' Dodds grimaced, 'But I can't. High grade intelligence has come in that two attacks are imminent from Ardoyne PIRA.'

Dodds paused. He had their full attention now.

'The first attack will be mounted within the next two or three days, against a static RUC target, as yet unknown. It will be mounted by Kane's shooting ASU, probably by Kane himself. There have been no sightings of Kane since Martin's funeral. Impress upon all your personnel that if he is seen it should be reported immediately in clear over the radio. As from today no, repeat no, police patrols are to enter Ardoyne without military back-up. I cannot emphasize this enough OK?'

There were nods of understanding from around the room. Nevin sat bolt upright in his chair. If his theory was correct then, not only would Kane attack a police patrol, but some time soon would also kill or attempt to kill an innocent girl as well. Absorbed by his own thoughts he almost missed Dodds's next words.

'We have much better intelligence on Ardoyne PIRA's next intended attack. An impeccable source, which I cannot divulge, has indicated that there will be a bombing attack carried out by Hughes's own bombing ASU, backed up by members of Clarke's Int. and Security boys. Now what I am about to tell you must not be discussed outside of this room.'

Dodds glanced around his audience, his eyes coming to rest on his Divisional Commander. He got a nod of consent. 'As soon as Kane's attack has taken place, hopefully without loss to ourselves, Ardoyne will go out of bounds to all police and military patrols. An E4A surveillance operation, code named

101

Operation Juliet will commence. Its object will be to house members of Hughes's ASU with weapons if they can, and I think their chances are good. We will have an SAS team on stand-by and authority to use them.'

There was an excited buzz of conversation around the room. Dodds held up his hand for silence. 'So you see, gentlemen, we are faced with the dilemma of having to face Kane's attack before we have a chance of nailing Hughes's ASU, any questions?'

Nevin raised his hand.

'Yes Nevin?'

'Why don't we just pick up Kane?'

Dodds laughed. 'If you can tell me where he is, I'll pick him up right away. The man is like a ghost. I don't think even his own side know where he is half the time, let alone us. That's why I want any sightings of him reported straight away. We might get lucky and catch him carrying a weapon; if not I'll find some reason to hold him and hope Hughes's ASU carry on with their operation.'

'Why don't you just put the whole of Ardoyne out of bounds, as of now?' an unseen voice asked.

Dodds scratched his head. 'We've thought of that, but if we stop all patrol movements too soon, the opposition may smell a rat. It's a tough decision, but we think we have an excellent chance of putting Hughes's team out of action permanently. We may not get another such opportunity. That's why we either have to pick up Kane or ride out his attack. Any more questions?'

Silence greeted him. 'Right then, gentlemen, in the immortal words of Hill Street Blues, let's be careful out there.'

☆    ☆    ☆

CID, General Office, 5 pm same day.

Nevin could not remember how long it had been since he had only one file on his desk. It sat there in front of him, its buff cover with a single, stencilled name across its top, LYNN MOODY. He turned it, twisted it and studied it from cover to cover, and still all he had was a lot of unsubstantial suspicions. No real facts, very little hard evidence.

102

That morning, after Inspector Dodds's briefing, he had sent out an MSX, to all Belfast stations, asking that they report immediately to him any attempted or actual sexual assaults within the next seventy-two hours.

For a second he thought of going into Brian Cotton's office and telling him the whole story. Even as he thought of it, he rejected the idea. Every police officer in North Belfast was looking for Kane. He was a 'lift on sight' suspect. What more could he do? Maybe, just maybe, if he was right about Kane, somebody might catch him in the act of attacking some girl. Then he would have all the proof he needed.

He was still turning ideas around his mind, when Inspector Cotton burst out of his office. 'Nevin, Dessi!' Both detective sergeants looked up. Cotton's voice was edged with urgency. 'Both of you get up to the Ballysillan Arms. There's been some kind of bar fight, a bad one. Uniformed members are at the scene, they say there's at least one dead!'

Ballysillan Arms Public House, Crumlin Road, fifteen minutes earlier.

It had all started out as a welcome home party for Martin Mickmichael's father, John, just arrived back on holiday from Australia. What had started out as a celebration had ended up as a drinking contest between Bing and the elder Mickmichael.

Bing had come off the worse, by far. Slumped across a table, he looked unable to stand. Peter Mickmichael still looked as fresh as when he had started. 'Ah, the younger generation isn't what it was.' He slapped Bing on his back. 'Why when I was your age, I could drink an old man like me under the table.'

There was a general ripple of laughter around the bar. Crowded up against its far wall, Billy Dixon, Andy Prentice, the younger Mickmichael and several other members of Tyndale's UDA sniggered.

Bing raised his head and for a second stared at Peter Mickmichael, trying to focus his eyes. Then he heard the laughter; swinging his head around he looked at his laughing men and his low brow curled up with concentration. Staggering to his feet, he looked Peter Mickmichael directly in the eye. 'Don't take it to heart, lad,' the older man said, placing a hand

103

on Bing's shoulder. 'Either you can drink, or you can't.'

For a second, Bing stopped perfectly still, then with a scream of rage he head-butted the old man. Blood poured from Mickmichael's nose. He tried to step back, but Bing followed him, swinging murderous blows with both hands. Unable to defend himself against such a ferocious onslaught, Peter Mickmichael fell, but still Bing did not stop. He began to kick and stamp on the already unconscious man.

Martin Mickmichael, seeing his father's plight, tried to restrain his incensed commander. 'For God's sake, Billy,' he pleaded, putting a hand on Bing's shoulder and trying to drag him back, 'can't you see he's had enough?'

Like some enraged animal, Bing turned on his friend and comrade. Throwing terrible punches he battered the young Mickmichael across the bar. Briefly, Martin tried to defend himself, but Bing's attack only increased in intensity. Stunned, Bing's UDA cohorts, held back by Billy Dixon, watched in horror as their commander kicked his helpless lieutenant out into the street.

For a second Bing looked down at his defenceless former aid, then he walked to a nearby building site and picked up a heavy, industrial breeze block. Carrying it with ease, he walked back and quite deliberately dropped it on Mickmichael's head.

Seeming suddenly calm and sober, Bing looked at his awed audience. 'None of you saw anything, right?' He snarled, staring at each one in turn. Turning he ran for Tyndale and home. Ann Bing heard a frantic knocking on her armoured front door. Looking through its peep hole she was surprised to see her husband standing outside; she had not expected him back until much later.

Opening her door she said, 'You're back ear . . . '

'Get out of the fucking way,' Bing snarled, brushing past her.

Rushing upstairs, he quickly changed clothes. Running back downstairs he threw his blood-stained clothes on an open fire. They were well alight when heavy knocking sounded on his front door. Bing heard his wife's voice raised in anger, then Nevin, Dessi Anderson and two uniformed constables burst into the room. 'William John Bing?' Nevin asked.

'Yes.'

'I'm arresting you for the murder of Martin Mickmichael.

You're not obliged to say anything, but I warn you that anything you do say will be taken down in writing and given in evidence against you!'

Bing looked from Nevin to his burning clothes. Nevin followed his gaze. 'That won't do you any good this time, Bing.'

Bing smiled and looked back to Nevin. 'You want to bet?'

☆    ☆    ☆

Tennant Street, CID General Office, 1 pm Tuesday.

Nevin and Dessi Anderson sat with DI Cotton, reviewing Bing's case. Both detectives had spent the entire night interviewing everyone present during Mickmichael's murder. They had arranged a special sitting of Belfast Magistrates Court that morning and had got Bing remanded in custody, on a charge of murder and attempted murder.

'All right,' Cotton said, 'give it to me straight, can we convict the bastard on what we've got?'

Dessi Anderson sighed. He had been a detective for ten years before taking his sergeant's exam and was much respected by both men. He was actually handling the investigation, with Nevin's assistance.

'None of the UDA men present have said a thing; we have three witness statements, one from the barman Brian Arthur and two non-UDA men, Russel Maylor and Harry Peterson.' Dessi paused and rubbed his eyes, obviously tired. 'Their statements all match.' He shrugged, 'If they stick to them, we should get a conviction.'

'The trouble is,' Nevin put in, 'that we have no forensic evidence to back up their statements. If they retract, our case goes straight out of the window.'

Dessi nodded his head in agreement. 'I don't think there will be any intimidation. I've been talking to Special Branch this morning, while you were at court. Inspector Dodds says that the UDA aren't going to back Bing. Apparently the word has come right from the top. For Christ's sake, he killed his own second-in-command; no level-headed man is going to lift a finger to help him.'

'I don't know,' Nevin said, his voice doubtful. 'The Tyndale

UDA had always been mavericks, and even if they don't back Bing there's always that animal Billy Dixon. The only way you could describe Dixon as being level-headed is because he dribbles from both sides of his mouth at the same time.'

'Well,' Dessi Anderson said, rising, 'all we can do is hope for the best. I'm away to write up some reports.'

Nevin too started to rise, but Cotton stilled him with an upraised hand. 'A moment please, Nevin.'

The Inspector waited until Dessi left, then looked Nevin directly in the eye. 'You want to tell me about it?'

'About what?'

Cotton sighed, 'About why the hardest working and most dedicated detective sergeant I know, who has the highest detection rate in this Division, is sitting with only one file on his desk?' He paused, continuing to stare at Nevin. 'And why this same detective put out an MSX yesterday to all stations in Belfast, asking that all sexual or attempted sexual offences during the next seventy-two hours be reported to him.'

Cotton tilted his head slightly, studying Nevin closely. 'And why this normally devoted police officer hands over a juicy, open and shut murder investigation against one of the worst villains in North Belfast, to another detective?'

He held both hands palm upwards towards Nevin. 'Tell me?'

Nevin closed his eyes for a moment. When he opened them he exhaled sharply. 'I have reason to suspect that the man who murdered Lynn Moody is going to strike again shortly.'

For several seconds neither man spoke. Then Cotton said softly, 'Nevin, I hope you're not getting in over your head; do you want to tell me about it?'

For a second he almost did, then he shook his head. 'You promised me two weeks. If I haven't got a lead by Friday, I'll tell you all I know.' He laughed without humour. 'Correction, all I suspect.' He looked his superior squarely in the eye. 'Deal?'

Cotton nodded, 'Deal.'

Nevin stood. 'Now if it's all right with you I'll take the rest of the day off on TOIL, because if what I think is going to happen actually happens, then I'm going to be very busy over the next few weeks.'

With that he turned and left, leaving behind a very perplexed Inspector.

☆   ☆   ☆

Ardoyne, Wednesday 12 pm.

Mary O'Niel checked the pram again. Her sister's baby
gurgled happily as she walked around it, studying it from every
conceivable angle. Satisfied she said, 'There's no way you can
see the gun, no way at all.'

Sitting across from her Sean Hughes agreed. 'Everything
set?' he asked.

'Yes.'

'What time do you meet Kane?'

'Two thirty, in the park.'

Hughes nodded. 'Kane's going to hit them around 3 o'c-
lock?'

'That's right,' she confirmed.

'Where is he now?'

She shrugged her shoulders, fussing over the child. 'I don't
know, away on his own. You know what he's like before an
operation, he has to be on his own.'

'I don't like it, he should be here in a safe house, not
wandering about on his own.' Hughes was angry, and he let it
show. 'Mr high and mighty Butcher Kane, is going to have to
tow the line, now that I'm OC.'

She rounded on him, like some vixen defending her cubs.
'He's the best man the organization has got. When has he ever
let us down?' She spat angrily, 'You have no right to interfere
with his ways.'

'My God,' Hughes thought, 'she's in love with him.'

Holding his hands up to placate her he said soothingly, 'All
right, all right, no offence meant. I'm just a little edgy, that's
all. This is my first operation as OC. I just want everything to
go smoothly, that's all.'

Satisfied she turned back to her pram, cooing and coddling
the baby, and without turning she said, 'Don't worry, Kane
never misses.'

☆   ☆   ☆

Tigers Bay, 1 pm, same day.

107

Mary Kirkpatrick slammed her front door shut. She stretched to her full height, almost screaming with ecstasy. 'What a day,' she said aloud, 'I'm glad that's over.'

Walking quickly to her kitchen, she began to fill her kettle; water pouring into it drowned out all sound in the tiny room. 'Just time for a cup of tea before *Neighbours*,' she said aloud.

Without warning a hand like steel clamped over her mouth, cutting off all sound. Terrified, she watched as a shining knife was passed backwards and forwards before her eyes. From behind her a voice as cold as ice whispered, 'Don't scream, don't struggle and I won't hurt you.'

☆      ☆      ☆

Antrim Road Playing Fields, 2.45 pm same day.

Mary O'Niel sat on a park bench, gently rocking her pram. She was getting worried. Kane was already fifteen minutes late. Suddenly there was a shout from behind her and turning, she saw him walking quickly towards her. She smiled and waved and he waved back. He sat beside her accepting her outstretched hand and kissing her lightly on her cheek. 'I was beginning to get worried. What kept you?'

Kane smiled. 'I got delayed.' He wore a long black wig and false moustache. Still smiling he said, 'Now take the baby and go.'

Sergeant Ian Gowdie checked his watch, 2.55 pm. 'Great,' he said to himself, 'just got time to change before briefing.'

He pulled his Nissan Sunny saloon car up to his station's security gates and reached inside his jacket for his warrant card to identify himself. In the playing fields, one hundred and fifty metres behind him, Kane watched his car come to a halt. With deliberate slowness, he stood, put his hand into the pram and drew out an AK47 rifle. Bringing it up swiftly, he sighted and fired in one fluid movement.

Sergeant Gowdie was just showing his warrant card to a security sentry when three 7.62 rounds hit the back of his head. Mercifully, he died instantly and did not feel his face smash into his steering wheel. Kane turned and ran for his getaway car, parked only twenty metres away. By the time police and soldiers reacted to his ambush, he was long gone.

☆　　☆　　☆

Carrickfergus, Nevin Brown's Home, 8 pm same day.

He was tired and depressed and sitting alone he contemplated
the day's events. Beside him on his sofa, King pricked up his
ears, then the doorbell rang. Getting up he checked out of his
window and he smiled; it was Marrianne.

'I thought you might need some company.' She smiled and
held out a bottle of wine. 'And I brought reinforcements.'

'Did you know him?' She asked as he poured them each a
glass of wine. He looked across; she held the *Belfast Telegraph* in
her hands. Its headlines read: Police Sergeant Killed In Gun
Attack.

'Not really.' He handed her a glass and sat beside her. 'I met
him once,' he shrugged. 'Nice man, married, two kids, all of it
wiped out in a couple of seconds.' He shook his head and
looked across at her. 'It was our friend Mr Kane.'

'Are you sure?'

He nodded. 'You can bet money on it. Special Branch told
us two days ago he was going to mount an attack; of course we
won't be able to prove a thing.'

He took a sip of wine as Marrianne continued to read the
paper. 'Where does that leave our theories about Kane being
some kind of double killer. He's killed again and no girl's been
found dead.'

'Are you sure?'

'Of course I'm sure. I sent a message to every police station
in Belfast, asking them to report to me any sex attacks. I
haven't had one report.'

'What about this?'

She handed him the paper. On its front cover, in letters so
small he'd missed it when he'd first read it, was a small
paragraph which read:

Woman killed in Tragic Accident.
Mary Kirkpatrick died tragically in her Tigers Bay
home in a freak accident. Neighbours, alerted by
water coming from her home, broke down the door
and found the thirty-two-year-old divorcee slumped
in an overflowing bath. Police believe she slipped on

109

soap getting into the bath, struck her head and drowned.

Nevin looked up, excitement driving away his depression.

'Tigers Bay,' he said. 'That's only a couple of hundred yards from where Sergeant Gowdie was shot.'

☆　　☆　　☆

Ardoyne, Gemma Court, Mary O'Niel's House, 9 pm same day.

His getaway car had dropped him off at the Shamrock Club and he'd left his wig, moustache and gun with its driver. Kane went inside and had a pint; there were eight witnesses inside who would swear on a stack of Bibles that he had been there all afternoon.

Now, several hours later, he lay in Mary O'Niel's spare room, alone in the darkness. He heard footsteps outside his door; it opened and Mary walked in, naked! She joined him in his bed.

He felt her hands on him, arousing him; her lips found his and she forced her tongue into his mouth hungrily. She straddled him, pushing him deep inside her. Her breathing became hoarse, moaning in a frenzy of passion. Suddenly, she stiffened, crying out as she climaxed violently. For the first time, he put his arms around her. Her head rested on his shoulder and she whispered meaningless words into his ear. Eventually she fell asleep in his arms. He lay awake, still aroused, still hard. His mind drifted back, back to where it all began. He remembered his mother.

☆　　☆　　☆

Ballymacarrt, Belfast, 9 August 1971.

Even though it was far away, he could hear the rioting. Occasionally there was an explosion, or a burst of shots. 'Mummy,' he shouted to his mother, 'can I go and watch the soldiers?'

'No you can't; you're staying inside until all this madness

110

ends,' she shouted sternly from the kitchen.

There was a pounding on the front door. His mother emerged from her kitchen, concern etched on her face. It became louder, threatening to splinter their fragile plywood door. His mother ran into the hall and he heard her scream. 'Oh my God!'

Then four men pushed her backwards into their front room. Three of them were masked, but their leader wasn't. Kane recognized him as a neighbour, Trevor Hinton. 'Where are the guns?' Hinton snarled, pushing a gun into Mary Kane's face.

'What guns? We don't have any guns.' His mother's voice was high with fear.

'Don't lie to me, you Fenian whore.' Hinton slapped her viciously across the face.

'Leave my Mummy alone!' Kane screamed leaping at Hinton.

One of Hinton's men clubbed him savagely to the floor. Hinton picked him up by his hair and pushed his gun into Kane's face. 'Tell me where the fucking guns are?'

'There are no guns; in God's name leave my boy alone,' his mother pleaded.

'You're Catholics aren't you?' one of the masked men said flatly. Kane could see the words UVF tattooed on his arm.

'No,' his mother protested, 'we're Protestants, like you.'

'Oh yeah?' Hinton smiled slyly. He looked at Kane. 'Get me your Bible boy.'

Only semi-conscious Kane staggered to a nearby sideboard and, opening a drawer, pulled out a Catholic missal; from it dropped his mother's rosary beads.

Hinton smiled. 'Protestant's eagh?' He leered at Mary Kane. 'Take off your clothes.'

'No!' screamed Kane and launched himself again at Hinton.

This time, Hinton pistol whipped him savagely. From a far distance he heard his mother's screams as she was repeatedly raped. He felt himself being dragged upstairs and thrown on his mother's bed. Through a red haze, he saw Hinton raise his gun, aiming at his mother lying beside him. He flung himself across her, trying to protect her. He felt himself hit and then hit again; everything went black.

He woke ten days later in Belfast's Mater Hospital and his uncle Leo Scullion was by his bedside. He learnt later that he'd

111

been there for the entire ten days. He tried to speak, but his mouth was too dry. Leo Scullion held his head gently, and helped him to drink some water. When he'd had enough, he nodded his head. 'Where's Mummy?' he asked.

Scullion leaned closer to him and very softly, he said, 'Your Mummy's dead; she died before any help could get to her.' Scullion looked around to make sure no one could hear him, then he put his lips close to Kane's ear. 'Do you know who did it?'

Kane nodded weakly. 'One of them was Trevor Hinton; he only lives a few doors down our street, he shot Mummy.'

Leo Scullion, Commanding Officer of the Provisional IRA's Third Battalion, nodded his head. 'Don't tell anybody else, especially the peelers.' He patted Kane on his shoulder. 'Your Uncle Leo will take care of it.'

Kane turned his head. He didn't want his uncle to see him cry. It was the last time he ever cried.

☆   ☆   ☆

Ballysillian Arms Public House, Thursday 2 am.

Brian Arthurs locked up. Being senior barman meant extra money, but also meant staying late and cashing up. He gave the bar door a final tug to make sure it was secure and turned for home. He was almost at his car when he felt a tap on his shoulder. Turning he received a smashing blow to his stomach. He collapsed to his knees, only to be pulled back up again and hit again, this time in his face.

'Hello Brian,' Billy Dixon said conversationally. 'I hear you've been talking to the peelers.' Dixon hit him again, this time in his mouth. 'If I was you I'd reconsider giving evidence against Billy.' He kneed Arthurs in the groin and let him drop. 'Consider this your first and last warning.'

☆   ☆   ☆

Tennant Street, CID General Office, 9 am same day.

'What do you mean, retracted?' Cotton said.

Dessi Anderson shook his head. 'Just that, Inspector, he rang

112

five minutes ago; he wants to take back his statement.'

Cotton threw his hands up in disgust. 'Did you warn him he could face prosecution?'

Anderson nodded. 'Yes,' he sighed. 'He said he'd rather be prosecuted than killed.' He shrugged. 'For what it's worth I think he's scared out of his wits.'

Cotton shook his head. 'Did you offer protection?'

Anderson grimaced. 'Of course.' He shook his head again. 'He said you can't protect me and my family for ever. I have to live and work here.'

Cotton's anger showed on his face. 'What about our other two witnesses?'

'Nothing yet, but,' he made a dismissive gesture, 'once one's gone, word gets around.'

'It's that bastard Dixon,' Cotton spat.

'Undoubtedly,' Anderson agreed.

'Pull him in.'

'On what charge?'

'Attempting to pervert the course of justice, suspected intimidation, anything you like, just get him off the street.'

'OK, but for what it's worth,' he shrugged again, 'I don't think it will do any good.' Anderson turned to leave.

'Have you seen Nevin this morning?'

Anderson turned back. 'No, it's not like him to be late.'

Even as the words left Anderson's lips, Cotton's phone rang. 'Yes,' Cotton almost shouted as he picked it up.

'Are things that bad, Brian? It's Nevin.'

'Just a second.' He looked back up at Dessi. 'Go and pick up our friend Mr Dixon.' Once alone he spoke to Nevin. 'Sorry it's not been a good morning so far.' Quickly he outlined the morning's events.

'Where are you? Don't tell me you're sick or something.'

'I think I've found the lead I was looking for. Don't ask me to explain anything just yet, but I'm going to need a couple of days; if you want, I'll take leave or something.'

Inspector Cotton was quiet for a moment, considering what Nevin had said. 'No,' he said eventually, 'if you're convinced you've got a lead then I trust you to follow it up. You're on police time; if anybody asks, I'll cover for you.'

'Thanks Brian.' Nevin was touched by his superior's faith in him.

'Don't mention it, but do us both a favour ... find the bastard who killed that little girl!'

Nevin put down his phone and looked at Marrianne. 'It's OK, my inspector has given me a couple of days.'

'What time is her postmortem?'

Nevin looked at his watch. 'Ten o'clock, we just have time to make it.'

☆　　☆　　☆

Foster Green Hospital Mortuary, 10 am same day.

Mary Kirkpatrick's body, already prepared for her postmortem, lay exposed on the pathologist's slab. Constable Peter McCready, known throughout his Antrim Road RUC Station as 'The Ghoul', sat, notebook in hand, awaiting Dr Ealing. Constable McCready was one of the few, one of the very few, police officers who actually liked postmortems.

He had been known to rush to sudden deaths in order to attend the resulting postmortem. Unlike other officers, he always stayed, asking Dr Ealing questions and taking avid notes. Ealing, recognizing true inquisitiveness, took pains to point out the various parts of human anatomy and how, to a practised eye, you could detect whether or not they were diseased.

McCready learnt well, even reading books on anatomy and physiology. Legend had it that he had once performed his own postmortem on a cat whose owner claimed it had been poisoned. Peter had been able to prove, so the story goes, that it had not.

In all, Peter McCready had attended twenty-five of them. Once he had even surprised his friend and mentor, Dr Ealing, by suggesting an alternative to his initial findings, which turned out to be correct.

He heard a door open behind him and turned, expecting to see Dr Ealing. Instead he saw a burly man in civilian clothes and an extremely attractive lady walking towards him. McCready got to his feet quickly. 'Con. McCready?' Nevin asked.

'Yes.'

Nevin produced his warrant card. 'Detective Sergeant Nevin Brown, Tennant Street CID.'

McCready checked his identification, then accepted Nevin's outstretched hand. 'Pleased to meet you Skipper.'

'This is Dr Marrianne Sterling.'

'My pleasure Dr Sterling.'

'Marrianne, please.' McCready's face showed his surprise at her American accent. 'Tell me everything you know about this woman's death.'

McCready looked from Nevin to Marrianne, then shrugged and opened his notebook.

'Neighbours found water seeping under her front door at 3 pm, yesterday. They broke down her door and found the deceased lying in an over-flowing upstairs bath. They made efforts to render first aid and called the police. We arrived at approximately 4 pm.' He looked up at Nevin. 'As you know we had a sergeant killed yesterday and that held up our response.'

Nevin nodded, McCready carried on.

'I was the first officer on the scene. There was a doctor present and he pronounced life extinct at 3.20 pm.'

'So she obviously wasn't still in the bath when you arrived; did you ask her neighbours in what position they actually found her?' Nevin asked.

'Yes, first person to actually find Mrs Kirkpatrick was a Mr,' he checked his notes, 'ah yes, Mr Adams who lives next door; here's his statement.' He handed Nevin a white statement form. 'As you can see, Skipper, he states that he found her slumped, head and upper torso in the bath, feet and lower body lying outside.'

Before he could ask another question, a voice interrupted him. 'Sergeant Brown, you seem to be hounding me.'

Dr Ealing joined them. Nevin introduced Marrianne and the pathologist shook hands, then studied him coolly. 'I did not know this was a CID matter?'

'I have an interest in the case.'

'You seem to have an interest in a lot of my cases recently.'

'Well,' he inclined his head, 'I like to keep busy.' Nevin glanced at Kirkpatrick's body. 'When you carry out your examination would you look for signs of any possible sexual assault and take samples?'

Ealing's eyes narrowed. 'Of course.'

'We'll wait next door.' He took Marrianne's arm.

She looked at Con. McCready. 'Aren't you coming?'

Nevin looked back and smiled. 'That's "The Ghoul", he likes postmortems.'

'Weird,' she said, shaking her head.

It was a full hour later that both men rejoined them.

Dr Ealing walked quickly to a wash basin. 'Constable McCready has taken his usual extensive notes.' He turned to Nevin and smiled. 'I'll give you a brief rundown and you can ask what questions you like, OK?'

The detective nodded. 'Right, primary cause of death was drowning, although she had suffered a massive brain haemorrhage, which in all probability would have resulted in her eventual death. Any questions so far?'

'Two, were there traces of soap on her feet and are her injuries consistent with the reported facts of the accident?'

'Entirely consistent and, to answer the first of your questions, there were traces of soap on her right foot.'

Nevin thought for a second. 'Is it conceivable that someone could have smashed her head against the wall?'

Ealing laughed. 'Highly unlikely.'

'Why?'

'Because she suffered an impact injury, not a crush injury. If someone had held her head, there would have been bruising on the back of it; there was none.'

He shook his head. 'For someone to do what you suggest would mean actually picking her up and throwing her against the wall. She weighed close to eleven stones and it would . . . ' Suddenly the smile left his face as he remembered, 'It would take a man with an immense amount of physical strength.'

Nevin smiled grimly, 'Was she raped?'

Ealing was still slightly shocked. 'What?' Then he collected his thoughts. 'I can't say for sure; she'd had sex but it's impossible to determine whether or not it was a forced sexual entry.'

'Why?' Nevin asked, confused.

'Because of the hot water,' McCready put in.

Ealing beamed at his protege, and then glanced back to Nevin. 'He's perfectly correct; the hot water caused total muscle relaxation; it would be impossible to determine whether or not she had violent sexual intercourse.'

'You took semen samples, as I asked?'

116

'Yes.' He handed Nevin a sealed police jiffy bag.

Nevin took it and immediately signed his name on it. As he did so he said, 'Constable McCready you will please make a notebook entry that at,' he glanced at his watch, '11.20 am, on this date I accepted a sealed jiffy bag from Dr Ealing, and please include it in your eventual written statement.'

'Why did you do that?' asked Marrianne, as the constable carried out Nevin's request.

'To prove continuity of evidence; if I did not, this would not be admissible in any eventual trial.' He looked back up at McCready. 'I would also like Mary Kirkpatrick's file.'

Looking surprised, McCready handed it over. 'Tell your head of CID, your section sergeant and inspector and nobody else that this investigation is now in the hands of Tennant Street CID, and is part of an on-going investigation.'

'You can depend on me Skipper.'

'I know I can Peter, thank you Dr Ealing.' He led Marrianne back to their car.

'You think it was Kane?' she asked, once inside.

'Yes,' he replied, his face like stone. 'I think he raped her, dragged her upstairs, threw her against the wall and then held her head under the water until he was sure she was dead.'

Both were silent. 'Nevin, there's one thing you must understand about Kane, if you don't already. He is the worst type of psychotic. Not only is he highly motivated, but,' she turned to look at him, 'he's highly intelligent; his careful planning of this girl's murder shows that clearly. He took the time to rub soap on her foot and I'll also bet he left the hot water tap on deliberately to confuse any forensic examination.'

She put a hand on his shoulder. 'Whatever you do, don't underestimate him.' Nevin nodded, lost in thought. 'Where to now?' she asked.

'Forensic science laboratories,' he said as he started his car. 'I need this semen sample analysed as soon as possible.'

Tennant Street, CID General Office, approximately same time.

Dessi Anderson put down his phone and shook his head.

Sighing he walked to Brian Cotton's office, took a deep breath, knocked and went in. 'Yes, Dessi.'

'We've lost Russel Maylor,' he said flatly.

'What?' Cotton's anger was plain.

'He's just been on the phone. Apparently he got a letter this morning, something along the lines of,' he closed his eyes so that he could remember it correctly, 'We know where you work, your wife's name is Brenda and she's alone in your house all day. Your daughter, Susan, goes to Shortcross School. Need we say more? Retract your evidence.'

Anderson sighed. 'It was signed UFF.'

Cotton shook his head in disbelief. Before he could say anything, Anderson went on, his voice tired. 'I told him he could face prosecution and I offered protection. It's no go. He said if it was only him he'd go ahead but he's scared for his family; quite frankly, sir, can you blame him?'

Cotton shook his head again. 'No I suppose not, it looks like Bing walks.'

'Unfortunately yes,' Dessi shrugged. 'Win some, lose some, his time will come one day.'

☆   ☆   ☆

Northern Ireland Forensic Science Laboratories Belfast, noon same day.

'And I'm telling you again Sergeant Brown, there's no way you can get this sample analysed today. It will take three days; with luck you'll get it on Monday.'

Nevin was starting to lose his temper. 'Listen I haven't got three days, I need it done today.'

Before either of them could say any more, Marrianne stepped forward. 'Excuse me please,' she said sweetly, 'is Professor Moore still in charge of this establishment?'

The young lad technician looked puzzled. 'Yes he is.'

'Would you do me a big favour and tell him that Dr Marrianne Sterling would like a word with him.'

She smiled again and fluttered her eyelashes; what man could resist? Picking up his phone he rang his director. Nevin could not hear what was said, but a disbelieving look suddenly appeared on his face. He looked at Marrianne with something

118

approaching awe. 'He says he'll be right down.'

Nevin looked at Marrianne curiously and she tilted her head, a smug smile on her lips.

Suddenly there was a shout from behind them. 'Marrianne!'

She turned and screamed like a little girl. 'Uncle Freddy!' Running like a child she jumped into his waiting arms.

Professor Moore, a strikingly good looking and distinguished man in his late fifties, clasped her and swung her around. For a second they held each other like some long lost lovers. Then he held her at arm's length. 'Let me take a look at you; it's not possible, you're even more beautiful than the last time I saw you. How are your parents?'

'They are both fine, they send you their regards and say that you don't write often enough.'

Professor Frederick Johnson Moore, holder of three masters degrees in chemistry, science and physics, and one of the foremost experts in forensic science on either side of the Atlantic, hung his head like a scalded child. 'I've been very busy,' he said apologetically.

She smiled and, taking him by the hand, led him to an open-mouthed Nevin, behind whom an entire reception area had come to a halt. 'Uncle Freddy, I'd like you to meet a special friend of mine; this is Nevin, he's a police officer.'

Professor Moore extended his hand. 'Pleased to meet you my boy.' His grip was strong and firm. He had the same Bostonian accent as Marrianne.

'Nevin this is my second father.'

'Son, I went to school with her father and dated her mother before he stole her off me.' He draped an arm over Marrianne's shoulder. 'I attended this little girl's birth, christening and every other major event in her life, before I took up this position.' He looked at her in mock disapproval. 'Now I know you've been over here for at least a month; why has it taken you so long to come and see me?'

'I've been busy too.' She glanced shyly at Nevin; he followed her gaze.

'Oh I see,' he said with a knowing smile, studying Nevin with renewed interest.

She locked her arm around his. 'Uncle Freddy, we have a little problem.'

It took her only a few seconds to outline what they wanted

done. Moore looked at the young lab assistant. 'Foster,' he bellowed like an enraged bull defending his calf.

'Sir,' the hapless Foster answered.

'Get this young man's tests done for him . . . now.'

'Yes, sir.'

After Nevin had handed over his samples and explained what he needed done, he followed Marrianne to Professor Moore's office. She whispered in his ear, 'Don't let his shouting bother you, he's a pussy-cat really.'

They spent a pleasant half hour, sipping coffee and talking about their respective jobs. Professor Moore gently probed Nevin about his present investigation. With as much tact as possible he parried his questions. Marrianne came to his aid by talking about her lecture tour. They were interrupted by a gentle knock. 'Come in,' bellowed Professor Moore.

Foster entered. 'I have the results of your tests, Sergeant Brown.' He handed Nevin a typed sheet of paper.

He read it, then looked at Marrianne, his face stern. 'O-negative blood group.' For several seconds he sat saying nothing, his thumb nail rubbing his bottom lip. Then he looked up at Professor Moore. 'Several weeks ago a young girl, Lynn Moody, was raped and murdered. Can you cross check the samples taken from her with this sample and get a genetic fingerprint?'

'What's a genetic fingerprint?' asked Marrianne.

'It's a relatively new technique,' Professor Moore answered. 'Every human being's body has its own genetic make-up. If you take a sample of blood, tissue or in this case semen, you can get a genetic trace.'

'Just like a fingerprint,' Nevin added.

'So you can tell if the same man was involved in both cases?' she asked.

'Beyond a shadow of a doubt, but there is one problem,' Moore looked at Nevin, 'we don't have the facilities to run those tests here; they have to be done at the Metropolitan Police Crime Laboratories in London.'

'How long will it take?'

'Normally about six weeks.' Nevin looked horrified. 'But,' Moore glanced at Marrianne and smiled, 'I'm not without influence; with luck I can get it cut down to three weeks.'

'I'd be grateful,' Nevin swapped a quick smile with Marrianne.

'Foster, get these samples off by dispatch rider, with the necessary paperwork, in time to catch tonight's secure flight.'

As his young assistant hurried off, Moore explained. 'We have a secure flight each night for forensic samples. I'll arrange for another dispatch rider to pick them up at Heathrow and ring my opposite number in London. Even so,' he shook his head, 'it will take three weeks.'

Nevin stood and extended his hand. 'I can't thank you enough, sir.'

'Think nothing of it my boy.' He smiled and winked at Marrianne. 'After all, what are friends for?'

'What now?' Marrianne asked as they sat in his car.

He shook his head. 'All we've got at the moment is a lot of theories and suspicions but no real proof. If we go to my authorities they might pull Kane in, but the IRA has a lot of very smart lawyers. They'll think it's some kind of dirty tricks campaign against them and their top killer.'

He looked at her. 'Remember, to his people he's a big hero, just like Kramer was to the Americans. If they get him out Kane will disappear into their network and we'll be lucky if we ever catch him.'

'We have to stop him Nevin, otherwise he will go on killing girls like Lynn Moody.'

'I know, I know, but it's proof we need; it's not going to be easy; look how we almost missed Mary Kirkpatrick's murder and we were watching for it.'

He thought for a second, then nodded his head. 'There might be one way of doing it. We have to find out every terrorist act Kane has been involved in since 1973, and then cross check those dates with any mysterious female deaths.'

'Can you get access to that type of information?'

He shook his head. 'No.' Then he turned to her and smiled. 'But I know a man who can.'

# 5

Tennant Street, Special Branch Briefing Room, 9.30 pm Friday, week five.

They looked anything but police officers, scruffy, unshaven and badly dressed. Most wore their hair long and unkempt and all gave the appearance of needing a bath. They were an elite E4A surveillance team.

Bill Dodds stood in front of a large-scale map of Ardoyne; around its edges were photographs of main IRA 'players' in Ardoyne PIRA. He was giving them a final local briefing for Operation Juliet.

'Right, gentlemen,' Dodds began, 'this briefing is to update you on our latest intelligence on your targets and local PIRA activity.' He turned to point at a photo on his map's edge. 'These are your main targets, Anthony "Luger" Hardy and Brian Keenan. They are members of Sean Hughes's bombing ASU. Hughes is now effective OC Ardoyne PIRA, after Larry Martin's late but unlamented demise. Pay particular attention to this woman.'

Dodds pointed out Mary O'Niel. 'She is their weapons carrier and will probably carry any weapons that will be used.'

He turned to face his audience. 'Now your main job will be to set up a running surveillance on these targets with the object of housing them with weapons. We believe their intended attack will be in the form of a Drouge bomb thrown by Hardy with Keenan backing him up. We have an SAS team at Antrim Road; they will take these people out and provide you with an immediate back-up should you run into trouble.'

The SB man's face hardened. 'A word of caution, since Martin's death, Clarke's Int. and Security ASI are out in force; they have immediate access to guns, but don't usually carry.

We have lost five officers in as many weeks in that hell hole. If you think, even for a second, that you're blown, then get the hell out of there.'

He paused to let his words sink in. 'Ardoyne will go "out of bounds" to all regular police and army patrols at 10 pm; be careful in there,' he smiled grimly, 'let's do it to them, before they do it to us.'

To a gentle ripple of laughter he handed them over to their own team commanders for individual taskings. Returning to his office he was surprised to find Nevin and Marrianne waiting for him. 'Nevin, a pleasure as always, and this must be the famous Dr Sterling.'

'Marrianne, please,' she said extending her hand.

Dodds smiled as he accepted it. 'You know people have been telling me a lot of lies about you.' He inclined his head to study her. 'They told me you were pretty.' He lifted her hand to kiss it. 'Nobody told me you were beautiful.'

Marrianne laughed. 'Flattery will get you everywhere Inspector.'

'Bill, please, sit down.' He extended a hand. 'I hope this is about that dinner invitation, Nevin, my wife's been making my life hell trying to meet this lady.'

'I'm afraid not Bill. This isn't social, we need your help.'

Nevin's tone wiped away Bill's smile. 'Tell me about it.'

With a quick look at Marrianne for confirmation, he took a deep breath and told him everything, starting with Lynn Moody's murder and ending with Mary Kirkpatrick's death. When he had finished Bill Dodds's face was like stone. 'How sure are you of all this?'

'Absolutely sure, but I can't prove a thing yet. I don't have to tell you what will happen if we move too soon. We risk losing him, perhaps for ever. Kane's a . . . ' he looked at Marrianne.

'He's a true psychopath.' She briefly explained the medical term. 'If he's not stopped, he will be compelled to carry on killing.'

'That's why I've come to you Bill. It will take three weeks to get a genetic fingerprint match. In that time I want to put together a strong enough case to get Kane arrested and remanded without bail. Good heavens, if he's been killing girls since 1973, he must have left some clues; you have access to information I could never get hold of. Will you help?'

Bill was silent for a second and Nevin threw an anxious glance at Marrianne. 'What do you want?' he said eventually.

Nevin let out his breath in a sigh of relief. 'Two things, first I've got Hart on my back and I need him off it.'

'That's not a problem. I'll get you a temporary secondment to Special Branch, he can't touch you here.'

'I'll need my aid Billy Boyd as well.'

'How much does he know?'

'Nothing about Kane, but I need somebody to help me with the leg work.'

'OK I'll get him seconded as well, but don't tell him about your suspicions unless you have to; the less people know about this, the better. What else do you want?'

'I want access to Kane's Special Branch file.'

Dodds shook his head. 'You know what you're asking?'

'I know.'

A Special Branch file contained names of informers, details of confidential sources of information and other highly secret information. For anybody unauthorized to be given access to it was a breach of the Official Secrets Act. In effect Nevin had just put his entire police career in danger, and was asking Bill to do exactly the same.

'I'll have to think about that.' He scratched his head. 'Go home now, I'll get in touch with your DI and get you and young Boyd seconded. Stay at home tomorrow, I'll contact you there.'

Nevin nodded and stood. 'I'll be waiting to hear from you.'

Outside Dodds's office door Marrianne linked her arm in his. 'What do you think?'

Nevin rubbed his bottom lip with his thumb nail. 'Bill will do one of two things, either he'll come in with us, or he'll report me for trying to subvert a superior to commit a gross breach of discipline.'

He turned to her and smiled. 'By tomorrow you could be going out with an ex-detective sergeant in the Royal Ulster Constabulary.'

She smiled and patted his cheek. 'Never mind, you could always work for me.'

He laughed, 'Doing what?'

She leaned forward and whispered in his ear. Nevin pulled his head back and looked at her with mock horror. 'Where in

124

heaven's name did a well brought-up lady like you learn language like that?'

☆    ☆    ☆

Carrickfergus, Nevin Brown's Home, 11 am Saturday.

'You know Nevin,' Bill said as he sat down, 'when you told me your story last night, I almost had you suspended, especially when you asked to see this.'

He lifted up a two inch thick red bound file. 'What stopped you?'

'Two things, I know how good a detective you are and this.'

Bill handed Nevin a typed sheet of paper; it was a Special Branch source report, dated May 1973. Nevin read it. Suddenly, sitting bolt upright and handing it to Marrianne, he pointed to its third paragraph. She read it out loud.

'Cahill reported that Anthony Kane and Terrance Heeny killed Margaret Hamilton on the orders of their OC, Martin O'Keefe, because she was believed to be an informer. Kane was also involved later that night in an ambush in the New Lodge in which Marine Corporal Ian Hunter was killed.'

'That report was given to us by a top level informer in Ardoyne PIRA, Brian Cahill. Unfortunately he was blown and head jobbed.'

Marrianne looked puzzled. 'Shot in the head; the IRA do that to any informers they find,' explained Bill. 'Heeny's doing ten years in Portaise Prison for explosive offences.'

'So you believe us now?' asked Marrianne.

Nevin laughed. 'He wouldn't be here if he didn't, what now Bill?'

'To save time I've drawn up a list of all the terrorist incidents we know Kane has been involved in.'

He handed them another typed piece of paper. 'It's in chronological order.'

22 April 1973 – Murder of Margaret Hamilton and Corporal Hunter.

19 June 1973 – Murder of RUC Sergeant Walker Cuthbert,

Agnes Street, Belfast.

14 February 1974 – Murder of two soldiers, Brompton Park, Ardoyne.

8 July 1974 – Murder of part-time RUC constable, Ligonel.

11 November 1975 – Murder of two RUC detectives, Belfast City Centre.

5 May 1976 – Murder of soldier, New Lodge.

26 January 1977 – Murder of UDR man, Forthriver, Belfast.

2 February 1979 – Murder of RUC constable, Crumlin Road, Belfast.

3 March 1979 – OTR Active in Fermanagh/Tyrone border. Believed to have received advanced training, possibly in Libya.

2 March 1982 – Murder of two RUC constables, Newry, County Armagh.

3 January 1983 – Murder of part-time RUC man, Warren-point, County Armagh.

25 January 1984 – Returned to Ardoyne, Belfast.

11 November 1984 – Murder of UDR man, Rathcool, Belfast.

2 February 1985 – Murder of RUC constable, North Queen Street, Belfast.

November 1987 – Believed sent to USA on orders of PIRA high command.

8 January 1989 – Suspected to have been involved in killing of ex-RUC informant, Brian Doherty, living under a new identity in Boston, USA.

10 February 1990 – Deported back to UK as illegal immigrant

by US authorities.


'This is horrific,' Marrianne said. 'You know he did all this and you can't convict him of anything?'

'As I told you before, knowing and proving are two entirely different things, isn't that right Bill?'

Dodds made a face. 'All too right I'm afraid; in total we believe our mister Kane has killed, or been involved in killing, twenty-four members of the security forces, including our four constables in the last five weeks. It could have been worse still if he had not gone OTR in March 1979 and to America in November 1987.'

'What's OTR?' Marrianne asked.

'It's short for "on the run",' Bill explained. 'In 1979 we turned a top IRA player in Ardoyne called Black. With his evidence we managed to break practically the entire PIRA network in Ardoyne. It was the first of the so called, "Supergrass" trials. In all we gaoled twenty-eight top players, for everything from murder to bombing.'

'But you missed Kane?'

'Unfortunately yes, he fled across the border and continued to be active,' Dodds sighed. 'To make matters worse Black's evidence was eventually discredited, that's why he was able to return to Belfast.'

'What about him killing this informer, Doherty, in America?' Nevin asked.

'Yes I remember that,' Marrianne put in, 'there was a big feature about it in the *Boston Herald*. CBS did a special report on it as well.'

'PIRA high command wanted to show that informers were not safe anywhere, so they sent Kane over to hunt him down. As you can see he was successful. Unfortunately your authorities could not prove anything against him and deported him as an illegal alien.'

'I never thought there would be so much; we'll never be able to check all these.' Nevin's voice held a note of concern.

'I know,' Dodds conceded. 'I have a plan, of sorts.' He looked from one to the other. 'I suggest we forget about the early 70s. Nevin, you concentrate on Kane's activities in Belfast since November 1984 and I'll take those two incidents while he was OTR in the south. I have a friend in Garda Special Branch who'll help me. Unfortunately I can't get down there until Tuesday as I have to attend a briefing in Armagh on Monday.'

'What about this incident in Boston?' asked Marrianne.

'What about it?' Dodds asked, a smile on his face.

'I could look into that for you.'

Both men looked at each other with amusement. 'Marrianne, you're a doctor of criminal psychology, not a detective; this is a job for a trained investigator.'

It was Marrianne's turn to look amused. 'I didn't mean that I would investigate it. I know I couldn't do that,' she smiled sweetly at them both, 'but I know a man who could.'

'Who?' both men said at once.

'Special Agent Henry Tyler, Boston FBI. We went to college together; if Bill would give me a letter outlining what he wants done I'm sure he'd help. I could ring ahead and make an appointment, fly out on Monday and be in his office first thing on Tuesday morning. What do you say?'

Nevin looked at Bill. 'What do you think?'

The SB man shrugged. 'Can't do any harm as long as he's willing to help.'

Marrianne clapped her hands like a little girl. 'Oh I'm sure he will.'

Dodds stood. 'Well we all have something to do; you and your aid are now officially seconded to Special Branch. Marrianne, I'll see you get your letter before Monday.'

'Thanks for everything Bill,' Nevin clapped his friend on the shoulder, 'let's hope we nail this animal for good.'

Bill nodded without speaking. Turning, he managed to hide the savage look that had come onto his face.

☆     ☆     ☆

Ardoyne, 11.35 pm, same evening.

It had started to rain again. Anthony 'Luger' Hardy, turned up his collar against its driving force and leaving the Crumlin Star social club, he walked down Brompton Park towards Sean Hughes's house. His mood was bad.

'Why did Hughes have to pick a fucking Saturday night for a briefing?' He thought angrily to himself. Weaving his way a little unsteadily up Hughes's garden path, Hardy knocked on the IRA commander's heavily armoured front door. There was a brief flash of light at its spy hole, then it opened to reveal a smiling Hughes.

'Come in Tony, the others are here already.'

As Hardy walked past his commander both men failed to notice a scruffily dressed man pass by across the road, seemingly uninterested in them.

'That's Hardy into Hughes's house,' he muttered. His Miter throat mike automatically transmitted his message to his E4A controller, who repeated his exact words. A tiny radio receiver in the undercover police officer's ear, hidden by his long hair, picked up his acknowledgement.

At Antrim Road RUC Station, forward command centre for Operation Juliet, the controller turned to a tall uniformed RUC senior officer. 'Looks like a briefing sir.'

The ACC for Belfast, operational commander, nodded. 'If our information is correct the job will be on Tuesday; it's starting to look promising.' He turned to a hard looking man in civilian clothes, sitting behind him. 'Do you want to pass this on to your people?'

Without answering the SAS liaison officer stood and left.

☆   ☆   ☆

Tennant Street canteen, midday Sunday.

Billy Boyd tucked into a hefty meal of steak, egg and chips. He had long ago given up the losing battle to keep his weight in check and had decided that fate had meant him to be pleasantly plump. A single man, he had a room almost above the canteen and Sunday was a favourite day for him. The station was quiet and he could eat and read his *Sunday Times* in peace.

'Anybody sitting here?' Billy looked up to see Eddy Gardner standing above him.

'No Eddy, help yourself, what are you doing in at this time of day?'

'I had a couple of things to sort out,' the part-timer explained as he sat down.

'You're keen, Eddy, if I didn't live here you wouldn't see me

129

for dust on my days off.'

Billy resumed his eating and reading. Across from him Gardner wet his lips and trying to keep his voice casual, he said, 'I hear congratulations are in order.'

Billy looked up puzzled, 'How do you mean?'

'Your secondment to Special Branch; not many CID aides get seconded to SB.'

'Oh that,' Billy laughed, 'it's only temporary. I'm helping Nevin Brown with an investigation.'

'Would that be that wee girl Lynn Moody's murder?'

Billy's eyes narrowed. 'You should know better than that, Eddy; once you're attached to SB, you can't discuss what cases you're working on.'

Studying Gardner's face, Billy saw concern flash across it. 'Why are you interested in Lynn Moody's murder anyway?'

'Just curious, that's all,' the part-timer said, a little too quickly. 'She was a local girl, people are concerned about her killing.'

Billy nodded and, as the silence grew between them, he saw sweat break out of Gardner's forehead. 'I, I have to go.' Standing swiftly he almost knocked over his chair. 'I didn't mean any offence Billy.'

'None taken, is there something wrong?'

'No, no, I haven't been feeling well, maybe a touch of flu, see you Billy.'

Turning, Gardner walked hurriedly away. Billy watched his retreating back with suspicion, then gave himself a mental shake. 'I've been attached to CID too long, I'm starting to suspect everybody.' Shaking his head, he resumed eating his interrupted meal.

☆　　☆　　☆

Jacky Hewitt's home, twenty minutes later.

Hewitt depressed the receiver with his index finger and as soon as he got a dialling tone he rang Colin Jackson. 'Colin this is Jacky. I've just heard from our mutual friend at Tennant Street.'

'Yes?'

'It seems that Special Branch are involved now.'

130

'Is that a fact, now that is interesting, come round and see me.'

☆   ☆   ☆

Tennant Street, station sergeant's office, Monday 11.30 am.

Nevin sighed and rubbed his tired eyes. He'd been at it for three hours with no success at all. Coming straight to work after dropping Marrianne off at Aldergrove Airport, he'd gone through everything he could think of. Station incident books, missing persons registers, even old radio logs! There was nothing recorded that was even remotely suspicious on the dates he was interested in. He shook his head with disgust.

'No luck?' Bob Duncan, Tennant Street's station sergeant, asked.

'No.' Nevin looked across with a smile. Bob had thirty-five years in the job, nearly all of them at Tennant Street. He was immensely liked and respected by all.

'I might be able to help, if I knew what you were looking for,' Bob offered.

Nevin considered his offer. 'Why not,' he thought to himself. What Bob didn't know about Tennant Street wasn't worth knowing.

'I'm interested in two dates, 11 November 1984 and 2 February 1985. Did anything unusual happen on them?'

'Like what?'

Nevin shook his head. 'I don't know really, a sudden death, a disappearance.' He shrugged and shook his head, 'Anything that involved the death of a woman.'

Duncan folded his hands across his stomach. 'The 2 February 1985, that rings a bell.' He tilted his nearly bald head as he concentrated, then a smile of triumph spread across his face and he looked at Nevin directly. 'Would a house fire be of interest?'

'Was a woman killed in it?'

'Yes.'

'Where was it?' Nevin's voice betrayed his eagerness.

'Highfield Estate.'

Nevin looked puzzled. 'Why isn't it recorded in the station records?'

131

Duncan gave Nevin a withering look. 'You've been in CID too long, you should know the top half of that estate belongs to Grosvenor Road.'

Nevin slapped his hand against his forehead. 'Of course,' he exclaimed.

It suddenly occurred to him that Kane could have struck in any one of half-a-dozen sub-divisions, and across at least three divisional boundaries, without leaving North Belfast. He could even have killed in another part of Belfast entirely. The enormity of his task suddenly struck him. It had only been by good luck, and Bob Duncan's excellent memory, that he had got a lead at all.

'Thanks Bob, I owe you a favour.' Pausing at the door he looked back. 'If anybody wants me, I'll be at Grosvenor Road.'

Grosvenor Road RUC Station, 1.30 pm same day.

It had taken him over an hour to get Constable Ian Johnstone in from a mobile patrol of West Belfast. It had been Johnstone who had investigated the fatal house fire on 2 February 1985. A further thirty minutes had been wasted as he had searched for his old file. Now Nevin sat reading it in a spare interview room. 'Is there some question about the way I conducted my investigation?'

Nevin looked up. Johnstone's face was stern and his voice betrayed both anger and concern. 'None at all, Ian isn't it?' Johnstone nodded. 'It's just that some new evidence has come to light that is making us look again at several cases, not just yours, OK?'

Johnstone smiled his relief. 'Thank God for that, it's not every day you get pulled off a patrol and asked to get a file you had almost forgotten about for a detective sergeant from SB. I thought I was for the high jump.'

Nevin laughed. 'You've no need to worry. I'm quite sure your investigation was properly conducted; now I'd like to go over some details with you.'

He looked back to Johnstone's file. 'The fire was reported at 2 am on the morning of 2 February, 1985, direct to the Fire Brigade?'

'That's right, a next door neighbour a Mrs . . . ' Johnstone flicked quickly through an old notebook. 'Ah yes, a Mrs Sheila Baird, she gave a statement, it's in the file.'

Nevin nodded without looking up. 'Fire Brigade arrived at 2.10 am, fast work, officer in charge was a Sub Officer White, is that correct?'

'Yes.'

'What time did you arrive?'

Johnstone checked his notebook. 'At 2.30 exactly, they had the fire out by then.'

Nevin looked up from his file. 'Now Ian think back, was there anything, anything at all, suspicious about the fire?'

'Not that I can remember.' He sucked his top lip with concentration.

'The deceased, Mary McDonald, went out every Friday night to the Highfield Club. She would drink with friends, then go home at about 1 am, regular as clockwork. She was divorced and lived alone, no regular male companion.' He shook his head. 'Evidence at the scene suggested that she had fallen asleep in bed with a lighted cigarette; her body was very badly burnt and collecting samples was difficult.' He suddenly clicked his fingers.

'There was one thing.' He pointed a finger at Nevin. 'That Fire Brigade Officer.'

'Sub-Officer White?'

'Yes him, he was concerned about how fast the fire had caught and spread and he ordered samples to be taken for forensic examination. But everything must have been OK. I got a report from him saying that nothing abnormal had been discovered; it's at the back of my file.'

Nevin quickly read it, then looked at Johnstone. 'Can I keep this file for a while?'

'I don't know Skipper, all my original statements are in it; if it gets lost my inspector will have my guts for garters.'

'I'll look after it,' Nevin held up a hand in mock solemnity. 'Swear to God.'

Johnstone laughed. 'OK, Skipper, it's yours.'

As Nevin walked towards the door Johnstone's voice halted him. 'This must be something pretty big Skipper.'

He turned to look at his junior comrade. 'If I told you Ian, you wouldn't believe me.' Shaking his head he left a puzzled and not a little confused Constable Ian Johnstone.

☆    ☆    ☆

Fire Authority HQ, Castle Street, Lisburn, 4.30 same day.

It had taken a lot more energy, not to mention some Special Branch clout, to track down Sub-Officer White. He had been promoted and posted since 1985. Nevin finally tracked him to an administrative post at the force's Lisburn HQ.

'2 February, 1985?'

'Yes,' Nevin urged, 'the deceased's name was Mary McDonald of 102 Highfield Crescent.'

White scratched his thinning grey hair; he was a distinguished looking man, who could have been a well preserved fifty or badly worn forty, it was hard to tell. His tunic bore three medal ribbons, one of which was the Queen's Gallantry Medal. Standing, White walked to a nearby filing cabinet. 'You're lucky,' he said over his shoulder, 'being in admin. allows me to keep my own files up-to-date.'

He hummed a tuneless song to himself as he rifled through his files. 'I keep all my files here.' He glanced over at Nevin and smiled, 'All the important ones anyway.' He looked back and continued his searching and humming. 'Ah here it is,' he said eventually and returning to his chair he opened a red file. 'Now what exactly did you want to know?'

'Well Officer White . . . '

'Call me Chalky, everybody does,' White interrupted.

Nevin smiled. 'Well Chalky, you took samples for forensic examination, you told Johnstone.' White gave him a curious look. 'The constable in charge of the police investigation,' Nevin explained.

White nodded. 'Yes I remember him now, tall blond haired lad, very keen.'

'Yes that's him; you told him you thought the fire had spread too fast; what made you say that?'

'Well let's have a look.' He read his file, humming his maddening tune to himself. Eventually he looked back up at Nevin, his face serious. 'I remember now.' His finger tapped the file as he spoke. 'The fire had consumed most of the girl's body. I thought it had spread too fast and too fiercely. I

134

suspected some kind of accelerant had been used.'

It was Nevin's turn to look confused. 'Accelerant?'

'It's a Fire Brigade term,' White explained. 'It means some kind of outside agency, introduced to accelerate the fire.' He looked back to his file. 'In this case the room, especially the bed, had been consumed very quickly, too quickly in my opinion.'

'And that's why you had tests done?'

White looked back into Nevin's eyes. 'Yes, I had all the blankets and rugs tested for accelerants, paraffin, petrol, white spirits etc. All tests were negative.' He handed Nevin a forensic report.

The detective read it thoughtfully. He checked his watch; 4.45 pm, he might just catch him! 'Can I use your phone, Chalky?'

'Help yourself.'

Nevin dialled and waited anxiously for an answer. 'Hello.'

'Professor Moore?'

'Yes.'

'This is Nevin, Marrianne's friend.'

'How are you my boy?' Moore's voice boomed its friendly greeting.

Nevin couldn't resist a smile. 'Fine sir. I'm afraid I'd like to ask you another favour.'

☆    ☆    ☆

Ardoyne, 6.30 pm, same day.

She had been woken from her comfortable afternoon sleep and taken from her warm bed out into the cold evening. In anger she cried and squirmed, kicking her blankets off her on to the pavement's floor.

Mary O'Niel paused to recover them. 'There, there,' she cooed, trying to mollify her angry charge. Slowly her sister's baby settled and she continued her journey towards Valsheda Park. Pausing outside a nondescript house, Mary checked around her. All was quiet, she turned her pram up its garden path. A lone car cruised past, its driver seemingly unconcerned, singing to himself. His foot moved to a radio transmitter button concealed on the car's floor.

135

'That's Mary O'Niel into the safe house pushing a pram.'

Back at Antrim Road, his E4A controller repeated his exact words back to him and turned to ACC Belfast. 'She'll have the grenade and rifle.'

'Anybody else in the house?'

The E4A controller checked his log. 'Just Sean Hughes.'

Satisfied he turned to his head of Special Branch. 'What do you think, should we hit the house as soon as Hardy and Keenan show up?'

Belfast's head of Special Branch shook his head. 'I wouldn't recommend it. O'Niel will put the weapons into a temporary hide; chances are we wouldn't get them actually holding them. It would be difficult to prove anything in court. Also,' he locked eyes with his superior, 'it might compromise our source.'

ACC Belfast took a deep breath, realizing his next decision might put a member of his force in terrible danger. 'So we stick to plan A?'

'Yes, it will mean inserting a "trigger Op" as soon as it's dark, but I think it's worth the risk.'

For a second, he considered his options, then agreed with his SB head. He spoke first to his E4A controller. 'Tell your people to go ahead with their covert OP insertion.' Then he turned to his SAS liaison officer, 'Could you get your men stood to please.'

Unaware of the joint police and army operation being mounted against his ASU members, Sean Hughes checked his weapons, an AK47 and 9 mm Browning pistol (both 'donated' to his organization courtesy of Colonel Gadaffi's Libya) and a Drogue bomb. The Drogue bomb was a hand thrown impact grenade, copied by an enterprising IRA volunteer from an illustration in a World War Two magazine. Its successful use had caused both police and army mobile patrols to up-armour their Landrovers' protective covering.

Satisfied, Hughes placed all three weapons in a temporary hide, under a stove in the kitchen. 'Are you staying to meet Tony and Brian?'

Hughes shook his head and stood. 'No I briefed them on Saturday. I just wanted to check you got safely here with the weapons. I'm off now to brief Stiffer's people about their "come on".'

Mary nodded without replying. Hughes studied her. 'Have

136

you seen Kane recently?'

'No, not for a couple of days, you know what he's like between operations, he likes to be on his own, why?'

Hughes shrugged. 'It's probably nothing; one of Stiffer's people thought they saw him coming out of the Woodvale last night.'

'Thought they saw?'

'He was drunk, heading home after a party in Ligonel. He wasn't sure.' Hughes paused, 'What would Kane be doing in Woodvale?' he asked, suspicion heavy in his voice.

'You don't know if it was him. If it was him I'm sure he had a good reason. Why don't you ask him?'

'I might just do that, but until I do,' he locked eyes with her, 'don't say anything to him, all right?'

He held her gaze, trying to impose his will upon her. She returned his stare defiantly. Finally he turned and left; behind him concern flashed across Mary O'Niel's face.

☆    ☆    ☆

Tennant Street, Special Branch Offices, approximately the same time.

Nevin yawned and stretched. He had reviewed his day's findings. He thought he was on to something but, like so much in this case, he had nothing tangible. It was like chasing shadows, you knew something was there but couldn't grab hold of it. Tomorrow he had three meetings that might prove crucial; first with Professor Moore who had agreed to dig up what he could about Officer White's forensic tests. Then he had a meeting with Mary McDonald's sister, Sarah, who he had traced to Newtonards. His final meeting he did not relish at all – another encounter with Dr Ealing. He shook his head, if there had been any other way he would have avoided it. The last thing he needed at this time was to cross swords again with the state pathologist.

In front of him were a pile of reports and sightings on Kane, stretching back to 1980. He intended to read through them that night. He checked the time, 6.50 pm. 'To hell with it,' he said out loud. Gathering up his paperwork, he headed for the door. It looked like it was going to be a long boring evening.

☆　　☆　　☆

Ardoyne, Valsheda Park, 9 pm same night.

It was the most dangerous, difficult and, without doubt, most uncomfortable job in surveillance; a close quarters 'trigger OP'. His small Ford Escort van had been parked, two wheels on the pavement, less than fifty metres from his target house. Inside its confined space, the E4A man lay, covered by sacking, hardly able to breathe let alone move.

He continually flexed his muscles to avoid cramp. Starting with his right foot, wiggling his toes, then his calf, moving slowly up to his right arm. Once completed, he changed sides and duplicated his actions. Cramp was a killer, forcing you to move; it had to be avoided at all costs; movement meant death.

Around his mouth he rolled a cough lozenger. A cough heard by a passing pedestrian would spell disaster. While other operators waited several streets away, they'd be too far away to protect him if he was discovered. In his hand he held a Smith and Wesson 9mm automatic pistol with a twenty round magazine. Along his side lay a Heckler and Kock MP5K 9mm sub-machine gun, with a double thirty round magazine. In reality he knew that if discovered, his chances of using either were practically nil.

Light was poor but he kept his eyes moving, never looking directly at a fixed point for too long. Staring caused the eyes to water, objects moved and shadows jumped. Better to check his target area regularly, sweeping his eyes from side to side methodically. He smiled to himself. Many an army sentry had stared too long at a tree, seen it grow arms and legs and when finally it had moved, fired, only to find it was a tree after all.

To a casual observer, the van's back door would appear normal. Had they been able to examine it closely, however, it would soon become apparent that it was twice as thick as a normal van of its type. A small observation hole had been drilled into it and optical glass inserted to provide a magnified effect. Practically invisible to anybody outside, it afforded its hidden watcher a clear view of his target.

His biggest problem was that someone might become suspicious of the van itself and either call for police or, infinitely worse, ask local IRA men to check it out. They had parked his van in the same spot three nights running, before inserting him.

It was risky but, as far as they could tell, there had been no local reaction. His van had become part of the scenery. Should someone actually ring Tennant Street about a blue Escort van in Valsheda Park, they would be told it had already checked out and was OK.

Radio silence had been imposed since his insertion. Other operators would not break it unless it was a matter of their own life or death. Inside his van, he knew he had only two real weapons, silence and concentration. Unable to talk, he communicated with his controller by means of clicks. Depressing his transmitter button, two clicks for yes, three for no, rapid clicks meant a sighting.

Movement! Two men walked up Valsheda Park towards his target house. He depressed his radio transmitter button six times. 'Roger Echo 30,' his controller's voice was calm and reassuring, 'do you have a sighting?'

He depressed his radio button twice, 'Click, click.'

'Roger your yes, Echo 30,' his controller went into a practised routine, 'is suspect Anthony Hardy one of them?'

He checked both men walking towards him, then pressed his radio button again, 'Click, click.'

'Roger your yes, Echo 30; is suspect Brian Keenan one of them?'

'Click, click.'

'Roger your yes, Echo 30, are there any more suspects?'

'Click, click, click.'

'Roger your negative, Echo 30; are the suspects into target house?'

He waited, Hardy and Keenan had stopped outside their safe house. He tensed as their eyes swept the street, passing over his van. They spoke to each other. 'Get inside, get inside you bastards,' he thought fiercely to himself. For what seemed like an age, but was in fact only a few brief seconds, both men stood quietly talking, then they turned and entered his target house.

He depressed his radio transmitter, 'Click, click.'

'Roger your yes, Echo 30; I read back suspects Hardy and Keenan into target house, is that correct?'

'Click, click.'

'Roger your yes, Echo 30, keep us informed.' Without

turning, the E4A controller listened to his superiors behind him.

'What do you think, John?' ACC Belfast asked his head of Special Branch.

'I think it's on sir; our latest information is that they will try and hit one of our mobile patrols, at the Ardoyne shop fronts, between 1 am and 2 am.'

ACC Belfast pursed his lips, then inclined his head. 'Very well, get everybody stood to.'

Phones were picked up, orders given and upstairs twelve heavily armed men started to don equipment and prepare weapons.

☆     ☆     ☆

Carrickfergus, Nevin Brown's Home, 2.30 am Tuesday morning.

He had spent all evening reading Kane's personal Special Branch file and it had made grim reading. Orphaned at three-years-old, his father, a merchant seaman, had been killed at sea leaving his mother to bring him up alone. She had been a good woman, although a Protestant, she had brought Kane up in his father's Catholic faith. He had, apparently, been devoted to her. He read with particular distaste the reports of her rape and murder.

Special Branch had researched his childhood with particular care. Teachers had described him as 'a quiet child'. His academic qualities had been quite outstanding, with his headmaster going as far as saying that 'Anthony has the potential to achieve great things, the child has an amazing capacity to learn and digest information.'

Kane had only been eleven-years-old when that was written. He turned to his physical education reports. Kane had played for his school in the rough sport of Gaelic football, but boxing had been by far his favourite sport. He'd boxed for Saint Mary's Boy's Club on the Falls Road.

Nevin whistled softly as he read his record; thirty fights, only two defeats, both on points, against vastly more experienced boys. The Special Branch investigator had interviewed Kane's old boxing coach. It read: 'Tony was what every boxing coach

140

always dreams of finding, a boy with natural talent and skill, coupled with superb reflexes and enormous reserves of stamina and strength. But what really set him apart was his control, he never lost his head, even when he got hurt. I tell you this, if I could have had him for two more years he could have been a potential world champion.'

Nevin checked the dates on Kane's file. He'd dropped out of both school and his boxing club after his release from hospital, going to live with his uncle, Leo Scullion, at that time head of PIRA in North Belfast. Nevin grimaced. 'If it had not been for his mother's brutal murder, he could have been anything, a scholar, an athlete, anything!'

Instead his uncle had seduced him into the IRA and set off a chain reaction that not even that hard bitten Republican could have foreseen. Kane had stayed with his uncle until he too was shot dead, by Paras in the Ardoyne. Now his nephew was a monster, a killing machine striking out at innocent girls in some kind of insane desire to avenge his mother.

'But I'm going to stop you, you crazy bastard,' he said out loud.

Shaking his head again, he rifled through Kane's file, reading reports from a number of sources on the IRA killer's various terrorist outrages. His eyes were beginning to hurt when something caught his attention; it was a low grade report from a regular police patrol. He had missed it on his first time through. It read: 'A mobile patrol reports stopping Anthony Kane at junction Ballygomartin, West Circular Road at 1.45 am 2 February 1985. Kane stated he was visiting friends in West Belfast. In view of his involvement in the killings of two RUC constables later that day this may have been a visit to brief Brigade staff about his intended operation.'

Nevin checked the time again, 1.45 am. Only fifteen minutes before Mary McDonald's neighbour reported her house on fire and that road junction was only a couple of hundred yards from her home. 'I've done it,' he shouted, jumping into the air.

He allowed himself to fall back onto his chair. This was a major break. Kane had been placed near Mary McDonald's house at her approximate time of death. Now if he could only prove her death was not accidental, he had the beginning of a case. Elation filled him. Sleep was banished and ideas and possibilities crowded his mind. Nothing would have pleased him more than to pursue his enquiries immediately, like a hunting dog on a fresh scent, wanting nothing more than to follow it to its conclusion.

Taking a deep breath he forced himself to relax. There was nothing to be done now. Sighing, Nevin dialled on his remote control for the latest news headlines. It hit him like a thunderbolt. All hell had broken out back at Tennant Street.

☆ ☆ ☆

Ardoyne, Valsheda park, 1 am Tuesday morning.

Despite his constant muscle flexing, cramps were starting to stiffen both his legs, nothing serious yet but enough to be uncomfortable. It was an operational necessity for an operator to empty his bladder and bowels before insertion. Despite this, some four hours later, he was starting to feel irritation in both departments. He laughed without humour; it wouldn't be the first time he had pissed himself.

It had rained earlier; now, in dim light, Valsheda Park shimmered like a slowly moving river. All was quiet, not a dog barked or a child cried. All of Ardoyne seemed to be holding its breath.

He heard a noise. Mary O'Niel opened the door of her safe house and walked slowly down its short garden path. He pressed his radio receiver six times.

'Roger Echo 30, is that a standby?' His E4A controller's voice held just a hint of excitement.

'Click, click.'

'Roger your yes, Echo 30. Attention all stations we have a standby, I say again we have a standby.'

At Antrim Road RUC Station, six heavily armed men cocked their weapons and got into a blue unmarked van. Six others divided themselves equally between two civilian cars. In convoy, the van between its two escort cars, they rolled up to an outer armoured security gate and waited. Back at Operation Juliet control room, ACC Belfast burst in. 'What do you have?'

'Looks like movement at our target house sir,' the E4A controller answered him.

'Anything positive?'

'Negative sir, just a standby.'

ACC Belfast turned to a dark haired soldier with no obvious badges of rank. 'Are your people ready to move?'

'They're in vehicles and ready to go.' His voice was cultured and exuded quiet confidence and determination. 'All you have to do is hand over control to us.'

ACC Belfast nodded and looked away from the SAS liaison officer as his own head of SB entered, hastily pulling on a civilian jacket. 'What's up?'

'Just a standby John, nothing concrete yet.' He turned to his E4A controller. 'See what you can confirm, controller.'

'Yes sir,' he depressed his radio mike, 'Hello Echo 30, this is control, do you have a suspect out of the target house over?'

'Click, click.'

'Roger your yes, Echo 30, is it either Hardy or Keenan?'

'Click, click, click.'

'Roger your no, Echo 30, is it O'Niel?'

'Click, click.'

'Roger your yes, Echo 30, keep us informed.' He turned to ACC Belfast. 'That's O'Niel out of her safe house, she's probably checking the street before they come out.'

ACC Belfast nodded, his face grim. 'I want this clearly understood by all,' he swept the room with a glance, 'I will not countenance deploying the SAS unless I'm sure that both Hardy and Keenan are out of that house and that both are armed.'

All four men present stared at the E4A controller's radio as if it was a living being. Its stillness irritated them all. Suddenly it burst into life. 'Click, click, click, click,' a short pause and then repeated twice more, a pre-arranged emergency signal.

'Roger Echo 30, do you have someone approaching your van, over?'

'Click, click.'

'Roger your yes, Echo 30, is it O'Niel, over.'

'Click, click.'

'Roger your yes, Echo 30, out to you. Standby all vehicles suspect O'Niel is checking Echo 30's position.' Taking his hand off the transmission button he looked at ACC Belfast.

'If she spots him we'll have to go in fast, otherwise he's a dead man.' Without waiting for an answer he turned back to his radio and waited, his thoughts with a friend and colleague in real danger.

O'Niel had been standing by his van door for several minutes. Sweat poured out over his face and he tried not to look at her directly, afraid his own staring would attract her attention to his hiding place. Worse for him, she stood in front of his observation point, making it impossible for him to see the front of his target house.

Slowly she started to walk back towards her safe house and he took a deep gulp of air, suddenly aware he had been holding his breath. As O'Niel receded he was gradually able to see his target area. What he didn't know for sure was whether Hardy and Keenan were still inside or not. Mary O'Niel paused at the house's front door and gave a last careful look around, then she spoke to an unseen person in its darkened interior. With little warning both Hardy and Keenan stepped out; both men spoke briefly and started to walk towards the street.

He pressed his radio button six times.

'Roger your standby, Echo 30, do you have Hardy and Keenan out of the target house, over?'

'Click, click.'

'Roger your yes, Echo 30, can you identify any weapons, over?'

Silence. He watched as both terrorists checked the street. He could see nothing. Keenan said something over his shoulder and Hardy laughed out loud. Stepping forward Keenan banged his leg against the fence and involuntarily staggered and almost fell. As he regained his balance he lost his grip on an object under his coat; it sprang into view, it was an AK47!

'Click, click.'

'Roger your yes, Echo 30, can you confirm Hardy and Keenan out of target house and with weapons, over?'

'Click, click.'

'Roger your yes, Echo 30, well done, out.' The controller turned with a smile of triumph. 'Weapons confirmed sir.'

All eyes turned to ACC Belfast. He stood for several seconds staring, then took a deep breath and turned to the SAS officer. 'It's all yours.'

Without any visible sign of emotion the SAS man tilted his head and spoke into his radio. 'I have control, I have control, standby, standby. Go!'

Antrim Road's huge security gates swung open to allow the

three vehicle convoy to pass. It turned right and headed at speed for Ardoyne.

Hardy and Keenan walked quickly towards Ardoyne shop fronts. Every fifty metres or so, one or other of them would glance about but around them all was deathly still. Occasionally one of Clarke's Int. and Security ASU would pass and whisper all was clear. Ahead of them an alley entrance loomed, it ran behind Ardoyne shop fronts.

As they entered it, total darkness engulfed them. Clarke's men had knocked out adjacent street lights. Walking along in total darkness Hardy ran his hand along the alley wall, searching for a pre-positioned plank of wood he'd left as a marker. Their alley was nearly a hundred and fifty metres long and had two entrances, one opposite Brompton Park, at which Hardy and Keenan had entered, and one at Ardoyne Avenue. Ahead of them, a blue van pulled up at this entrance and its side door opened with almost no sound. From it emerged four men, each dressed and armed identically. From head to toe all wore black, flameproof overalls, gloves and boots, and black balaclavas hid their faces.

Around their waists hung black leather belts containing ammunition pouches and low slung holsters with 9mm Browning automatic pistols. Each pistol had anti-slip Patamire grips and were loaded with twenty round extended magazines. All carried 9mm Heckler and Koch MP5 sub-machine guns with torches fitted on top. Each torch was zeroed to its gun – where it shone, so went the gun's bullets. Swiftly they broke into pairs and, hugging separate walls, each pair started to slowly inch their way towards their intended targets.

Hardy had found his marker; he knew the door next to it was unlocked and that its garden offered easy access to the shop front's roof tops. He turned to Keenan behind him and whispered, 'Hole it there, I want to check the grenade before we climb.'

Kneeling Hardy removed his Drogue grenade and began to check and prime it, using touch only. Behind him Keenan pulled out his rifle and checked its safety catch. Both wore surgical gloves which did not impede sense of touch but prevented their fingerprints being left. Hardy was about to rise, when he heard a slight noise. He looked up into impenetrable darkness. Behind him he could hear Keenan fiddling with his rifle. 'Sssshhh,' he whispered hoarsely.

There was silence. 'What's the matter?' Keenan whispered eventually.

'I thought I heard something.'

They both listened in silence for over a minute. Hardy had dropped his grenade and pulled out his Browning pistol. 'You're imagining things,' Keenan said fiercely, his voice barely a whisper.

'No,' Hardy protested, standing; he was certain something was wrong, it just didn't feel right. When he spoke his voice was low, but no longer a whisper, 'There's something wrong, let's get out of . . . '

Two torch beams came on, catching both terrorists full in their faces. For a fraction of a second all was still, six men caught in a frozen micro-second of history.

Hardy tried to bring up his pistol. Four 9mm rounds smashed into his face. Their entry points could be covered by a 50p piece. Hardy's face and head seemed to explode as he was thrown backwards. The sudden noise was deafening in such a confined space. Keenan stood beside his now dead partner, and tried to make his legs and arms move; they wouldn't. He opened his mouth to talk, to shout, to scream, perhaps to beg, to plead, to ask for forgiveness, but no noise came out. With a supreme effort he forced his right arm, holding the rifle, to move; whether to raise it or throw it away would never be known for sure.

There was a second burst of firing, two four round bursts. Eight 9mm rounds hit him, literally picking him up and driving him back horizontally several feet. He was dead long before his body hit the alley floor.

Then again there was silence, as four torch beams searched across two crumpled bodies. Finally the four man SAS team were satisfied that their targets were no longer a threat. 'Move!' A single word of command sent two men rushing to cover past Hardy and Keenan.

From a distance came noise; screaming car tyres and slamming car doors heralded the arrival of two back-up cars. Each one sealed off an alley entrance. Three men in NATO camouflaged uniforms burst out of both cars, armed with Heckler and Koch G3 rifles, and took up covering positions. Hardy and Keenan's bodies were checked impersonally by an

SAS sergeant. Satisfied he depressed his radio transmitter. 'Hello Zero from Bravo One Contact, over.'

'Zero send over.'

'Bravo One, confirm ambush sprung, confirm two dead terrorists, confirm no own casualties. One improvised grenade, one hand gun, one AK47 rifle recovered. Send in relative agencies when ready, over.'

'Zero, Roger, well done, QRF on the way, out.'

Standing, the ambush commander walked to his cover man. From a distance both could hear sirens approaching. He turned and smiled beneath his balaclava. 'Piece of cake, Andy.' Both laughed, not with humour, not with remorse or even malice, but with relief that both were still alive.

☆    ☆    ☆

Tennant Street, Tuesday morning, 8.50 am.

Nevin felt it as soon as he entered; the atmosphere was electric. Everyone was on a high. Between parking his car and arriving at CID general office he was asked at least five times, 'Did you hear about last night? Great news eh?'

He managed to nod and smile to each of his questioners. As a professional police officer he hated killing, whether by para-militaries or security forces. Like many he longed for the day he would not have to carry a gun or check under his car every day. But he also was realistic enough to understand that officers in his sub-division, who had suffered so much in recent times, might feel a certain satisfaction that terrorists who had killed their friends had been brought before 'the ultimate court of justice'. Personally, it just made him sad.

In CID general office he found detectives, despite the early hour, already celebrating. Even DCI Hart's normally morose features broke into a smile as he entered. 'Did you hear about last night? Great news eh?' His assembled detectives had given a ragged cheer. It had taken DI Cotton's firm and steady hand to bring them to order.

'OK, OK,' he had said, emerging from his office as things looked like getting out of control. 'We still have a job to do, put away that drink, briefing in five minutes.' Slightly subdued, his plain clothes officers started to get back to reality. Nevin spied

Billy Boyd sitting at his desk. With a jerk of his head he led him to Bill Dodds's SB office.

'How is your house to house in Tigers Bay coming along?' he asked, once inside.

Billy shrugged. 'Not good, I've turned up nothing yet, but I still have a few houses to check.' He gave his superior and mentor a curious look. 'It might help, skipper, if I knew exactly what I was looking for.'

Nevin considered Billy's question. He had originally given him only a scant brief, telling him to ask if anybody had seen or heard anything suspicious in relation to Mary Kirkpatrick's death. It had been one of Bill Dodds's conditions. Now he felt this case was going to blow wide open any day, it was time to take a few chances; besides he trusted his young aid's judgement and discretion.

'What I'm about to say must not be discussed with anybody else, even DI Cotton and especially DCI Hart OK?' Billy nodded, his face serious. 'You are looking for a tall well-built man, with blond hair, blue eyes, aged in his middle thirties. Is that specific enough for you?'

'More than enough,' he took a deep breath, 'it's an even better description than Lynn Moody's killer.' He looked at Nevin directly. 'You think both deaths are connected,' he bit his bottom lip, 'and you know who the killer is?'

'Yes, but don't ask me who it is. Nobody must know that these two deaths may be linked.' He put his hand on Billy's shoulder. 'There's a lot more to this than just two girls' murders, a lot more. I'm trusting you Billy.'

A determined look crossed the young detective's face. 'You can rely on me,' he said firmly and with a quick thumbs-up sign he left.

Alone, Nevin sat and rubbed his eyes; sleep had not come easily to him last night, too much on his mind. It was all coming together, he sensed it, today could be crucial. He checked his watch, time to go, he had a meeting with Professor Moore at 10 am.

☆　　☆　　☆

Ardoyne, Fidelious Clarke's house, approximately the same time.

It was a sombre group who gathered in the veteran Republican's front room. Gathered were all of Ardoyne's leading PIRA activists . . . Sean Hughes, Kane, Clarke, Robert Fennel and Mary O'Niel. She had just finished recounting her story of last night's operation. All had listened with silent intensity.

'How could they have known?' Clarke said bitterly. 'The fucking SAS were waiting for them, how could they have known.' He hung his head.

For a second nobody spoke, then Kane asked, 'Have your people noticed any strangers over the last few days or any unusual activity?'

Clarke looked up quickly. 'No, since Larry was shot I've had my boys out in force, they haven't spotted anything.'

'Just because they didn't see anything doesn't mean that there wasn't anything to see.' Kane's voice was at its usual unemotional level.

Clarke opened his mouth to make an angry reply but was interrupted by Hughes. 'One thing is for sure, it was no accident; they don't bring in the SAS unless it's on very good information.' He glanced around, 'They knew Tony and Brian were coming, it's that simple.'

'What do you mean?' Kane asked.

Hughes pursed his lips. 'Brigade were on the phone this morning; as of now all operations are suspended.' He looked at each face in turn. 'They believe we have an informer amongst us.'

Clarke jumped to his feet, his face red with anger. 'What? That would mean it would have to have been one of us; only we knew, and poor Tony and Brian.' He pointed an accusing finger at Hughes. 'Are you accusing one of us of being a tout?' He spat his last word like a curse.

Hughes held up a placating hand. 'I'm not accusing anybody, but we have to find out what happened before we can get back to hitting the Brits.' The IRA leader paused to allow his head of security to sit down. When he was sure Clarke had his temper under control he went on. 'Now nobody take this personally, just answer as best you can. I have to ask these questions. Stiffer, your people were to smash some shop windows to draw in a police patrol, what did you tell them?'

'Nothing,' Clarke spat, still obviously angry. 'I briefed Robert, he briefed them. I checked the area myself with two lads at midnight. I told them we were just patrolling the area, not that a job was on. Then I rang Mary at the safe house to tell her all was clear.' He fixed Hughes with an unswerving stare. 'It was clear.' His voice was a low growl.

Hughes nodded and turned to Fennel. 'What did you tell your people?'

'Nothing much.' He shrugged and lifted his hands in a helpless gesture. 'I told them we were going to break some windows to see what reaction the peelers would take.' He glanced around in desperation. 'I never said anything about Tuesday's operation, honest.' His voice held a note of pleading.

Hughes studied him for several minutes, then he shrugged. 'I believe you.' He looked at Mary O'Niel. 'That leaves you, who did you tell?'

'Nobody,' her voice was indignant. 'I picked up the weapons, transported them here and handed them over to you.'

'And you told nobody about last night's job?'

'Of course not!'

Hughes's eyes narrowed. 'Not even him.' He jerked his head towards Kane.

She opened her mouth to make an angry retort, but Kane beat her to it. 'Mary didn't tell me anything, she knows better than that.' His voice was quiet, almost soft.

'I don't know that.'

'What are you suggesting Sean?'

Despite himself, Hughes felt a stab of fear. 'I'm not suggesting anything, just trying to get things straight, that's all.' Even to himself, his voice sounded unconvincing.

Kane sat back and his icy blue eyes bored into Hughes, studying him for several seconds. When he spoke eventually, his voice was a gentle purr. 'I think you've got something on your mind Sean, let's all hear it.'

'He thinks you were over talking to the Prods, one of Stiffer's men thought they saw you coming back from Woodvale last Monday,' Mary O'Niel blurted out, pointing at Hughes.

'You stupid bitch.' The IRA chief jumped out of his chair and advanced on O'Niel, his manner threatening. 'I told you to keep your mouth shut.'

Kane exploded from his chair, his body moving with speed and power that was truly awesome to behold. Grabbing Hughes by his throat with a single hand, he levered him into a wall. A hand like a vice stopped all air getting to his lungs and both feet kicked helplessly, inches off the floor. Hughes tried desperately to pull Kane's hand away with both of his own, but that only increased the pressure on his throat.

Slowly Hughes's face turned from red to an ashen grey; his eyes bulged and strength ebbed from his arms. Kane smiled, his face like a mask of death. 'So you think I'm a tout?' His voice remaining low, calm almost conversational. Kane loosened his chief a couple of inches and slammed him back. Hughes was close to unconsciousness. 'Think I'm a tout?' he repeated and this time there was an icy edge to his voice.

'For Christ's sake let him go,' pleaded Clarke, pulling ineffectively against Kane's right arm. He pushed his face closer to him and lowered his voice. 'Anthony you'll kill him.'

Mary O'Niel came up to Kane's left side and put a gentle hand on his left arm. 'Please let him go, Tony.'

He turned to look at her, his eyes as cold as death. For several seconds they exchanged stares, then Kane released his grip. Hughes fell making choking noises as he tried to draw air into his lungs. Kane studied him for several seconds with obvious distaste. Finally he knelt next to his barely conscious commander. 'If you ever say anything like that to me or Mary again, I'll kill you.' Standing he walked out. O'Niel threw a venomous glance at Hughes and ran after him.

Clarke and Fennel helped Hughes to his feet. He drew huge gulps of air into his lungs, trying desperately to ease his pain. Clarke shook his head, his face grim, and looked from Fennel down to the gasping Hughes. 'You're a fool, Sean, don't you know he could never betray us.' Shaking his head he helped Fennel drag their OC out for some fresh air.

Many miles away, two MI5 listeners looked at each other. One smiled, 'Looks like a falling out amongst the troops.'

His section chief nodded. 'With any luck they'll kill each other.'

The radio bug planted inside Clarke's TV set was paying remarkable dividends. Removing a cassette recording of what they had just heard, the section chief stood. 'I'll get a written transcript of this made out and passed to Special Branch,' he smiled grimly, 'I'm sure they'll find it interesting.'

☆　　☆　　☆

Forensic science laboratories, Beevers Park, Belfast, 10 am.

'The questions that have to be asked are, was a warning given before these men were shot? Did one of them try to surrender? Witnesses have spoken of hearing shouts before the army opened fire. These questions must be answered and until they are, the soldiers concerned must be removed from active duty . . . .'

Nevin turned off his radio with a sigh of disgust. It was all very well for politicians to preach from their safe seats in parliament; they had no idea of the complexities of life in Ulster. If you put a band of heavily armed terrorists and equally heavily armed but specially trained squad soldiers in a Belfast back alley, then it would be unrealistic to expect either side to take prisoners. He gave a mirthless laugh as he opened his car door. If politicians wanted to stop killings like last night's then they had to take proper steps to stop the root causes of the IRA's present murderous campaign.

Showing his warrant card, Nevin was ushered through security and up to Professor Moore's office. The eminent forensic scientist rose with a beaming smile. 'Come in, come in, my boy.' He advanced with an extended hand and slapped Nevin on his back. 'Good to see you.'

Looking over Moore's shoulder, he saw a slightly bashful young man sitting in a corner. The professor followed his gaze. 'This is Robert Shaw; he's the analyst who carried out your tests.'

'I hope there is nothing wrong, Detective Sergeant Brown?' Shaw advanced nervously, clutching a buff coloured folder in his left hand as if his life depended on it.

Nevin could not help but smile. 'There's nothing to be alarmed about, Robert, this is part of a much larger, on going investigation. Please sit and let me explain.'

Once all were seated, Nevin went on. 'Now what I am about to say must be kept in the strictest of confidence. I must warn you that any premature disclosure may contravene the Official Secrets Act.'

Shaw's eyes widened. Nevin was not sure if he could back up his threat, but he needed something to scare the young man into silence. Professor Moore smiled benignly; he guessed that it would take a lot more than the Official Secrets Act to scare

152

this hard boiled professor.

Having paused for dramatic effect, he went on, 'It is my belief that Mary McDonald's death was not accidental and is connected to several other similar deaths.' Shaw's eyes now held a mixture of fear, surprise and awe. 'Now in view of this Robert, could you review your analysis of the sub-officer's request for a search for any accelerants?'

'Detective Sergeant Brown . . .'

'Please call me Nevin.'

Shaw smiled shyly. 'Nevin, I was asked to search for any sign of things like petrol, white spirit,' he shook his head, 'anything suspicious at all that could have been used as an accelerant. There were none.'

Nevin rubbed his bottom lip, then spread his hands in supplication. 'Could you check your file again? There must be something.'

He bent to read his file. Nevin looked at Professor Moore, who gave a non-committal shrug. Shaw looked up eventually. 'I'm sorry Nevin, there's just nothing unusual.' He looked back down to his file and shrugged, 'Except that she ate in bed.'

'What?'

'She ate in bed, there were some grease stains, not significant, but enough to suggest that she ate in bed.'

Nevin tried to keep his voice calm. 'Could I have that file?'

Professor Moore interrupted. 'We don't allow that, but Robert,' he looked at his young analyst, 'go and make a copy, a comprehensive copy of that file for Sergeant Brown.'

Alone, the sharp eyed scientist studied his guest. 'I think you want to ask me something?'

'Could grease, food fats, be used as an accelerant?'

'Of course, if used in sufficient quantities they would make an excellent one, but Shaw said he only found a small quantity, not enough to suggest that it had been used as you suggest.'

Nevin thought for a second. 'What would happen if a person poured fat over a human body and then set it on fire?'

It was Moore's turn to think; finally he said, 'Yes it's possible, the body would be consumed and only a small amount of fat would get onto the actual bedclothes themselves.'

He pursed his lips, and lapsed into silence for several seconds. 'At the postmortem they would be unlikely to be able to ascertain what were fat burns and normal human fat tissue burning; they certainly didn't send us any samples for analysis.'

'I'm not surprised,' Nevin's voice was grim. 'To them it was just another normal sudden death.'

'There's just one thing; according to Shaw's file Mary McDonald was alive when the fire started. What kind of man would pour animal fat over a live woman and set her on fire?'

'I think I already have the answer to that question.'

Moore's face hardened. 'You know who did this?'

'Yes.' There was no uncertainty in Nevin's voice.

Before either could say more, Shaw returned. Nevin accepted his copy file. Professor Moore walked with him to his car in silence. As he opened his car door, the older man put a hand on his shoulder. 'Nevin, make sure you get this, this . . .' he searched for words but could find none, 'nail this son-of-a-bitch.'

'You can bet on it sir.'

Newtonards, midday, same day.

His drive to Newtonards had given him enough time to collect his thoughts. When he knocked on Sarah Lawson's door he knew exactly what questions he wanted answering. The door was answered by a tall, slim attractive woman, in her early thirties.

'Sarah Lawson?'

'That's right.'

'Detective Sergeant Brown.' He showed his identification. 'I rang you yesterday.'

'Oh yes, please come in.' She showed him into her front room. 'You said you wanted to talk to me about Mary's death. I thought all that had been settled. It was an accident, wasn't it?'

Nevin thought for a second before answering. 'That's what I'm trying to establish. I hope you can help me.'

'Of course, anything I can do; please sit down, would you like some tea?'

'That would be nice, thank you.'

While Sarah made his tea, Nevin glanced around. Her room

was neat and comfortably furnished and there was a photo of a man in UDR uniform on her mantelpiece. When she came back he nodded towards it, 'Your husband?'

A look of intense pain flashed across her face. 'Yes, he's dead, he was . . ., they . . .' She looked up with tears in her eyes and took a deep breath. 'They put a bomb under his car. I saw it, he lost both legs.' She shook her head. 'It took him three weeks to die.'

He swallowed involuntarily. 'I'm sorry, I didn't know.'

She smiled. 'Don't be, I'm just being silly; now what did you want to ask about Mary?'

He took a sip of tea. 'According to the postmortem your sister had been drinking heavily on the night of her death. Was that unusual?'

'How do you mean "heavily"?'

'Well according to the constable who investigated her death, witnesses said she had at least six or seven half pints of lager.'

Sarah laughed. 'That wasn't heavy for Mary; she could drink most men under the table. People used to say that she had hollow legs.'

'So that amount of alcohol wouldn't have made her fall asleep?'

She snorted in derision. 'It wouldn't have fizzed on her.'

Nevin made a note. 'Did she normally smoke in bed?'

'Well I never saw her do it, she never kept an ashtray in her bedroom.' She shrugged, 'But that doesn't mean she didn't; for all I know that could have been her first time.'

Nodding sympathetically, he readied himself for his most important question. 'Did your sister eat in bed?'

A look of confusion passed over her face. 'Eat in bed? What do you mean?'

'Fish and chips, stuff like that.'

Sarah laughed openly. 'Mary eat fish and chips, are you joking? She always used to say that she drank and smoked, so the least she could do was eat properly. Mary was a health food nut; muesli for breakfast, salads for lunch, boiled fish for supper. She wouldn't eat butter or cheese, she used to drive me nuts with it.'

Nevin sighed and sat back. That was what he needed. A smile of satisfaction crossed his face. Sarah studied him curiously. 'Just what is this all about?'

155

'I'm sorry, there were a few facts in your sister's file that needed clarifying.' Standing he extended a hand. 'I'd like to thank you, could I be rude and ask to use your phone?'

'Yes, of course, it's in the hall.'

He called Tennant Street and asked for Billy but he was still out on enquiries. Leaving word he could be contacted at Foster Green Hospital he rang off, bade farewell to Sarah Lawson and made his way back to his car. Now for the part he really wasn't looking forward to, his interview with the eminent Dr Ealing.

☆     ☆     ☆

Foster Green Hospital, 2 pm, same day.

To say that the state pathologist was not amused, was like saying a rain storm didn't get you wet. Anger showed clearly on every line of his face.

'This is the third time in as many weeks that I have had to deal with what I regard as unreasonable behaviour on your behalf, Detective Sergeant Brown. First you practically blackmail me into giving you confidential information on my predecessor, then you arrive at one of my postmortems and hijack it; now you want to go over a case that has been officially closed for more than six years.'

He took a deep breath, fighting to contain his anger. 'I am the state pathologist for Belfast; unless I get some straight answers, then there is no way that I'm going to discuss this.' He tapped a folder on his desk. 'No way at all.'

Nevin pondered a second, then locked eyes with Ealing. 'I believe that Lynn Moody, Mary Kirkpatrick, Mary McDonald and perhaps as many as twenty other girls, were raped and murdered by the same man over the last twenty years. Is that straight enough for you?'

Ealing was appalled. 'My God! Are you sure?'

'Practically certain; now do I get some co-operation?'

'Yes, yes, of course.' He opened his file with a slightly shaking hand. 'What do you want to know?'

Nevin opened his own notebook and took notes. 'How much alcohol was in Mary's blood; in your report you said it was a "significant amount".'

Ealing checked. 'About 145 milligrams of alcohol in 100

156

millilitres of blood.'

He did a mental calculation. 'Roughly equivalent to six or seven half pints of lager?'

'Perhaps a little more.'

'And you considered that a significant amount?'

'For a woman, yes.'

Nevin shook his head. 'Not for Mary; according to her sister she had a high tolerance for drink and could drink most men under the table.'

Ealing started to pale. 'Nobody told me.'

'Could you tell me, without being too technical, what exactly was the cause of death?'

'Massive internal shock, due to heat.' He looked up, his face grim. 'She was quite literally burnt to death.'

'Could she have been dead before the fire was started?'

'Not a chance; her bodily functions were operating fully before she died; that much was established without doubt at the postmortem.'

'Please check your notes again doctor, there must have been something out of the ordinary.'

Ealing scratched his head. 'Well in most fires the victims usually die from smoke inhalation, before the fire gets to them. Mary didn't.'

'You mean there was no smoke in her lungs?'

'No, there was smoke, but not enough to kill or even incapacitate her.'

'What conclusion did you come to from this?'

'That she was breathing shallowly due to the effects of alcohol and that the fire caught hold rapidly.'

'Well I've already established that she was not in a drunken stupor; what else could have caused her to breath shallowly?'

'She would have to have been unconscious.'

'There were no marks or bruising on her face or neck?'

'Of course not. If there had been I'd have reported it and I can anticipate another question before you ask it, there was no way to determine whether or not she had been sexually assaulted. The lower half of her body was too badly burned.'

Nevin was silent, rubbing his bottom lip. 'Just because you can't prove she was, doesn't mean she wasn't.' He took a deep breath. 'I think my man raped Mary McDonald, then rendered her unconscious, probably by using a pillow or cushion,

157

poured animal fat over her body, making sure very little was spilled on the bedclothes, then set her on fire.'

'Jesus Christ. Can you prove all of that?'

'Most of it.'

'The man must be a monster.'

'Yes, can I have a full report of your findings in writing, concentrating on the lack of smoke in her lungs and alcohol levels?'

'Of course, I'll have it done immediately and sent over to your station. If there's . . .' The telephone rang. Ealing answered it. 'It's for you, Sergeant Brown.' He handed it across.

'Skipper, it's Billy. I've found you a witness.'

Tennant Street, Special Branch office, one hour later.

She was what he always imagined the ultimate mother-in-law would look like: about fifty years of age, big, busty, red-faced, even her hair had a blue rinse to it. She could have stepped out of any current soap opera on television. Her name was Betty Carlisle. Nevin was introduced to her by Billy, and was surprised when an unusually gentle voice replied. 'Pleased to meet you Sergeant Brown.'

'Could you please tell Sergeant Brown what you told me Mrs Carlisle.' Billy tried, and failed, to appear professional. The excitement was clear in his voice.

'Well you see, Sergeant Brown, I sort of keep an eye on our street, you know we have terrible trouble with youngsters coming down from Antrim Road and breaking windows.' She leaned forward and lowered her voice and patted his knee. 'Not that ours are any better, mind you.'

Nevin nodded sympathetically, resisting the urge to ask her to speed up her story.

'Well about a month ago I saw this fellow in the street, a big hard looking man, with fair hair.' She shook her head and shivered. 'He looked a bad sort. At first I thought nothing of it, but then I saw him again the following week and the week after that. Always at the same time and on the same day.'

'What day was that?' asked Nevin.

'Wednesday, always on a Wednesday.'

158

Nevin and Billy exchanged glances. Nevin looked back to Betty Carlisle as if she was a golden prize in a raffle. 'Did you know Mary Kirkpatrick?' he asked.

'Yes, that poor woman who drowned in her bath. I sometimes baby-sat for her, she was divorced you know.'

'Yes I know,' Nevin tried to keep his voice calm, 'have you seen this man since her death?'

Betty's brow furrowed. 'No I haven't; was he related to her?'

Nevin ignored her question. 'If I showed you a picture of this man do you think you would recognize him?' Behind Betty's back a look of incredulous surprise appeared on Billy's face.

'Of course I could. I may be getting old but my eyesight is still perfect.' Betty's voice held a note of pride.

Nevin looked at Billy. 'Get Mrs Carlisle a cup of tea. I want to get a photographic display set up.'

Billy followed him into the corridor and grabbed his sleeve. 'Skipper to show her photographs, you have to have a suspect.'

He looked at his young aid's concerned face. 'I have a suspect Billy.' Nevin's voice was grim. 'Believe me I have a suspect.'

Police rules for showing photos of suspects to potential witnesses are very strict. There had to be no less than twelve, and all had to be the same size, colour and clarity. The subjects in them had to be roughly of the same age as the suspect and have roughly the same hair and facial colouring. Where possible, all should be shown dressed in roughly similar clothing.

It took Nevin nearly thirty minutes to collect and put together the necessary photos. It took Betty Carlisle exactly thirty seconds to point unerringly to just one. 'That's him!'

'Are you sure, no doubt at all?' asked Nevin.

'Absolutely positive, that's him.'

Nevin looked at a startled Billy Boyd, then both looked down at Betty's pointing finger; it rested on a photograph of Anthony 'Butcher' Kane.

☆ ☆ ☆

Tennant Street, Special Branch office, Wednesday.

He checked his watch, 4.55 pm; only five minutes to go before

Marrianne phoned him from America. He sat next to Bill Dodds's secure telephone and waited for her call. They could speak on that line in perfect safety. It was all a bit of an anti-climax now; no matter what Marrianne and Bill found out, he had more than enough evidence to arrest Kane and hold him until he was genetically fingerprinted. However he had promised Bill not to break the case until his return. Besides, he believed there was time to spare; since the SAS shooting, Ardoyne PIRA had been stood down while an 'internal inquiry' was conducted into Hardy and Keenan's deaths.

If the IRA didn't order Kane to kill, then he in turn would not be triggered into killing any more girls.

'And before that happens I'll have you behind bars, you murdering bastard,' he said softly to himself. His thoughts turned to Marrianne and a smile crossed his face. He was looking forward to hearing her voice. As if on cue, the telephone rang. He picked it up immediately. 'Is that you Marrianne?'

'Yes my love.' Even from afar her voice sounded beautiful.

Nevin smiled and began to tell her his news. 'I've missed you darling, you'll never guess how much I've found out . . . .'

'Nevin, please listen,' she interrupted him, urgency in her voice. 'I've discovered something terrible . . . .'

His smile vanished as he listened to her. He had to get this information to Bill Dodds immediately!!!

# 6

---

Boston, Federal Building, previous Tuesday, midday.

Marrianne was still slightly jet lagged as she walked through a huge set of doors into FBI headquarters. She spied a counter marked, 'All Visitors Report Here', and made directly for it.

'Yes, can I help you?' enquired an attractive young woman in her early twenties.

'My name is Doctor Marrianne Sterling. I have an appointment to see Special Agent Henry Tyler.'

'Just a second please,' she checked a typed list in front of her, then looked up swiftly and smiled. 'Yes you're expected Dr Sterling, please take a seat, I'll have an escort sent down for you straight away.'

Several minutes later a very handsome young man stepped out of the elevator, walked directly to her and held out his hand. 'Dr Sterling.' Marrianne nodded, standing to accept his hand. 'My name is Agent Stewart Brosco. I'm to escort you to Special Agent Tyler; you'll need this.' He handed her a triangular badge marked 'Visitor' and waited while she pinned it to her jacket lapel. Nodding with satisfaction he extended his right arm. 'This way please.' He led her towards the elevator. Once inside he turned towards her with a ready smile. 'We're on the twelfth floor, you're a native Bostonian aren't you?'

Marrianne returned his smile. 'Yes, four generations.' She was aware that he was looking at her with frank juvenile admiration.

'I have only just been posted here myself, perhaps you could show me some of your city's culture some time?'

Marrianne smiled, this one was a fast worker. 'I don't think that will be possible. I'm giving a lecture tour in Britain and have to return shortly.'

161

A flash of disappointment crossed his face. Marrianne guessed he didn't get turned down very often. They glided to a halt, the doors silently opening to reveal a door directly in front of them marked 'Special Agent Henry Tyler'. Brosco walked over and knocked politely. It was opened swiftly. 'Marrianne!!' Henry Tyler held out his arms in welcome. 'It's been too long.' He kissed her on both cheeks.

Looking over her shoulder he said, 'Thanks Agent Brosco, that will be all.' Brosco remained looking at Marrianne. Tyler smiled and put a hand on the younger man's shoulder. 'You can go now Brosco.'

Brosco looked round quickly, blushed and left hurriedly. Tyler smiled and closed the door behind him; looking at Marrianne he said, 'Looks like you've made a conquest.'

'He's cute but not my type and besides,' it was her turn to blush, 'I've met someone rather special.'

'I'll have to hear all, otherwise Kathrine will never forgive me, please sit down.' He indicated a chair opposite his and then sat observing her over his fingers. Henry Tyler was an extremely imposing man, his prematurely grey hair adding to, rather than detracting from, his good looks. Slightly slanting eyes and high cheekbones gave him an oriental appearance many women found fascinating. Unfortunately for them he was, and had been for ten years, a happily married man.

'How is Kathrine?'

'Wonderful as ever. We've had another boy since you last visited us.' They exchanged gossip for several minutes, then a silence developed between them. Tyler took a deep breath and decided to get down to business.

'Marrianne, your phone call was, to say the least . . .' he searched for the right word, '. . . intriguing; you said you had information about murders, Irish terrorists.' He studied her. 'If it had been anybody else I'd have called for the men in white coats.'

'You still might, what I'm about to tell you is very strange and disturbing, so I think you had better read this first.' She handed him a hand-written letter from Bill Dodds. Tyler read it and looked up, clearly impressed.

'This is some recommendation and from an RUC Special Branch inspector no less.' He looked down again at Bill's letter, and read from it. 'Could you as a favour to our force extend

162

any help you can to Dr Sterling?' He looked back up and smiled. 'What exactly can I do for you?'

Marrianne told him her story, omitting nothing. Tyler's smile froze; for several seconds after she had finished he said nothing, lost in thought. Finally he locked eyes with her, concern evident on his face. 'I don't suppose you could be wrong about all of this?'

Marrianne shook her head. 'No, I don't believe we are. I've talked this over with Nevin and Bill. We want you to find out if a girl was raped and murdered on the same day as Brian Doherty was shot. You see, in Ulster Kane has been covering up his killings, disguising them as suicides or accidents. But over here he may not have bothered to do that.'

'Sounds logical,' Tyler said. 'Come with me.' He led the doctor through the outer office to the lift. 'Our records department is upstairs,' he said pushing the lift button. Two floors up Marrianne followed him to a door marked 'Criminal Records Department', and Tyler went in without knocking. Marrianne found herself in a long room filled with filing cabinets. Behind a computer terminal an elderly man stood up and walked towards Tyler. 'Henry,' he said extending a hand. 'What can I do for you?'

'Matt this is Dr Marrianne Sterling. Marrianne this is Matt Hastings.' They shook hands.

He looked enquiringly at Tyler. 'I want you to check and find out if we had an unsolved female rape/murder on 8 January 1989,' Tyler said.

Hastings nodded his balding head. '8 January 1989. No problem. That sounds familiar,' he said, walking swiftly to the computer terminal. He flicked buttons with practised ease. Eventually he said, 'Ah yes,' and looked up at Tyler. 'I thought so. It was the last of the so called "prowler" killings.'

'Of course!' Tyler exclaimed moving round to look over the old man's shoulder. 'I should have remembered.'

'Prowler killings?' Marrianne asked.

Tyler looked up and answered her. 'Yes. It was the name the papers gave him. It was a series of four very brutal rape killings. None of the victims had anything in common – it completely baffled us.'

Marrianne thought for a second. 'Did they start after November 1987?' she asked.

Hastings pressed a button and looked up. 'Yes,' he replied.

'And the last one was on 8 January 1989, right?' Marrianne said again.

'That's right again – what is this?' he asked.

'Do you have a record of the attacker's blood group?' she asked.

'Of course,' replied Hastings. 'In case we get a suspect, then we can . . . '

'Genetically fingerprint him – I know,' Marrianne said interrupting with a smile. 'I'll bet you his blood group is O-neg.'

Hastings pressed a button then looked at the doctor, a surprised look on his face. 'You're right! How did you know? It was never in the papers.'

Tyler interrupted him. 'Never mind that. I want everything you have on the prowler killings. And on a man called Anthony Kane. He was an IRA terrorist we arrested and had deported.' Back in Tyler's office they sifted through the files. 'So what we have is this,' Tyler summarized. 'The killings started after Kane arrived. They ended after he left and they follow the same MO as the Lynn Moody killing in Belfast.'

'There's also the blood group,' Marrianne pointed out.

'Yes, I haven't forgotten that.'

'There's one thing that puzzles me,' she said.

'What's that?' enquired Tyler.

'Kane's psychological profile indicates that he kills the girls as a prelude to an assassination for the IRA. Therefore, if he's followed that pattern in this case, he must have been involved in at least three other killings.'

Tyler nodded. He looked at Kane's file before answering. 'Kane entered the country illegally through Canada. He had false identity documents. We only discovered him by luck. One of our agents spotted him in a bar on the west side called Paddy's Place. He recognized him from an intelligence circular sent to us by the RUC.' He thought for a second. 'I think we'll go over there and ask a few questions.'

'OK,' Marrianne said, 'let's go.' She half stood up.

'Just a second,' Tyler said, holding up a restraining hand. 'It's in a very rough neighbourhood – we're going to need some back-up.' He pressed a button on the office intercom. 'Do you know where Agent Baxter is?'

'I believe he's in the gym sir,' his secretary answered.

'Can you get him for me?' He looked at Marrianne and smiled. 'You'll like Baxter.'

There was a lot of Special Agent Baxter to like. Standing at just under 6'3" tall in his stockinged feet he weighed in at around 220 lbs – and none of it was fat! In college he had played running back – his coach describing him as the next Walter Patton. Instead the black athlete studied law, graduating from Law School with honours. He had been offered the chance to join one of Boston's most prestigious law firms but instead he joined the FBI, graduating third in a class of a hundred and thirty.

Tyler introduced Baxter to Marrianne and briefly outlined their plans. 'I want you to drift into the bar ahead of us, Leon. Don't get involved unless we need you.'

Baxter nodded. 'Paddy's Place,' he mused. 'That will probably mean the Westsiders.'

'Who are the Westsiders?' asked Marrianne.

Getting up Tyler replied, 'I'll tell you in the car.' During the drive across town Tyler outlined the history of the Westsiders. 'They started off twenty years ago as just another Boston street gang. They still have a youth gang called the Shamrocks. In the early 70s they started to graduate to more serious things – racketeering and drug running. It wasn't long before they had eliminated every other street gang and effectively controlled the streets on the west side – hence the name Westsiders.

'In the 80s their sphere of influence had extended so much it brought them into conflict with our local branch of the Cosa Nostra. A vicious gang war broke out between them in 1986. Nobody gave the Westsiders a chance against the Sicillians. At first everything went the Mafia's way and the Westsiders suffered badly. It wasn't that they lacked men, guns or guts. It was just that the Mafia were more experienced and better at fighting the sort of all out war they were in.

'Gradually, however, the tide changed. In 1988 the West-siders managed to kill the Mafia's top hitter, Joe "The Animal" Bassario. From then on it was all one way traffic. The war was effectively ended when they nailed the local Capo, "Big Paul Castellano". Now they control everything on the west side – drugs, unions, prostitution, racketeering, loan sharking – everything.'

They pulled up outside Paddy's Place. Tyler looked at Marrianne. 'And this bar is one of their favourite hangouts, so let's be careful,' he said seriously.

Paddy's Place was surprisingly clean and well furnished, its walls decorated with Irish memorabilia. Marrianne noted Baxter sitting quietly at the bar sipping a beer. Tyler showed his identification to the barman. 'I want to see Heavy,' he said.

The barman nodded without replying and moved off. Tyler guided Marrianne to a vacant corner table. Presently the owner of the bar, Heavy Doyle, joined them. Marrianne's flesh crawled as the fat man undressed her with his eyes. 'Waddaya want?' he enquired after checking Tyler's identification.

'It's about a man who worked in this bar. You knew him as Sean Hall. His real name is Anthony Kane and he is in the IRA,' Tyler said.

'I been through all this before with you Feds, and the people from Immigration. I'll tell you what I told them. He had a green card – I thought he was legit!' Doyle protested.

'I know all about that Doyle. What we want to know is who he was friendly with – what did he do in his spare time?' asked the FBI man.

Heavy Doyle spread his fat arms. 'What am I – his keeper? Look, he turned up for work, he served drinks, I paid him. That's all I know and all I want to know.'

As he spoke Doyle's eyes continually darted towards a nearby table where three youths sat, obviously interested in what Doyle was saying. They wore green jackets emblazoned with gold shamrocks. Tyler followed the bar owner's gaze. Dropping his voice he said, 'Listen Heavy, if I don't get some co-operation I might take it into my head to get the IRS to have a check through your records. Now you wouldn't want that would you?'

Doyle stood up quickly. 'You do what you want!' he spat angrily. 'I've got nothing to say to you.' He stormed off towards the bar.

Tyler turned to Marrianne. 'He's scared but I don't think we'll get anything out of him.'

Marrianne nodded then sat upright in her chair. The look on her face made Tyler look quickly around. The three youths were coming towards their table. A squat powerfully built youth with cropped hair and a gold earring in his left ear swaggered up to them. He placed both hands flat on the table top, openly leering at Marrianne, and said to Tyler, 'You seem to be giving our friend Heavy a hard time Mister – what's your beef?'

Tyler showed him his FBI identification. 'You're mixing with the government boys – now why don't you back off?'

'That badge don't mean squat here.' He pushed his face closer to Tyler. 'What are you going to do if I take if off you and shove it up your ass?' he spat.

Tyler seemed to be taking the proposition seriously. He thought for a second and then said to the grinning youth, 'I don't suppose I would do anything, but Mr Baxter might.'

'Who the fuck is Baxter?' the youth said. He felt a tap on his shoulder and turned. His eyes were just about level with Leon's chest. He slowly looked up into the sombre black face. Leon grabbed him by the front of his jacket with one hand. With seemingly effortless ease he lifted him single handedly until his eyes were level with the youth's. The other two youths saw their leader visibly gulp.

'I'm Mr Baxter,' Leon said. 'Don't you have somewhere else to go?' The youth nodded vigorously. Baxter replaced him on the floor. Slowly all three of them backed away from the table.

They left the bar, Leon bringing up the rear. As they walked into the afternoon air Marrianne said, 'You know Henry, you're right – I do like Mr Baxter.'

All three of them adjourned to a nearby coffee house for a counsel of war. Over a coffee Tyler said, 'I don't think it would be any good putting more pressure on Heavy – he's too scared to talk.'

'What do you think he's scared of?'

'Who knows. There's a strong Irish population in this part of the town. Half the Westsiders are of Irish descent. Maybe Kane made some friends who are putting the arm on him,' he shrugged.

'Well what do we do now?' asked Marrianne.

'We find somebody who's more scared of us than he is of them. Trouble is – who?' Tyler mused.

'What about Manny Scheler?' asked Baxter, speaking for the first time.

Tyler smiled and nodded. 'He's a loan shark for the West-siders. He knows everything that goes on in this part of town, but more importantly we know something about him – don't we Leon?'

Baxter nodded and flashed a broad grin at Marrianne. 'That we certainly do,' he said.

Manny Scheler's office had none of the charm of Paddy's Place. It was a run down office in a run down part of the town. The two storey tenement in which it was housed was littered with decaying garbage. Just being in the building made Marrianne feel dirty. Walking up the rickety steps to Scheler's office they were confronted by a heavy set man in a dark crumpled suit. 'Yeah, can I help you?' he asked, his eyes going to all three in turn.

'I want to see Manny,' Tyler said.

'Mr Scheler doesn't see anybody without an appointment,' the man said. Tyler showed him his badge. 'You got a warrant or something?' the man asked.

'No,' replied Tyler.

'Then you still need an appointment,' the man said, a note of triumph in his voice.

Tyler pursed his lips. 'I don't need an appointment – I've got a Baxter.'

Scheler's face was livid when they walked into his office. A small man with a completely shaved head, he hopped from foot to foot with anger. It did not abate after Tyler showed him his badge. 'I'll have your badge for this Tyler. Harassment, illegal entry, trespass – I'll see they kick you and your trained gorilla out,' he shouted.

'Sit down Manny, this is a social call,' Tyler said. Baxter put a huge hand on the loan shark's shoulder and lowered him into the chair. His face now bright red, the small man said, 'You won't get away with this.'

'Won't get away with what?' Tyler asked, spreading his arms in a gesture of innocence. 'Listen Manny, I want to tell you a story.'

'I don't want to hear it,' interrupted Scheler.

'Oh yes you do,' Tyler said. 'Like all good stories it starts . . . in the beginning there was an industrious little loan shark and money launderer called Manny. He worked very hard for his bosses. So hard in fact that they gave him the whole loan shark franchise on the west side. What they didn't know, however, was that he was ripping them off.' Tyler's voice lost its mocking tone. 'We know about your bank account in the Cayman Islands, Manny. By our reckoning you've ripped off the Westsiders by more than a million dollars in the last five years! If they find out, there won't be a hole deep enough for you to hide in.'

Scheler's face was ashen. 'You wouldn't tell them. You're Feds, you're supposed to protect people,' he said.

Tyler smiled at the little man. 'I might not, but this little lady is a civilian and she might if you don't tell us what we want to know.'

Scheler dropped his head into his hands. Without looking up he said, 'OK, OK. What do you want to know?'

'I want to know everything about a man called Sean Hall. He used to work at Paddy's Place.'

'You mean Kane?' Scheler said looking up.

'How did you know his real name?' Tyler said abruptly.

'They'll kill me if they find out,' he moaned.

'They'll kill you if they find out you've been ripping them off. Talk,' Tyler ordered, raising his voice.

Rolling his head in his hands the little Shylock said in a beaten voice, 'OK. I'll tell you everything.'

☆      ☆      ☆

Paddy's Place, Boston, February 1988.

'These OK for you Sean?' Archie Hamilton asked. The Westsider's eyes followed every movement as the man he knew as Sean Hall broke down the Ingram M10 machine gun. Despite never having used this type of weapon before it took Kane less than a minute to take it apart and put it back together again. His hands moved with the practised precision of a trained soldier. 'It's fine,' he said without looking up.

Beside the Ingram on the table lay an M16 rifle with a Browning pistol. Supplying Kane with the weapons he needed to kill the informant Brian Doherty had been part of the deal the IRA had struck with the Westsiders. Archie watched fascinated as the Irishman then checked the Armalite and pistol, his hands moving like they had a mind of their own. Despite being the Westsider's top enforcer and brother of the gang's boss, Carl Hamilton, Archie was awed by the big Mick.

'You must be a real heavy hitter back where you come from,' he said.

Kane did not answer, busy checking his weapons. 'How many guys you bump off in Ireland?' he asked, his voice rising with excitement. 'Five ... ten?' Kane still did not reply. Archie's voice dropped to a confidential level. 'Come on. You can tell me. More than ten?' he asked.

Kane stood up and walked over to the gangster. His face only inches from Hamilton's he spoke in a voice as cold as ice. 'My people pay you to supply me with weapons, identity documents and a cover, not to ask me questions – do I make myself clear?'

The menace in Kane's voice chilled Hamilton's blood. He threw both hands up in a gesture of supplication. 'OK, OK. No offence meant,' he spoke quietly. 'Jesus H Christ I'm only trying to be friendly.'

Kane made no reply only continuing to stare at Hamilton. 'Well I gotta go,' the enforcer said, fighting to keep his voice under control and appear unaffected. 'If there's anything you need, anything at all, just ask Heavy, the bar owner. He'll get it for you.'

Kane said nothing but turned and went back to his weapons. Archie left the back room. Putting his back to the door he drew a handkerchief and mopped his brow. He looked at his hand and found it was shaking. He walked to the bar and jerked his head to Heavy. The fat man hurried over. 'I want to use the phone,' Archie said.

'Sure Archie,' Heavy replied and produced the phone from beneath the counter. Hamilton dialled a number from memory. It took eight rings before a voice said, half asleep, 'Hello.'

'Uncle Pat, it's Archie. How are you?'

'Archie – you know what fucking time it is?' the voice replied angrily.

'Never mind that – there's something I want you to do for me ... you got a pen?'

☆　　☆　　☆

'The bastards,' Carl Hamilton screamed, storming round his penthouse apartment in fury. Watching, his right hand man and adviser Phil Diamond let him blow off some steam. He'd just told him two of their best men had been found in Boston Harbour, shot in the head, their balls shoved in their mouths – a traditional Mafia killing.

'It's that bastard Bassario,' Diamond said when Hamilton had calmed down. 'I'll tell you this Carl, if we don't get that mother fucker he's going to fix us all.'

Carl sat down opposite him. 'I know, I know. I'm working on it but the last time we tried to hit him we got chewed up.'

Diamond nodded. He thought to himself, 'Yeah, you're working on it but you're not out on the street. You're up here in a penthouse with six fucking bodyguards.' Out loud he said, 'We gotta do something Carl. The boys are starting to get real jumpy.'

Carl nodded and looked around the room. 'Where the fuck is Archie?' he asked. 'He should be here.'

Diamond shrugged. 'I don't know. He's been acting strange for the last two days – making a lot of phone calls to Europe – I don't know what he's up to.'

As if on cue the private lift arrived and Archie stepped out. Behind him were two of Carl's bodyguards. 'Hi ya big brother,' he beamed, looking pleased with himself. He sat down next to Diamond and smiled at his elder brother.

'You heard the news about our two boys in the harbour?' Carl asked.

'Yeah. One of the boys told me in the lift.'

'Then what are you so pleased about?' Carl exploded. 'You won the lottery or something?'

'Better than that. I got the answer to all our problems,' he said grinning broadly at both men.

'Well what is this – twenty questions?' Carl said angrily throwing his arms wide. 'Tell me.'

'You want to get rid of Bassario, right?' Archie asked. He held up a hand to prevent Carl's angry outburst. 'I know the guy who can do it.'

'Who?' both Carl and Diamond said at once.

'Kane,' Archie said triumphantly.

'Who the fuck is Kane?' Carl said, his voice rising.

'You know him as Sean Hall,' Archie answered.

'The guy over at Heavy's place we're hiding for the Micks?' Diamond said.

171

Archie stood up excitedly. 'Yeah, that's him. Now before you both say anything, listen.' He looked from Diamond to Carl and back. 'I checked up on him with Uncle Pat over in Dublin. He's well connected. He's the IRA's best hitter. According to Uncle Pat he never misses. He's a fucking legend over there. Christ he's killed twenty cops and soldiers – he's a real pro.'

Carl and Diamond looked at each other and then at Archie. 'OK wise guy,' Carl said sarcastically, 'suppose what you say is right. How do we get him to ice Bassario? I know these Mick terrorists – he won't work for money.'

Archie smiled in triumph. 'He'll do it because his bosses will tell him to,' he said.

'And why would they do that?' Carl asked, suddenly very curious.

'Because,' Archie said, 'we got something to trade!'

Micky Fennel was a third generation American, but proud of his Irish roots. He regularly marched in the traditional St Patrick's Day Parades and was a prominent fund raiser for all matters Irish. As a lawyer he successfully lobbied Congress into banning all arms sales to the Royal Ulster Constabulary. This was well known to the general public. What was not so well known was that he ran the Provisional IRA's American network.

He stared angrily at Carl and Archie Hamilton. Behind them Phil Diamond leaned against the office wall, casually menacing. 'I don't know how you found out Kane's real name,' Fennel said angrily, his fingers tapping the desk top as he spoke. 'But this absurd idea of having Kane . . .' Fennel paused searching for the word Carl had used. 'To hit, I believe you said, some Mafia killer for you is out of the question. Volunteers in the Irish Republican Army do not get mixed up in petty gang wars.'

Carl looked at Archie and then smiled at the Boston lawyer. 'Not even for twenty Red Eye surface to air missiles?' he asked.

Fennel sat bolt upright in his chair. 'Have you got them?' he asked.

'Yes, replied Carl. It was our guys who hit that National

172

Guard armoury two months ago. We didn't know what they were when we stole them, we were just after guns. But from what I hear, you guys really want them bad. Do we deal?' he asked.

☆　　☆　　☆

Kane didn't like it and said so. 'I'm a soldier, not a gangster,' he shouted angrily at Fennel.

'I know, my boy, I know. But war makes strange bedfellows,' he sighed. 'I don't like it anymore than you, but this has come straight from the high command.' He placed a hand on Kane's shoulder and dropped his voice. 'They really want those missiles Kane. This is as important as finding Doherty.'

Kane said nothing for a while then looked over Fennel's shoulder to the waiting Carl and Archie Hamilton. 'OK,' he said. 'Who do you want killed?'

☆　　☆　　☆

It had taken Kane six weeks to set up Bassario. The Mafia mobster was extremely careful, never going anywhere without a screen of personal bodyguards. During that time he had organized his own ASU along the lines of the IRA. He wanted and got four new recruits into the Westsiders, schooling them in terrorist tactics and weapons. He also got the Hamiltons to stop all attacks on their opposition. 'I want them to think you're beaten,' he told Carl Hamilton. 'Start negotiations through a third party. It will make them careless. There's nothing easier to kill than an over-confident enemy.'

It had not been easy but the Hamiltons managed to restrain their men. Swaggering Mafia button men openly walked into Westsiders bars, boasting they had the Irish gang beaten. The Westsiders took it and waited. Kane's young recruits watched Bassario, never getting too close, trying to spot a pattern. Eventually they found one. The notorious hit man had a weakness for the spaghetti bolognese served in a small Italian restaurant on the east side of Boston . . . as well as a soft spot for one of its waitresses. Every second Wednesday in the month his wife would visit her mother. Bassario would take the opportunity to sample the bolognese – and the waitress.

173

'Let's go through it once more OK?' Kane said to the three youths sitting beside him in the car. Their faces clearly showed their fear. 'Amateurs,' Kane thought and shook his head. He went on, 'Bassario has four men with him – two at the front who check everybody coming into the restaurant, and two in the kitchen, OK?' The three youths nodded without replying. Kane went on, 'I go in alone and walk up to Bassario. Once I shoot him you two . . .' he pointed at the two youths in the back seat, '. . . Timmy and Mike, come in fast. I'm counting on you to shoot the two bodyguards at the door and to cover me as I run back in case the two goons in the kitchen come out. Remember, if you see the kitchen door start to open, blast it, OK? Don't wait to see who's there – just open fire – right?' The two youths nodded. One carried an M16 and the other a pump action shotgun.

'Tommy, when you see Timmy and Mike start to open fire you drive the car up to the front of the restaurant. Be fast and be ready to get out of here in a hurry. We'll be coming out a lot quicker than we went in – OK?' The driver nodded his head quickly in reply.

'OK you two, out you get. Make sure you keep your guns under your coats and don't for God's sake get seen from the restaurant until I go in or you'll blow the whole thing.'

The two youths got out. Alone with the driver Kane checked the Browning high power automatic he carried, making sure its action worked and checked the magazine for spring. Satisfied he cocked it and shoved it in its holster. 'We were all looking for you today Sean,' the driver said. 'Christ, Carl and Phil thought you had run off or something when you disappeared like you did. Where'd you go?'

In the darkness of the car he failed to see the faint flicker of a smile pass across Kane's face. 'I had something personal to attend to,' he replied. Kane checked his watch. 'It's time,' he said. Stepping out of the car he stripped off his overcoat and threw it in the rear. Putting on his hat he walked towards the restaurant.

'Ah Maria you make the best bolognese sauce in the whole world,' Bassario said smacking his lips loudly in appreciation. Beside him the pretty waitress giggled, studying the diamond ring he had given her to show just how much he appreciated her talents. Bassario dropped his hand beneath the table and

174

cupped her firm thigh. Lowering his voice he whispered coarsely, 'It's not the only thing you do best in the world, eh Maria.' She giggled even more, shooting him a look of open invitation.

In front of him, near the entrance, his two bodyguards stiffened as the door opened. They relaxed when they saw it was a cop. 'Who owns the car outside?' he drawled, his voice Irish Bostonian.

One of the bodyguards jerked his head towards Bassario. 'It's the boss's car but I wouldn't bother him – not if you want to keep your badge,' he replied with a mocking grin.

Giving the gunman a withering stare the policeman walked the length of the restaurant to Bassario's table. Bassario looked up as he approached the table, his cruel eyes holding a look of contempt. 'You own the car outside?' he asked.

'Get lost pizzano – I own your captain,' Bassario said with a flick of his hand, hardly glancing at him.

'Your name Bassario?' asked the cop.

'That's right,' Bassario said, looking up and staring into the eyes of the cop. He felt one brief wave of fear as he looked into the coldest pair of eyes he had ever seen. Then with practised speed Kane drew the Browning and shot him twice in the forehead. The mobster's head fell forward into the spaghetti bolognese he loved so much.

Kane pivoted fast holding the Browning in two hands. Behind him Maria was screaming hysterically. The two body-guards by the door were on their feet, one drawing a sawn-off pump action shotgun from under his coat, the other an automatic pistol. Kane went for the shotgun knowing he would never get both in time. He fired three times in quick succession. All three hit the shotgun holder in the chest as he brought up the weapon, knocking him backwards.

The entrance door burst open. The second bodyguard spun round as Mike burst in carrying the M16, giving Kane enough time to alter his aim and fire again. Two shots – the gangster's head exploded like an over-ripe watermelon. Kane ran for the exit. Behind he heard the kitchen door open. 'Fire FUCK YOU, FIRE!' he shouted at Mike. The Westsider opened up, the M16 spraying the kitchen door. Kane burst out into the street almost knocking over Timmy still standing outside. He grabbed him and threw him into the waiting car. Behind him he heard Mike's M16 stop firing and pivoted round. 'Move it – get the hell out of there Mike,' he shouted.

The Westsider stumbled out of the restaurant entrance, fumbling with the magazine of his M16. Shots rang out from inside, almost hitting Kane. He fired back, emptying the Browning one handed. The other hand pushed Mike into the car. Kane turned and dived into the back seat on top of the other two Westsider gunmen as the car sped off at full speed.

'Great. Fucking A-one great,' Carl Hamilton said, pouring champagne into glasses held by Phil Diamond and Archie Hamilton. He looked over his shoulder at Kane. 'You're as good as they say you are buddy,' he said.

Archie, his glass filled, weaved his way to a sitting Kane. The IRA gunman had said nothing since he had returned to the back room of Paddy's Place. 'Come on, buddy, join the party! Have a drink,' Archie said drunkenly.

Kane reacted with frightening speed. Levering himself out of the chair he brushed aside the startled Archie. Before anyone could stop him he picked up Timmy by the throat and slammed him into a wall. 'Where were you?' he said, repeatedly hitting Timmy on the wall. 'I almost got wasted because of you. Why weren't you with Mike coming through the door?' Although clearly angry Kane's voice still sounded quiet and calm, almost as if he was discussing the weather.

Mike grabbed Kane's arm as Timmy's face turned white, then red, for lack of air. 'Let him go Kane for Christ's sake – you'll kill him,' Mike pleaded tearing at his arm.

Kane dropped the semi-conscious youth. He dropped his elbow as Mike pulled the arm back. Using this leverage he thrust in and up with the elbow driving it with incredible force into Mike's solar plexus. Air exploded out of his mouth and he crumpled on to the floor next to Timmy. Kane squatted down beside them. 'Now listen to what I have to tell you,' he said in a voice as calm as a village pond, 'when I tell you to do something you had better do it. The only reason I don't kill you is that I would have to train somebody else and I have more important things to do. But gentlemen – believe me when I say this. If you screw up again then nothing will stop me from blowing the pair of you away. Understood?'

Neither was in a fit state to reply and Kane turned to an open mouthed Carl Hamilton. 'Amateurs. They nearly got me

176

killed. Instead of drinking that you should be considering your next move.'

'Like what?' a still startled Hamilton asked.

Kane sighed and spoke slowly as if he was explaining something difficult to a child. 'Like the Sicillians are going to want to hit back at you fast. You've killed their best shooter – they'll want revenge. A smart man could use that to his advantage.'

'How?' Carl Hamilton asked, his voice betraying both curiosity and respect.

Kane looked at Archie Hamilton and smiled a totally humourless smile. 'Offer them a target,' he said.

☆    ☆    ☆

'I tell you it's a cinch boss,' Vito Mazzerella, Bassario's replacement said. 'My boys have been tailing him for a week.'

In the four weeks following Bassario's killing Paul Castellano's mobsters had been continually scouring the west side seeking a target for retribution. Now at last they had found one – Archie Hamilton, the chief enforcer for the Westsiders and brother of its leader. The upstart Irish gang would be taught a lesson they would never forget. 'He visits the broad every Tuesday?' Paul Castellano asked.

'Right. It's an apartment block. It's got an underground car park. It's perfect for us,' Mazzerella said. 'He arrives at the same time every Tuesday but leaves at different times, so it's best to hit him on the way in.'

Big Paul Castellano smiled his agreement. 'OK set it up. Let's show these punks who really runs this town.'

'It's on for tonight Kane,' Phil Diamond said over the phone.

'You're sure?' Kane asked.

'Positive. We trailed Mazzerella to a flat in the east side. Three of his top hoods just drove up. I checked the car with a friend down town – it's hot. Looks like they're going to try and hit Archie tonight.'

Kane thought for a moment. 'OK. Tell Tommy to get the truck and load up the boys. I'll meet them in the car park at 7 pm.' There was silence on the other end.

'You're not going to travel with them?' Phil asked in

surprise.

'No. I'll make my own way there. Tell Archie to drive in promptly at 8 pm OK?'

'Sure Kane. I'll pass it on,' Phil said.

☆     ☆     ☆

Tuesday 5 pm, Carl Hamilton's apartment.

'It's OK for you to say everything will be all right,' Archie Hamilton said, walking angrily up and down the room. He took a gulp of whiskey. 'It's not you with your neck out.'

Carl Hamilton sat on the sofa watching his pacing brother. 'Don't worry,' he said, 'Kane and his boys will be there.'

Archie stopped pacing and stuck his face closer to his elder brother's. 'And what happens if they hit me outside the fucking car park? Answer me that,' he shouted in his face.

Carl smiled to placate his younger brother. 'Kane says the guineas are pros. They won't try anything in the street – too many people and cars. They'll try to hit you in the car park.'

'Kane says this, Kane says that. I've had that big Mick up to here,' Archie made a chopping motion against his neck with the edge of his hand. 'Where the fuck is the son of a bitch anyway?' he asked.

Carl stood up and put a soothing arm round Archie's shoulder. 'He likes to go away on his own before a job. You know, sort of get himself in the mood. Don't worry – he'll be there.'

☆     ☆     ☆

5.30 pm, Tuesday, West Side of Boston.

Ring! Ring! Ring! 'OK I'm coming,' she called and hurried to the door. She checked through the peep hole. A surprised look crossed her face when she saw the figure of a police officer standing in the hall. She opened the door. 'Yes?' she said.

'Maureen Kelly?' the officer asked.

'That's right,' Maureen replied.

'We've had a complaint about malicious phone calls being made to residents of this building. Have you had any such calls?' he asked, his voice a pleasant Irish American.

178

Maureen shook her head. 'No, thank God, I haven't,' she replied.

He tipped his hat and smiled. 'Well in that case I won't bother you anymore. If you do receive any calls please don't hesitate to contact us.' He turned as if to leave, then looked back. 'I couldn't use your phone?' he asked. 'Our radio isn't working and I want to check in with the station.'

'Sure come on in,' Maureen said, turning. She led him into the apartment and heard him close the door. 'The phone's in here . . . .' The words were choked off as he grabbed her from behind. She felt a knife pressed against her throat.

'Don't scream, don't struggle and I won't hurt you,' a voice as cold as ice said.

She relaxed, going limp in his arms. He spun her round to face him. Using the impetus of his turn she launched a forward punch. It struck the uniformed man just above the heart. Taken by surprise he lost his grip on her. She stepped back and tried a snap kick for his groin but caught him high on the thigh instead. The leg nearly buckled and he lost his grip on the knife as he held on to it with his right hand.

Keeping up the attack she threw a throat punch. Too high, it struck him on the chin. She stepped back and took up a classic karate pose. 'Not so easy is it,' she breathed through clenched teeth. 'You're going to have to fight for it big man and I'm a black belt.'

She circled him, trying to edge for the door. He cut her off and started to close with her. Instead of backing away she stepped towards him and threw two forward punches. She connected with the right but he caught the left between his right arm and body. As she tried to pull it free he launched a vicious short uppercut which hit her flush on the jaw. He released her left arm. Only semi-conscious she tried to fend him off with her right arm. He threw a violent right cross which smashed into her left cheek and jaw, breaking both. She slumped to the floor. He stood above her motionless body, breathing heavily. Then he went and picked up the knife.

☆    ☆    ☆

7.30 pm, Tuesday, basement garage.

His footsteps echoed in the emptiness of the subterranean

179

garage. Stopping at an unmarked panel van he looked right and left, then knocked on the side door. It opened to reveal Mike's worried face. 'Kane! Thank fuck. We thought you weren't coming. What kept you?' he asked in a low worried voice.

'I got delayed,' Kane said calmly and got in. Mike handed him an M16 and he checked it. 'Everybody set,' he asked in the darkness. There was a chorus of whispered yeses. 'Fine. Let's hope Archie's on time,' Kane said.

Archie drove his convertible towards the apartment block. His heart leapt as the entrance of the garage loomed in front of him. He almost went past it but, summoning up reserves of courage, he turned into the dark entrance. Across the street Mazzerella said, 'That's him, let's go!'

His driver turned the four door sedan across the street. Inside Mazzerella took the safety catch off the Remington pump action shotgun he held. In the rear his two best men, similarly armed, did likewise. Archie parked his car next to the van. Getting out fast he started to walk towards the service lift. Behind him there was a screech of brakes. Mazzerella's car roared into the garage, squealing to a halt in front of the petrified man. The doors swung open and Mazzerella and his men started to pile out.

The two back doors of the panel van swung open. Kane, Mike and Timmy knelt, M16s levelled. A shattering burst of gunfire erupted from the back of the van. Mazzerella's car practically disintegrated under the fusillade, the mobster and his cohorts riddled by a withering sheet of lead. In the silence that followed the mayhem Kane shouted to Archie, 'Over here! Move man – we haven't got all day.'

The words stung the paralysed man into movement. He stumbled to the rear of the van and Kane pulled him in. Swiftly Tommy reversed and roared out of the car park. Outside the street lights threw shadows across the faces of the men in its rear. Kane opened his overcoat. 'Why have you got a cop's uniform on again?' Mike asked.

Kane's face was expressionless in the darkness. 'I thought it might come in handy,' he replied. Mike and his friends were impressed – Kane was always one step ahead of them.

☆    ☆    ☆

Carl Hamilton's penthouse, 12.00 noon, next day.

'Have you seen the paper boys?' Phil Diamond said, handing the *Boston Times* to Carl. Its banner headline read, 'FOUR KILLED IN RENEWED GANG WAR'.

'Yeah – fucking great. We got them on the run now. Hey, did you see this? A girl was murdered in the same block. Lucky her body wasn't found until the next day or Kane and our boys would have run into a mass of cops.'

Diamond sipped a cup of coffee by the bar. 'Yeah, real lucky,' he said thoughtfully.

In the four months following Mazzerella's death Castellano's family were savagely mauled by the Westsider's gang. An appeal to the organization's commission for assistance had been bluntly rejected. Castellano had started the war against their wishes – it was up to him to end it, they had stated. Castellano himself became a virtual prisoner in his two storey east side mansion, surrounded by an army of security men. With hope of military victory all but gone, he used the church as a mediator, trying to get some kind of deal set up with the Hamiltons. 'What do you mean Father, they don't want to negotiate?' Castellano said to Father Bonneti.

The small Italian priest shrugged his shoulders in a gesture of despair. 'I'm sorry Mr Castellano but Carl Hamilton said he sees no need to talk or compromise with you. I can do no more my son.'

He took the small man's hand in his and kissed it. 'You did your best Father. I could ask no more. Please say a mass for me.'

Father Bonneti smiled and nodded, patting Paul Castellano's hand. 'I will, my son, I will. You will be in my prayers.'

With the priest gone he turned to his long-time bodyguard, Jonny Rico and said, 'So they won't negotiate and the commission won't help.'

Rico, a huge hulking man, said, 'What are you going to do now Mr Castellano?' concern obvious in his voice.

Castellano walked to the open window. With his back to

Rico he said, 'I've been in touch with the Cleveland mob. They're willing to help – at a price.' He sighed and shook his head. 'They're animals. They want my whole waterfront operation.' He threw his arms wide as if to embrace the sky. 'But what can I do? I'm a desperate man!'

'You should maybe stay away from the window Mr Castellano,' Rico said, voicing his fear for his boss.

Castellano glanced over his shoulder and smiled. 'Nonsense Rico. The grounds are full of men and it's three hundred metres to the perimeter fence.' He took a deep breath. 'Ah, it's a fine morning.'

Four hundred metres away Kane sighted down the telescopic sight of the Woodmaster hunting rifle. From the low hill he was on he had a clear view of his target. Adjusting his aim slightly to allow for the slight breeze he fired. Castellano was enjoying the morning air as the .30 calibre soft lead bullet smashed into the bridge of his nose. Kane dropped the Woodmaster and ran the hundred metres across country to where his getaway car was parked. Opening the passenger door he jumped inside. 'OK Tommy – it's done. Let's go.'

Turning to the driver he was surprised to see Phil Diamond sitting by the wheel, a Colt .45 automatic in his hand. 'Hello Kane,' he said without any warmth. 'I've been waiting for you.'

'Where's Tommy?' Kane asked.

'I sent him home. Told him I wanted to drive you.' He looked Kane directly in the eye. 'I know Kane,' he said.

'Know what?'

Diamond shook his head smiling. 'About the girls. I followed you this morning. I saw you kill that nurse outside the hospital. Don't try and act innocent.'

Kane said nothing, just stared at Diamond, who, despite holding the gun, felt uneasy next to the killer. Finally Kane broke the silence. 'What are you going to do?'

'Why, kill you of course. You make my flesh crawl, creepo. I'm going to blow you away, then tell Carl and Archie – I'll be a hero.'

Diamond brought the Colt up level with Kane's head. Outside there was a squeal of brakes as a car skidded to a halt twenty metres away. Diamond's head flashed round to look. Two of Rico's security guards were firing at Kane's car. One hit Diamond in the shoulder spinning him half around in his seat. Kane grasped the .45. Kicking open the passenger door he rolled outside. Kneeling outside the car he looked back at Diamond. There was a lull in the firing. Diamond's frightened face turned towards him. 'If you're going to shoot, shoot,' Kane said quietly and fired twice with the .45. Both shots hit Diamond in the head. Keeping low and using the car as cover he ran for the nearby woods.

☆    ☆    ☆

Boston, Manny Scheler's office.

'So,' said Tyler, 'it was Kane who killed Bassario and Big Paul.'

'Yeah, that's right,' Scheler said. 'Carl Hamilton offered him a fortune to work for him but he turned it down. Christ he was some real bad dude.'

'Worse than you will ever know,' Marrianne said.

They drove back to the federal building in silence, each busy with their own thoughts. Tyler had radioed ahead and Hastings was waiting for them. It took just seconds to cross-check. 'It all fits. Each of the prowler killings coincides with one of Kane's,' Baxter said.

'If you check the details of the girl's background I'll lay money they were all of Irish Protestant descent,' said Marrianne.

The FBI chief looked at her. 'I think we'll be wanting a word with your Mr Kane,' he said.

'It could take some time,' Marrianne replied. 'I think the RUC have a prior claim. Those Hamiltons have a lot to answer for.'

'Only one of them left to answer for anything.' Marrianne looked questioningly at Baxter. 'Archie Hamilton was blown up in a car bomb about three months ago.'

# 7

---

Dublin, Shannon Airport, Tuesday 10 am.

Chief Inspector John Flanagan was waiting for Bill as he passed through security. 'Well, well – 'tis the famous Special Branch man from the RUC,' he said.

Bill gave him a disapproving look. 'You can cut that out for a start,' he said, his voice stern.

'Now what would that be?' Flanagan asked in mock serious-ness – throwing his arms wide. The small Irish SB man was a picture of hurt innocence.

'The thick Paddy act,' Bill said poking his southern Irish counterpart in the chest with an outraged finger. 'Save it for the tourists.'

The Irishman held the look of injured pride for a few seconds more, then burst out laughing. 'OK, OK. I have to get some practice in you know.' Still laughing, he led Bill to his waiting car. As he turned onto the main Dublin Road he said, 'Well now, tell me what was so important you couldn't say anything over the phone.'

Bill looked out of the side window. 'If you don't mind, Flan I'd rather wait till we get to your office.' The tone of his voice made Flanagan flash a concerned look in his direction.

'That bad,' he said.

Bill nodded without replying. They drove in silence for a while, each absorbed with their own thoughts. Bill broke the silence. 'How are things with the Garda anyway?' he asked to relieve the tension he felt.

'Not so good,' Flanagan replied. 'Underpaid, undermanned and overworked. Things are particularly bad in Dublin. We have a real drug problem here,' he said, shaking his head sadly.

'Thank God that's one problem we don't have in the North,'

Bill commented.

Flanagan nodded and went on, 'We never used to have one until early in the 80s. Our local drug barons, the Dunns, only pushed marijuana and pills. That was bad enough but we could contain it with our resources.

'Then in 1981 a Yank came to work for the Dunns – man by the name of Pat Hamilton. He had a dual Irish and American nationality so we couldn't deport him. He brought in a consignment of heroin from the States. Provos shot him last year – probably as a warning to the Dunns.

'At first the Dunns couldn't offload the drugs – their customers were happy smoking grass and popping pills. But the Dunns were nothing if not enterprising and decided to give it away to regular customers free and for gratis.'

Flanagan shook his head and glanced at Bill. 'In effect they created their own market. When the customers came back for more they had to pay. Gradually the price went up and up. Now we have one of the worst drug problems in Europe and everything that goes with it – crime, junkies holding up shops and banks to get money to pay for drugs, health problems, AIDS, hepatitis, everything. Oh yes, the Dunns really put Dublin on the map all right.'

He was silent for a while, lost in thought, then went on, 'Apart from that, our main problem is Republicans robbing banks to finance their operations north of the border. They grossed two million pounds alone last year. It's crippling our banks, but I'm sure you don't need me to tell you that, do I?' Bill smiled in agreement. They passed the rest of the journey swapping stories about work and mutual friends and enemies. Arriving at Dublin Castle Flanagan led Bill to Special Branch offices on the second floor. Opening the door to his small but comfortable office he let Bill in.

'Now,' he said, settling himself behind his desk, 'what is it you want to tell me?'

Bill placed both hands under his nose, as if in an attitude of prayer. Gathering his thoughts he told Flanagan everything, omitting nothing. Flanagan rubbed his hand across his eyes, clearly disturbed by what Bill had said. Standing, he thrust his hands into his pockets and walked to the window. With his back to Bill he continually raised himself up on his tiptoes and then dropped his weight back down on his heels. He was lost in

185

thought, considering every detail of what the RUC man had told him. Eventually he turned and said, 'You realize the implications of what you've just told me?'

'I do,' Bill replied, 'and I realize what will happen in Belfast when this story breaks.'

'Is there anything you can do to minimise the damage?'

Bill shook his head sadly. 'Not really. I'll try, of course, but . . .' he shrugged his shoulders helplessly, '. . . I think it's going to be very bad.'

Flanagan pushed his hands deeper into his pockets and slowly walked back to the desk, his head down as if studying the carpet's pattern. He sat back down with a sigh. 'OK. What do you want from me?' he asked.

'First I want you to run a check on these dates.' He handed Flanagan a piece of paper. 'These are two dates when we know Kane was living in the south but actively involved in operations north of the border. Check and find out if you had any suspicious female deaths or homicides which coincide with them.'

Flanagan studied the paper briefly and then pressed the office intercom. 'Yes sir,' a female voice answered.

'Could you step in Mandy?' he said.

Mandy O'Flynn, an attractive dark haired woman stepped through the door. Flanagan handed the piece of paper to the Special Branch secretary. 'Take that up to records. Tell them it's from me, highest priority. I want to know if there were any suspicious female deaths on either of those dates, especially if rape or sexual attack was involved.'

Mandy glanced at the paper and nodded. As the door closed behind her Flanagan turned back to Bill. 'What else?'

'I want you to arrange for me to see Terrance Heeny in Portaise Prison,' Bill said.

Flanagan pursed his lips. 'That might be more difficult,' he said, standing up. 'I'll have to go and pull a few strings.'

Bill heard the door close behind him. Alone he picked up Kane's file and turned to the report on the Silverbridge shooting. Two RUC officers dead and one seriously injured. 'And they weren't even your intended targets, were they Kane?' he said aloud to the empty room.

☆    ☆    ☆

Silverbridge, 2 March 1987.

'What time is it?' McCartan asked.

Kane checked his watch. 'Two o'clock. Ten minutes after you last asked,' he said, his voice as calm as ever. 'You're going too fast,' Kane said as they entered the town centre. 'We don't have to be there until 3.30 – that's when the UDR man delivers the coal.'

McCartan smiled nervously at Kane. It was his first job. 'Sorry. I'm a little tight that's all.'

'Pull over,' Kane said, indicating a paper shop on the opposite side of the small main street. McCartan obediently did as he was told.

'Why have we stopped here?' he asked, his voice high and nervous.

Kane sighed deeply. 'Because we have time to kill and this is less suspicious than cruising around,' he said, looking around the nearly empty street. Turning to McCartan he went on, 'Now I'm going into the paper shop. Just sit here and relax.' A faint smile touched his lips. 'Try and look natural, OK?' McCartan nodded vigorously shaking his head. Kane got out and walked into the shop.

'I've run out of cigarettes,' Sergeant Logan said to his observer, Constable Andrews, from the rear seat of the un-marked RUC Granada.

'You smoke too much Skipper,' the driver, Constable McKee said, laughing. 'Those coffin nails will kill you!'

From the back Sergeant Logan replied in mock seriousness, 'Once I gave up smoking, drinking and chasing women. It was the longest two minutes of my life!'

They all laughed. Logan handed a five pound note to Andrews. 'Do your old sergeant a favour and get me a pack of Benson and Hedges, king size, will you? There's a shop in Silverbridge.'

McCartan was smoking a cigarette, taking the opportunity with Kane gone. The big man did not like people smoking in his presence. He glanced in the mirror and stiffened. A police car was driving up behind him. Logan noticed the car in front had a damaged rear light. 'Check the driver of that car out, Andy,' he said as Constable Andrews started to get out. 'If he's OK, warn him his back light is defective.'

Constable Andrews nodded and got out of the car.

Sweat broke out on McCartan's brow as he saw the uniformed man walking towards him. He had a short barrelled Smith and Wesson .33 revolver in his coat pocket but could not seem to make his shaking hands obey the order to draw it. Andrews knocked politely on the window. McCartan rolled it down. 'Something wrong officer?' he asked.

'No sir,' Andrews said, smiling. 'Just a routine check. Can you tell me your name and address please?'

'Dermot Coyle,' McCartan said, using the name of the ringer whose vehicle he was driving, '125 Ballantrain Road, Carrickmore, County Tyrone,' he continued, giving the address Kane had made him repeat over and over again.

'Thank you sir,' Andrews said. Stepping back he called in the details on his personal radio.

'I wish he'd hurry up, I'm dying for a fag,' Sergeant Logan said, watching Andrews inspecting the car. 'I didn't want him to be all day telling the driver he had a bloody defective tail light.'

McKee grinned at the big sergeant's impatience. 'He doesn't half get irritable when he wants a cigarette,' he thought.

'Tango 24 from base,' the controller came back.

'Tango 24 send, over,' Andrews answered.

'Reference your car check, it's a . . . '

Andrews was in the middle of writing down the controller's response when Kane walked down the store's steps, paper in hand. 'Base from Tango 24, wait,' Andrews said and then to Kane, 'I'll be with you in a minute sir.'

Kane looked at Andrews, head down writing, and then the two men sitting in the car, and back again. 'This is a piece of cake,' he thought to himself. Dropping the paper, he pulled a 9mm Browning from a shoulder holster under his coat and shot Andrews over the roof of the car.

Pivoting on the toe of his left foot and the heel of his right, Kane swung sharply towards Logan and McKee in the car. In the back seat Sergeant Logan tried to do two things at once – cock the Sterling sub-machine gun on his lap, and open the back door. He failed to do either. Kane fired four shots in quick succession – three hit the RUC sergeant in the chest and one in the head. In the front seat McKee tried frantically to free his revolver, hampered by the steering wheel and the two restraining straps holding it in its holster. He'd just got it free when Kane, altering his aim and adopting a classic combat stance, fired his remaining eight rounds in rapid fire. McKee was hit by six of them and slumped sideways across the front passenger seat. The back of his head was a gaping mess.

Kane pressed the Browning magazine release catch, allowing the empty magazine to fall free. He inserted a spare magazine, clicked the slide lever allowing it to go forward and, reloading, jumped into the car next to a shocked McCartan. 'Don't just sit there. Drive damn you, drive,' he shouted. Numbly McCartan started to obey his shouted command. Pushing down on the clutch he slammed the car into first gear.

Lying on the road Constable Andrews had been knocked semi-conscious. Sitting up and using his left arm to support his right he, with great difficulty, started to draw his Ruger revolver. McCartan stalled the car and looked with horror at the flickering red lights on the dash board. 'Put your foot on the clutch, depress it . . . that's it,' Kane spoke slowly as if to a child. 'No, don't take it out of gear. Now start it again.'

Andrews lifted the revolver with great difficulty. It seemed to weigh a ton. When he got it level with his shoulder he opened fire. McCartan realized rounds were hitting his side of the door. He took his foot off the clutch and the car jerked forward. As the car started to move away, Andrews emptied the revolver into the driver's door. The soft lead semi-jacketed rounds, designed to prevent ricochets, mushroomed on impact. Only one actually penetrated the door, missing McCartan's foot by less than an inch. The car sped off down Silverbridge High Street at full speed.

Andrews got slowly and painfully to his feet. Light headed and groggy he staggered towards the patrol car. He slumped over the car bonnet and looked inside. Sickened he reached into it and pulled out the radio handset. 'Contact, contact,' he shouted and gave a quick contact report.

'Hold on Tango 24. Hold on . . . we're on our way,' the controller answered.

Andrews dropped the radio handset and, putting both arms on the top of the car, he started to cry.

☆      ☆      ☆

Behind him the door opened and closed. Flanagan crossed the

room in quick strides. Bill looked up from the file. 'It took a bit of doing but I finally managed it,' he said, sitting down opposite him. 'You're booked in to see Heeny tomorrow at Portaise.' He grinned at Bill. 'Took a phone call from my superior (who's only one step down from God himself) but we finally managed it.'

'Thanks. Tomorrow – I'll have to find somewhere to stay,' Bill began to say.

Flanagan held up a hand. 'Sure I'll hear none of it. I've got a big place all to myself, being the confirmed bachelor that I am. It will be a pleasure to put you up. I might even spring to a bite to eat later on,' he winked, 'on the old expense account.'

Before Bill could make any protestations there was a knock at the door. 'Come in,' Flanagan shouted. Mandy walked in and handed him several pieces of paper. Flanagan read them, his face losing its normal ruddy colour. When he looked up he said, 'Thanks Mandy – I'll give you a call if I need anything else.'

He let her leave the room before he spoke to Bill. Sitting back in his seat he brought his pen up between both hands. Looking over it, he said, 'On 2 March, 1982, Janet Munroe, a Protestant nurse, working in St Mary's Hospital was raped and stabbed to death on her way back to the nurses' residence. Identity of the attacker never discovered.' Flanagan looked again at the paper in front of him. 'On 3 January, 1983, Mary Ann Briant, a Protestant tourist was found dead in her car near Dundalk. The car was found on its roof in a ditch. The cause of death was a broken neck. From the skid marks on the road it was assumed she took a bend too fast and lost the car. We kept the file open because of this.' He handed Bill an extract from the pathologist's report.

Bill read it aloud. 'The subject had sex not more than one hour before she died. Entry was violent and may have been forced. This could have been a sexual assault and I recommend it be looked into.'

Bill looked up at Flanagan. 'And was it looked into?' he asked.

Flanagan looked at the ceiling and back to Bill. 'Dundalk CID asked a few questions. She wasn't local. Nobody knew anything.' He tugged his ear. 'She'd been staying at a local caravan park. Nobody could remember anything suspicious.'

190

Bill leaned closer to his southern Irish counterpart. 'And that was that?' he said tersely. Flanagan shrugged philosophically. 'They had no real proof anything out of the ordinary had occurred in respect of Miss Briant's death.'

'No proof,' Bill said, raising his voice. 'No proof! The bloody girl was raped, God damn it!'

Flanagan half stood out of his chair and slammed the flat of his hand on the desk top. 'Now wait a minute Mr High and Mighty RUC man,' he shouted back angrily. 'For a start the report said "could have been" *not* "was" sexually assaulted.' He walked round the table to stare defiantly up into Bill's face. 'Secondly I don't need a man with possibly twenty unsolved female homicides telling *me* how bad *my* force is.'

For a second each of them locked eyes, anger crackling in the air. Then Bill breathed through his nose. 'Sorry Flan,' he said. 'This is starting to get to me.'

Flanagan nodded his head in understanding and threw a mock punch at Bill's jaw. 'What are friends for,' he said grinning, 'if not to shout at each other? Come on, I'll take you home, then buy you the best dinner in Dublin.'

☆     ☆     ☆

Dublin's Westburn Hotel, off its main Glaston Street, was one of Ireland's finest, with a fine a la carte restaurant.

'You're pushing the boat out Flan,' Bill said, cutting into a superbly prepared veal in red wine sauce.

Flanagan shrugged nonchalantly. 'I reckon my expenses can run to it,' he said smiling. 'After all, it's not every day I get to entertain a real top class SB man from the north.'

Bill inclined his head, accepting the compliment.

A waiter arrived and displayed an expensive bottle of French white wine. Flanagan studied the bottle. 'Mattins '58, excellent choice.' He looked up at the waiter and his face lost its smile. 'But I didn't order it.'

'No sir,' the waiter replied, inclining his head to the far end of the dining room. 'It's compliments of the gentlemen at that table.' Bill followed the waiter's glance. At a large table sat six men and three women. Three of the men were clearly related, their faces all bore the same stamp of casual cruelty and arrogance. The other three looked like professional thugs.

'Dunn,' Flanagan said, contempt plain in his voice. Grabbing the bottle of wine he walked towards the table. Bill followed. As they neared it the three heavy set men got up. 'Obviously bodyguards,' Bill thought.

One of the women tittered. Flanagan gave her a scornful glance. 'You send this Dunn?' he asked the eldest of the seated men.

'Just trying to be friendly Flanagan,' Eamon 'Bull' Dunn, the squat, powerfully built head of the crime family replied. 'And it's *Mr* Dunn to you – I'm a taxpayer!' There was a rumble of laughter around the table. Flanagan pursed his lips. With deliberate care he poured the bottle of wine over the table. The three women jumped up with shrill screams. Dunn's bodyguards started forward, but Eamon Dunn restrained them with an upraised hand. Still seated, he wiped some of the wine from his lap, and looking at Flanagan, said, 'That was a bad mistake Flanagan.'

Flanagan leaned both hands on the table and the bodyguards shifted uneasily. Bill tensed. 'Then make no mistake about this. If you *ever* send me over anything again in a restaurant I won't pour it over the table – I'll shove it where the sun doesn't shine. Understand?' Flanagan's voice was calm and deadly serious. For a second there was violence in the air, then reason returned to Eamon Dunn.

'Come on,' he said harshly to his entourage, 'something in this place stinks.' Flanagan turned to leave as Dunn stood. 'Flanagan,' Dunn said through clenched teeth, 'you haven't heard the last of this!'

The Chief Inspector smiled humourlessly and replied with a noncommittal shrug, 'I won't hold my breath.'

Angrily Dunn turned and, followed by his party, stamped out of the restaurant. Flanagan led Bill back to their table. The manager, a personal friend of Flanagan's, appeared. 'I'm sorry Chief Inspector, but one cannot choose one's patrons.'

'Eat your veal – it's getting cold,' Flanagan said as Bill cut into the meat. He went on in deadly earnest, 'One day it will give me great pleasure to put that whole rotten family behind bars.'

The waiter appeared with another bottle of Mattins '58 in his hand. 'Compliments of the house, sir,' he said.

Flanagan smiled at Bill. 'Now this one we'll drink.'

Later, Flanagan said as they walked towards his parked car, 'We have a long trying day tomorrow but,' he patted his stomach appreciatively, 'at least we're well fortified.'

As the small detective inserted his key in the door a voice from behind them said, 'We've been waiting for you.'

Both men turned. In front of them stood Raill Dunn, Eamon's youngest son, and the three thugs from the restaurant. 'This is stupid, even for your father.'

'My father doesn't know about it,' Raill Dunn replied. 'It's my idea.'

Flanagan glanced at the three thugs. 'I'll get you all five years minimum for this,' he said.

Dunn laughed. 'Don't try that. I'll have them out of here and across the water before the night's out – we're international now. I can get them abroad if I want. You'll never be able to find them.'

Flanagan stepped to within a foot of the grinning youth. 'I can find you,' he said.

'Me?' Dunn put both hands to his chest in mock innocence. 'I'm just going to walk to the car. It's the lads here that will do the business.'

Flanagan smiled grimly up at the youth. 'I don't think so,' he said quietly.

Dunn leaned down towards the smaller man. 'And what's going to stop me?' he said mockingly.

'Me,' said Flanagan, 'and the .38 Smith and Wesson revolver I've got pointed at your gut.'

Dunn looked down. The ugly little gun was inches from his stomach. His face lost its colour. 'Now,' Flanagan continued, 'if you don't want the contents of your stomach to shake hands with your spine, tell those three gorillas to get into their car and fuck off.'

'You wouldn't dare,' stammered Dunn.

'Try me,' Flanagan answered firmly.

Dunn hesitated only a minute. 'Don't just stand there. Get the hell out of here.'

The three goons swapped glances, then jumped into their car and sped off. With their departure Flanagan replaced the Smith and Wesson in his pocket. He looked up at Dunn, slapped him lightly on the face twice and said, 'Let this be a lesson son, never step out of your class.' He turned and left a still shocked Dunn standing alone.

Laughing, Bill joined him in the car. They drove in silence for a while. Bill broke it with a question. 'Would you have?' he asked.

Flanagan shrugged behind the wheel. 'I don't know. I've never shot anybody before.' He seemed to consider it. 'Probably not,' he said. Bill was not so sure.

☆      ☆      ☆

Portaise Prison, 12 noon, Wednesday.

The huge metal gate of the inner security barrier closed behind them. Bill and Flanagan found themselves in an enclosed courtyard. 'Follow me please,' a prison officer said, leading them to a door in one corner of the yard. Three steel doors and two security checks later they found themselves in the interview room. Heeny swaggered in accompanied by a prison warder. He slumped into the metal chair opposite Flanagan.

'Flanagan,' he said in his thick Belfast accent. 'I might have guessed. And who's this?' he jerked his head in Bill's direction.

'Sure that's no way to be talking to a member of the Royal Ulster Constabulary is it,' Flanagan said, his voice an uncultured country twang. Heeny sat bolt upright.

'I'm not talking to any black bastard,' he snarled. Flanagan put both hands under his chin and rested his elbows on the metal desk, looking for all the world like a school master about to admonish an unruly pupil.

'Such talk I'm hearing,' he turned to Bill, 'sure the man's not worth bothering about.'

'Fuck off Flanagan and take him,' he pointed at Bill, 'with you.' He leaned across the table and whispered, his voice harsh with hate, 'When we win, there won't be enough lampposts to hang you all on.'

Flanagan studied him, unmoved, his chin still resting on his hands. 'Is Peter McCormack still OC of your wing?' he asked.

Heeny's forehead furrowed, surprised by the question. 'What's it to you?'

Flanagan smiled. 'A very violent man is our Peter, very unstable.' He paused and looked at Bill. 'I hear he hung one fella in this very prison.' He looked back at Heeny. 'Now why

194

did he do that?' he held up a hand. 'No, don't tell me. Yes, I remember. He found out he'd been sleeping with an IRA lifer's wife when he was outside. Very moralistic is Mr McCormack.'

Heeny looked worried. 'What's that to me?' he asked.

Flanagan smiled grimly. 'What do you think he would do if he found out you'd been fucking his wife before you came in here?'

Heeny jumped to his feet and the metal chair riveted to the floor almost caused him to fall. 'That's a lie,' he shouted, pointing an accusing finger at Flanagan.

'Is it?' Flanagan asked innocently, without taking his eyes off Heeny. He leaned over and took a buff coloured folder from his briefcase. 'Do you want to see the photos?'

'You bastard,' Heeny spat.

Flanagan nodded. 'Quite probably. Now are you going to answer my friend's questions or not?'

Heeny turned to Bill. 'What do you want?'

'It's about the murder of Margaret Hamilton in 1973,' he said. Heeny sat back in his chair trying to remember. 'You were with Anthony Kane,' Bill offered.

Heeny jumped up and walked to the door and back to the table in agitation. Leaning on the table he said, 'Fuck you. I'd rather take my chances with McCormack than stiff Kane.'

'We're not asking you to give evidence. Just confirm some details for us – things we already know. I'll ask questions, you just answer yes or no, OK?'

Heeny looked at Flanagan. 'I have your word this is off the record and won't be used against me?' he asked. Everyone knew, whether Republican, criminal or police officer, that if Flanagan gave his word he would stick to it.

'That's right,' Flanagan said.

Heeny pointed at the file. 'And you won't try to use that against me again?'

Flanagan looked at the file and back at Heeny. 'You drive a hard bargain, but OK.'

Heeny sat back down and folded his arms. Looking at Bill he said, 'OK, ask away, but only yes and no and only about Margaret Hamilton's execution. She was a tout.'

'Martin O'Keefe ordered you and Kane to kill Margaret?'

'Yes,' replied Heeny.

'Kane actually killed her with a knife?'

195

'Yes, I wanted to use a gun but Kane said it would make too much noise.'

'Kane raped her before he killed her?'

'No,' Heeny said. Bill looked puzzled. Heeny smiled. 'She thought if she let Kane screw her he'd let her go. Ha! He hates Prod girls. Kept calling her a Prod bitch every time he stabbed her.'

Bill was quiet for a time. 'Kane enjoyed killing her?' he asked.

Heeny smiled viciously. 'Yeah. He really did. First time I ever saw him excited. Christ he was on a high. Took full ten minutes to come down.'

Bill nodded studying Heeny's face. 'Then you went with him to the New Lodge and he shot a marine?' he asked.

Heeny shook his head. 'I said only the tout's murder, nothing else.'

Bill stood up slowly and gathered his papers. Before Flanagan could stop him he grabbed Heeny by the throat, pulling him across the table. He spoke through clenched teeth, 'Listen you heap of shit and listen good. You've got two years to go. Flanagan might have given you his word, but I didn't.' He thrust Heeny back into the chair and walked to the door followed by Flanagan. He paused at the door and, looking back, said, 'Sleep well Heeny and hope I don't write McCormack a letter.'

☆     ☆     ☆

They sat in Flanagan's office, both with a stiff drink in their hands. Bill said, 'I'm no expert but I would say the killing of Margaret Hamilton probably triggered Kane off. He became a double killer. The girls were a preparation for his IRA operations. It's all probably linked to his mother's murder. In his warped mind he was reinforcing his hatred and renewing his strength every time he killed a Protestant girl.'

Flanagan sipped his drink. Looking over the rim he said, 'I'll have to inform my superiors. We'll have to be ready for what happens after you arrest him.'

Bill massaged his eyes. 'It could be the 70s all over again,' he said.

There was a knock on the door. Mandy came in. 'Two

things sir. There's a phone call for Inspector Dodds on the secure line, and this is for you.' She handed Flanagan a piece of paper.

As he read it he said, 'You can use that phone over there Bill – it's secure,' indicating a phone in the corner.

'Bill,' a familiar voice sounded.

'Nevin! How are you – making progress?' Bill asked.

'Yes, a lot. But I've got some urgent news for you. It's from Marrianne in Boston.'

Bill's face went to stone as he listened to Nevin. 'OK, now listen. I can't get a flight until tomorrow.'

'When is Marrianne due back?'

'Tomorrow night at eight o'clock.'

'Right. We may have to break this thing a week earlier. I'll see you in my office at the airport tomorrow. I think there's a flight at 2 pm, OK?'

Bill waited for Nevin's acknowledgement then replaced the phone.

'Bad news?' Flanagan asked.

'Terrible,' Bill replied. He outlined what Marrianne had found out in Boston including the fact that the IRA had acquired twenty Red Eye surface-to-air missiles.

'They got them from a bunch of Yank gangsters called Hamilton? I wonder if they were related to Pat Hamilton – the guy who was shot last year?'

Bill shrugged. 'Do you think it's important?' he asked.

'At this stage we're grasping at straws. Anything might be important. I'll check.' He stood up to leave. 'Meanwhile here's some more bad news,' he said, throwing the paper to Bill. He read the typed note. A third possible female homicide had been discovered. Carol Anderson, a university student found hanging in her room at Dublin University. A postmortem had revealed violent sexual intercourse prior to death but enquiries had been negative and friends had stated that she was suffering from depression. Blood group of sexual partner O-neg., same as the other two.

Bill threw the paper onto the desk. 'Chalk up another one for Kane,' he thought.

It was a full hour before Flanagan returned. 'Bill! Pat Hamilton was the uncle of Carl and Archie Hamilton,' he said his voice high with tension. 'Something else – Archie Hamilton was blown up by a bomb under his car three months ago. I checked with the Boston police. The explosive used was semtex.'

Bill stood up and read the report. 'You think the Provos killed *both* Hamiltons? Why would they do that? According to Professor Sterling they sent twenty SAMs over here for them.'

Flanagan thought for a minute then looked at Bill. 'Maybe they screwed up,' he said.

☆    ☆    ☆

She walked with a confident, provocative step, her short skirt revealing shapely curved thighs and firm long legs. Male heads turned as she passed admiring the sensuous curves of her young body. As she passed the van Bill gave a low whistle. 'He's got taste, I'll give him that,' he said.

Beside him Flanagan gave a nod of agreement. 'Yes, mind you, he has the pick of the entire Dunn range of whores,' he said.

The girl disappeared into the apartment building in front of them. 'Richard runs the family's prostitutes. He's been seeing this one for three months now.' Flanagan checked his watch and turned to the three other men in the van's interior. All were exceptionally large members of Dublin's CID. 'We'll give them a few minutes to settle,' he grinned.

Flanagan, Bill and the CID men walked into the foyer of the apartment block. A uniformed porter started to lift a phone. 'Now don't disturb anybody,' Flanagan said, showing his warrant card. One of the CID men removed the phone from his hand and replaced it in the cradle. Flanagan said, 'Stay here and keep him company. He looks lonely.' They paused outside number 22B. Flanagan cocked his head. 'Did you hear a girl scream?' he asked one of the CID men.

'I did indeed sir,' he answered.

Flanagan tapped the door with his index finger. 'This is the police,' he whispered barely audibly. 'Is there any trouble?'

The second CID man said, 'I think I heard another scream.'

Stepping back, Flanagan said, 'Kick it.'

The huge CID men hit the door at once. It disintegrated under the assault. Lying on a huge sofa was Richard Dunn. Astride him was the girl, wearing nothing but a pair of black stockings and a suspender belt. 'What the fuck,' he said, jumping up and spilling the girl on to the ground.

She screamed. 'Shut up,' he snarled at her and turned to Flanagan. 'You've done it now Flanagan. I'll have your job for this.'

Flanagan smiled. 'We had a report of a woman being sexually assaulted,' he said, and looked at the girl. 'Were you being sexually assaulted Miss?' She sobbed, not answering. In a slightly softer tone he said, 'How old are you Miss?'

'She's old enough,' snarled Dunn.

Flanagan turned to one of the waiting CID men. 'What's the lady's name and age Sergeant?' he asked.

The CID sergeant produced a notebook. 'Lady's name is Maria Doyle. Age fifteen years sir,' he replied.

Dunn rounded on the cowering girl. 'You stupid slut,' he shouted, lifting his hand, 'you fucking lied to me.'

Before he could strike a blow, the CID sergeant stepped forward and delivered a short right cross to his jaw. He fell heavily to the floor. 'Get the lady dressed Sergeant and take her back to the station. Put some clothes on please Mr Dunn.'

With Dunn fully dressed Flanagan and Bill sat down opposite him.

'Wait outside please. I'll call you if I need you,' Flanagan said to the remaining CID man. With the room empty he said to Dunn, 'Well Richard, this is a fine mess you've got yourself into.' He held up his hand, counting off his fingers. 'Let's see. We have unlawful sexual intercourse with a girl under sixteen, statutory rape, procuring a minor for immoral purposes, assault with intent on a female, resisting arrest, assault on a police officer. With your record you'll be lucky to get less than five years.'

'You'll never prove all that,' Dunn retorted.

Flanagan cocked his head. 'Maybe not,' he smiled, 'but I'll have fun trying.'

Dunn ran a hand over his face. 'What do you want?'

Flanagan looked at Bill, a huge grin on his face. 'Now that's what I like. Public co-operation.' He looked back at Dunn, deadly serious. 'Why did the Provos blow away Pat Hamilton?'

Dunn looked up, surprise on his face. 'So that's what all this is about.' He shook his head from side to side, a disgusted look on his face. 'I told Da not to get mixed up with that Yank, with all his big talk and big ideas – he was always nothing but trouble.' He lapsed into a sullen silence.

'Well you're a good judge of character, I'll give you that Richard, but you still haven't told us anything,' Flanagan prodded.

Dunn looked up, anger plain on his face. 'Neither he nor his stupid brothers ever understood. They thought the bloody Provos were just like the Mafia.' He shook his head. 'It was all to do with an agreement his brothers had made.'

Bill interrupted. 'To ship twenty SAM missiles to Ireland?' he asked.

Dunn looked stunned. 'So you know about that?' His shoulders slumped and he looked at the floor. 'I'll tell you what I know.'

☆   ☆   ☆

Donegal Coast, 26 January 1990.

A slight breeze ruffled the grass which ran down almost to the water. A small beach, barely twenty metres wide slashed the water's edge. Behind them a low range of hills tumbled upwards to a distant road. Kane stood with two other men on the narrow shore, a shielded torch in his hand. In the distance a light flashed. Kane answered it with two quick flashes. Beside him a squat, thick-set man who looked like a farmer said, 'Looks like they're on time.'

Sean 'Slab' Murray was the commanding officer of the IRA's most active unit, the South Armagh Brigade. He was without doubt one of the IRA's most dedicated and ruthless commanders. It was to be his unit's responsibility to hide, familiarize with, and eventually use the incoming SAM missiles.

Kane turned and flashed his torch three times. A lorry on the distant road flashed its headlights twice in reply. Clearly the sound of a distant outboard motor could be heard approaching them. 'I'll check them on the beach. There's no telling how they've been packed,' the other man said. Peter Andrew Stevenson was a professor of electronics at Dublin University. Tall, grey haired and in his late fifties he was an expert in electronics and weapons systems, having once worked in the research department of a Short Guided Missile Department.

Slowly a black painted Zodiac inflatable cruised into view. It beached and two men jumped out and walked towards the three waiting men, while behind them two others began to unload several boxes. 'I hope we didn't keep you waiting?' the leading man said, approaching Kane. An Ingram M10 could be seen clearly in his right hand.

'No, you're right on time,' Kane replied.

'You didn't need that "slab",' Murray said, indicating the M10.

'What – this?' The man said, looking at the M10 as if somebody had sneaked up and put it in his hand while he wasn't looking. Grinning he replied, 'I never go anywhere without it.' His accent was central American. Even in the darkness Kane could tell he was swarthy.

'We want to check the merchandise,' Kane said.

'Help yourself,' the man said, sweeping an arm towards the now unloaded boxes. Stevenson took a small torch from his pocket and went to the first box. Levering up the lid he checked the contents. He looked at Kane and swiftly checked the other boxes. Kane knew instinctively something was wrong.

'They're all there,' he said, standing up, 'but the power units have been removed. They're useless.'

The man lifted the M10. Beside him his partner produced a Berretta automatic. Kane felt Murray stiffen. 'What's this?' he asked.

'Unfortunately there have been some additional expenses in transit. Your organization will have to pay US$2 million for the power units,' the man said grinning.

Murray cursed. Kane put a restraining hand on him. 'Where do we take the money?'

'Not where – who! Pay it to Mr Pat Hamilton in Dublin. He will give you the details of where your power units are.'

Slowly the two men backed towards the Zodiac. In seconds they were in the boat and gone.

☆    ☆    ☆

Dublin Docks, three weeks later, 12 midnight.

In the distance a ship's horn sounded the midnight hour. Its echoes resounded in the empty warehouse. The drip of water could be heard clearly, like the ticking of some giant clock. Kane walked towards three men, half hidden in the shadows.

'You came alone,' Pat Hamilton said, stepping into the light.

'Of course,' Kane said softly.

'Where's the money?' asked a new voice. Kane recognized it as belonging to the man from the beach.

'Patience, patience, Carlos,' Hamilton said over his shoulder. Turning back to Kane he grinned, 'My nephews recruited Carlos from a rather nasty Columbian cartel,' he said.

Carlos stepped in to the light. Darkly handsome, his features were marred by a vicious knife scar running through his left eye. 'Ah Mr Kane, I'm a big fan of yours,' grinned Carlos. 'You have a big reputation back in the States.' His face lost its grin. 'I'm better,' he said seriously. The M10 shook slightly as he spoke.

'Easy Carlos. Mr Kane has come to make us rich men.'

Kane studied Hamilton. 'Was this your own idea or were your nephews in on it too?' he asked.

'Only Archie. Carl is scared shitless of you,' replied Hamilton. 'You see Archie wants to invest in a project outside his brother's sphere of influence, shall we say. Columbian cocaine to be exact.' He patted Carlos's shoulder. 'My friend here helped set it up. Look at it this way Kane. Your $2 million will be an investment. In six months it will be worth twenty million bucks.' His face lost its smile. 'Now, where is the money?'

Kane reached up and scratched his ear with his left hand. 'So it was you and Archie who had the idea. That's all I wanted to know.'

A thunderous crash sounded as an armoured truck ripped apart the two metal doors behind Hamilton's group. Carlos spun around, bringing up his weapon. Before he could fire Kane drew a Browning and shot him twice in the head. The other Columbian dropped his Berretta and threw his hands in the air. From the back of the truck armed and hooded men spilled out. They formed a semi-circle around Hamilton and his hired gunman. Hamilton's face was deadly white. 'What the fuck are you up to Kane?' he said.

Kane made no reply. Letting the hand holding the Browning drop to his side, he started to walk around Hamilton. 'I won't talk, you stupid Mick shithead,' screamed the sweating man. 'I know you'll kill me if I talk.' He followed the slowly walking Kane with his eyes, spinning his head as Kane strolled around the ring of armed men.

Kane stopped in front of the Columbian. He looked at Hamilton. 'Are you a technical man Pat?'

'What?' Hamilton asked.

Kane looked at the Columbian who was still standing with his hands in the air. A nervous smile was flashed at Kane. He smiled back then brought the Browning up and shot the still smiling Columbian between the eyes. The sound was deafening. Hamilton jumped involuntarily. 'My God,' he moaned as he involuntarily lost the contents of his bowels.

Kane waved his left hand in front of his nose. 'Phew,' he said as he started to walk back in front of Hamilton. He thrust his hands behind his back, talking to Hamilton like a teacher giving a lesson. 'I asked if you were a technical man Pat? Probably not, I'd say. I'm not, I must admit – I'm a soldier. But you see we have this guy called Stevenson. Now he *is* a technical man. He used to work in anti-aircraft missile research. Actually he's been trying to develop some kind of anti-aircraft missile for us. Do you know what the most difficult part of a missile is to manufacture?' Hamilton's face was drenched in sweat. His eyeballs had diluted with fear to a point where the whites were barely visible. He shook his head numbly in answer to Kane's question.

Kane tipped his head back as he answered. 'The guidance system. Without it the missiles are useless. Unfortunately for you, when you removed the power units from the Red Eyes you destroyed their delicate guidance systems.' He smiled and leant closer to Hamilton. 'They're useless now Pat – you fucked them up.'

'Oh my God,' Hamilton said and dropped to his knees. He brought both hands up in an attitude of prayer. Kane lifted the Browning from behind his back and fired three quick shots into his head.

'What do you want done with them?' Murray asked, coming to stand next to Kane.

'These two,' he gestured with the Browning towards the

Columbians, 'they had better disappear. Feed them to the pigs on your farm. Hamilton we'll dump in the town centre. He's a known drug dealer. We'll say we killed him in the public interest.' He looked at Murray. 'We might as well get some good press out of this.' He shook his head angrily. 'I knew we should never have worked with these people.'

☆ ☆ ☆

'So Hamilton's greed stopped the Provos getting their hands on the SAMs. No wonder they killed him and Archie,' Bill said.

Flanagan stood and walked to the door, followed by Bill. 'What about the girl?' Richard Dunn asked.

At the door Flanagan turned and considered the question. 'As far as we're concerned, unless she makes a complaint we'll let it go for now.' He turned to leave and paused. 'I suppose you know who her father is?' he asked.

Dunn looked confused. 'No. Should I?' he asked.

Flanagan grinned at Bill and turned back to Dunn, a vicious grin on his face. 'It's Kieran Doyle,' he said, laughing as he walked out of the door.

In the lift a puzzled Bill Dodds asked, 'Who's Kieran Doyle?'

Flanagan grinned at the CID man knowingly and said to Bill, 'Dublin's main IRA enforcer. He's kneecapped more people than I've arrested.' All of them laughed.

☆ ☆ ☆

Thursday, 2 pm.

Flanagan saw him off at Shannon Airport. Bill grasped his outstretched hand. 'Thanks Flan, I don't know what I would have done without you,' he said.

'Think nothing of it m'boy,' Flanagan said in his best thick Paddy accent. Then seriously, 'I'll give you a couple of days before I brief my people – it'll give you time to get things set north of the border.'

Bill nodded. 'Thanks. I could use all the time you can give me.' He looked Flanagan in the eye. 'You know I'll do all I can to stop innocent Catholics getting hurt.'

'I know that Bill,' Flanagan said, slapping him on his shoulder. 'I know that.'

☆    ☆    ☆

Belfast Crown Court, Crumlin Road, Thursday 1 pm.

Judge Matthew Howell looked down his glasses disapprovingly at the Crown Prosecutor. 'You wish to withdraw all charges, Mr Powell.' he asked.

'Unfortunately yes M'Lord. All the witnesses have retracted their evidence.'

'Very well. I direct you to instruct the police to investigate these matters.' He turned to the man in the dock. 'William John Bing, much as it is against my wishes, I direct that the charges against you be withdrawn. You are free to go.' Bing grinned broadly. He glanced around the court and in the public gallery saw Billy Dixon. He gave him a clenched fist salute. Smiling, Dixon acknowledged the salute with one of his own.

☆    ☆    ☆

Tennant Street, Special Branch office, 3 pm, same day.

Nevin had picked Bill up from the airport. They'd exchanged what they each learnt during the drive to Tennant Street Barracks. Now they both sat in Bill's office. The SB man was going through some recent intelligence reports – he looked up at Nevin. 'There are reports of unusual activity amongst the Shankill UVF.'

Nevin looked surprised. 'What kind of activity?' he asked.

Bill glanced back down at the papers on the desk. 'Moving arms about, getting some of their "Doomsday" weapons out of caches, calling up stood-down volunteers, etc., etc.' He looked at Nevin. 'It's almost as if they know some bad news is about to break and are getting ready.'

Nevin looked concerned. 'How could they know?' he asked.

Bill sighed and looked back at the ceiling. 'Who knows Nevin, who knows. But one thing's sure.' He looked at Nevin. 'We can't delay any longer. I'll have to brief my boss today.

205

We'll all have to see the Chief Constable tomorrow.'

There was a knock on the door. A familiar face peeped round it. 'Ah Bill.'

Bill stood up and extended his hand. 'Ronnie. How are you?' he said.

Inspector Ronnie Calder, Head of Special Branch for Andersonstown pumped the outstretched hand. 'Fine Bill. I'm glad I've finally got you in. Can I have a word?' he glanced at Nevin.

Nevin stood. 'It's all right Inspector, I was just leaving.' He turned to Bill. 'I'll see you at my place at ten o'clock tonight.' Bill nodded.

'Sit down Ronnie,' he said as Nevin left, 'what can I do for you?' He rubbed his eyes with his hands. 'I hope it's not bad news.'

Ronnie looked concerned. 'Things that bad?' he asked.

Bill looked through his hands and replied, 'That bad and likely to get worse.'

Ronnie smiled. Reaching into his briefcase he extracted a buff coloured folder. 'Maybe this will cheer you up,' he said.

Bill took the folder curiously. He read it – slowly at first, then more quickly, flicking pages and studying photographs. Eventually he looked up, a wide grin on his face. 'I'd never have believed it. He's married with two kids!'

Ronnie nodded, giving a low chuckle. 'I know, it's dynamite isn't it?' he laughed.

A flicker of concern passed over Bill's face. 'Does anybody else know about it – TCG, Division?'

Ronnie shook his head. 'No, only the DS who took the photos. It was a routine surveillance.' His eyebrows shot up as he beamed. 'Turned up trumps, eh?'

'And you're just giving it to me?' Bill asked in surprise. 'What's the catch?'

Calder laughed as he stood up. 'No catch Bill – it's your patch. You can make best use of it. Besides,' he paused at the door and looked back, 'you'll owe me a favour,' he grinned.

With the door closed Bill studied the file again, his lips pursed in concentration.

☆    ☆    ☆

Tennant Street canteen, 7 pm, same day.

'Do you know,' Garry Howe said, grinning over the top of his *Belfast Telegraph* at Billy Boyd, 'there's an article in here about this southern Irish civil rights campaigner. He'd campaigned for the Guildford Four, the Birmingham Six and the Winchester Three. Somebody asked him what he thought of the Renault 5 – know what he said?'

'No,' Billy said, waiting for the punchline.

'He said, "Another classic case of British injustice – they're definitely innocent and should be released immediately".'

They both laughed. 'It's pretty close to the truth,' Billy said, half seriously.

Gary nodded, 'Aye, a lot of people believe that the English police caution should be "Anything you say will be taken down in pencil, rubbed out, scrubbed out and *then* used in evidence against you".'

Billy broke into another fit of laughter. He was still laughing when Eddy Gardner sat down next to Gary. 'What's the joke?' Gardner asked.

Billy shook his head. 'You had to be here to get it. You on duty tonight?'

'No, I've just come in to get a few things from my locker.'

'You're keen Eddy – you wouldn't see me near this place when I'm off duty.' The big Scotsman yawned and stretched. 'I'll have to be going,' he said, standing. 'I'm on patrol in five minutes.' He handed Billy the *Telegraph* and left.

'You still attached to Special Branch?' Gardner asked Billy, trying to sound nonchalant.

Billy was reading the paper. He glanced up at Gardner. 'Only for today. I'm back with CID tomorrow.'

Gardner fidgeted for a second then asked, 'So you've got a result as far as Lynn Moody's murder is concerned then?' He still tried to sound casual but even to himself his voice sounded strained.

Billy didn't look up immediately. Alarm bells were going off in his head. Nevin Brown had told him on no account to mention the Lynn Moody murder to anyone, or the fact that Kane had been identified. He looked up slowly, his eyes searching Gardner's face. 'You're taking a keen interest in my career all of a sudden Eddy. Why the interest?'

Gardner shrugged. He lifted his hands in a casual gesture, but his voice quivered as he spoke. 'Oh, you know – just curious. I live in the area you know and people are concerned,' he said, trying to control the quiver. Billy said nothing. 'About Lynn Moody's murder I mean,' he added quickly.

Billy studied the part-timer's face. He could see strain etched in every line. He grabbed Gardner's arm. 'Is there something you want to tell me Eddy?' he asked, his voice low and full of concern. For a second it looked like Gardner was going to blurt something out. His lips moved but no words came out. Instead he ripped his arm from Bill's grip.

He stood suddenly. 'I was just trying to be friendly,' he shouted. Billy thought he was close to tears. Around the canteen people turned to stare. Gardner looked down at Billy. He opened his mouth to speak, thought better of it and, spinning on his heel, half walked, half ran out of the canteen.

Billy sat for a second. Around him there was a hub of noise as people discussed the scene at his table. Making up his mind he quickly left the table and walked upstairs to Bill Dodds's office. Stopping outside the door he took a deep breath and knocked on the door.

'Billy,' Dodds said, 'come on in.'

The CID aid shuffled awkwardly into the office and sat down. 'This may be nothing sir.' He gave a half hearted laugh. 'I don't really know where to begin,' he hesitated.

Bill Dodds sat back in his chair. He eyed the CID aid carefully. 'Take your time Billy. Start at the beginning.'

Billy took a deep breath. 'Well it began last Sunday . . . '

☆    ☆    ☆

Carrickfergus, Nevin Brown's home, 11 pm, same day.

It was all there on the table in front of them. Each of them had retold their stories. All now knew the facts. 'What's the next step?' asked Marrianne.

Bill Dodds took a sip of the whiskey Nevin had given him before answering. 'I've briefed the head of Special Branch this evening at nine o'clock. He didn't believe me at first,' he glanced at Nevin and laughed. 'In fact I think he was going to suspend me from duty for having a mental breakdown.'

'But you managed to convince him?' Nevin asked.

Bill nodded. 'It took some doing but yes, finally he took me seriously.' He took a deep breath. 'Tomorrow we face the RUC's equivalent of the Spanish Inquisition.' He looked at Nevin and Marrianne in turn. 'We have an appointment with the Chief Constable, the ACC for Belfast and the Head of Special Branch at RUC Headquarters.'

They were silent for a second then Marrianne reached out and grabbed Bill's arm. 'Don't worry Bill. We have plenty of proof. We can easily prove our case.'

Bill laughed bitterly and took another sip of whiskey. 'I'm not worried about proving our case against Kane,' he said, his voice harsh.

Nevin leaned forward concerned. 'What is it then Bill?' he asked seriously.

Bill glanced at him, his eyes full of suppressed anger. 'A police officer in Tennant Street has been leaking information to the UVF. That's why they've been getting all their men and guns ready. I think they're going to use Lynn Moody's death as a trigger to launch a major series of attacks against the Catholics in the Ardoyne. When they find out it was a Provo gunman who killed her and that there were many other Protestant girl victims, all hell with break loose.'

Nevin looked stunned. 'How do you know a police officer leaked information to the UVF?' he asked incredulously.

Bill shook his head as if trying to rid himself of the memory. 'Because,' he said, staring Nevin in the eyes, 'I know who he is.'

# 8

Knock Headquarters, 10.45 am, Friday.

There was silence in the room, each of the six occupants absorbed with their own thoughts. Nevin, Bill and Marrianne had all told their individual stories. Documents littered the table in front of the Chief Constable. Sworn affidavits from varied sources, FBI, Garda Special Branch, Professor Moore and Dr Ealing. Reports from the English forensic science labs, newly arrived by special courier confirming that Lynn Moody and Margaret Hamilton had been killed by the same man. Witness statements from Billy Moffit, Ann MacDonald, Constable McCready, Johnstone and many others added to the weight of evidence.

'This is monstrous,' the Chief Constable said, breaking the silence. He ran a hand through his thinning hair, obviously shaken. 'How could this have gone on for so long and not be detected?'

Before anyone could answer the Head of Special Branch asked another question. 'How many dead girls are we talking about?'

Nevin looked at Bill. The Inspector took a deep breath and spoke. 'To answer the Chief Constable's question first,' he said, speaking slowly and looking the Head of the RUC in the eye, 'Kane is a very unusual man, as Dr Sterling has already confirmed.'

Marrianne nodded without speaking.

'He's highly intelligent and knew if he simply shot, stabbed or strangled his victims it wouldn't have been long before somebody somewhere connected him and the killings. So he decided, at a very early stage, to disguise them as accidents and suicides. When we finally check up we may even find that some

210

girls simply "disappeared". For our part, we as a police force were too busy fighting a terrorist war, especially in the 70s and 80s to notice.' Bill's face contorted in a grimace of distaste. 'Also we had no experience of this type of crime. If it hadn't been for Nevin we might *still* be in the dark.'

There was a general murmur of agreement around the table. Nevin bowed his head modestly. Bill turned to his Special Branch Chief. 'As to your question sir,' he said, taking another deep breath, 'the simple answer is we just don't know. Nevin has discovered three, Marrianne four, and myself another three. But if Kane's kept to a pattern, and Dr Sterling thinks it would be impossible for him *not* to,' – he glanced at Marrianne for support – she nodded in agreement and Bill went on, 'then it's probable that we have at least twenty, maybe more undiscovered deaths.' He shook his head sadly.

'Maybe we will never know for sure how many innocent girls this bastard has really killed.' Bill glanced at Marrianne and smiled apologetically. 'Excuse my language Marrianne.'

'You're excused,' she replied with a smile.

'What I don't understand,' the ACC for Belfast said, speaking for the first time, 'is why he didn't try to hide the murders in America and Eire. He certainly went to great lengths to hide his crimes in Ulster.'

'That's fairly easy to explain,' Bill said. 'In America and Ireland he thought of himself as being "invisible". He was, after all in both countries illegally. He thought nobody would connect him to the killings. Obviously nobody did – or at least nobody who ever came forward.'

The ACC nodded in agreement. Another question popped into his mind. 'Why did he make no attempt to conceal Lynn Moody's murder – why did he just stab her?'

'I think I can answer that,' Marrianne said, leaning forward in her seat, 'I believe there were a number of factors involved. Firstly Kane was still probably "hung up" on his American cycle of violence. The physical act of stabbing and raping Protestant girls reaffirms his hatred. Every time he does it he re-enacts his own mother's brutal death.' She paused collecting her thoughts. 'From studies we have undertaken in America it would seem that these types of psychopaths also believe that by reliving their hatred they become some sort of invincible weapon of vengeance. As Bill has said Kane is highly intelligent. He gambled he could get away with the isolated rape and stabbing before he went back to covering up his crimes.'

The Chief Constable considered his next question carefully. 'In your opinion Doctor, would Kane be convicted in a court of law? I mean is he insane, unable to know right from wrong?'

Marrianne considered her answer. She tilted her head to the right in a characteristic gesture of concentration. 'Obviously I would have to study and question him at length before I could give you a definite answer. But from my studies of the case, my first inclinations are that Kane is criminally insane and unfit to either plead or stand trail.' Beside her Bill snorted. His mouth opened to make an angry reply.

He was stilled by a gesture from the Chief Constable. 'Thank you Doctor Sterling. I just wanted a guideline.' He straightened and looked round the room. 'The next question is obviously where do we go from here?' he said.

'Before we do,' Bill said abruptly, 'I think it's advisable that Sergeant Brown and Dr Sterling leave the room.'

Nevin and Marrianne turned to stare at their friend, obviously taken aback. Bill gave them a weak smile. 'I'm sorry, please don't take offence,' he said, making a helpless gesture. He looked back at the Chief Constable. 'There are matters of a highly sensitive nature I wish to discuss. I think it would be better if my two colleagues were to withdraw.'

The Chief Constable glanced at his Head of Special Branch. He got the briefest of nods in reply. Turning back he spoke to Nevin and Marrianne. 'Very well, Sergeant, Doctor if you would excuse us. But before you go I want you both to know that your efforts have been deeply appreciated by us all.' There were nods of agreement from his two colleagues. 'All of us owe you a debt of gratitude.'

Nevin and Marrianne both stood. Each was slightly embarrassed and with a last curious look at Bill they left the room. The Chief Constable let the door close before he turned to Bill. 'Well Inspector Dodds,' he said, knowing the Special Branch man had something important to say, 'what is it?'

Bill went straight into it, with no preamble. He outlined the UVF's preparations on the Shankill, told them of his belief that Reserve Constable Gardner had leaked information to them on the Lynn Moody investigation, and voiced his fears for the future in the aftermath of Kane's impending arrest. 'The best we can hope for is an outbreak of civil unrest and rioting. At worst the UVF will use this as an excuse for an outbreak of random sectarian killings. The Provos won't stand idly by – they'll hit back – hard!'

He paused to let his words sink in. 'It will be a return to the early 70s – violence on a scale unseen in years, dozens, maybe hundreds, of innocent lives lost – all because of Kane.'

There was silence in the room. Bill's words hung in the air like some portent of doom. The Head of Special Branch took a cigarette from a packet on the desk and lit it. Through the smoke he looked at Bill. 'You have some sort of suggestion to make Inspector?' his voice measured and calm.

Bill hesitated. He knew what he was about to say might cause him his career. Making up his mind he bent swiftly and took a sheet of paper from his briefcase. 'This is a copy of an MI5 document.' He handed the paper to the Chief Constable who read it and passed it to his Head of Special Branch. 'It's a transcript of a conversation picked up by a radio bug in Fidelious Clarke's house after Hardy and Feenan were shot by the SAS.'

The Head of Special Branch shrugged as he read it. 'So?' he said.

'Sean Hughes and Kane had a fight.'

He shrugged again. 'What has that got to do with this situation?'

'It's not the fight I'm interested in,' Bill said, his voice edged with excitement, 'it's the reason for it.'

All three men stared at him. 'Don't you see – Kane had been spotted coming back from the Woodvale – probably setting up his next female victim – but the point is his own people are already suspicious of him.'

The Chief Constable stiffened slightly. He locked eyes with Bill. 'I think I see where you're heading Inspector and I don't like it.'

Undaunted, Bill pushed home his point. 'Sir, with all due respect, I think this offers us a way out of our predicament.'

'What *exactly* are you proposing?' the Special Branch Chief asked.

Bill leaned forward as he replied. 'I'm proposing we tell the Provos everything – about all the girls' murders.' He threw his hands wide. 'They have almost as much to lose as us. Let them handle Kane. It will be quick and clean *and*' – Bill emphasized the word – 'we won't have the fall out from the Prods.'

The Chief Constable sat back in his chair, a look of concern on his face. For long seconds nobody spoke. When he did speak his voice had an icy cutting edge. 'I'm going to pretend I didn't hear what you just said Inspector.'

'But sir . . .' Bill protested. His outburst was stopped by an upraised hand.

'Inspector,' the Chief Constable continued, 'we owe you a debt of gratitude for your part in bringing this matter to light, but your suggestion is totally, *totally* out of the question. Do I make myself clear?'

Bill nodded without answering. 'I know you mean well Bill,' the Head of Special Branch put in, 'but even if we tried it there's no guarantee the Provos would buy it. Kane might well be tipped off by a friend and we'd lose him.'

Bill sighed. 'I suppose you're right sir, but I did think it would be for the best.'

'I know you meant well Inspector, so we'll say no more about it,' the Chief Constable said, 'now we'd better get down to business. First we'll have to arrange for an arrest operation. Next . . . '

Bill stopped listening as they laid their plans for Kane's arrest and the fall-out from it. 'Oh well,' he said to himself, 'so much for Plan A' – he gave a mental shake. 'It will have to be Plan B after all!'

☆　　☆　　☆

Ballysilyian Arms, 1 pm, same day.

Noise was subdued in the bar as William John Bing and Billy Dixon walked in. Talk all but stopped and anxious glances were exchanged as the two UDA men strode to the bar. Bing glanced around, his eyes searching each face in turn. 'What's the matter?' he said loudly. 'Aren't you glad to see me?' His gaze swept the bar as one by one conversations started up again and the noise level rose. With a dismissive gesture Bing turned his back on the crowd and leaned on the bar.

'It's good to have you back,' Billy Dixon said touching Bing's arm in an almost childlike way. Bing nodded as two pints of lager were placed in front of him. Brian Arthurs, the bar man, avoided looking at Billy Dixon – his face still bore marks from a savage assault.

'It's good to be back,' Bing said, sipping his lager. 'I knew the organization would stand by us.'

A look of concern crossed Dixon's face. 'They didn't stand by you,' he said. 'I did.'

Bing put down his glass with an audible thump. 'What do you mean – they didn't, you did?'

'It came down from the top – the inner circle itself – not to back you. McCrum, Prentise – all of them said you were to stay inside.' Dixon put a huge paw on Bing's shoulder. 'But I didn't listen,' he said proudly. 'You'll always be my CO.'

Bing was thoughtful for a second. He had wondered why no one had come to see him since his release. He'd thought everybody was just taking it a little easy. Now he knew the truth of it – his organization had disowned him. If it had not been for Billy he would still be inside.

All talk suddenly ceased in the bar as four men walked in. Two were well known to Bing. One was Andy Tyman, head of the powerful East Belfast wing of the UDA and a leading member of the organization's inner circle – the other was his second-in-command, Robert McCrum. Behind them strode two huge men, as big as Billy Dixon, if not bigger. They had the look of professional thugs. 'Hello William,' Tyman said, grinning without humour. His eyes flicked to Billy Dixon. 'What about you Billy – keeping well?' he asked.

Bing could feel Billy tense beside him as he answered, 'Fine Mr Tyman, fine.'

'It's not often we see you in this part of the world Andy,' Bing said, trying to sound casual.

Tyman shrugged his shoulders. 'These are unusual times.'

Around them the bar had gone deathly quiet, as if everybody was holding their breath. The two huge men with Tyman moved to flank Bing and Dixon. Bing tensed, readying himself to fight. Tyman held up a hand as if to forestall violence. 'I'm here to deliver a message from the inner council,' he said, stepping close to Bing, his voice firm and level. 'You're out of the organization Bing. You no longer belong to us.'

Bing blinked twice and stepped even closer to Tyman. 'You can't do that,' he hissed through clenched teeth. 'It's been tried before. Tyndale will back me. I'll go it alone – take them over to the UVF. How would you like that?' He poked Tyman in the chest with his finger. Tyman's bodyguards shuffled closer but Tyman again held up his hand to restrain them.

'The UVF don't want you Bing. You're too . . . ' he searched for the right word, 'unstable.'

'As for Tyndale backing you – tell him Robert.' He turned his head to McCrum.

Bing's former second-in-command sneered as he spoke. 'Nobody wants you after what you did to Mick Michael and his dad. For fuck's sake – he was one of your best men.' McCrum's face contorted with anger. 'You couldn't get any-body but this,' he jerked his head at Billy Dixon, 'dickhead to follow you.'

'Who are you calling a dickhead?' Dixon snarled pushing himself off the bar.

Before he could take a step one of Tyman's bodyguards unleashed a haymaker against his jaw. There was an audible crunch as he fell semi-conscious to the floor. Tyman looked down at the fallen man and shook his head. Looking back at Bing he said, 'You're out.' He nodded to McCrum. 'Roberts is OC now and he has both the area and the council's backing.' He smiled at Bing. 'You have one week to get out of the province. If you're here after that you're a dead man.'

Bing looked around the room wildly. He saw nothing but hostile faces. He started to edge for the door. 'You can't do this Andy. After all I've done for the organization, you . . . '

'One week – not a day more,' Tyman cut in, openly laughing at him. Others began to laugh – McCrum, the bodyguards, people in the room. Bing turned and fled as if the hounds of hell were after him.

☆　　☆　　☆

Special Branch Office, Tennant Street, 1.30 pm, same day.

Bill poured each a glass of whiskey and sat down behind his desk. He'd been unusually quiet on the return journey as if carrying some heavy burden. Nevin and Marrianne, on the other hand, were bright and happy – relieved their nightmare was coming to an end.

'What's the matter Bill?' Nevin asked, concern for his friend clear in his voice. 'You haven't said two words since we left the briefing.'

Bill closed his eyes as if tired. He massaged the eyelids with his left hand. 'I'm sorry Nevin, just worried about the future.' He opened his eyes and gave Marrianne a weak smile. 'You'll have to forgive me – pressures of the job.' She gave him a smile of conciliation.

'What's going to happen next?' asked Nevin.

Bill took a sip of whiskey before answering. 'Well, our lords and masters have planned a huge arrest operation,' he said, his voice tinged with bitterness. 'They're going to follow that with a press release blowing the whole thing wide open.'

'Well what's wrong with that?' Marrianne said, her face filled with curiosity.

Bill shook his head and smiled sadly. 'It would take too long to explain,' he replied.

'What about the leak to the UVF – what's to be done about that?' Nevin asked.

A look of disgust crossed Bill's face as he answered. 'The officer concerned will be interviewed by Complaints and Discipline on Monday. After that,' he shrugged, 'who knows?' He was silent for a second as if reflecting. Forcing a smile on to his face he said, 'Well enough doom and gloom. I've persuaded the Sub-Divisional Commander to give you three days paid leave. I suggest you use it to good advantage and show this lovely American visitor of ours some of the nicer parts of our city.'

Nevin smiled broadly and finished his drink with a gulp. 'That's one order I'll be pleased to obey,' he beamed and held a hand out for Marrianne to accept. As he opened the door for her he looked back. 'What about you Bill – care to join us later for a drink somewhere?' he asked.

Bill smiled wanly. 'I've got a bit too much on – maybe tomorrow.' Nevin gave him a parting grin and closed the door. For several seconds Bill eyed the door then, opening his desk drawer, he removed a red folder. He clasped his hands over it, almost in an attitude of prayer. 'Time for Plan B,' he said out loud and reached for the phone.

Ardoyne.

'For fuck's sake shut that bloody kid up will you,' Sean Hughes roared to his wife. He took a long angry draw on his cigarette. His mood had been ugly since his confrontation with Kane. It had not been helped by the arrival of the Brigade Command's investigation team – two veteran, hardline Republicans from West Belfast. The crying got louder. He jumped to his feet, hardly able to contain his anger. 'Can't you keep him quiet?'

His harassed wife appeared on the hall landing, the crying baby in her arms. 'I can't help it Sean,' she pleaded, looking dishevelled, 'he's teething.'

Hughes muttered an obscenity and stormed back to the sitting room. Pouring himself a beer he flopped in his armchair. 'Fucking Kane,' he muttered out loud.

He'd hated it when the two West Belfast investigators had met him. They had fawned and praised the North Belfast gunman, calling him 'the IRA's most effective weapon'. 'They did everything but kiss his arse,' Hughes snarled to the empty room. He took a deep swig of beer. 'I'll fix you Mr Fucking Kane – you just wait and see,' he spat.

Even as he said it Hughes knew it was a lie. Kane terrified him. The memory of his steel-like grip and those icy blue eyes made his stomach churn. The phone rang. Cursing, Hughes lifted the receiver. 'Hello,' he said harshly.

'Sean Hughes?' an unknown voice asked.

'Who is this?' Hughes demanded, his tone less sharp.

There was a low chuckle on the other end of the phone. 'We've never actually met but let's say I've always had an interest in you.'

'What the hell is this?' Hughes demanded, his voice now worried.

'I want to meet you,' the man answered.

'Why should I meet you?' Hughes demanded, alarm now in his voice.

There was silence, then another low chuckle. 'If I was to mention the name McGowan, followed by the address 114 Ballymurphy Crescent – and follow that by mentioning the date Wednesday 14 of last month, would I have got your interest?'

Holding the phone Hughes turned pale. His voice shook as

he replied, 'How do I know I can trust you?'

'You don't. But if I wanted you dead I'd only have to turn this information over to your Brigade Commander – you'd be dead in less than a week.'

Hughes closed his eyes, fighting for control. 'OK, OK. I'll meet you,' he said eventually. 'Where and when?'

'Oh somewhere nice and public,' the unknown man paused as if searching his memory. 'Let's say the public bar in the Europa Hotel at 5 pm tonight. Don't be late.'

The phone went dead. Hughes stood listening to the dialling tone, his face deathly pale.

☆    ☆    ☆

Mountain View Bar, Shankhill Road, 4 pm, same day.

People milled around the bar, many having escaped early from work. Laughter echoed around the half-filled room. Seated at a corner table Eddy Gardner did not share the general humour. Depression hung over him like a visible cloud. He was waiting for Jacky Hewitt.

He spotted the UVF man pushing his way through the crowd, acknowledging an occasional welcome from various acquaintances at the bar. Approaching Gardner, Hewitt broke into a smile – it made his face look like a skull.

'What about you Eddy?' he said, extending his hand. Gardner ignored it. Hewitt shrugged and sat down beside him. He studied the reserve policeman curiously before speaking. 'Now what was all the emergency?' he asked, a faint smile on his face.

Gardner continued to stare at the table top, his face leaden with despair. Without turning he said, 'They know,' his voice completely flat – void of any emotion.

Hewitt's eyebrows raised slightly. He touched Gardner's arm. 'Know what?' he asked.

Gardner pulled his arm away roughly. He turned, anger now replacing despair on his face. 'They know I've been giving information to *you*.' He pointed an angry finger at Hewitt.

The UVF man glanced around the bar anxiously before replying. 'Keep your voice down Eddy,' he said softly, his voice hard. 'How do you know you've been found out?'

'I know. I've been told I'm suspended and that Complaints

219

and Discipline are coming to interview me on Monday.' He was silent for a few seconds then rounded on Hewitt again. 'It's all your fault,' he said angrily, his voice starting to rise again. 'I only wanted to get back at the Provos for my friends. You made me ask all those questions about Lynn Moody.' He shook his head, tears starting to form in his eyes. 'They'll send me to prison. I'm ruined,' he all but sobbed.

Hewitt scratched the back of his neck as he studied the distraught man. He felt little pity for him. 'Listen to me, little man,' his voice was measured and low. He made no attempt to hide the contempt he felt. 'It was *you* who came to us begging for "justice" didn't you? We shot Larry Martin for you – didn't you feel good about that?' Hewitt sat back and studied Gardner over his glasses, then leaning forward again he went on, 'Now, when the going gets a little rocky you come whining to me.' His voice was low and venomous. 'You're pathetic.'

Gardner rounded on his tormentor. He grabbed Hewitt by the shirt front and raised an angry fist.

'Ah, ah,' Hewitt said, his eyes moving to the bar. Gardner followed his gaze. Standing with their backs to the bar were three rough looking men – all tensed, ready to intervene. Gardner recognized them as local UVF men. With a slight shove he released Hewitt and dropped his fist. Hewitt nodded smiling. 'That's better,' he said smugly. 'Now you're starting to show a little sense.'

Gardner closed his eyes and leant back in his chair. He seemed almost to shrivel in front of Hewitt. 'What am I to do?' he said again, his voice bitter and despairing, all anger gone.

'Well it's not really my problem is it?' Hewitt said brightly. He turned and smiled at the three men at the bar. 'I've only got one piece of advice for you and this is one piece of advice you had *better* take.' He leaned close to Gardner to emphasize his words. 'Keep my name and the organization's name out of it – understand?'

Gardner made no reply, his eyes remaining fixed on the table. 'I'm sure you do Eddy,' he said, nodding with a final backward smile at the distraught police officer. He turned and left the bar. Behind him Gardner put his head in his hands and began to cry softly to himself.

☆     ☆     ☆

Europa Hotel, Belfast, 5.20 pm, same day.

Voices were muffled and laughter subdued, as befitted the public bar of Belfast's finest hotel. Visitors to the city were often told, with some sort of twisted pride, that the Europa was the most bombed hotel in Europe. Despite this somewhat unwanted distinction it remained a popular meeting place for Belfast's more distinguished visitors. Familiar faces from television, sporting stars and prominent business men all mixed at its bars.

Sean Hughes had arrived early for his mysterious appointment. He had waited thirty minutes for his unknown caller to make contact with him – cursing the unseen man for not showing, and at the same time fearful of him doing so. He checked his watch, nodding to himself, 'Another ten minutes. No more – I'll give the bastard only ten more minutes.'

A tall, broad shouldered man with red hair pushed himself from the bar and strode over to his table. 'Sean,' he said, his ruggedly handsome face breaking into a smile of welcome. 'I'm glad you could make it.' He sat down next to Hughes, not offering a hand. 'I'd have been over sooner,' he continued in a slightly lower voice, 'but I wanted to make quite sure you were on your own.' He smiled again at Hughes with little humour.

'I know you,' Hughes said, his lips curling in a snarl, 'you're an SB man.'

Bill Dodds nodded. 'That's right,' he said, still smiling.

Hughes's eyes narrowed. He jerked his head back. 'What do you want?' Before Bill could answer he went on, 'Before you try, I'm not going to be your fucking tout, SB man,' he hissed, his voice full of hatred. 'I'd rather take my chances with Brigade Command.'

Bill studied the IRA man with grim humour. He pinched his nose between thumb and forefinger, a slight smile playing about his lips. 'I don't think you would have much of a chance,' he said, taking a brown envelope from his inside pocket and handing it to Hughes, 'not with Maquire being Brigade Commander.'

Hughes studied the photographs he found in the envelope, his face losing all colour.

'It's amazing the detail you can get with good quality cameras, isn't it?' Bill asked. 'Do you know, the guy that took those pictures was nearly five hundred metres away.' He shook his head and laughed. 'You really should have closed the curtains, Sean.'

'You bastard,' Hughes said holding the photos, his hands shaking.

Bill nodded as if in agreement. 'Probably,' he said lightly. He pointed at the photos. 'By the way, you can keep those – I've got plenty of copies.'

Hughes sat stunned, unable to talk for several minutes. Slowly he turned his head and looked Bill full in the face. 'I still won't be a tout,' he said slowly.

Bill pursed his lips. 'Actually, I don't want any information,' he shrugged smiling. 'At least not at the moment.' He reached into his side pocket and withdrew a white envelope. He handed it to Hughes. 'Read this.'

Hughes opened the envelope and read its contents. His eyes grew wide as he flicked through the neatly typed pages. 'Is this all true?' he asked, his voice tight with excitement.

Bill glanced around the room before answering. 'Oh it's all true. We probably won't ever know the full story.' He fixed Hughes with a steely gaze. 'Now Sean,' he said firmly, 'this is what you're going to do.'

☆     ☆     ☆

6 Gemmab Court, Ardoyne, 7.30 pm, same day.

Unsure of her emotions Mary O'Niel lay with her head in Kane's lap. He aroused so much in her – wants, needs, longings – yet he returned so little. Even when they made love she felt he was not totally there. It was as if a part of him withdrew, shutting out the emotions she so desperately wanted him to feel for her. She opened her eyes and searched his face. He sat with his head back, eyes closed as if asleep, but she knew he wasn't. It was as if he never relaxed. His body always felt tensed. She jumped as the phone rang. Kane opened his eyes as she answered it. 'Hello,' she said, then looked at Kane. 'It's for you – I think it's Sean.' Kane stood without speaking and padded to the phone. Watching him move Mary was reminded of a lion she'd seen once in Belfast Zoo. He took the receiver from her hand.

'Yes,' he said with no emotion in his voice.

'Kane?' he heard Sean's voice. He didn't answer immediately. He didn't like his name being mentioned on the phone.

'What do you want?' he said eventually.

'I need to see you straight away. We have an emergency,' Hughes said.

There was something in Hughes's voice Kane didn't like. What it was he couldn't put a finger on. Puzzled he asked, 'Is something wrong?'

'Yes,' Hughes replied. 'But I can't tell you over the phone. I need to see you – ' his voice sounded strained.

'OK,' Kane said. 'Where and when?' He listened to Hughes's directions. 'OK. I'll be there.' He replaced the receiver. Looking at Mary he said, 'I have to go out. I don't know how long I'll be.'

☆    ☆    ☆

Cambria Street, Shankhill Road, 9.30 pm, same day.

He'd been drinking all day heavily. After his confrontation with Hewitt he'd wandered from bar to bar, getting drunker and drunker. The last two bars he'd gone into had refused to serve him. Unsteadily he'd walked back to his car which was parked in Cambria Street.

Now he sat, too drunk to see past the car's bonnet, tears streaming down his face. He began to talk to himself. 'I did it for you Billy. I couldn't let them get away with killing you,' he sobbed huge great wracking sobs – his shoulders rising and falling with each intake of breath. 'And for you Peter. Good God in heaven you didn't do anybody any harm, did you?' He wiped his face with his cuff. 'You didn't deserve what they did to you.' He was shouting now, the bitterness and anger welling up in him. He shook his head trying to clear the fog which clouded his brain. 'But I got them back lads,' he said gesturing to his unseen friends. 'That bastard Martin won't blow the head off any more RUC men.'

Across the road Thelma Watt, attracted by the noise, glanced though the curtains. Tutting to herself she went to the phone.

'Hello, Police, Tennant Street, can I help you?' a pleasant voice answered.

'Yes Officer. This is Mrs Watt, 12 Cambria Street. There's a drunk man in a car opposite my house. He's ranting and raving to himself. Could you send somebody please?'

'No problem madam,' the pleasant voice answered. 'I'll have a patrol check it out.'

At the other end the Station Controller replaced his phone and picked up a radio transmitter. 'Delta Tango 70 from Zero, over,' he said.

'Delta Tango 70 send, over,' a strong Scottish voice answered.

The Controller smiled briefly before answering. 'Delta Tango 70, can you go to Cambria Street. Report of a drunk man in a car, over.'

'Roger Zero, on our way, out.'

Gary Howe turned to his driver. 'He must have started early, it's only just after nine,' he said as the driver turned the powerful Sierra towards Cambria Street.

He'd stopped crying but still addressed his imaginary audience. 'What am I going to do? he shouted. He twisted his head left and right. 'I wanted to be a Regular. I wanted to help people. Now they're going to put me inside,' he screamed. Gardner subsided into a sullen silence. Staring fixedly out of his car window he became aware of a weight in his pocket. Numbly he put his hand inside and withdrew his issue Walther 9mm automatic pistol. He looked at it as if seeing it for the first time.

Coming into Cambria Street Gary spotted the car. 'That's Eddy Gardner's car isn't it?' he said to his driver. As his car stopped Gary peered through the windscreen. The car in front of him had its windscreen heavily misted but a figure could be vaguely seen behind the wheel. Gary's cover man got out of the rear and ran to the opposite side of the road.

'What the fuck's Eddy up to,' Gary said, glancing at his driver. 'It's not like him to be drunk at this time *and* attempting to drive. He must be off his head.' The driver shrugged, making no reply. Gary took a deep breath. 'Well no use putting it off. I'll go and have a word with him.' Putting on his cap he got out of the Sierra and walked towards Gardner's car.

Eddy had dimly seen the Sierra pull up in front of him. Numbly he watched the front door open and a vaguely familiar figure get out and start to walk towards him. 'I wanted to be a

Regular,' he said, softly lifting the Walther and putting its barrel against his head. Walking towards the car Gary heard the shot. Instinctively he drew his own revolver. Across the road he heard his cover man cock his weapon. There was no hostile movement from the car. Gingerly he walked the short distance to it and pulled the front door open fast. Eddy Gardner lay slumped across its front seat, a bullet wound to his head. Gary felt for a pulse. His cover man and driver ran to join him. He shook his head and turned to look at them. 'It's Eddy Gardner.'

'I'll get an ambulance,' his driver said, running back to the Sierra.

'I doubt if that will do much good,' Gary said to his ashen-faced cover man. 'He's dead.'

☆    ☆    ☆

Upper Crumlin Road, 9.30 pm, same day.

Traffic was light as they drove slowly towards the Horseshoe Bend. Hughes drove a two-year-old Ford Cortina. It was a 'ringer' vehicle – the number plates matched an identical car belonging to an Andersonstown man with no connections with the organization. Ardoyne PIRA kept it for emergencies, hidden in a lock up garage. 'This is a bit unusual,' Kane said, his voice held more than a hint of suspicion.

'I've told you,' Hughes answered, his voice tight and drawn, 'it's the way Brigade wanted it.'

Kane stared out of the passenger window, making no reply. He thought back to the story Hughes had told him. The West Belfast investigators had discovered an informer who was highly placed inside the Ardoyne PIRA. They also feared that certain houses belonging to other members were bugged. The Brigade Commander himself wanted to speak to Hughes and Kane immediately about the situation.

'Why this God forbidden place for a meeting?' Kane asked as they rounded the sharp bend.

'Because nowhere in the Ardoyne is safe,' Hughes replied. He glanced quickly at Kane in the darkness. 'After all our operations in the Ardoyne it's easier for him to come to us than for us to get into West Belfast and see him.'

225

Kane turned to look at Hughes. 'You were given no clue who the tout is?' he asked, his voice deadly calm.

Hughes shook his head. 'No. I was told just to bring you with me and come up to the quarry as soon as possible.'

Kane shook his head, slowly returning his gaze to the front. 'I don't like it. This isn't like Brigade at all.'

Hughes turned the car into the quarry. It was the same one Eddy Grady had been shot dead in only a few short weeks before. Hughes's car headlights picked up the outline of another car already parked in the disused depths of the quarry. 'Looks like he's already here,' Hughes said. His voice trembled slightly.

Kane stared fixedly out of the window. Without turning his head he said, 'What's wrong Sean – you sound scared.'

Hughes shrugged and forced a weak smile on to his face. 'I am worried, Butcher. We have to find out who this traitor is.'

Kane turned to stare at Hughes. The IRA Commander could not meet his eyes. Instead he got quickly out of the car. Hughes took three quick gulps of cold night air as he left. He looked at his hands. They were shaking. Behind him Kane sat, seemingly in contemplation. Slowly he got out of the car and checked the silent gallery. His gaze finally came to rest on Hughes, who shrugged nervously under the cold blue eyes.

'Maybe he went for a walk,' Hughes said limply.

Kane walked slowly round the car, menace in every step he took. He stopped only inches from Hughes. With no warning he grabbed Hughes by his shirt front and slammed him against the car. With his free hand he quickly searched his IRA Chief.

'Wwwwhat's wrong?' stammered Hughes. Kane took a two handed grip on his shirt front. Twisting he easily cut off air to Hughes's lungs.

'What are you up to Sean?' he asked almost conversationally. 'Why did you bring me here? What little game are you playing?' Kane pushed his face only inches from Hughes. 'This has nothing to do with Brigade does it?' he asked, twisting harder.

'You're quite right Kane,' a voice said behind him. Without releasing Hughes Kane turned his head towards the voice. A tall, broad shouldered man with red hair stood holding a pistol trained on him. 'Let Mr Hughes go, there's a good fellow,' the man said. With a contemptuous shove Kane threw Hughes

226

from him. Hughes gasped, trying to draw air into his lungs.

'You took your fucking time about it?' he shouted hoarsely. The man shrugged. 'I was rather enjoying it,' he replied.

'Bastard,' Hughes spat.

'Tut, tut,' the man admonished. 'That's the second time you've called me that today.'

Kane stared fixedly at Hughes's tormentor. 'I know you,' he said, 'you're an SB man from Tennant Street,' he accused.

Bill Dodds smiled in acknowledgement. 'Ah, what it is to be famous,' he said. Watching his step he moved slightly closer to Kane.

'What is this?' Kane asked. Outwardly he looked relaxed but his body was tensed, like a spring ready to uncoil.

'What this is,' Dodds said, a tight smile on his face, 'is the end of the road for you Mr Butcher Kane.' The smile left his face. 'No more dead little Protestant girls for you.'

'For fuck's sake get on with it,' Hughes said harshly.

Dodds glanced at him with distaste. 'Not so fast Mr Hughes. I want to have a little word with our friend first.' He gestured towards Kane with the gun. Kane turned to look at Hughes.

'You fucking traitor,' he said, his lips curling with contempt.

'Don't be so fucking high and mighty,' Hughes shouted back throwing his arms up. 'I know all about the girls you've raped and killed, both here and in America.'

For the first time Kane showed emotion. Surprise was clearly etched on his face.

'Ah,' Hughes said triumphantly, 'you didn't think anybody would ever find out did you?' he sneered openly. 'The organization is well rid of the likes of you.'

Bill Dodds laughed. 'Now, now Sean. Don't be so moralistic.' He shook his head. Still laughing he looked back to Kane. 'Do you know how I got him to agree to all this?'

'Shut up you black bastard,' Hughes screamed starting to move towards the Special Branch man.

'Ah, ah,' Dodds said, gesturing towards him with the gun. Hughes froze. 'That's better.' He looked back at Kane. 'Your friend here has a little playmate he screws every time he visits West Belfast.' Bill shrugged still smiling. 'Now normally that wouldn't be too bad, but in this case the playmate is a fourteen-year-old boy.' Dodds paused for effect, '– who also happens to be the son of your Brigade Commander. Isn't that great?'

Kane turned his head to look at Hughes. He gave a short, humourless laugh. 'I always thought you were bent,' he said.

Hughes shook his head. 'I don't have to justify myself to you,' he snarled. Looking back at Dodds he said, 'As for you, a bastard like you would never understand.'

Kane locked his eyes with Dodds. Despite himself Bill felt a little uneasy. 'So,' Kane asked, 'you're going to kill me?'

Bill nodded, the smile still tight on his face.

'I think it's the best thing all round. See this?' he indicated the gun he held in his right hand. It was a reproduction of a Colt Government .45 automatic. 'A friend of mine in the Parachute Regiment gave me this, a present from the Falklands War. It's untraceable.' He jerked his head towards Hughes. 'Our mutual friend here is going to explain everything to your superiors – make sure there's no retaliation.'

Dodds paused, matching Kane's stare. 'Do you know why I'm going to kill you?' he asked.

Kane shrugged. 'Does it matter?' he asked.

'It does to me,' Dodds said, his voice firm and steady. 'I'm not going to kill you because of all the police and army men you've killed.' As Bill talked Kane flexed and relaxed his right arm. 'I'm not even going to kill you because of all those girls you raped and killed.' Bill shrugged. 'You're just a sick, twisted lunatic.'

A long double edged, extremely sharp knife slipped into Kane's hand, hidden from Dodds's view by his leg.

'I'm going to kill you to stop other animals like you from killing any more innocents in your name.' Dodds was silent. His finger started to tighten on the trigger.

'Can I ask one question?' Kane asked, his voice cold and calm.

Dodds shrugged. 'Sure, ask away.'

Kane inclined his head slightly to one side measuring the distance to Dodds. 'Was it you who found out – about the girls?'

Bill laughed. 'No. I can't claim the credit. A young detective sergeant in Tennant Street called Nevin Brown tied it all up. I'm going to see he gets a medal for it.'

Kane nodded. 'That's all I wanted to know.'

With almost unbelievable speed Kane dropped to one knee. At the same time he threw the knife underarm at Dodds. Bill fired but too quickly. The bullet almost parted Kane's hair but left him unharmed. A smashing pain erupted in Bill's chest. The knife thrown with incredible strength embedded itself to the hilt in his chest.

Numbly he looked down at it. Taking a step back he stumbled and fell against his car. In an instant Kane was on him, wrenching the .45 from his grip. Bill feebly tried to rise but Kane lashed a savage kick into his ribs and he subsided with a groan. Hughes stood, transfixed by the few seconds of furious action. Kane rounded on him, the .45 in his hand. 'Well Sean,' he said, his voice level despite his heaving chest. He walked slowly towards his former chief. 'It hasn't worked out quite as well as you'd planned has it?'

Hughes shook himself from his reverie. Placing both hands palms up towards the advancing Kane, he backed away. 'Anthony please, I thought it was for the best. It was for the movement, for the good of the organization.'

Kane stood barely an arm's length from him. Slowly he started to raise the .45. 'Wait, wait,' Hughes said quickly pushing his hands. 'I can help you.'

Kane cocked his head to one side, a thin smile on his face. 'Help me?' he asked softly. 'How?'

Hughes's face contorted with relief. 'I can get you out of the country. Don't you see. You can't stay – they've got enough on you to lock you up for the rest of your life.'

Kane studied him, letting the silence develop. With a very faint shrug he asked curiously, 'How will you get me out of the country?'

Hughes forced a smile onto his face. 'There's an escape route. It's for emergencies only – a boat.'

'Where from?' asked Kane.

'Larne Harbour. It's run by a Prod named Deans, John Deans.'

Kane shook his head slowly. 'No – I don't buy that. What's a Prod doing working for us?'

'He's a sympathizer. He believes in a Republic – that's why he's so useful to us.' Kane still looked unconvinced. 'I can prove it,' Hughes said quickly, 'you remember "Fats" McDonald, the Derry man who broke out of the Crumlin Road jail?' Kane nodded without speaking. 'Well we got him out of the country on Deans's boat. That's how I found out about it. I hid him and took him to the boat.'

Kane considered what Hughes had told him. 'How do you make contact with him?' he asked.

Hughes smiled, trying to look friendly. 'There's a telephone number. Larne 27575. You say your name is Harvey and ask about hiring his boat. Deans will do the rest.'

'Larne 27575 – Harvey – ask to hire the boat?' Kane repeated.

'That's right,' Hughes said ingratiatingly. 'I can get you false documents, passport, money, anything you need.'

Kane smiled and shook his head. 'Naw,' he drawled grinning. Nodding his head he said, 'I've already got all that.' Tilting the .45 he fired two quick shots. Hughes was slammed backwards by the heavy bullets. Slowly he slid down the car, coming to rest with his back against it. Kane bent down. Looking into Sean's still open eyes he asked softly, 'Does it hurt?' and gently slapped Hughes's face. 'I'll make it better.' Standing he sighted carefully down the .45's sights. He fired three times slowly and deliberately. All the rounds hit the slumped figure in the head, practically obliterating Hughes's face.

Silence descended on the grim gallery walls. Kane heard a grown behind him and his head spun around. Behind him Dodds moved, more dead than alive. Smiling he strode quickly to the felled SB man. Grabbing him by his jacket front he levered him into a sitting position. Dodds moaned.

'Hurts huh!' Kane grinned as he spoke to the semi-conscious man. He started to search Dodds. In a shoulder holster under his arm he found a second gun. He withdrew it from its holder and let out a low whistle. 'A Smith and Wesson .44 automatic. Fancy,' he said, softly turning the gun in his hand. Satisfied he tucked it into his waistband. He continued his search. Inside his inside pocket he discovered the SB man's warrant card and an address book.

'What have we got here?' he mused out loud. He flicked through its pages and went to disregard it, then paused thoughtfully. Moving his thumb to the letter B he thumbed it open. A smile sprang to his lips. 'Brown, Nevin.' He looked down at Dodds still form. 'Carrickfergus. That's on my way to Larne,' he smiled.

He took hold of the knife is Bill's chest and wrenched it out, blood from the wound, spraying the shirt red. 'Sorry I can't leave you this,' Kane said, pushing the knife into its sheath on his arm, 'I've become rather attached to it.'

Standing, he kicked the helpless man in the face. Getting into Bill's car he sped off, back towards the Ardoyne.

☆   ☆   ☆

Larne, 10.30 pm.

Walking a little unsteadily John Deans made his way home. He remembered the conversation at the bar with distaste. Larne was a Loyalist town, dominated by conservative hard line Protestants. When talk got around to politics the line was always the same. 'Shoot them, hang them, gaol them.' Deans shook his head in disgust.

'Don't the fools realize that Britain is the common enemy,' he thought angrily to himself. 'Nobody had anything to fear from a thirty-two county, all Ireland Socialist Republic. All could be free, safe from the shackles of British colonization.' In his anger he slammed the door behind him. God, how he had to bite his tongue listening to the mindless bigotry of his fellow Protestants.

'Thank God I went to University in Dublin,' he said out loud.

It had been at Dublin University, where he had studied political history, that his conversion to Republicanism had taken place. On his return to Ulster he had contacted the Provisionals through a fellow Republican classmate. Suspicious at first, he had been given little of interest to do, carrying the odd message to Scotland via his boat. His job as a freelance journalist gave him an excellent excuse for frequent journeys, often at short notice.

Slowly his worth to the movement became apparent. He helped to ferry men and arms to the mainland ASUs, carried wanted men to the relative freedom of the mainland UK, and kept a pipeline of communication open to activities all over the UK and abroad. As he entered the sitting room, the phone rang. He picked it up.

'Larne 27575,' he answered.

'Hello,' a cold voice said on the other end. 'My name is

231

Harvey. I'd like to hire your boat.'

Deans sobered immediately, and thrill of anticipation ran through him. 'That would be OK. When do you want it?' he asked.

There was silence. 'About 2 am in the morning,' Kane said eventually.

'That's short notice.'

'This is an emergency, can you handle it?'

Deans considered for a second. 'Just about. I'll have to fuel up and get port clearance, that's always a danger especially at such short notice.' He paused considering. 'There's no way you could leave it till say about 8 am?'

'No it has to be 2 am, no later. Like I said this is an emergency, it's important, perhaps the most important thing we have asked you to do.'

Deans felt his chest fill with pride, the organization had turned to him in their hour of need. Trying to keep his excitement out of his voice, he replied, 'OK, if it's that important I'll have the boat standing by.'

'Good man, where will I meet you?'

'By the ferry passenger terminal at exactly 2 am. I'll be in a green Cortina.'

'Fine, I won't be late.' Kane hung up and, looking at his watch he smiled to himself. Plenty of time to settle with Mr Brown, before he caught his boat to safety.

☆      ☆      ☆

Carrickfergus, 12 midnight.

They lay together, passion spent. Marrianne's head rested on his shoulder, her right arm draped across his chest. An empty bottle of wine lay, discarded, next to Nevin's trailing right arm.

'Nevin?'

'Yes,' he answered, more than half asleep.

She lifted her head and looked at his closed eyes mischievously and, rolling a finger in his ample chest hairs, she gave a sharp tug. Nevin's eyes flew open. 'Ah that hurts,' he said with the air of an injured martyr.

'Serves you right. I want to tell you something important.'

Nevin looked down; her face, only inches from his held a

232

worried look.

'What is it?'

'I've been offered a permanent position at Queens University. It means I could stay over here.'

'So what's the problem?'

'Do you want me to stay?' Her eyes were wide; in the soft light of his bedroom she looked like an angel from heaven. 'I mean permanently.' Both knew what she was asking.

'I want you to stay, I never want to be without you again.' Enfolding her in his arms he kissed her long and deep. Their kiss was disturbed by King's barking below.

He broke of and raised his voice angrily, 'Be quiet King.' The barking got louder. He looked at Marrianne apologetically. 'It's probably just a cat, I'll check.'

Rolling out of bed he pulled on a pair of slacks and, picking up his Ruger, walked to the door. As his hand touched its handle the barking stopped. He froze for a second, a puzzled frown on his face. Going quickly to the stairs he switched on the landing light. 'King,' he called softly. He could see the huge Doberman was curled up by his front door, apparently asleep.

'What's the matter boy?' Walking quickly downstairs he approached the still animal. Bending slowly he picked up King by the collar. His head hung limply, its neck broken. Behind him a voice said, 'Very careless of you leaving the back door open.'

Startled he started to turn. 'Drop the gun or you're a dead man,' his unseen assailant said. Nevin considered his alternatives, perhaps if he spun quickly enough he might get a shot off. As if to answer him the voice said, 'Don't try it, you'd never make it.'

Nevin dropped his gun and turned round. Kane stood a few feet from him, an automatic pistol in his hand. 'Shall we join your guest,' he smiled, his face looking like a death mask. Nevin turned and led him upstairs.

'What's wrong, I heard voices is . . .' Her voice faltered as she saw Kane.

'Now isn't that cosy,' he leered at Marrianne. 'This is going to be more fun than I thought.' Nevin faced the killer.

Playing for time he said, 'You'll never get away with this; we know everything; nobody, not even your organization will help you.'

Kane cocked his head to one side studying the detective, as if he was an interesting toy. 'I know I'm blown,' his face hardened slightly. 'I've got you to thank for that.'

'Then you know you've got nowhere to run,' Marrianne said sitting up.

'Wrong I've got a boat waiting for me in Larne. I'll be out of the country by morning. I've got fake identity documents, passport, money waiting for me in England.'

'Then what?' Nevin asked. 'Nobody will hide you.'

'Oh I don't know,' he gave a dismissive shrug, 'maybe I'll go back and work for the Hamiltons, or the Mafia.' He smiled evilly. 'Somebody will want my talents.'

'How did you find me?' Nevin asked, still playing for time.

'Your friend Dodds told me everything,' – he stared directly into Nevin's eyes, his voice dropped becoming almost silky – 'before I killed him.'

Nevin tensed and took a half step towards the killer. 'Come on, come on,' Kane said softly, motioning him with his left hand to step forward. Nevin forced himself to relax, hoping for an opening in Kane's defences.

Marrianne spoke again. 'Why did you kill all those girls?' she asked, trying to keep her voice controlled.

Kane's eyes flicked towards her but his concentration never left Nevin. 'Because they were Protestant bitches just like the first one I killed.'

'Margaret Hamilton?' Marrianne prompted.

Kane grinned. It made him look demonic. 'That's right. She tried to buy her freedom with her body, the slut. But I had other ideas.' Marrianne was about to ask another question but he went on, 'That night I killed my first Brit and I knew what I had been doing wrong. I knew my mother wanted me to kill those Prod sluts and she would make me strong and invincible . . . to take my revenge for her.'

There was silence for a second, Kane's words shocking both Nevin and Marrianne. 'You killed Lynn Moody, Mary Kirkpatrick and Mary McDonald as well?' Marrianne asked.

Kane nodded, his eyes never leaving Nevin. 'That's right. I never thought you'd link one stabbing and rape to me,' he laughed. 'I was wrong, wasn't I? You put it all together didn't you,' he said softly.

Nevin saw his finger begin to caress the trigger of his gun and tensed, ready to throw himself at Kane and give Marrianne a chance to escape. 'How did you kill the other two girls?' Marrianne asked quickly.

'I smashed Kirkpatrick's head against the bathroom wall and drowned her. McDonald I half suffocated with a pillow, then set her on fire. I had brought a bottle of liquid fat to pour over the bed – I didn't think your forensics would spot that.' His eyes flickered over once more to Marrianne and once again his voice dropped to a silky purr. 'But there were many others; you'll never find them all,' he grinned. 'Only I know,' he said softly, seeming to be in an almost sexual state. Again his finger caressed the trigger.

'Your mother wouldn't want this Anthony. She was a good woman,' Marrianne said softly.

Involuntarily Kane spun towards her, pointing his gun at her. 'Don't mention my mother's name you Prod slut,' he screamed manically.

Nevin saw his chance. Stepping forward he lashed out with the edge of his hand against Kane's wrist. The gun fell free. Almost immediately the killer reacted. With his free hand he backhanded Nevin. The force of the blow drove Nevin backwards into the wall. Kane stepped forward and drove a violent short jab against the already winded man's ribs. There was an audible crack as one of them broke.

Behind Kane Marrianne scrambled from the bed towards the gun. With lightning reactions he spun and lashed a foot against the girl's head, dropping her over the gun. Roaring with anger Nevin threw a roundhouse right cross which caught Kane unprepared on the jaw. The big gunman staggered backwards half a pace, but did not go down. The two men glared at each other, separated by less than a metre.

'I don't need a gun to kill you, you black bastard,' Kane snarled. He advanced on Nevin, his hands outstretched like talons. Nevin slammed two punches into Kane's stomach with all his strength. The man's body was like iron. Then Kane had his hands round Nevin's throat, almost immediately cutting off the air to his lungs. Nevin tried to break the hold but Kane's grip was too strong. His hands squeezed like a vice. In desperation Nevin brought his thumb up and drove it with all his force into Kane's left eye. The madman's head rocked back and he howled like a wolf. With a sudden wrench he threw

Nevin from him. Nevin's legs hit the bed and he tumbled onto it. Still hardly able to breath, he watched Kane lift a hand to his eye and look at it in amazement. It was covered in blood.

Kane's right arm bent sharply and came back up. It held a knife. He glared at Nevin lying on the bed. Looking more animal than human he advanced. Nevin sat up and tried to lash a kick into Kane's groin. The killer easily avoided it and again backhanded Nevin, knocking him back onto the bed. Kane knelt on the bed astride his nearly helpless victim.

Nevin reached up and grabbed Kane's knife arm with his left hand. He tried to punch Kane with his right fist but Kane caught the blow easily and forced Nevin's arm back onto the bed. Slowly Kane started to lean on Nevin's arm, driving the knife inch by inch towards Nevin's face. Suddenly he wrenched his hand free and plunged the knife with unbelievable force into the detective's shoulder. Nevin screamed in pain; Kane pulled the blade free and raised it upwards in both hands. Then a gunshot froze both men!

Kane looked down, a puzzled look on his face; blood began to appear on his shirt front. He struggled free from his badly wounded adversary and looked round at Marrianne. She held Bill Dodds's Smith and Wesson automatic in a shaking hand. Kane took a step towards her. She pulled the trigger again. A 'click' was the only sound. Marrianne looked in panic at her unfamiliar weapon; it had jammed!

In the distance there was the sound of an approaching police siren. Kane swore, then staggered past Marrianne, still only barely conscious. Behind him Nevin rolled off his bed and grabbed Bill's automatic from Marrianne's unprotesting hand. Working its slide, to free the jammed gun, he lurched out after Kane.

He had one brief view of his quarry, silhouetted against the open door. Bringing the gun up quickly, he fired two quick shots. There was a howl, more animal than human, from the darkness. Half crawling, half falling he moved towards the doorway. As he reached it, he was aware of figures running towards him, someone cocked a rifle, then a voice shouted, 'Don't shoot he's a police officer.'

He fell forwards, into the arms of two uniformed RUC officers. Looking up, he tried to tell them about Marrianne, hurt upstairs, about Kane, wounded somewhere close by. As he looked into their concerned faces, a cloud of darkness enfolded him in a warm embrace.

☆ ☆ ☆

Musgrave Park Hospital, Secure Wing, one week later.

'You were very lucky,' DI Cotton was explaining through a mouth full of grapes, 'a neighbour heard the fight start, then Marrianne's shot . . . she rang the local station. A police patrol was close by and responded immediately, their siren probably saved both your lives.'

Nevin opened his mouth to speak, but his superior read his mind, 'She's OK, just a few bruises, nothing serious,' he nodded towards the closed door, 'she's outside, waiting to see you.'

Nevin smiled, then tried to speak again, Kane's hands had crushed his larynx, the doctors had said it would be weeks before he would talk normally again.

Cotton put his head close to the detective's lips, then straightened and shook his head. 'Bill Dodds is in intensive care, only a fifty-fifty chance I'm afraid.' He shrugged, 'We still don't know why he and Kane met that night.'

For several seconds neither man spoke, then Nevin croaked a single word. 'Kane?'

Cotton shook his head sadly and took a deep breath. 'We found Inspector Dodds's car abandoned in Larne, there was blood all over it. Later Scottish police found a Larne registered boat floating adrift about a mile off the coast.' He looked at Nevin, 'Its owner, a man called Deans was dead on board, he'd been strangled. Kane's blood was all over it.' He shrugged, 'If it's any comfort the doctors say he was very badly hurt in his struggle with you, with the amount of blood he'd lost there's a good chance he might not have survived.' He stood, 'Don't you worry about it. It's not your problem anymore. Here's someone much more important.'

He opened the door; Marrianne stood there, beautiful despite her bruises. As she sat beside him Cotton left. Nevin opened his mouth to tell her how much he loved her, that he never wanted to be parted from her again, that she was his whole world.

Marrianne placed a single finger on his lips and smiled, 'Shush my darling, I know. You don't have to say a word. Do you want to know a secret?'

Nevin nodded. She leaned closer and kissed him softly on his lips, 'I feel exactly the same way.'

# AFTERMATH

The death of Hughes caused an initial uproar amongst Republicans; threats of violent retaliation were made and accusations of a 'shoot to kill' policy were levelled, both in parliament and media. Gradually some little of the truth was leaked to the IRA and wiser counsels took over.

A threatened offensive by the UVF against Catholics in North Belfast was forestalled; a major police operation recovered massive arms hauls and many arrests were made. However no evidence was ever found to link either Colin Jackson or Jacky Hewitt and both remain active in the Shankill UVF.

Bill Dodds survived Kane's attack, although severely wounded. His, and the official story, was that he had met Hughes with the intention of recruiting him as an informer and both had then been attacked by Kane. No charges were ever brought against him and in fact he was awarded a Queens Gallantry Medal. Unfortunately his injuries were so severe he was not able to resume his police career. However MI5, impressed no doubt by his handling of the Kane affair, recruited him. He now works in London.

DCI Hart was moved to administration and his place as Divisional Head of CID was taken by Inspector Cotton. Nevin Brown was promoted to Inspector and moved to head Regional Crime Squad; he also was awarded a Queens Police Medal. Marrianne accepted a permanent position at Queens University; the word on the streets is that she and Nevin will be married shortly.

Ulster remains much the same; people still die either 'for God and Ulster' or 'The Republican Dream'; perhaps many more will. The IRA has spread its campaign to mainland UK and Europe to shatter the lives of people who have never heard of Ireland. In truth Ulster is a country whose future and present have been destroyed by the seeds of the past.

Kane was never found, despite an extensive search by police forces as far apart as Ulster and the USA. His fate remains unknown.